A Lesser Form of Patriotism

A Novel of the King's Carolina Rangers
and the American Revolution
in the South

by G.G. Stokes, Jr.

Printed in the United States of America

ISBN: 13 - 9780615558868
ISBN: 10 - 0615558860

First printing, 2008
Reprinted 2011, Chattahoochee Publishing

Interior design by
Nadene Carter

Cover by
Heather McGrath Design
www.heathermcgrathdesign.com

Dedication

To Helen

Visit the Author's website
www.GeorgiaWriter.com

Chapter 1

The Ceded Lands, Georgia
Tuesday, February 24, 1779

The late afternoon sun cast slanting shadows through the thick forest, illuminating the knot of tired and travel-stained refugees as they sloshed through the shallow river ford and slipped quietly into the protective shadows of the primeval southern forest. The man in the lead suddenly stopped and threw up his hand, signaling an urgent warning to the others. They halted in their tracks, as fearful and skittish as a dray of squirrels in the shadow of a passing hawk.

The man detached himself from the group and crept forward, slowly and cautiously, shuffling along in the stiff, crouching gait of a hunted man. His face was haggard and drawn, his body tense and hunched forward, drawing in on itself as if he would spin about and burst into flight at the slightest hint of danger. He held a battered doglock musket, the stock pressed against his hip and the muzzle thrust forward in nervous anticipation. His clothing was ragged, his face and hair filthy.

Twenty paces ahead he paused to listen. Lifting his nose like a hound dog on a scent, he tested the air as he studied the trail that snaked away into the distance. He grunted, grounded his musket, and frowned. Other than the faint, watery rippling of the nearby river the only sound was the wind, but when it shifted and blew from the south, it carried with it the smell of wood smoke and horse dung.

Holding a finger to his lips, the man motioned for the others to move into the trees. As they blended into the underbrush, he pulled his feet from the wreckage of his scuffed, cracked, and broken shoes, exposing grimy toes thrust forlornly through the strained seams of worn and filthy stockings.

Keeping the wind in his face, he crept ahead with silent, tentative steps, bent at the waist like an aged man and shifting his foot whenever a leaf or stick threatened to betray his presence with a crackle or snap.

Closing to within a musket shot of the strange camp, he sank to the ground and crawled forward on hands and knees, halting behind the remains of a once stately oak from which he could look into the camp of strangers that lay no more than a pistol shot away.

There were three soldiers in the camp. Dressed in buckskin trousers and dark green jackets they moved about indolently, preparing the campsite for the night. Clearly, they anticipated no danger. Their uniform jackets were cut short, with light green lapels, and crimson collars and cuffs. One of them wore a black rifleman's hat with the left brim tacked up. He smiled. These were Provincial Troops, King's men, like himself.

The wind suddenly shifted, carrying the sounds and smells of civilization to him; the ring of metal striking metal sounded unnaturally loud and out of place in this wooded wilderness. He could smell the sweet scent of gun oil, the tanginess of sweat.

"Watch that noise, Jacob!" one of the men cautioned a tall, giant of a man. The large, boyish-faced individual gave him a penitent smile as his only answer. The big man began to move more carefully as he continued to unwind the leather padding from a copper pot. The copper caught the sun as it moved, flashing brightly burnished tattoos of reflected sunlight into the surrounding forest. The flashes caught the eye of the other soldier. He frowned and shook his head, but said nothing.

On the far side of the camp two Cherokee warriors, stripped to breechcloths, stood at the edge of the Savannah River. The right arm of one suddenly drew back and shot forward, driving a sharpened shaft into the surface of the river. Both men laughed as he drew a struggling fish from the water and forked it from the end of the makeshift spear onto the bank. It landed, flopping and twitching, alongside three of its cousins.

Handing the spear to his companion, the fisherman said something in his own language and laughed. His words were foreign, but their inflection contained the unmistakable sounds of challenge. The other man took the weapon and waded knee-deep into the river, his arm cocked and his head aswivel as he sought a target.

The erstwhile spy closed his eyes and took a deep breath to muster his courage before rising cautiously to his knees to hail the camp through cupped hands. "God save the King!" he shouted. "And God bless Loyal Americans!"

His words spurred the camp into a flurry of activity. With silent, disciplined grace, the soldiers and warriors melted into the surrounding foliage. The sharp, metallic clicking of muskets being drawn to full-cock filled the air.

Half a minute passed in eerie silence as both sides appraised the situation.

"Advance and be recognized!" one of the soldiers called from his hiding place near the bank of the river.

The intruder stepped from behind the fallen oak. He left his musket on the ground and held his hands out, well away from his sides.

"Who are you?" the soldier demanded.

"My name is John Stokes, late of Ninety-Six, in South Carolina," the stranger called back.

"Are you alone?"

"No. I've eight others with me, refugees; driven from the colony by a bunch of damned rebels over a week ago!"

John heard the men conferring quietly, deciding what to do with this unexpected guest.

A decision was made. One of the men rose and advanced in his direction. The man moved with deliberate purpose, alert for any sign of treachery. He held a shortened Brown Bess musket at an angle in front of him, the muzzle was pointed upward, but it could be lowered quickly and discharged if necessary.

He stopped at arm's length from John and studied him for a moment before lowering the weapon and motioning him towards the camp. The other men rose in response to some silent signal, sprouting from the forest floor like giant, green-coated mushrooms. They moved back in the direction of their fire, their eyes wary, nervous at having been caught off guard by this intruder. The two Cherokees eyed him with grim curiously before shrugging their shoulders and going back to their fishing.

"Have a seat," one of the men offered. John sat cross-legged on the ground next to the fire.

"Well," the man drawled. "You've scared the wits out of us. What's your story?"

John looked across at the other man, silently appraising him. Out of the corner of one eye, he saw the other soldiers fade into the forest, moving cautiously in the direction from which he had come. He took a deep breath before beginning.

"As I said, my name is John Stokes. Until two weeks ago I ran a gristmill in Ninety-Six, for Mr. Thomas Fletchall. You know of him?"

The other man nodded. "A good King's man."

"That, he is. I served under him back in '75 during the battle at Ninety-Six. Since the truce I have been an honest, law-abiding citizen, ready to aid King and country if needs be. Last month, Zachariah Gibbs and Colonel Boyd let out a call for the Loyalist Militia. Over six hundred men turned out. They had so many that Colonel Boyd owned he didn't need me, so I stayed behind to tend the mill with the wife and young'uns." John stopped and studied the other man closely. "I suppose you know about Kettle Creek?"

The soldier nodded. "Aye, we heard about it. Bad tidings, sure enough.

Some of the Rangers was there, but not us."

John nodded. "After Augusta was occupied, I renewed my oath of allegiance to the King. Then, directly after the damned rebels brought the prisoners from Kettle Creek to the gaol at Ninety-Six, they started howling to high heaven, blowing like a bunch of bleeding heroes about how they were going to clean the Loyalists and British out of the country. I woke in the middle of the night to find my house ablaze. Outside was a mob of rebels - scum and lowlifes, I've no doubt you know the type. They came on like animals after a wounded beast! My own wife's family among them!" John spit into the fire and let out a short, humorless laugh.

"I don't know that I could laugh at something like that," the soldier observed.

"You could, had you been there. You see, Andrew DeLoach was one of the ringleaders."

The soldier thrust his chin into the air and toyed with his chin for a moment. "Andrew DeLoach," he said, sounding out his words slowly and nodding in thought. "I've heard tell of him. None of it good."

John snorted. "And all of it true! I could see in his little pig eyes what the bloody *cut purse* was wantin'. He was thinking that once my house was confiscated and sold at auction, he could buy it cheap. But he made one mistake; he had given his brave and loyal Patriots too much rum to get their loyalty. Some of his lads set a torch to my house. You should have seen the face of that fat bastard drop, knowing he could do nothing but pat them on the back for their bravery, all the while watching seven-hundred-pounds worth of property go up in smoke."

John looked up as the soldiers who had drifted into the trees returned, herding the rest of his party into the camp. His wife, Egrain, moaned as she dropped a tattered blanket stuffed with their belongings and stumbled into his arms.

"Sit here, love," John said, his voice heavy with concern. He held her arm to steady her as she sank to the ground. She sat on her hips, with her thighs drawn up to her breast and her arms wrapped around her knees. Slowly, she lowered her head into the space between her arms. Her shoulders began to shake with silent sobs. Faintly at first, then growing more pronounced as the enormity of her loss crept over her.

John lay a hand on her shoulder and brushed the back of her neck with a kiss. "Everything's fine, Grainy," he said softly. "We've found friends, our nightmare is almost over."

As the pent-up anger and frustration of her ordeal burst forth, Egrain continued to sob. The other women of the party began to wail also.

Ruth Weatherford, the eldest of the women at age forty-two, stepped forward and grabbed the soldier's hand.

"God bless you, sir!" she cried, looking up to him with eyes that seemed to worship him as a savior. Those eyes quickly overflowed with tears. "May we at least know the names of out deliverers?"

The soldier smiled down at her. "Certainly, ma'am. I am Sergeant William Hopkins, Captain Johnston's Company, King's Carolina Rangers. These two men are James Dobbins and Jacob Fenton, also of that worthy regiment."

Ruth eyed the men with curiosity. "What, pray tell, brings you three fine gentlemen into this wilderness?" From sheer habit she suddenly gave the men a quick curtsey.

Sergeant Hopkins presented her with a slight bow in return. "We have been sent by Colonel Brown, bearing dispatches to the Cherokee towns up north of here." He waved his arm, vaguely indicating a direction of travel.

"Colonel Brown?" Ruth's husband, Roger, chimed in. "The one what was tarred and feathered over around Augusta?"

"One and the same. And I'm bound to say that those so-called Patriots rue the day they did that dirty deed! I almost ended up the same way." Loosening his stock, Sgt. Hopkins pulled it away from his neck, exposing a puffy red scar running from just below his cheekbone, down his neck, and out onto his right shoulder. "The dirty buggers almost did me in a few years back, but Dobbins here put a musket ball through one of 'em's head just as they started pourin' the tar." He jerked his head to indicate one of the soldiers standing off to one side. "I pulled free and made my escape. They nigh chased the two of us all the way to Florida before we gave them the slip. Hey, what? James?" he directed his question at the soldier, Dobbins.

"That's the God's truth, ma'am," Dobbins assured her solemnly. "I've never seen such a fuss about one damn rebel! A body would think that the buggers was growing scarce the way they carried on about him!"

"They're no way scarce enough to suit me," Ruth assured them. "God bless you boys, we were nigh on tuckered out." With a sigh she sank to the ground and blew a long breath. "I'm a mite hungry, too. If you fine gents have any food, tired as we be, the three of us women will gladly fix up a meal for the whole company."

Hopkins smiled. "We've not been on the trail long, so we're still well-stocked. We would be mighty pleased if you would see to our meal." Turning his head, he called over his shoulder to one of the Cherokees spearing fish in the river. The warrior gave a short, guttural answer and leisurely forked another fish onto the bank.

"Thunder's Child says we'll have plenty of fish. I'll go get some corn meal and tea from the saddle bags."

While the women worked, the Rangers and their male guests withdrew to the edge of the camp. Playing the good hosts, they produced several short-stemmed clay pipes and a bag of tobacco. The travel-stained refugees eagerly accepted the hospitality.

"You say that you're heading into the Cherokee country?" John asked through the pungent cloud of tobacco smoke he had just exhaled. "We were hoping that you were heading towards some settled area still controlled by the Crown."

"Not any time soon," Sergeant Hopkins said. "But we'll be happy to take you with us to either Little Chota or Long Swamp. That might be the safest place to go for the time being. With the way things are shaping up around these parts, there's going to be a sight of fightin' in the next few months."

"Oh?" John waited for someone to voice an opinion. When no one else spoke up, he asked, "What about the Indians?"

"They're lukewarm," Hopkins said, "Some will help, some won't. Of course these fiascoes at Kettle Creek and Augusta won't give them any faith in us. They don't want to get caught in the middle of a war that's none of their concern." He shrugged and rolled his head to loosen a stiff neck. "But the families at Long Swamp have gotten along well. That's where Dobbins and I have our families. 'Course, we were already licensed traders when all this nonsense started." Indicating the third member of their group, he added, "Jacob here doesn't have a family, but Dobbins and me are on the lookout for some likely wench for him. I expect that he'll be starting one just as soon as we locate a strong, buxom lass for him. Ain't that right Jacob?"

Jacob's ears burned bright red. John realized that he had not heard the young man, no more than seventeen, say a word since he had come into the camp.

"Jacob's a good Ranger and stronger than an ox, but he's might shy." Hopkins emphasized his statement with a hearty slap to the young man's muscular back. It sounded like he had slapped a side of beef. Jacob grinned at the ground, embarrassed by the public praise.

"If you're interested in joining the Rangers," Hopkins said, "we'll be glad to have you. Your family will be safe at Long Swamp while you're out soldierin'." With a smile, he gave the young soldier's massive shoulder an affectionate shake. "How 'bout getting the women some firewood, Jacob?"

The young giant jumped to the task. Hopkins waited until he had disappeared into the underbrush before turning back to his guests. "Jacob's family was all hung by the rebels back in '77. He weren't but about fourteen, watched from the underbrush while they murdered his mother and father along with his eight-year-old sister. Hung 'em all." He shook his head in distaste. "What bastards! Me and Dobbins was leading a patrol of Florida Rangers up from St. John's when we found him, sittin' under a cedar tree, no more'n an hour after it happened. He's never talked much since we found him." He raised one shoulder in a dismissive gesture. "But then, I suspect he's never been much of a talker."

"They hung an eight-year-old girl?" John's face mirrored the horror he felt.

"Yep, but our company made good Patriots out of them. Lucky for us, we came along before they had a chance to get away." He shook his head sadly.

"Unfortunately, that type of deviltry is getting more and more common. I'm surprised you folks got off with no more hurt than you did." He nodded towards the old musket the wretched group had dragged along with them. It lay canted against the tree trunk alongside John. "At least you weren't put out without some means of getting game every now and again."

John reached out and retrieved the musket. Laying it across his thighs, he rubbed it affectionately. "This belonged to my great-uncle. He carried it at Bloody Marsh against the Spaniards, and my father-in-law carried it against the Cherokees at Montgomery's defeat back in the French wars. Now, I guess, I'll be carrying it against our own people." John rubbed his hand plaintively across the weapon's scarred and pitted stock.

"They're not your people anymore," Hopkins warned him. "You better get that out of your head, right now! Those Patriots would just a soon shoot you as look at you. That goes for your wife, too. Hey, didn't you say that you had young'uns?"

"We do." John's lips compressed into a thin line. "Grainy's father grabbed them, wouldn't let 'em come with us. Said they was to be raised as good Patriots." John gave a short, bitter laugh. "Patriots? The rebels have some nerve calling themselves that. Aren't we the Patriots?"

"That's how we see it," Dobbins said earnestly.

Hopkins nodded his agreement. "I reckon they'd argue that we who honor the King serve a lesser form of patriotism, but if them damned rebels think they are patriots, then what are we loyal folks? They're the traitors, not us. I'll be happy to watch them all swing once we win this war."

* * * *

The soldiers and Cherokees rose before dawn the next morning. While John sat up in his blanket, savoring the last of its warmth and watching the Rangers scout the perimeter of the camp, the two Cherokees disappeared into the darkness, searching farther out for any signs of the enemy. They were gone for half an hour before they returned and nodded to Sergeant

Hopkins that all was clear. Satisfied, the three Rangers moved about the camp, shaking the men awake and instructing them to be ready to move out immediately.

"Aren't we going to have a bite of breakfast?" Ruth asked.

"No, ma'am," Dobbins told her. "We'll eat later, after we put some distance between us and this campsite. It's not safe to stay put at dawn, just in case some enemy scout happened on us during the night. If so, they'll be howling down on a small party like this at first light." He smiled when he saw concern on Ruth's face. "Don't worry, ma'am, it's just a precaution. If Thunder's Child and Robin say there's no one about, you can be fairly sure that there ain't."

Sergeant Hopkins knelt next to John and inclined his head to indicate the ancient doglock. "That musket primed and loaded?" he asked.

John frowned. "It is, but my younger brother smuggled it to us on the road out of Ninety-Six. All he could get from the house before it burned was a half a horn of power and a bag of birdshot. It won't stop anything bigger than a rabbit."

Holding the musket by the barrel, Hopkins studied the bore. "Sixty-nine caliber," he observed. Reaching into his cartridge box, he pulled out three paper cartridges and handed them to John. "These may be a tight fit, but you should be able to ram them down in a pinch. They're buck and ball loaded. Use the buck shot out of them if nothing else." He gave John a reassuring pat on the shoulder. "We'll be at Colonel Waters's Fort on the Broad River the day after tomorrow. He may have a mould for that musket of yours lying around in his store. Now, if you're willing to join up with us, he'll issue you a new musket, along with powder and lead from the supplies of our good King, George III." He smiled good-naturedly and proudly blew out his chest. "Of course, you're not getting a fine uniform like this 'til you get to the regiment down in Savannah."

John nodded. "I'm leaning that way for the moment, but not 'til I get my wife and these other women somewhere safe." He thought for a moment. "This Colonel Waters, would that be Thomas Waters from Ninety-Six?"

"One and the same. He was appointed Deputy Superintendent to the Cherokees when Stuart died. He has a fort up on the Broad River and his own detachment of militia with him. You know him?"

"Yes, and no. I met him back in '75 when the loyal folks mustered at Mr. Fletchell's home. That was just before the battle at Ninety-Six. He was about the only one that knew what he was doing. He served alongside my father and uncle, as a lieutenant with the Georgia Rangers before the rebellion. We could use a hundred more like him."

* * * *

In response to Sergeant Hopkins's silent signal, the small party started north in the still darkness of early morning. Skirting the Savannah River, they moved ahead slowly, cautiously following seldom-traveled and ill-defined trails; signs of rebel activity were common. The refugees followed behind the mounted Rangers on foot, leading the packhorses and casting anxious eyes at the surrounding underbrush.

Late in the morning, the small column emerged from the onerous shade of the never-ending forest and into a small, sunlit clearing littered with stumps. A partially burned cabin sat in the middle of it. The smell of wet, charred wood hung heavily in the air. The Rangers seemed shaken by the discovery, Jacob more so than the others. He appeared almost physically sick, his face paled noticeably, and he swayed slightly as if he would slide from his saddle at any moment.

Sergeant Hopkins signaled a halt just beyond the tree line. He sat in his saddle, surveying the scene and pointing out the signs as he unraveled the story of this small tragedy. He guessed that the cabin had been burned no more than four days before. It had rained heavily that day, he said, probably the reason why the cabin had not burned to the ground.

"Were these some of our people?" John asked.

"The McDougals," Hopkins replied soberly. "There was five of them." He pointed to four fresh graves at the rear of the cabin. "I wonder who survived?" He spit and pursed his lips thoughtfully. "Hope they weren't taken prisoner." Rebel treatment of their prisoners was notoriously unpleasant.

They halted in the clearing to kindle a small, smokeless fire and boil water to which they added ground corn meal and salt. The resulting Hasty Pudding would barely satisfy their hunger.

John ate without tasting his food. As he sat quietly, resting his back against a fire-scarred tree that stood at one corner of the cabin, a slight movement in the underbrush along the far wood line caught his attention. He jumped to his feet and assumed a defensive posture. The lock of his musket clicked ominously as he pulled the hammer to full cock.

Alerted by his movement, the Rangers sprang into action. Throwing themselves behind the nearest cover, they readied their weapons and peered across the clearing, muscles taunt, eyes alert, ready for a fight as the Cherokees faded off, one to each flank, where they merged into the underbrush. They glided forward silently, all but invisible against the heavy brush that lined the edges of the small clearing.

An uneasy hush settled over the clearing. A slight whisper of wind wafting through the leaves of nearby trees produced the only sounds.

Jacob, kneeling just inside the doorway of the deserted cabin, suddenly grounded his musket and walked out into the sunlight. "Hold on just a minute," he said, shading his eyes with his hand. "I think that's Miss Judith out there." He cupped his hands and called across the clearing. "Judith! It's Jacob and Sergeant Hopkins, girl, come on out!"

Ever so slowly, a thin young girl, covered in freckles and with flaming red hair, no more than seventeen years of age, emerged from behind a holly bush. She clutched a wicked-looking Scottish Claymore tightly in both hands, straining mightily to keep the point of the heavy sword turned upward in a defensive posture.

Leaving his weapon behind, Jacob moved towards her, halting about ten yards short of the wood line. The instant Judith recognized him, she exhaled a sigh of relief and sank to the ground. The sword dropped alongside her with a dull thump as Jacob leapt forward and swept her from the ground into his arms. He carried her effortlessly back to the cabin where she leaned heavily against his muscular frame as he gently set her on her feet. Hopkins rifled through the pack saddles in search of food. After gobbling down a handful of dried venison, Judith, speaking with a heavy Scots accent, told her story.

"It was a group of five men," she said, gazing at the ground while still chewing on the tough meat. "They came four days ago, during the rain. Bastards! Every one of 'em! My poor Da, Christian soul that he was, he fed 'em and let 'em lay by our fire during the night." She laughed a quick, humorless laugh. "Us with barely enough to feed ourselves and Da sharing with the likes of them?" She suddenly looked up, her eyes boring into the sergeant's face. "The next mornin', as they was gettin' ready to ride out, another group of them came thundering across our field. Hard men! Angry lookin' imps of Satan! Driven north by our men comin' up from Savannah." She spit derisively onto the ground. "Bloody bastards jumped off their horses and commenced to ransacking our cabin and corncrib." Her lips curled back into a sneer, exposing even white teeth as she mentally relived the tragedy. "I can see 'em now, strutting about and prowling through the place like they owned it. When Da tried to stop 'em, they…" She paused to sniff back a tear. "They knocked him to the ground and commenced to kick him like a dog. Ma couldn't take it. She screamed at them and threw herself across Da. That's when one of the bloody murders called her a 'damn Tory bitch' and sank a hatchet into the back of her head." Overcome with rage, Judith jumped to her feet and looked about for something to vent her spleen upon.

"Where's Da's sword?"

"It's safe," Dobbins said. "It's propped against the cabin over yonder."

With a sigh, she sank to her knees. She closed her eyes and wrapped one arm around Jacob's leg, hugging it like a child clutching its mother in the dark of night. "Bloody bastards started shooting then," she said softly. "First Da, then my brother, then me." She lowered the neck of her tattered smock, exposing a swollen purple streak left by the musketball that had grazed her upper arm. "I lit out. One of 'em chased me all the way to the bloody woods!" A shiver racked her body and she slid to the ground, sitting on her hips and holding a pale, freckled hand to her chest as she panted laboriously, trying to regain her breath. Lightheaded, she swayed slightly from side to side.

Grainy pulled a blanket around the girl's trembling shoulders. With John's help they lifted the girl to her feet and guided her to the bed inside the half-burned cabin. Jacob followed them inside, his long, troubled face giving him the appearance of a loyal hound.

Grainy eased the girl onto her back and lay a hand on her sweat-beaded forehead. "Feels like you've come down with a fever, young lady," she said with a worried expression.

Jacob disappeared through the door. He returned a few moments later with a blanket. "Here," he said, shyly holding it out. "Use mine, it's a might warm for me this time of the year. I'll be just fine."

Grainy smiled at the young man. "So you can talk! Can you also fetch water?"

"Yes, ma'am," Jacob stammered as he continued to stand there, looking with deep concern at Judith's flushed face.

"Then don't just stand there blushing like a timid schoolboy!" Grainy snapped. She made a shooing motion with one hand. "Get us a bucket of cold water."

* * * *

The next morning, Judith woke drenched in sweat.

"You're fever's broken," Grainy said as she gently sponged Judith's forehead, "but I don't think you should travel just yet. It'll be a few days 'fore you get your strength back."

"She'll need to travel today, strength or no strength," Sergeant Hopkins said from the doorway. "With all these rebels being pushed northward into the ceded lands, this is no place for decent folks. It's not safe." He inclined his head in Judith's direction to emphasize his point.

"But she can't walk!" Grainy protested. "She's much too weak."

"I'm sorry, ma'am," the sergeant said apologetically, "but it's simply too dangerous to stay here. The banditti will be thick as fleas around here now that the sun's up."

A quiet, "Excuse me," drew their attention as Jacob stepped through the door. Hat in hand, he mumbled an apology for intruding on the women's domain. He cleared his throat. "Miss Judith could ride behind me." He cut a quick glance in Sergeant Hopkins's direction and added hastily, "She don't weigh enough to tire the horse."

"But you do, you side of beef!" Hopkins laughed. "You alone weigh almost enough to break the poor animal's back." He studied the young man's features for a few moments. "Oh, go ahead and put her on your horse," he said, dismissing the subject with a wave of his hand. "Let Mrs. Stokes ride behind to support her while you lead the bloody nag. With us already having to nursemaid these civilians, we won't travel any slower with you slogging along on foot. But…" he wagged his finger to emphasize his next point, "…if I see trouble and signal you to mount up, they come right off. No dilly-dallying around. Understand, private?"

Jacob grinned and bobbed his head. "Yes, sir! I'll have my musket loaded and ready."

They trudged ahead, relying on the morning mist to conceal them from unfriendly eyes. Wary, on the lookout for any sign of trouble, the Cherokees and Rangers rotated to the front and rear of the little column, always alert for any sign of approaching danger.

Grainy sat behind Judith, who rocked lethargically in the saddle, clutching her father's Claymore as if she expected to have some bandit snatch it from her at any moment. A single blanket covered both women. Judith's protector plodded alongside the mare's head, holding the reins and looking back often to check on his two charges. It was obvious to Grainy that Jacob thought very highly of the recently orphaned Miss Judith McDougal. She smiled down at him and asked quietly, "You seem to set quite a store by Miss Judith. Did you know her before … well, before yesterday?"

"Yes, ma'am," Jacob responded. "I've known Miss Judith for quite a spell. Her Ma and Pa often fed us and gave us a place to sleep whenever we were passing through." A quick frown screwed up his face. "They was mighty fine folks. King's people, like us."

"Do you think their murderers will ever be brought to justice?"

"Yes, ma'am, I do. If me and the sergeant don't get them, the Sheriff will find them after we win this war and make sure that they pay."

"I'm quite sure of that." Grainy smiled down at him. She, like Jacob, had no doubt the lawless rabble of low-classed rebels would be no match for the King's forces. Once they moved inland from Savannah, they would make short work of these petulant people who used patriotism as an excuse to prey on innocent victims. On sudden impulse she added, "What makes the rebels so cruel, Jacob? The King's people don't act like that."

"I can tell you the answer to that." The sergeant's voice startled Grainy. She flinched, and then smiled over her shoulder as the soldier laid his hand on the horse's rump.

"The fact is, ma'am, they do it because they're scared. They're not sure they've backed the right dog in this fight. Most of 'em have been talked into it by someone hoping to make a profit out of selling our property if they win."

"But they won't win, surely!" Grainy asserted.

"I don't see how they can. And they don't either, that's the problem. The Yankees up north have been driven from pillar to post. They've only won one battle when General Burgoyne blundered into a trap. Now, the same King's troops that have given Mr. Washington such a trouncing are heading this way. The rebels are scared. They should be. Why, I would wager that by this time next year, the war down here in the South will be won." He waved his arm in a sweeping motion to emphasize his next point. "Just look at this fix we're in. The rebels are thick as thieves around here simply because the army marched towards Augusta. There's been no fighting to speak of, and there won't be. They know they can't win, so they skedaddle up here into the forest, picking on those they know can't hurt them. Had there been a Corporal's Guard wearing the red coat in Ninety-Six when your home was burned, they would have prevented that mob from ever having formed in the first place."

Grainy shook her head. "If only that Corporal's Guard had been there!" Arching her back to loosen her stiffening muscles, she added. "Are we stopping soon? My back could use a rest."

"No, ma'am." The sergeant smiled. "We won't stop 'til we get to Waters's Fort. That should be no more that four or five more hours."

Sometime around three o'clock that afternoon, the small group halted beside the trail. Sergeant Hopkins spoke a few quick words to the two Cherokees, who hurried ahead. He helped the two women dismount. "We'll wait here for a bit while our scouts check the road ahead. We're mighty near the fort and the chance of running into a group of rebels scouting around here is fairly good. No sense in getting careless this near to safety."

Twenty minutes later, a group of mounted Loyalists thundered into view. They didn't slow their charge until they were abreast of the waiting refugees. Reining in their mounts, they slid to a halt alongside the elated travelers.

"Welcome!" the leader of the group called out as he looked down on the exhausted refugees. He touched his finger to the brim of a gold-laced tricorn and bowed gracefully from the saddle. "Lieutenant Daniel Ellis of the East Florida Rangers. At your service!" With a mischievous smile, he peered down at Sergeant Hopkins. "That's a mighty fancy outfit you have on sergeant. Did you transfer to another regiment?"

"No, sir!" Quickly coming to attention, the sergeant explained, "This, sir, is the uniform of the King's Carolina Rangers, lately known as the East Florida Rangers. We've been renamed, and our good King George has uniformed us in the finest style. I also have a mighty fancy uniform that Colonel Brown has sent to Colonel Waters, along with his new orders."

The lieutenant sat his horse, silently eyeing Sergeant Hopkins, obviously waiting for some further response.

Hopkins cleared his throat. "Sorry, sir, he only sent the one. Said that even though Colonel Waters isn't technically a Carolina Ranger, he is the Deputy Superintendent of Indian Affairs, and the uniform may impress the Cherokees when they meet with him. You'll get yours in Savannah."

"I see," the lieutenant said with good-natured grin. He reined his mount about, facing it in the direction of the fort. "Come along now, ladies and gentlemen, if you please," he said, sweeping the hat from his head and bowing to the ladies from the saddle. "I'll lead the way."

Chapter 2

Waters's Fort
Friday, February 26, 1779

John and Grainy felt hope for the first time in weeks. The first order of business Colonel Waters had seen to, upon their arrival at his fort on the Broad River, was feeding the refugees and issuing cloth for making new clothing. The eight refugees from Ninety-Six were surprised at the efficiency that went into their relief.

"Yours is an unfortunate story that we've seen played out many times," the colonel had informed them once their immediate needs were seen to. He had politely insisted they join him in his evening meal, during which he talked patiently with them, discussing their situation at great length, giving the men his undivided attention as they told their stories. He was one of those rare individuals who listened well and spoke sparingly, giving the refugees the impression that their problem was of paramount importance to him, and that he would give it his undivided attention until some suitable solution was discovered. Although he had served with John's father as an officer in the Georgia Rangers before the war, he did not mention it, nor did John think it proper to remind him of it, since the Rangers had all deserted their officers and joined the rebel cause early in the conflict.[3]

Colonel Waters was a fastidiously dressed man, gentry born and accustomed to the finer things in life. He possessed extensive property and wealth, but at the same time, he seemed at home among the tradesmen and soldiers he came in contact with on a daily basis. Only after all of their questions had been answered, and their most urgent needs had been seen to, did he take his leave of them. Extending his hand to each of the men in turn, and giving the women of the group a courtly bow, he retired to his quarters, along with their rescuers, to read dispatches and discuss the military situation to the south.

Among the militiamen at the fort were two old acquaintances of John and Grainy. They had immediately invited the refugees to share their cabins with them and offered the services of their own wives to help make new clothing. Relieved that they were once again among friends after almost two weeks of wandering in a hostile wilderness, John gratefully accepted the invitation of Matthew Nowland, while Roger and Ruth Weatherford paired off with James Books and his wife, Jenny. Jacob volunteered to escort Judith to the home of Sergeant Hopkins's sister, where she found immediate acceptance.

Rebecca Nowland literally leapt for joy on the arrival of one of her oldest friends. Throwing her arms around Grainy's neck, she laughed out loud, threw back her head, and praised God.

Matthew Nowland smiled. "We've got company for a while 'Becca. These two just refugeed in from Ninety-Six today, along with the Weatherfords, Swineys, and Morgans."

"Poor child!" Rebecca said. "I know how awful it must have been. Hardly a month goes by that we don't have three or four families come in with the same sad tale." She shook her head angrily, her mouth set in a firm line of disapproval. "I can't believe our old friends and neighbors have sunk so low. I guess what they say is true; *the scum has risen to the top.* This liberty they crow about doesn't seem to get spread around very far, does it? I'm thinkin' their idea of liberty is confined to those who think like them. Shoo!" Dismissing the idea with a wave of her hand, she led Grainy through the low door of the rudely built cabin. Matthew and John remained outside, under the lean-to porch.

While John took a seat on a puncheon bench, Matthew straddled a shaving horse that was pulled under the overhang to protect it from the weather. He looked sadly at John. "Other than the obvious, what brings you here?" he asked.

John poured out his story, full of vim and vinegar towards the rebels. Nowland nodded his head in agreement. "At least it will be over soon. With the British army moving around the countryside, the rebels are fleeing like rats into this area. We've begun to call it the *Hornet's Nest.*" With a nonchalant wave of his hand, he indicated the thick forest that began a hundred yards away from the fort. "I'm amazed your party made it through the Ceded Lands without at least one brush with those *Crackers* out there."

"We did have one run-in, so to speak," John said. He gave an account of the slaughter of the McDougal family and the rescue of their daughter, Judith.

Frowning, Matthew shook his head. "I can't believe it's gotten so bad. The McDougals were good Scots people. They were too old to fight, but they do have two sons with the Highlanders down towards the coast. They'll be sore missed." He spit on the ground. Then with the practicality born of living in an uncertain world, he added, "We should get a cart and go retrieve whatever is left out at their cabin. Judith could use it when she gets back on her feet. She'll need to find a man to marry up with. Having everything to start a homestead will certainly help her find one." He shrugged his shoulders. "A woman out here, alone? Won't work for her or anyone else."

Grainy and Rebecca stepped through the door of the cabin.

Grainy eyed Matthew as if measuring his intelligence. "Surely that poor child isn't to be married off to the first man who comes by?"

"Why no!" Matthew corrected her. "She'll have her choice of any man in the garrison. Single women are rare as hen's teeth out here. These boys'll be beating a path to her door 'fore she can get settled in." He laughed, gave Grainy a look that said, *you'll learn,* and quickly added, "Be that as it may, have you two made any plans about your own future?"

John shook his head. "On the way up here we talked to Sergeant Hopkins. With all this rebel banditti moving up from the south, he seems to think this is going to be a rough place to live for the next few months. I've been thinking of moving west, to this Long Swamp Village the sergeant told us about. Once I have Grainy settled there, I'll come back and join the fight." His lips compressed into a straight line. "I should have done so long before now." He blew a long breath and added, "That is if Colonel Waters will have me. I don't have any experience fighting Indian style."

Matthew shrugged. "In that case, Colonel Brown will take you in his Rangers. But I warn you, from what I've heard, the enlisted men are a mighty hard lot. Many of those on our side are no better than the rebels. I shudder to think what they'll do if they ever think we're losing."

John's mouth dropped. "Surely it will never come to that!"

Matthew laughed. "I don't see how, I'm just saying *if.* I'll ask around, and see if there are any men willing to ride out with us to retrieve Judith McDougal's belongings. Ever hear of Daniel McGirth?"

John's eyes lit up at the mention of the Loyalist hero. "Certainly! According to the rebels around Ninety-Six, he's a one-man foraging detail for the British Army."

Matthew laughed. "He does have an eye for fine horse flesh!" Slapping his thigh, he chuckled before continuing. "He's a good fighter, I'll grant you that. Has about two hundred men—white, red, and black—with him here at the fort, and he told me today they'll be heading south to join up with Colonel Brown the day after tomorrow. They're to cover the British withdrawal back to Savannah. If you've a mind to go fetch Judith's things, he may be willing to escort us as far as the McDougal place."

Later that night, as the four old friends sat by the flickering fire in the hearth, talking quietly and watching the flames burn down into glowing embers, there was a light rap on the door of the cabin. Matthew looked over his shoulder. "That's McGirth."

A lean, plain-looking man dressed in a green hunting frock and butternut-colored breeches stepped into the room. He removed a fashionably well-made tricorn hat bearing a red cockade,[4] revealing a full head of black hair pulled tightly back from his face and tied into a stiff queue at the neck. The man held out his hand and greeted Matthew with a jaunty grin.

"Well, Matt," he said, at the same time he openly eyed the others in the cabin. "Here I am. Any vittles left?"

Rebecca jumped up and swung a blackened cast iron pot, suspended on a crane, out of the fireplace. Grainy retrieved a wooden trencher and handed it to her along with a Maplewood spoon.

Pushing an unruly lock of hair away from her face and tucking it securely under the edge of her mobcap, Rebecca pointed to the seat she had vacated by the fire.

"Please sit here, Mr. McGirth." Her eyes twinkled as the visitor claimed the seat and took the plate of steaming beans and bacon from her hand. Grainy quickly laid a piece of crackling bread on the side of the plate.

"We've already eaten, so you go right ahead," Grainy told him. She looked down to hide a smile of her own, amused by the way that Rebecca was fawning over their visitor.

"Please call me Daniel, ma'am," he said to Rebecca with a quick grin. Turning his smile on Grainy, he raised an eyebrow. "May I help you, Mrs…"

"Stokes, Egrain Stokes." She smiled back at him. "But people generally just call me Grainy."

McGirth nodded his head. "Pleased to meet you, ma'am." He rose from the stool, bowed slightly, and reseated himself before shoving a healthy spoonful of food into his mouth.

"Please excuse my boldness Mr. Mc… er, Daniel," Grainy stammered, embarrassed by having been caught staring at a stranger. She grinned mischievously, and added, "It's just that I was looking for your forked tail and horns!"

McGirth erupted into a boisterous laugh. "I see you've been talking to some damned rebel!" he howled, almost choking on a mouthful of crackling bread. Sobering, he added, "Excuse me for the profanity, ma'am."

"You're most graciously excused. What else would you call them?"

"Quite right." He smiled and continued eating.

Matthew reclaimed his stool alongside McGirth. "Daniel can tell you just about anything you would care to know about rebels."

"That is true," his guest agreed. "After all, I used to be one of them."

Grainy blushed. "I had heard that, Mr. McGirth," she admitted, adding coyly, "Of course the story I heard was from the lips of a *damned* rebel." She glanced defiantly at her husband, who frowned openly at her bold profanity. "Don't look so glum, John. Isn't that epitaph part of their name? At least it is when you men talk of them!"

"It does my heart good to hear a Tory woman speak her mind," McGirth quipped between bites of food. "Most of 'em I run onto, have been cowed by these Patriots who would deny freedom to any who disagree with them."

"I beg you not to think me too bold, but would you mind telling us the true story of how you were turned from the rebel cause, back onto the side of truth and justice?" Grainy asked. "Having heard it from you, it will truly be a tale to tell our children one day."

Looking over his shoulder at the curious eyes peering down on their elders from the loft, McGirth smiled and wiped his mouth with the back of his sleeve. "Why don't you call your young'uns down, ma'am, and I'll tell them myself."

Tears formed at the corners of Grainy's eyes. One trickled down her cheek, hung precariously from her chin, and dropped down the bosom of her loose fitting smock. "My children are prisoners of my family, rebels all!"

McGirth leaned forward, studying Grainy intently. "Matthew tells me you folks are from Ninety-Six."

"Yes, sir, we are."

"The boys and I are due to carry out a mite of foraging around that area. If you'll explain to me where your rebel relations live, we may just stop by one day and pay them a friendly visit. I'm sure they'll agree that your children are better off with you, than with them. I have some mighty persuasive fellas ridin' with me."

"Oh no! Please don't do them any harm, Mr. McGirth," Grainy pleaded. "I couldn't live knowing I'd hurt my family."

McGirth gave a genuinely friendly laugh. "Don't you worry, missy, we won't harm a hair on their rebel heads. Would that suit you, if it gets your young'uns back where they belong?"

"Thank you, sir. Yes, it would." She smiled through her tears.

"Then that's settled." He turned to the Nowlands and said, "Now, why don't you two get your brood down here, and I'll spin a yarn for them that they'll tell their grandchildren about one day."

Daniel waited until he finished his supper before beginning his story. He looked around with a sly smile at the upturned faces of the three children sitting expectantly in front of him. They were arranged in a semicircle on the puncheon floor.

"As you all know," he began, "I started this war as a rebel militiaman. I had my fateful mare, *Gray Goose*, with me even then. She was a magnificent animal, only two years old at the time. There was a lieutenant, name of

Gibson, who tried to buy the Goose from me, but, of course, I wouldn't part with her. One thing led to another and wham!" He punctuated his story with a jab of his fist into his open palm and smiled as the children jumped back in surprise. "The man hit the ground! Well, where I come from, when two men settle a difference like that, it's between them. But not the lieutenant! He had me court-martialed and then had me tied to a post in front of my friends and whipped like a slave!" He shook his head in remembrance. In front of him, little eyes lit up with the unspoken questions of childhood. A quick laugh escaped from the serious looking man.

He smiled and nodded. "Yes, I'll let you see them." Standing erect, he turned away from his audience and lifted his hunting frock, exposing a kaleidoscope of puffy red scars crisscrossing the pale white skin of his back. He smiled over his shoulder. "Go ahead, get a good look," he said to the engrossed children, who catapulted to his side to explore the marks.

Dropping his shirt, he turned around and resumed his seat. Leaning forward, speaking almost in a whisper, he said, "That was the result of the first whipping. But I was sentenced to get two! Well, sir, Daniel McGirth ain't no fool. That night I slipped out of the tent they had me confined in, stole my way to the Goose, and raced away into the night. I let it be known over my shoulder as I rode out of camp, and in no uncertain terms, that I would get even with that bunch!" He sat back and took a deep breath. "Well, I made my way to Florida where old *Burnfoot Brown...*" He leaned forward again and said in a conspiratorially low voice to the children, "Don't ever let him hear you call him that 'less you want to end up with a back looking like mine!" He smiled at their terrified expressions. "To make a long story short, when I made it back to Florida, Colonel Brown was more than glad to take me into his Florida Rangers. Made me a lieutenant colonel just like him!" He glanced quickly towards Grainy and added, "That's the true story of how a rebel becomes a loyal subject of King George III, ma'am."

Grainy looked wide-eyed with disbelief at the speaker. "But surely, sir, there must be more to the story than that! Didn't your own convictions of what is right and wrong weigh on your conscience?"

McGirth gave a quick, humorless laugh. "Why no, ma'am. You see, here in the back country people don't feel as strongly about these issues as you folks in the settled areas do. Take my own men for instance. I'm certain many of them would switch sides the instant a weakness is perceived in the British war effort. They," he indicated a vague mass of unknown humanity with a jerk of his head towards the cabin door, "fight for the winning side." He held up his hand to stay a response from the startled woman.

Grainy sat, open-mouthed, bursting to ask more questions as McGirth continued, "You see, these men have never paid any taxes, probably never will. Those rebels in the backcountry fight because of the Proclamation of 1763, which forbids the settlement on lands west of the mountains. If the rebels win, they'll be free to steal every last acre of this country from the Indian tribes. On the other hand, the ship owners on the coast want to be free of import and export restrictions, so they can become wealthy like their counterparts in England. And finally, the American-born gentry wants to rule a country—any country. They can't do that while Britain controls us; Colonists aren't allowed titles. Take their Mr. Washington for instance. Had the old King George[5] knighted him after he saved what was left of Braddock's army back in the French wars, he would be a Loyalist right now!" He shrugged his shoulders. "You see, ma'am, I'm not an overly educated man, but I do expect to be richly rewarded for my service to the King once we've whipped these miscreants back into their place. It's all a question of money and political power. We British and Loyalist have it, the rebels want it, and they plan to get it over our dead bodies!"

Grainy sat back, subdued, troubled. "Surely there's more to it than money and power. Doesn't what is right and honorable play into the decision?"

"For a very few, I'm sorry to say. Take for instance these two gentlemen here." He indicated John and Matthew with a clap to Matt's shoulder. "I'll wager all I have, they will fight for good old King George to the bitter end if it ever comes to that." His fleeting, humorless laugh erupted again, and ended quickly. "But, of course, it won't."

Having finished baiting her, he turned his attention to John. "Back to the reason for my visit. What are you of a mind to do about this McDougal business?"

"I will defer to your judgment, colonel," John answered. "However, I do feel some responsibility for the young lady."

"Hump! You'll get over that, sir, I assure you! If you start feeling responsible for every family that's burned out, you'll not have time left for killing off these rascally rebels."

John though for a moment. "I don't plan on that, but in this case, she is a very young and vulnerable woman, and orphaned so suddenly!"

"Surely there is something we can do Mr. McGirth, er… Daniel," Grainy interjected.

"Yes, quite. I have talked to Matthew here about the young woman's predicament. Normally, I would leave the matter in Colonel Waters's hands, but since my detachment will be heading back south the day after tomorrow, and we will be passing by the old McDougal place, if you've a mind to retrieve the girl's belongings and can get a wagon, you can ride that far with us. Getting back though…"

"I can get about five men to go with us," Matthew said. "Do you think that'll be a strong enough party to keep the rebels at bay?"

"Normally, no. But if we keep this a secret, I think you can pull it off. The rebels will be expecting us to head south together. They'll follow me and the boys. Most likely you can slip back undetected with the wagon. It is a chance though. Of course, Colonel Waters must approve this."

"Of course," they agreed.

Daniel nodded. "Until tomorrow then." He rose to his feet. "Mrs. Nowland, Mrs. Stokes." Throwing a quick bow to the ladies in the room, he disappeared through the cabin door.

* * * *

John and Matthew met with Colonel Waters late the next morning. Hesitant at first, the colonel gave his reluctant approval. "I don't see how we can abandon the child of a fellow Loyalist in need. Dangerous though I deem the request, you may proceed with no more than ten men, volunteers. Report back to me immediately. Dismissed!"

Turning to go, John halted abruptly and turned back to face the colonel. "Sir, if I may impose on you, I could use your advice?"

Waters eyed him for a moment. "Of course. At your service, sir."

"Thank you. As you know, I just arrived yesterday with Sergeant Hopkins."

The colonel simply nodded and waited silently for John to continue.

"He mentioned there were towns in the Cherokee territory where Loyalist families have taken refuge. I would like your opinion on their security, as a refuge for my wife."

"Are you going to be staying with her?"

"At first, but once she is safely settled, I plan on returning to join either yourself or Colonel Brown."

Waters had been looking down, studying the floor, his head shot up. "Are you certain of this?"

"Yes, sir, I am. But I must confess, I know absolutely nothing of the Indian's style of fighting."

"Are you a good horseman?"

"I can ride, but I am far from accomplished. I have spent the last few years running a gristmill. The most that I've had to do with horses was riding behind them in a wagon."

Colonel Waters held up a message. "New orders. The Florida Rangers are now designated as the King's Carolina Rangers." He paused, seemed to come to a conclusion within himself, and then added, "And made into a unit of foot. So you have a choice, walk or ride. I must confess that I could use more men, but the most I could promise you is duty as a courier until you hone your riding skills. Of course, with me you would be with the Indian

Department, which requires the ability to speak their language." He raised an eyebrow in a silent question.

John shook his head. "Sorry, sir, I don't speak a word of Cherokee."

"Too bad, it looks like the Carolina Rangers for you. Now, back to your original request. We do have several families of Loyalists living out in the Indian towns. I believe they are safer there, than here. I don't know if you're aware of it, but with the evacuation of Augusta, the rebels are migrating back into the Ceded Lands and bringing the war with them. So, to answer your question, yes, by all means take your family to the safety of those towns. I'm sending Sergeant Hopkins and Private Fenton out to them next week. I would not be averse to you accompanying them. Is that agreeable to you?"

"Yes, sir," John responded eagerly. Smiling widely, he followed Matthew from the room.

The two men were halted on the front porch of Waters's home by the drumming of hoof beats rapidly approaching from the south. A few moments later, a red-faced and dusty rider raced his heavily lathered mount through the fort gates. He catapulted from the saddle before the horse had come to a complete stop, raced past the two gaping men, and barged through the front door of the house, bellowing that he had important dispatches. Colonel Waters appeared and relieved the man of his dispatch case. Before disappearing through a side door into his office, he ordered one of his servants to see to the man's needs. A few moments later, Waters reappeared only long enough to order the two gawking men to send for the officers in the fort.

By that evening the news had spread to every man in the fort and outlying area. A group of Rangers had been captured and taken to the gaol at Ninety-Six. There, several of them, including one of their officers, a Lieutenant Hall, had been hanged as traitors. Another Ranger, Sergeant McAlister, who had been stationed at a paroled American officer's home to protect him from Loyalist vengeance, had also been killed and hacked to pieces by an American raiding party. All available men were ordered to move immediately down river with Daniel McGirth to help cover the withdrawal of the British Army, which was falling back on Savannah. Glum faces met John and Matthew at every turn.

"We better get that wagon quick! And be ready to move," Matthew advised John as the pair elbowed their way through the agitated mob milling about in front of the colonel's home.

Chapter 3

Colonel Thomas Waters's Fort
Sunday, February 28, 1779

The following morning they departed Colonel Waters's Fort in that false dawn that heralds the approach of the sun. Matthew, as the most experienced teamster among them, was elected to drive the borrowed wagon. Even with skills honed by a lifetime of constant use, he struggled to keep pace with the rapidly moving militiamen.

Hoping to catch the rebel army before it flew apart and went to ground, the cavalcade surged along the narrow trail, following Colonel McGirth down the west side of the Savannah River at a furious pace.

John, holding grimly onto the sideboards, sat in the bed of the wagon with Roger Weatherford and two other refugees from Ninety-Six. They were jolted and flung about unmercifully as it butted along the rutted and deeply washed trail. Sergeant Hopkins, along with the other Rangers and Cherokee scouts, appeared as vague apparitions in the heavy curls of dust that trailed the wagon. Like John, they had covered their faces against the choking clouds of dust. They looked like highwaymen in pursuit of a victim.

Ahead of the wagon, dust churned from the dry roadbed by the two hundred horses that preceded them clouded the air. Even the leaves of the underbrush along the margins of the trail were coated with a thin red layer. It was a world of dust, created by the riders who charged ahead recklessly, secure in the belief that their numbers would deter any rebels from firing on them.

By the time Matthew coaxed his jaded team to a halt in the McDougal clearing, the lead riders had finished watering their horses. Those who had arrived first had stripped the saddles from their mounts and were giving them well-deserved rubdowns. Southerners had learned the hard way not to work during the hottest part of the day.

John dismounted gingerly from the back of the wagon. As he walked back and forth to work the stiffness from his back and legs, he spied Colonel McGirth standing alone at the edge of the creek. McGirth was facing away from him, loosely holding the reins of the Gray Goose, letting the mare have her fill of the cool water. John walked over to thank him for the escort. Having great respect for the abilities of the man who had literally run circles around the rebel army for the past few years, he hesitantly asked him for any last minute advice.

McGirth gave John an appraising look. "Once you're loaded, move down the road about two miles and hold up for the night. Find a good spot well off the road to conceal the wagon. When you do move, keep those two Cherokees out ahead, and have the Rangers follow behind. Make sure every musket is primed and loaded. Don't take anyone's word for it, check them yourself."

John studied the edges of the nearby forest as McGirth spoke. For the first time in his life it looked dark and foreboding.

McGirth shook his head. "I have a bad feeling about this area. I can smell the stink of rebels, thick as thieves around here! Don't go to sleep tonight without a guard and keep those Cherokees out scouting the whole time you're loading that wagon. If they spot anything, light out! Leave the wagon; it won't do you any good if you're dead. And for God's sake, don't light any fires!"

A few hours later, John's small party watched anxiously as Colonel McGirth and his men splashed across the creek and disappeared into the tree line heading south. Left alone, they felt suddenly small and inconsequential.

Sergeant Hopkins looked at his companions. As the senior ranking man in the detail, he felt the hefty sense of responsibility for their welfare resting on his shoulders.

"Well," he said, "let's get to work and get out of here before a passel of rebels show up. This is a mighty unhealthy area for a handful of the King's men to tarry in."

They knocked the frame of the old rope bed apart and emptied the dry cornhusks from the mattress before loading it in the bed of the wagon. After lashing it into place, Matthew gave the bed frame a stout slap and winked at the other men. "This here is everything that a good man needs to start a family of his own." He looked at Jacob and smiled sheepishly.

They all laughed when Jacob's ears turned bright red with embarrassment.

The McDougal's lean-to shed had been overlooked by the raiders. There, they found such handy items as an adz, two axes, a set of chisels, and three awls.

"These tools will come in mighty handy," Matthew said, as he ran his fingers along the wooden handle of a froe. He flashed a quick smile in Jacob's direction. "They'll make Judith a good dowry when the right man comes along."

Thunder's Child, who had been scouting in the direction of Waters's Fort, returned two hours later leading a lumbering milk cow by a rope halter. The cow bawled miserably, its distended udder in need of a good milking. The aggravated expression on Thunder's Child's face clearly told that he would much rather eat the noisy creature than have its pitiful moans bring the enemy down around their heads. He exchanged some angry words with Sergeant Hopkins before handing over the animal's lead rope and sauntering to the edge of the creek, where he dropped to his knees and took a long drink.

"What did he say?" John asked

"He wants us to hurry up, and he also wants to get rid of that heifer. He says she'll slow us down." Hopkins looked around, taking in every detail of the clearing, tree line, and cabin. "We're about finished here. I reckon we'll be moving out in about an hour." He looked over one shoulder. "Jacob!"

Thunder's Child scowled at him from the creek. Jacob poked his head through the low doorway of the cabin.

"Fetch a bucket and milk this cow. It'll quiet her down and give us something to drink at supper."

With the wagon creaking in protest, the small convoy moved out two hours before sunset. John and Roger ambled along on foot, muskets held casually, confident that the Cherokees and Rangers would warn them of impending danger. As the sun dipped below the western tree line, Sergeant Hopkins motioned for Matthew to pull the wagon from the narrow trail. He maneuvered it through the closely spaced trees, far enough from the trail that it would avoid a cursory glance by passing rebels. After covering it over with freshly cut branches, the men sat in the gathering gloom, munching on stale cornbread and dried meat, and washing it down with the warm milk Jacob had coaxed from the cow before leaving the cabin. Roger pulled out his pipe and tobacco, but Hopkins shook his head. "No smoking tonight," he said, motioning towards the road that was barely visible through the thick underbrush. "Anyone passing by would smell it."

With a sigh, Roger replaced the fragile clay pipe in a small leather bag suspended around his neck. He shrugged. "Oh well, might as well get some sleep." He looked around at the other men. "Who's taking the first watch?"

* * * *

John woke suddenly in response to a hand placed urgently over his mouth.

"Shhh!" The dark outline of Sergeant Hopkins hovered over him. He felt the pressure of the hand slacken, then disappear. "Quiet," the sergeant whispered, "someone's coming, and I don't think they'll be taking tea with us."

John nodded. He sat up and checked the priming of his doglock while the sergeant shook Matthew's shoulder, administering the same quiet warning. In the darkness, John could hear the faint sounds of Dobbins and Jacob waking the others.

Thunder's Child materialized at Hopkins's side, whispered, and then melted wraithlike into the night. The sergeant looked at the groggy men. "Do *not* fire unless I do!" he hissed.

John moved quietly to the position the sergeant pointed out to him. He dropped onto his stomach and lay prone, concealed among the enormous roots of a stout hickory that had snaked their way upward, in some places rising as high as two feet above the ground. Through the course material of his hunting frock he could feel a slight tremor in the earth intensifying as the unknown riders drew nearer.

When the first rebels appeared there were only five of them. Their black outlines were clearly visible in the rapidly fading darkness. John felt his hands growing sweaty against the wooden stock of his musket. He cringed involuntarily and pressed his body lower to the ground. To his left, despite the chill of the morning, he saw Matthew wipe sweat from his forehead. Their eyes met briefly; John smiled and looked back towards the trail.

To the north, a loud rumble announced the approach of the main body of the enemy. The hidden Loyalists looked at each other, eyes wide, as the tightly bunched column of rebels burst into view. John recognized the man leading the troops as his old nemesis, Andrew DeLoach, the ringleader of the mob that had burned his home. Mouth compressed into a thin line, he ran his finger along his musket flint, testing its edge. To his left, Sergeant Hopkins frowned and shook his head. John relaxed his hand, leaned closer into the hickory root, and waited as the final group of riders pounded past.

They continued waiting even after the rear guard passed by. To the south, the sounds of the horsemen faded in the distance; the dust disturbed by their passing drifted down, settling onto the backs of the hidden men. They became uneasy, wondering what to do.

Stay put? Or move back to the wagon? The question was answered when Robin appeared from the south and indicated that all was clear. A moment later Thunder's Child came from the north with a similar report.

Sergeant Hopkins spoke to them in a low, almost inaudible voice, "Very quietly, move back to the wagon and get the horses into their traces. Dobbins, Jacob, saddle up. We're moving out of here just as fast as we can." He paused long enough to look down the trail in the direction of the vanished riders, then spit and shook his head. "This time last month, every damned rebel in this county was heading in the opposite direction, crapping in their pants, and looking over their shoulders. Now they're back like a band of rabid dogs on the trail of a wounded deer. Well, they'll be heading back quick enough once they twist the tail of the British Lion!"

Chapter 4

Unicoi Trail
Sunday, March 14, 1779

The small, two wheeled cart bumped along the trading path heading northwest. Every step of its two-horse team carried them farther from the war and the violence that continued to rage behind them. With the help of Colonel Waters and their old friends at his fort, they had managed to get their hands on most of the supplies that would be needed when they started their new lives at Long Swamp Village. The cart groaned under the weight of those supplies. Keenly aware that a broken wheel or tongue could cause them several days delay, John drove cautiously, carefully controlling the speed of the cart, nursing it over each obstacle while Grainy, Judith, and Ruth walked behind.

When the small group of travelers reached the ford at the Soquee River[6] they halted for the day. While the women collected dry wood and kindled a fire, and the men prepared the campsite, John roamed the river bottom in search of wild game that abounded in the area. He returned just before sunset with a small, field-dressed doe draped across his shoulders. Sergeant Hopkins and Dobbins wasted no time in stringing the carcass up for skinning. Once the butchering was done, the men skewered it with a freshly trimmed pole and lugged it to the camp, where they transferred the responsibility of cooking the meat to the women.

Their work done, the men knelt at the riverbank to wash the blood and dried meat from their hands and knives.

"When do you think we'll reach Little Chota?"[7] John asked Sergeant Hopkins. The sergeant sat on a large rock, leisurely smoking his pipe. He blew a smoke ring and watched it dissolve in the air as he mentally calculated an answer.

"Tomorrow, mid-afternoon."

"What's your plan when we get there?" John queried.

"Stay over a day or two, rest the horses, and check out the cart before we move on. There's another trail that splits off thereabouts and heads southwest to Long Swamp. We should be there inside of a week."

"Any English families in Little Chota?"

"A few. There's one white woman married to a Cherokee, and a trader that has a small commissary by the river. He trades for a few furs. Claims to get gold sometimes, but mighty little of it. What makes you ask?"

"I was just thinking that the sooner we get a crop in the ground, the better off we'll be. Maybe we should hold up at Little Chota?"

Hopkins nodded to himself as he thought about John's words. "It is a beautiful place, and with it lying right along the Chattahoochee, the ground is good. It'll grow about anything that you've a mind to plant." He looked sideways at John. "A body could do worse. But you had better ask the people there. They may not be happy havin' Loyalists living amongst them. Draws the attention of the rebels. Those bastards came through here early on in the war and burned a sight of towns. That's why they want us settled so far beyond them, in Long Swamp. It's kind of the border between the Cherokee and Creeks. That way, if the rebels get riled, the two tribes can blame us on each other."

The men headed back to the cart where Grainy, Judith, and Ruth Weatherford, assisted by Jacob, had the deer turning on a spit over a bed of coals. Judith stood to one side, critically eyeing the meat. Using a makeshift brush, she basted the meat every fifteen minutes with melted bacon drippings to keep it moist. Venison was mighty lacking in fat and tended to dry out something fierce when it was roasted.

Grainy answered the men's question before it was asked. "It'll be ready when the meat pulls away from the bone," she said and looked at Ruth. "We're going to need a pair of lanterns before we're done. It's going to be dark before supper's ready."

Ruth hustled to the wagon, where she trimmed two candles and placed them in glass-sided lanterns. She lit them with a twig from the fire and hung them by wires from the low branches of nearby trees.

"What else you women cookin' up?" Dobbins quipped, directing the question straight at Jacob. A huge grin formed around the stem of his clay pipe in anticipation of Jacob's retort.

"Potatoes," Jacob answered without the slightest hesitation, refusing to be baited into a bickering argument with the good-natured Dobbins. He licked his lips. "Mmm ... they're coated with bacon drippings and salt, and baking in a pot under the coals this very moment." He looked proudly at Judith and added, "That were Judith's doing, she's a right handy cook."

"She better be, to fill up a bear like you!" Dobbins laughed. He enjoyed embarrassing Jacob in front of the lovely Miss McDougal by making sport of Jacob's obvious worship of her.

Jacob looked at the ground, a blush of color creeping up his neck. Judith came to his rescue with a quick retort. "I guess I can handle that job, Mr. Dobbins!" she said defensively. "If'n I have too!"

Knowing glances passed from person to person. Grainy's eyes met John's and a contented smile transformed her face into a likeness of angelic rapture. Unable to resist a surge of overwhelming passion for his wife, John pulled her close and kissed her on the forehead, his face a portrait of love and contentment.

"Remember when we were like that?" he whispered.

A church-like silence descended over the group of travelers. The spontaneous show of emotion, as tender as it was genuine, had transformed the entire atmosphere of the camp. It felt suddenly charged with magic, energized with passion. Sergeant Hopkins stared into the fire, dreaming of his own wife, who he hadn't seen for almost a year, and who was waiting for him at Long Swamp.

Dobbins felt likewise. He drew contemplatively on his pipe. All was quiet except for the crackling of the fire and an occasional hiss as juices from the meat dripped onto the coals, producing spirals of greasy smoke. Ruth Weatherford gently nudged Judith, indicating with a nod of her head that she needed to keep turning the spit. The spell broken, conversation resumed as abruptly as it had ended a few fleeting moments before.

That night, while their companions slept, Grainy gently wakened John. He opened his eyes to find her propped on one elbow, smiling down at him. Around them, the night had grown intensely dark. He could see her as a mere shadow outlined against the blue-black of a moonless sky. All about their makeshift bed, scattered by the thousands along the forest floor, the katydids continued their eternal argument, competing with the crickets and frogs to fill the night with sounds. In the dim light of the fire, nothing more now than a few shimmering coals, John could detect the contented glow in his wife's eyes. She reached out, touching him gently with her fingertips.

"Why Mrs. Egrain Simpson Stokes, you naughty girl!" he whispered to her. "Just what do you have on your mind?" She pressed a finger to his lips for silence. Then, leading him by the hand, they crept softly into the night. The katydids, unconcerned, continued their song: *Katy did, Katy didn't, Katy did, Katy didn't … but Grainy did!*

* * * *

"Oh! How beautiful!" Grainy exclaimed the next afternoon, as she viewed the Nacoochee Valley for the first time. The narrow, level plain, nestled between low mountains, looked like a scene from a fairy tale.

"What mountain is that?" She pointed, childlike, to a large mountain that dominated the skyline to the south.

"That's called Mount Yonah, ma'am," Sergeant Hopkins said. "If you ride up that sloping spine on the east side, you can see for fifty miles! My wife and I will ride back this way one day and take you two up there. It's well worth the effort."

"It's about the most beautiful spot that I've ever seen!" Judith inhaled deeply, enjoying the crisp air and mountain vistas. "Jacob, why didn't you tell me about this?"

The young Ranger, walking beside her to rest his mount, merely smiled. All five of the refugees were awestruck by the sight of the valley. John could only muster a single word to describe the area, and that word was, "Beautiful."

Thunder's Child and Robin, who had ridden ahead two days ago, warmly greeted them as the cart rolled to a halt in front of the small log smithy.

"We'll make camp here," Sergeant Hopkins said. "Let the smith know of any repairs the cart needs, and he'll see to them." He next cautioned them firmly. "Make certain that you do not insult these people. Like it or not, you are the King's representatives in this country. What you do reflects on all of England."

The sergeant left the immigrants to make arrangements for a handful of minor repairs to their cart. He returned an hour later. Blackstone Mullis, the English trader in the town, had extended an invitation for John and Grainy to stay at his home.

"You see," the sergeant explained, "the Loyalist folks out here are starved for news from back home. Blackstone will feed you well, but you'll have to do a might of talking to earn your room and board." He thought for a moment and nodded in Judith's direction. "Miss McDougal, you best go along with these folks." Jacob's mouth flew open, but the sergeant looked directly at the young Ranger. "You'll sleep in the wagon to make sure everything stays safe." Jacob dropped his head like a sad puppy.

Grainy, seeing the young man's distress, looked plaintively at the sergeant and said in her sweetest voice. "Of course, sergeant, you wouldn't mind if I had Judith bring a trencher of food out to the private, would you?"

Hopkins guffawed. "Why no, ma'am," he said smoothly. "After all, the private is a soldier performing a *dangerous* assignment. By all means, see that he is well fed. Can't have him growing faint from hunger can we?"

Both Grainy and Judith presented the sergeant with their most enchanting smiles before they turned to follow John in the direction of the trading post. Behind them, they could hear Sergeant Hopkins informing the Weatherfords where they were to stay for the night.

Late that afternoon, a young Loyalist girl named Sally Chambers appeared at the wagon carrying three large bundles and a bar of freshly-made lye soap. She introduced herself as the niece of Blackstone Mullis, the local trader who had invited John and Grainy to share his cabin during their stay at Little Chota. Blackstone had allowed Sally to close the store early so she could guide the three women to a secluded bathing spot on the Chattahoochee River. The river's chilly waters flowed between low, heavily forested banks as it wound along the edges of the valley and curled past Little Chota. Sally, who was the about same age as Judith, explained that the downstream section of the river was reserved exclusively for the use of the village women, while the upstream side was strictly for the men.

Laughing and frolicking like children, the four women scrubbed themselves until their skin turned pink. Afterward, as they stood in the waist deep water, giggling and squeezing the excess water from their freshly washed hair, two women—one middle aged with dusty blonde hair, the other a young girl of about fourteen with mixed European and Cherokee features—appeared on the river bank. Both wore loose fitting but elegantly-decorated, doeskin smocks. Sally turned and called to them, explaining to Judith that the woman was called *The Forgotten One*. Since The Forgotten One spoke no English, Sally had taken it on herself to teach their language to the woman's daughter, Molly. Sally called to the two hesitant women and motioned for them to join her. The mother dropped a small package, wrapped in buckskin, to the ground before the pair stripped off their short shifts and stepped into the water. The Forgotten One yipped and said something in a teasing tone to her daughter. Even without understanding the language, the four Loyalist women clearly understood the words. The water had been shockingly cold when they had first stepped into it, also.

Their scrubbing complete, the six women, chattering like magpies, sunned themselves on the tops of a pair of large boulders that barely jutted free of the swift current. During a rare pause in the conversation, the Forgotten One suddenly turned to Molly and spoke in Cherokee. Molly hopped into the water and splashed her way towards their clothing, which was strewn about on rocks and hung from the lower branches of trees along the river's bank. She rummaged through a small bag, found what she was looking for, and, with a shout of success, turned and made her way back to the other women.

"My mother asks that you please accept these gifts," the young girl said. She held out a trio of hand-carved, bone combs to the three surprised women. When they hesitated, Molly added with a coy smile, "To refuse a gift is an insult to the Cherokee Nation!"

"Thank you!" the English women exclaimed as they reached for the treasures.

The women remained perched on the rocks, combing their tangled hair as they exchanged stories of their pasts. Molly interpreted for her mother, with Sally stepping in to help with those words that had no equivalent in the Cherokee tongue. With undisguised curiosity, Grainy and Judith asked for and received the story of The Forgotten One. Before beginning the tale, Sally told them that the older woman was in no way emotional about her past, having forgotten her first life, somehow endured before becoming a Cherokee.

The Forgotten One freely repeated the story told to her by her Cherokee father. He had brought her to the Real People, as the Cherokees called themselves, during the old French wars when she was no more than two years old. He had found her wandering alone in the forest after a war party had surprised a group of white settlers far to the north on the Susquehanna River in Pennsylvania. She had boldly walked up to him, stood toe to toe with the fiercely painted warrior, and raised her hands, silently demanding to be held. In response to this undisputed omen, he had scooped her into his arms and returned to Little Chota, adopting her into the Blue Holly Clan.[8] Obviously, her parents had forgotten her in their panicked flight, hence the name, The Forgotten One.

When Grainy reached back and began to wind her hair into a bun at the back of her head, the Forgotten One spoke to Molly, who translated. "My mother says you have beautiful hair. When the sun shines on it, it shimmers like a raven's wing. She thinks you should wear it loose, like Cherokee women. She also wants to know why white women hide their beauty by tucking it under an ugly cap."

"Why … I don't rightly know," Grainy answered. "I suppose it's just to keep it out of our way as we work." She smiled broadly. "Of course, if it's an insult to refuse a suggestion…"

Molly roared with laughter. She turned to face her mother, and, after a lengthy explanation, both women heed and hawed with merriment while Sally tried her best to explain the joke to the English women. "They know what Sergeant Hopkins said about your being representatives of the King. They think it hilarious that the actions of one person would sway their opinions of an entire people."

After a moment of thought, Grainy agreed. "But it would be foolish to disregard advice in a strange country from the people who live there. Tell her that I'll leave it loose." She smiled a knowing smile. "I see that gossip travels as fast in a Cherokee town as it does in the settlements!"

"Faster!" Molly said. "Surely, much faster!"

Their baths finished, the women waded ashore through the knee deep water. As Grainy reached to retrieve her one-piece shift from the fork of a narrow tree, Sally stopped her with a grin. "Here," she said, holding out one of the packages she had brought with her, "These are gifts from Blackstone and me."

Hesitantly, Grainy accepted the package, a questioning look on her face.

"These are for you," Sally said, as she handed Judith and Ruth a package of their own. The three women stood speechless. They were even more surprised when Molly and The Forgotten One unwrapped their own buckskin bundles and handed each of the women a small, neatly folded present.

"What?" Grainy began, "Not another present! How shall we ever repay you?"

Sally held up her hand and said puckishly. "It's a Cherokee custom to give visitors gifts. It would be an insult to turn them down." She laughed at her own joke. Then added, "It really is a custom!" Reaching for the package in Grainy's hand, she produced a small clasp knife and deftly severed the twine.

The three women gasped, awestruck at the richness of the gifts. From each bundle they pulled out an apron of either red, blue, or green; a gray bodice made of fine linen, and a white chemise and petticoat. None of the materials were locally made, all must have been imported from English mills at great expense.

Tears formed in the corners of Grainy's eyes. "We really can't..." she mumbled with a shake of her head. "What will our husbands say about accepting gifts from strangers?"

"But you must!" Sally assured her.

Grainy burst into laughter, sighed, and shook her head. "Then we have no choice, do we?" She grinned quickly in Ruth's direction. "It's our duty to accept."

Judith, who had no compunction about accepting the gift, was already pulling a chemise on over her freshly washed and goosepimpled skin. She looked around and grinned.

"What are you two biddies looking at?" she asked flippantly. "Myself, I don't have any husband to worry about." She grinned wickedly. "Mama McDougal didn't raise no foolish children!"

The Forgotten One stepped forward next and presented each woman with a soft pair of plain Cherokee moccasins. Molly, interpreting for her, added a lively, "Of course it is an insult to refuse!"

Grainy felt more light-hearted and refreshed than she had at any time since this ordeal had begun. She literally bounced with enthusiasm as the women made their way across the cleared fields of the town. She carried her mobcap loosely in her hand, letting her waist-length hair blow freely in the wind while the soles of her feet felt the texture of the ground through new moccasins.

"What a strange hill that is!" Grainy proclaimed suddenly. She pointed to a low, tree-covered mound at the edge of the village. "I noticed it when we first arrived."

Molly quickly corrected her. "That's not a hill, it's a mound left by the Ancient Ones."

"The Ancient Ones? Who are they?"

"We don't know, we just know that there were people living here before the Cherokee came. They left their mounds all over the land."

"How long ago was that?"

"No one knows." Molly shrugged, indicating that she had reached the extent of her knowledge on the subject.

"How do you know that it's not just a flat topped hill?" Judith said. "It would take a heap of time for folks to pile up all that dirt."

Molly, smiling at the ignorance of the women, decided to educate them. "Come on," she said, "I'll show you."

The group followed Molly to the edge of the mound where she stopped and conversed with her mother in what seemed more of an argument than a discussion. Both women made jerky motions with their hands as they talked. They acted nervous, wary of something unseen.

Sally looked about uncomfortably. "See?" She pointed up into a slight rain-eroded fissure that cut down the side of the mound. It looked uncannily like a jagged knife cut, as if some giant had at one time slashed the mound with his knife purely out of spite. "See those broken pots with those white sticks next to them?"

"Yes," the women all agreed.

"They're not sticks; they're the bones of the Ancient Ones."

"Are you sure?" Ruth asked skeptically. She took a step towards the mound. Both Molly and The Forgotten one yelped and grabbed an arm.

"No!" Molly commanded sharply. "This is the grave of the Ancient Ones, we dare not disturb them!"

The women stepped cautiously away from the mound as if distance increased their security from the unseen shades of the vanished race. All except Ruth Weatherford.

"Just a bunch of superstition, I say," Ruth mumbled. All five of her companions gave her a quick, hostile stare.

"Ruth!" Grainy snapped. She glared at the older woman for a moment before turning with the other women and continuing towards the town.

Ruth looked down, avoiding their eyes as they walked on in silence, but inside she boiled at what she considered an insult.

John, stepping from the shade of the smithy, paused—stunned into inaction, as was Roger Weatherford—at the sight of their well-dressed wives approaching. The women walked towards them in a tight, leisurely knot, strolling down the center of the dusty lane, prattling pretentiously, totally absorbed in their conversation. John frowned; Jacob simply smiled and smiled.

Face frozen into an irritated scowl, John marched out. Seizing Grainy rudely by the arm, he steered her to the cramped space between the smithy and the cart.

"What's the meaning of this?" he snapped. "We have no money for this! Where did it come from?" He seemed to choke for a moment. "And for decency's sake, cover your head woman!" He looked around as if she were a hunted felon in imminent danger of discovery.

Before she could answer, The Forgotten One strode confidently up to John. She stopped toe-to-toe with the taller man. Looking up, she scolded him profusely in Cherokee. Molly stood by, patiently waiting for her mother's tirade to end before she interpreted the angry message. John, stunned by the temerity of a mere woman administering a caustic tongue lashing to a grown man, stood dumbstruck, thinking *And she is a complete stranger to boot!*

The Forgotten One stopped abruptly, but continued to stare brazenly at the dazed man while Molly interpreted.

"My mother says these are gifts from the Cherokee people. It would be an insult to refuse them. She also wants to remind you that you are in the land of the Cherokees. A man does not lift his hand in anger to his woman." Her eyes twinkled mischievously as she added, "It is an insult!"

Grainy bit the inside of her lip to suppress an impish grin. "It is, John," she agreed meekly. "I tried to turn them down, but Sergeant Hopkins told us we are the King's representatives, and that we can't afford to insult our hosts." She looked down contritely. "I'm sorry, but I must keep them for the good of our country." With superhuman willpower, Grainy forced herself to remain outwardly serious as a silent, unrepentant giggle struggled to be released. Her shoulders convulsed slightly as she kept her head bowed in penitent repose. She could not trust herself to look into her husband's face.

Blowing a breath through tightly-pressed lips, John turned and stalked away. "God give me the strength to deal with willful women!" he snapped Grainy thought that The Forgotten One gave her a quick wink before turning to depart.

That night, after John had been given what was left of Grainy's new bar of soap and directed to the men's area of the river, they announced themselves at the door of Blackstone Mullis's home. The trader opened the door and held out his hand in welcome. He was a short man, rather rotund with unruly salt and pepper hair that framed a heavily-jowled, clean-shaven face. His rich blue eyes seemed to twinkle when he talked. The three guests took to him immediately. Sally stood to one side with a friendly smile.

"Do you have a wife, Mr. Mullis?" Grainy asked. She looked around at the neat, one-roomed cabin.

"Please, ma'am, call me Blackstone. As to a wife, the answer is yes, and no. I do have one, but she and her parents fled to Halifax from Charleston early on in this war and I have not seen her since. I do, however, receive a letter every once in a blue moon. It's the small price that I pay for my loyalty to King George III. God bless him!" Blackstone thought for a moment, seeming to weigh his next words carefully before adding, "I was able to save a few of her things. I've recently put them to a better use." He smiled knowingly at Grainy and then motioned for Sally and the three visitors to take a seat at a rude wooden table.

Molly bustled about the room, busily setting the table for the meal: cornbread baked from finely ground meal, smoked pork, navy beans simmered with bacon, molasses, and brown sugar, baked sweet potatoes, and, for dessert, apple pie. Steaming cups of tea were poured to wash it all down.

Blackstone looked at Grainy. "You've met Molly," he said. "I employ her to take care of my domestic chores." He looked towards John and added hastily, "You may lean your musket against the wall by the door, sir. We're quite safe here." He motioned for John to sit in an unpainted ladder-backed chair that sat at one end of the table and claimed its mate at the far end for himself. The women sat opposite from each other on the long benches that flanked both sides of the table.

Grainy's eyes sparkled as she surveyed the cornucopia spread out before them. "I almost feel guilty sitting here while the Weatherfords are taken, God knows where," she confessed.

"Don't you worry about them, ma'am," Blackstone consoled her. "They, like you, will be well taken care of. You must understand that the Cherokees are not overly fond of either side in this war. But they are acutely aware of the disaster that will befall them should the rebels prevail. They are very cognizant of the sacrifices that people such as yourselves have made. They know, quite well, that it could just as well happen to them one day. Isn't that right, Molly?"

Molly was sitting a trencher of biscuits on the table. Grainy noticed with surprise that the biscuits were made with real wheat flour. A wooden bowl of ham gravy was placed alongside the other foods on the table. Molly smiled, quipped a quick, "Yes," and left the room on another errand.

"Molly is half white," Blackstone explained. "Her mother is a white woman captivated back during the old French wars. She was so young when she was taken that she doesn't even remember her own name. But she can't hide that light hair of hers, no matter how much she wants to keep it hidden from the rebels."

"I met her this afternoon," Grainy answered. "She seems like a fine young woman."

"Is she wanted by the rebels?" John asked.

"No, they probably don't even know about her. But if they find her, they'll drag her, kicking and screaming, back to a civilization that will neither understand nor accept her."

"I see," John said. "But would she not be better off in the white world once this rebellion has been put down?"

Blackstone laughed. "Why, Lord no! Women rule the roost in a Cherokee town!" He patted the back of Grainy's hand before continuing. "Once you've been here a while you'll see, even this fine young lady will be corrupted."

A crimson stain crept up John's neck and spread itself across his cheeks, highlighting the small sprinkling of smallpox scars that pitted his upper neck.[9]

Sensing that he had inadvertently angered his guest, Blackstone was quick to repair the damage.

"My apologies, sir!" he blurted out with more than a hint of contrition in his voice. "I did not mean to insult you, or your wife. Please forgive me." He rose from his chair and gave a quick half bow to his guest.

"I sincerely pray that you two gentlemen will remain friends," Grainy interceded. "Please! Let us eat! My mouth is fair watering at the sight and smell of this food!" She turned her face to Blackstone, batting her eyelashes innocently. "Would you be so kind as to say Grace for us?"

After the meal, while the women cleared the table and scrubbed the trenchers, Blackstone led John out onto the small, dirt-floored porch that ran along the front of his cabin. He motioned for John to have a seat on a block chair[10] placed on one side of the door and then sat on a low puncheon bench[11] that was pushed back against the wall on the opposite side. While Blackstone rested his back against the hand hewed logs behind him, John leaned forward, elbows resting on knees, tamping the tobacco into his pipe with his thumb. Blackstone stood and carefully pushed open the glass on one side of a candle lantern that hung from a low rafter above his head. He removed the candle, lit his pipe, and passed the taper to John. Both men sat idly blowing streamers of smoke into the darkness as they gazed into the night.

A natural symphony of katydids, crickets, and frogs filled the air. Mosquitoes buzzed about the lantern, bumping against the glass with tiny tapping sounds in their suicidal efforts to merge with the candle's flame.

Above the open fields lining the river, bats darted silently overhead, feeding on unseen insects, while fireflies floating indolently on the night air flicked their tails on and off in slow, melancholy rhythm.

The two men stood respectfully when Grainy and Judith stepped from the doorway and crossed into the night bearing food and drink for Jacob. They watched them walk away, the womanly curves of their bodies accentuated by their newly acquired finery and faintly illuminated by the dull glow of the candle lantern.

Blackstone could not help but admire Grainy's form as she stepped lightly along in the night beside her companion. She was an intriguing young woman. Although at first glance only mildly attractive, with eyes set too closely together and separated by what could only be termed a Roman nose, men could not help but admire her. If a master artist were commissioned to paint her exact likeness, and succeeded in doing so, it would show an unremarkable face. But she was one of those rare individuals that all people encounter at some point in their lives. They have an aura of some unknown mystique about them. Grainy's lithe movements, her totally feminine mannerisms, and her amiable personality combined with this almost magical aura, so that once she had departed from a person's presence, they were left with the unmistakable impression of having been in the company of a very beautiful woman. Blackstone shook his head to force himself out of his reverie and returned his attention to her husband.

"What's the news from the settlements?" he asked. "Any end in sight?"

John exhaled a stream of pungent gray smoke and shook his head. "No. We moved into Augusta, but pulled back for some reason. No one seems to know why. Some of our militia took a whipping at a place called Kettle Creek."

"That's what Hopkins told me," Blackstone said. "The British are always slow to do something. It was just like that during the old French War. We took a beatin' for years before they finally sent ole' Wolfe up to Canada to finish 'em off." He took a puff, drew it into his lungs, and held it for a moment before blowing it out in a long gray stream. "Looks like the same thing's going to happen here."

"I hope so, the sooner the better. My wife and I have lost about everything we owned by not turning traitor like Pickens and Clarke." He shook his head sadly. Like all Loyalists, John would never be able to see how people who turned on their own king and country could call themselves "Patriots" without feeling a touch of hypocrisy.

"You know either of those two gentlemen - Pickens or Clarke?" Blackstone asked.

"Just as acquaintances. I used to run a mill back in Ninety-Six District, and I would see Pickens once of a blue moon when we was milling for him. He seemed like nice sensible folk. I don't know what turns men like him into rebels."

Blackstone guffawed. "Money and power!" He took the pipe from his lips and held it in his hand, rubbing his fingers over the smooth bowl. "Mark my words. If either of them two don't end up as a governor, or with some type of title, they'll rebel again and start a third country. Rebel's are all alike, wanting to take by force what they can't get legally."

* * * *

Across the way, Grainy and Judith casually approached the wagon. Judith felt her heart jump when Jacob recognized them and stepped forward to meet her.

"Here you go, Private Fenton," she said as she handed him the trencher heaped with hot food, "as promised!" Spying a pair of empty nail kegs alongside the smithy wall, she laid a board over one and wiped the other with a damp cloth. She indicated the top of the keg. "Your table and chair, sir."

Jacob took one bite of the ham and closed his eyes, a smile of pure ecstasy on his face. "Now that's good meat!" he exclaimed before forking in another piece.

Grainy held out a pewter mug full of steaming tea. "Wash it down with this," she said. "I added a bit of cream to it before we left."

"Why thank you, ma'am!" Jacob said. Judith gave Grainy a pleading look as Jacob took a hearty gulp of the warm liquid.

Grainy smiled through her most convincing counterfeit yawn, slowly curled one arm upward and stretched her body in an exaggerated display of lassitude. "I think I'll sit on the seat of the wagon for a while, I'm a might tired today. Do you two think you will be all right by yourselves?" she asked, flashing the couple a knowing, secretive smile.

Jacob sat mute; Judith approved the idea with a quick grin.

Poor Jacob, Grainy thought to herself as she strolled towards the wagon, *He doesn't stand a chance.*

* * * *

The next day, the smith pronounced the cart fit for travel. Sergeant Hopkins declared they would start for Long Swamp at first light the following morning.

When Roger Weatherford urged them to move on that day, Hopkins rationalized his decision by telling him that the animals needed another days rest.

Immediately after finishing the afternoon meal, Grainy and Judith disappeared in the direction of the river with Sally and Molly, who had promised to teach them how to swim. Like many women in the settlements, they rarely had time for such luxuries. The women spent the entire afternoon splashing and frolicking in the shallow rapids of the river, paying little heed to the passage of time.

When they returned, strutting gaily along and laughing together without a care in the world, the sun hovered barely above the tops of the western mountains.

Blackstone spied them and called from the door of his commissary as they passed on the dusty street. "So this is why the oven's cold and there's no supper, is it?" Hands resting sternly on his hips, he gave the four women a caustic look, then erupted into laughter. "Never mind! We'll eat whatever's handy," he said something over his shoulder to a customer in the building and stepped back inside.

Embarrassed at having failed in their duties, the women rushed to get the evening meal ready by candlelight. Just as they were laying out the food on the table, Blackstone stepped onto the front porch. Leaning against a hand-squared post, he peered intently to the east, studying the dark trail that entered the village from that direction. When his curiosity was satisfied, he nodded his head.

"Set some extra places, ladies!" he called to them through the opened door. "It looks like my wagonload of supplies has arrived at last."

Ten minutes later, amid the snorting of draft animals and the rattle of trace chains, the wagon groaned to a halt in front of the commissary.

"Hey, Blackstone!" the driver called from his perch on the wagon's seat. "Where do you want this load parked for the night?"

"Right where it is'll be fine," Blackstone said. He walked to the side of the wagon and extended his hand to the driver. "Andrew, good to see you." He nodded to the other man who remained motionless, arms across his knees, cradling a loaded blunderbuss in an attitude of utter exhaustion. "Caleb."

Caleb returned the nod, raising his hand to acknowledge the greeting.

"We've been going since before dawn," Andrew said. "Too close to stop and too far away to keep goin'. You know the feeling." He grinned. His gap-toothed smile looked like a narrow checkerboard. The teeth that remained were unnaturally bright against a dust-stained face. "Know any refugees around here by the name of Stokes?" he asked, raising his head to look around, as if he could spot a person by that name based solely on appearance.

"As a matter of fact, I do," Blackstone answered. He turned to point to Grainy, who had come to the door of his cabin along with the other women to stare curiously at the newcomers.

"Are you John and Egrain Stokes of Ninety-Six?" the driver called to her.

"That's me," Grainy said and nodded.

"Well, ma'am, then we have a couple of deliveries for you. If you'll step to the back of the wagon I'll get them out." He fished around inside his shirt and held a wrinkled and travel-stained envelope out to her. "Colonel McGirth sent this here letter to you along with a couple of small packages."

Speechless, Grainy followed the man to the rear of the wagon, her mind racing in an attempt to guess what the partisan colonel would be sending her. The driver untied the canvass cover and peered in. As he leaned forward, his head and arms disappeared. Grainy could hear him mumbling something inaudible beneath the canvass as if he were giving directions to someone within. When he reappeared he held a sleeping child in his hands. "I reckon this here bundle belongs to you," he said.

Grainy felt as if she had been struck by lightning. She swayed, felt herself falling, and caught herself against the tailgate of the wagon.

"Lynn Celia!" She grabbed the child and crushed her to her chest; the sudden movement woke the baby. It squalled in angry protest.

"Here's the other one," the man announced as he sat two-and-a-half-year-old Simpson[12] on the ground. Simpson yawned and wiped his sleep-filled eyes with his fist. He looked up, jubilation registering immediately on his face. Even in the darkness he instantly recognized his mother. "Mama!" He leapt forward and attached himself to her leg like a tiny leech. Grainy burst into tears as people flooded out of nearby cabins to see what the commotion was all about. John came running at full speed from the direction of the smithy, calling his children's name as he ran. He slid to a stop at Grainy's feet and pried Simpson away from her leg, hugging him so fiercely that the boy cried out in pain.

"Here! Here!" Blackstone shouted. Pulling both parents by the arm, he guided them towards the door of the cabin. "Bring those young'uns into the light so's we can get a good look at them." He cast a quick look back in the direction of the two drivers. "Come on in, boys," he called over his shoulder, "the table's set. We can always feed two more!"

"We'll be right with you. Got two more passengers to unload."

Blackstone moved back to the wagon as the two drivers helped a young black woman, holding a baby of her own, down onto the ground.

"This here woman's husband has gone and got himself killed serving with Colonel Brown and the Rangers. Rebels captured him at Kettle Creek and stretched his neck down to Ninety-Six. She hid out in the woods, and then made it all the way to Waters's Fort by herself. The colonel said to tell you he's sent her along to take care of the Stokes child, but I'm thinkin' he just didn't know what to do with her. Probably afraid if the rebels got a hold of her they would return her to her old master. He's some Carolina rebel that her and her husband run off from two years ago. The colonel said for me to deliver her to a Sergeant Hopkins and have him see to her. I've got it all writ'n down right here." The man waved a second grimy envelope in Blackstone's face. "Know where I can find the sergeant?

"He's here in town," Blackstone said. He looked at the woman. "What's your name?"

"Seley Smith, sir," she answered.

"Well, Seley Smith, you go on in, and we'll get you something to eat. I'll be damned if I'll turn away the widow of one of the King's soldiers, regardless of what color she is!"[13]

The woman's mouth trembled slightly at the unexpected courtesy. She forced a smile through tears that welled up involuntarily and coursed down her dusky cheeks. "Thank you, sir," she said before disappearing into the cabin.

Unable to be parted from their children, John and Grainy held them in their laps long after sleep had stolen them away. They sat staring into the red, flickering flames that curled across the backlog, casting shadows that danced around the interior of Blackstone's hearth. Both sat in crude rocking chairs, as did their host. The other guests sat on the puncheon floor in a semicircle, using any space they could wiggle, or cajole, from their neighbors. The small cabin seemed packed with the dozen bodies it had been called on to shelter for the night. In the shadows, one of the drivers suddenly began to snore softly through his open mouth.

As the time neared midnight, much later than anyone present would have normally stayed awake, Blackstone cleared his throat. He looked at Grainy, who returned the stare, her lips parted slightly as awareness flickered in her face. "Why I near forgot!" Against the far wall, the sleeping driver opened an eye before drifting back to sleep. Holding the sleeping child in the crook of one arm, Grainy reached into her apron pocket and withdrew the envelope the drivers had given her when they arrived.

"John, this is a letter that Colonel McGirth sent along with the children."

Cradling his son carefully in one arm, John reached out and took the letter. Aroused from his slumber, Simpson frowned and rubbed his face roughly against the front of John's hunting frock. John waited until the child's breathing quieted again before he canted the envelope to catch the shimmering firelight. He studied the outside carefully. "Fancy," he remarked. "Sealed with wax." He opened the letter slowly and moved it around, testing various angles, in an attempt to catch the light. "Can't hardly read it though."

Blackstone rose and fetched a candle lantern. He stood directly behind John, holding the light over his shoulder. Seeing that one lantern would not be sufficient, he turned to Sally who sat beside the stone fireplace. "Sally, would you get that other lantern, please?" He spoke the words softly, so as not to wake the children.

News on the frontier was a rare and chancy thing. John knew it was almost considered a duty to share the contents of a letter with the others. He looked up. "If you'll permit me, I'll read it through first to myself, then tell what it says."

He looked down, pursing his lips. "Says here it's from Colonel McGirth, dated four days after we left for the Cherokee country." He moved his head from side to side as he scanned the document, pausing often to hold the paper closer to his face to make out a word. At one point he chuckled to himself. "I should say so," he mused aloud. He separated the top sheet from the second and took a quick look. "There's another letter in here from Colonel Waters." He lowered the pages to his lap and looked at his wife. "I'll get to that later," he said, sensing the growing impatience of his audience.

Waving the first letter, he announced triumphantly, "Colonel McGirth says that our troops have thrashed the rebels at a place in Georgia, called Brier Creek. Ever heard of it?" He looked over his shoulder at Blackstone, who shook his head. "Don't know as I have."

"There's a Brier Creek that runs into the Savannah, about half way between Augusta and Savannah," one of the drivers volunteered. "Ain't that right, Caleb?" he directed the question to his snoring partner. There was no response. Reaching out with his foot, he gave the sleeper a hearty shove. Caleb came awake suddenly, looking around, temporarily disoriented. "Ain't that right?" The driver repeated the question again, oblivious to the fact that the other man had no idea as to what the question was.

"Ain't what right? Damn it!" Caleb bellowed. He looked towards the women in the room, and added with an embarrassed gulp, "Sorry, ma'am."

"Brier Creek," he continued without a pause, "Ain't that about half way from Augusta to Savannah?"

Caleb rubbed his head sleepily and yawned. "Yeah, I seem to recall that it is." He gave a sudden angry leer at his partner. "What about it?" His lips poked out. He was sorely aggrieved at having been awakened for something as trivial as this. John and Grainy exchanged a humorous glance. In the darkness one of the women giggled softly.

"Well, Mr. Sleepy Head," the first man said, pulling himself erect. "As it turns out, we give the rebels a licking down there the first of March. Ain't that right?" He looked towards John to corroborate his story. "It were a terrible whipping too! I bet. Go on mister, tell him!" With a wave of his hand, he urged John to continue.

John chuckled, rechecked his facts, and continued, "Says here that they defeated some North Carolina General, name of Ashe, at Brier Creek. Captured all of his artillery and ammunition and inflicted about four hundred casualties on them." He looked down and reread the passage to be certain, before he continued. "That's what it says all right, four hundred rebels killed, wounded, or captured." He shook his head. After pondering on the enormity of the numbers, he added, "That's a passel of men to be kilt!"

"How many does it say we lost?" Blackstone tapped him on the back of the shoulder, to urge him on.

"Sixteen."

"Sixteen!" Blackstone exclaimed jubilantly. "Why at that rate this war'll be over before you know it!" Around him the news was greeted with similar enthusiasm.

"Thank the Lord!" Seley shouted, raising her hands to heaven. "There ain't nothin' in the world sweeter tempered than a dead rebel," she avowed. "I can't recall a soul that's ever been hurt by one in that condition."

"What else does it say?" Blackstone asked.

"The colonel also sends his complements to you, Grainy. Says that you must have misunderstood your family. Why, according to him, when he and his men dropped in for a visit, your old father was the most obliging *Loyalist* that he ever met." John paused to give his listeners a roguish grin. "He says the old gentlemen couldn't do enough to help the King's cause. Even fed all two hundred of McGirth's men for free."

"Well, I reckon a yard full of the King's soldiers would make even that old devil, Mr. Washington, act like a Loyalist," Grainy observed dryly.

"It ends like this," John said, reading directly from the letter. "'If I can ever be of any further service to you…'" he looked up quickly. "He means you, Grainy. '…I would consider it an honor and a privilege to be of service.'" John smiled. "I reckon I ought to be jealous of that there fellow."

Blackstone thumped his guest on the back with a friendly hand. "What's the other letter say, the one from Colonel Waters?"

John refolded McGirth's letter, then perused the second sheet of foolscap. Finished, he looked up. "Oh, not much. He just explains that he felt it unwise to dispatch such young children without a responsible female hand. He asks that we do all in our power to help Sergeant Hopkins in aiding Seley to start a new life out here." He looked gently down at his son, studied the cherub-like face of the sleeping toddler for a moment, and then announced to Grainy that it was time to climb into the loft.

"I think I'll step out for a while. It's a mite stuffy in here," Judith said nonchalantly.

Grainy laughed at the other woman, her teeth flashed in the reflected firelight. "You be sure to stay near the wagon. The Rangers are taking turns guarding it. I'm quite certain they'll keep you safe."

Although Grainy couldn't see it, she knew the young woman's face had flushed with embarrassment. Judith threw her head back, her unbound hair cascading freely across the back of her Chemise. "That's quite all right!" she snapped. "I can take care of myself!" Snatching a woolen shawl from a wall peg, Judith wrapped it about her head and shoulders. Thoroughly miffed, she stalked from the cabin.

"Now what do you suppose all that's about?" John asked, his face puzzled.

Grainy studied him for a moment to make sure the question was as innocent as it seemed. She smiled fondly and kissed him lightly on one cheek. "John, sometimes I find it hard to believe that we've been married three years and you still know almost nothing about women." Shaking her head in disbelief, she climbed the ladder into the loft.

Chapter 5

Long Swamp Village
Monday, March 22, 1779

John swiped the sweat from his brow with the back of one hand and slung it in a downward arch, spraying the moisture that flew from his fingertips onto the brown blanket of last years leaves. He took a step back, craning his neck and shading his eyes as he looked up at the beautifully formed black walnut tree towering above him, gauging the path of its imminent descent. Satisfied, he tightened his grip on the ax handle and swung the blade against the rich, purple-colored wood that his hacking had exposed beneath the giant's rough bark. Ever so slowly, the tree leaned into the cut as John circled around to the rear of the tree and sank the head of the ax into the backside of the notch. With a snap, followed by a series of crackles and pops, the tree began to lean into the notch, gaining momentum as gravity took hold and crashing to the ground amid the snapping sounds of breaking branches and loud thumps that jolted the earth beneath his feet. He took a deep breath and walked along the trunk to where the first branch sprouted. There, he began separating the upper branches of the tree from the smooth trunk. The top of the tree would be used for firewood. His main concern now was building a cabin as quickly as possible.

To his left another of the stately walnuts crashed to the ground, taking the top of a smaller tree with it as their branches became entangled during the fall. Through the underbrush he could see Jacob moving slowly along the fallen trunk, his finger testing the edge of his ax.

Sergeant Hopkins and Private Dobbins guided a pair of horses alongside a smooth log to his right, a long chain snaking its way through the leaves behind them. Using a cant hook, Hopkins rolled the trunk of the walnut onto a short section of wood that had been split down the middle. The motion raised one end of the trunk from the ground, allowing him room to wrap the chain around the log before dragging it to the building site where Roger Weatherford stood ready to dovetail the ends of the logs. John could see him tapping the straight piece of sapling he used as a ruler to keep the cuts evenly spaced against his leg as a signal for the other men to hurry up.

While he waited for Hopkins and Dobbins to return, John cast a critical eye along the slight rise of ground that extended along the banks of the Etowah River. He felt extremely lucky in finding this site. The trees were uniformly ten-to-twelve inches in diameter, easily handled. The land had been a field at some time in the past. Abandoned when it had stopped producing, probably fifty years before, it had been reseeded naturally by black walnut, oak, hickory, and chestnut, some of the most useful trees on the frontier. Behind the building site there was a game trail leading down to the river, carved into the bank by untold generations of deer, bison, dogs, bears, and humans.

To the east stood the village of Long Swamp, inhabited by several hundred people, mostly Cherokee with a smattering of Creek Indians from the south, and a few families of banished Loyalists. The English families tended to cluster on the west side of the village in a tightly knit community, acutely aware that their survival depended on each other and infected with more than a touch of suspicion that if the war ever turned in favor of the rebels, they could very well find themselves isolated in a hostile country.

John and Roger had decided to build a double cabin with a common roof and a breezeway through the center that could be used to house the horses in the winter. When not in use, it would make a comfortably shaded spot for the women to cook in. Each cabin would be roughly twelve feet wide by sixteen feet long. A steeply angled roof would allow an upper story that could be used for sleeping and storage.

Everyone worked. While Grainy tended the children and prepared a meal of stew, concocted of squirrel seasoned with wild onions, Ruth used a bow saw to section a smooth-grained cedar log into two-foot lengths. Judith then used a froe and a wooden mallet to split shingles from the fragrant wood. A small pile was already building at her feet.

Several Cherokee men stood at a distance, watching with folded arms and talking to each other in low voices. They seemed neither friendly nor hostile, appearing to accept the presence of a new white family in their midst as a matter of course.

"Are they upset about something?" Grainy asked Sergeant Hopkins as he unrolled the chain from a freshly delivered log. She inclined her head slightly to indicate the spectators.

Hopkins studied the group for a moment, and smiled. "No ma'am, just curious, like folks everywhere. If they do decide to come in and visit, make sure you give them some of that stew you're tending to, and don't be stingy! They expect visitors to be fed, even if you have to do without." He smiled at the stubborn set that appeared on Grainy lips. "Don't worry. Mor'n likely they'll only talk to us men. Their womenfolk will see to y'all, in time." He suddenly snapped his fingers. "By the way! My woman and Mrs. Dobbins will be over sometime this morning to get acquainted. I expect that you women will get to know each other pretty well while us men are away."

"Oh? Has John definitely decided on joining you?" Grainy's right eyebrow arched suddenly. This was news to her.

"Can't do much else. Taking the King's shilling is the only way that any of us will ever see hard money out here."

"I suppose so," Grainy agreed. She avoided looking into the sergeant's eyes, pretending that the stew needed sudden attention.

By late afternoon, the men had cut enough logs to outline both cabins. Judith's pile of cedar shakes had grown to knee high. Trudging up the slight hill, with feet dragging and shoulders slumped in total exhaustion, the four men stumbled into the building site. Dobbins dropped to the ground and looked around, surveying their progress. He groaned as he rolled onto one side and propped himself up on his elbow. "I'm thinking I'll jump in that river over yonder," he announced to no one in particular. "Clothes and all!"

"You know, that ain't a bad idea," Hopkins agreed. He looked at the other men. "You boys comin'?"

Hands on hips, the women watched the men amble towards the cool, clear river. Judith shook her head. "Like they're the only ones that put in a day's work!" She barked the words incredulously at the backs of the men as they walked away. Pulling the kerchief from around her neck, she used it to swipe the dirt and perspiration from her face. The task completed, she looked around at the faces of the other women, searching for signs of support. Seeing only blank stares, she glared in the direction of the river.

"Come on ladies!" She barked to the other women who shuffled about docilely, waiting for her to cry *havoc!* as their signal to mutiny. "What's good for the goose is good for the gander! I'm going to cool off, too!" She let out a puff of exasperation and headed for the river.

Grainy called to Simpson, and, gathering Lynn Celia into her arms, fell in behind the other woman. After a moment's reflection, Ruth shrugged her shoulders and followed the crowd.

Judith marched towards the river like a mother goose followed by a string of trusting goslings. Before the astonished eyes of the men, all three women descended the low bank and waded fully dressed into the river. Grainy held Lynn Celia by both hands and dipped the squealing child into the cold water. Beside her, Simpson flopped about like a stranded fish before heading towards his father and the other men who were lying, bare-chested, in the shallows. John grabbed the boy, tickling his stomach before he gave him a quick dunk. Simpson emerged spitting and smiling.

Giving Jacob a haughty glance, Judith waded out into the current, found a spot up to her chest and disappeared beneath the surface. She reappeared a good thirty seconds later, cool and refreshed. Turning, she slapped the water with both hands, spraying Jacob playfully.

This was the signal that spurred the two sides to battle. The entire river was suddenly filled with splashing, screaming, and laughing men, women, and children. For a few fleeting minutes, the war and the troubles of the world were totally forgotten amid a watery battle of the sexes.

When the dripping clan returned to the cabin, they were met by the wives of Sergeant Hopkins and Private Dobbins, flanked by what appeared to be the majority of the three hundred inhabitants of Long Swamp Village. Along the foundation of the double cabin were arranged a variety of meats, vegetables, fruits, and pastries.

"Why bless their souls!" Ruth exclaimed. "They must have been preparing this feast all day!"

"Welcome to Long Swamp!" Sergeant Hopkins's wife, Elizabeth, called out as the stunned group gazed around in wide-eyed amazement.

"I thought it was about time for you to show up," Hopkins said to his wife. When he bent to give her a hug, she returned the gesture and added a quick peck on his stubbled cheek. She looked towards Grainy and the other women. "I declare! I hope that y'all didn't think we was unsociable, waiting so long to come over. But this took a while." She motioned towards a two-wheeled cart that had pulled alongside that of the refugees. A pair of burly Cherokee men where straining to remove a complete hog, still steaming hot after a full day of being roasted over a pit of hickory coals. To one side, a matronly Cherokee woman gave explicit directions to the two men in their own language. Each of them placed their end of the spit on the sideboards of one of the wagons, leaving the bulk of meat suspended between the two conveyances, ready for slicing.

"We've had to dig into our root cellars for all of this," Elizabeth explained. "Most of what was saved from last year's crop is just about gone." Catching sight of something out of the corner of her eye, she turned and waved.

"Nat!" She called to a young black man who had appeared from the direction of the village. He walked with a slight limp and wore a new green jacket of the Carolina Rangers. Grainy noticed that he had the most innocent looking face of any man—white, red, or black—that she had ever met. His skin was a deep, shiny black; the curly hair on his bullet-shaped head had been freshly cropped, very short, and was beginning to show a hint of gray along both temples despite his obvious youth.

"Nat has been with Colonel Brown since the beginning," Elizabeth said. "He's been here since the battle at Kettle Creek. He nearly lost his left leg to a musket ball."

Nat removed his hat and tipped his head respectfully. "Mrs. Hopkins," he said looking at the ground. "Excuse me, ma'am." He stood erect and continued speaking hesitantly as he turned his attention to Grainy. "I heard that there was a young colored woman who would be traveling with you. Could you introduce me?" His ivory teeth, framed by a set of full lips, glinted brightly.

"My! News does travel fast out here!" Grainy said to Elizabeth. She smiled at the nervous solder. "I'm sorry, but she remained behind in Little Chota."

Nat's face, that had been so animated a moment before, dropped immediately. He looked as if he had suddenly lost all of the hope that he had so recently possessed. He stammered an apology and turned to leave.

"Not so fast, Nat!" Elizabeth commanded. "You're not leaving without a full stomach."

Nat turned his sad face back to the woman. "Thank you, ma'am," he said softly. Giving the brim of his hat a respectful tug, he turned away.

"Poor Nat," Elizabeth said when he was out of hearing. "From the looks of that uniform, he spent all day getting it cleaned and pressed."

The welcome party lasted well into the night. As it grew darker, the men banded together and collected an enormous amount of dead wood and underbrush to build a bonfire. Its flames at times reached thirty feet into the air; a highway of glowing cinders drifted up to heaven from its fiery fingertips. The people laughed and socialized in its red glow while they waited for Nat to go *git his fiddle*. Once he returned, Nat's disposition lightened rapidly as he scratched out familiar tunes on his battered instrument.

Around him, the Cherokee couples created a makeshift dance floor by standing in a ring, clapping and stomping in time while his fiddle provided the cadence for any couples bold enough to venture into the grassy circle. All of the Loyalists jumped in and cavorted for the benefit of their hosts, animatedly dancing jigs, reels, and hornpipes. Judith, drawing on the Scottish heritage of her murdered parents, produced her father's Claymore and flawlessly performed a Highland Sword Dance to the amazement and pleasure of their Cherokee allies.

Panting and sweating, Grainy managed to disengage herself from the group after almost an hour of nonstop capering. She dropped in smiling exhaustion alongside one of the notched logs that had been so laboriously dragged into the building site that morning. John dropped beside her. The perspiration on his forehead glistened when it caught the light of the fire. Leaning his back against the log, he stretched his legs out straight and rested the back of his head in his cupped hands. His feet continued to jerk in rhythm with the music. Neither of them spoke, they simply smiled and enjoyed the temporary company of one another.

Almost without a pause, the Cherokees moved into the Welcome Dance[14] as soon as their visitors surrendered the field to them. Musical instruments of their own—flutes, rattles, and drums—appeared magically in their hands.

Grainy looked at John, her eyes glistening in the glow of the fire; she smiled, exposing straight white teeth. They sat and watched the Cherokees who were now deeply involved in a dance of their own. One young Cherokee woman, dark tresses loose and waving in the night, came and signaled insistently for them to join in. Resigned to their fate, the couple followed the woman back to the circle of dancers. She laughed as she showed them the steps. They executed them poorly.

When the Cherokees finally rested, it was a signal to their guests that it was their turn to entertain. Accompanied by Nat's fiddle and a fife played by Dobbins's wife, Sarah, they serenaded their new neighbors with the longing strains of *Michael Row the Boat Ashore*, followed by the foot tapping tune, *Brighten Camp*,[15] before ending with the plaintive spiritual, *We Gather Together.*

The full moon was directly overhead, illuminating the area like a cool sun when Dobbins bent and whispered to Sarah and Nat. Both grinned mischievously as Dobbins moved into the center of the crowd and bawled for everyone's attention. When everyone had fallen quiet and all eyes were trained on him, he turned to Judith McDougal and, with a courtly bow, addressed her.

"Miss Judith, I have heard you sing on several occasions during our trip from the east." He looked around at the other members of his party. "Is there anyone here who has heard the lovely Miss McDougal and who will not agree that she has the voice of an angel?"

"Here! Here!" Hopkins shouted, clapping his hands forcefully. "Give us a song girl!"

Urged on by the other members of both groups, Judith sheepishly stood alongside Sarah and Nat, head bowed modestly while she searched her memory for just the right tune. She looked up and laughed. "If you want a song, then I'm of a mind to give you one!" Turning to Sarah, she conversed quietly for a moment before turning back to face the audience. Behind her Nat and Sarah launched into the lively strains of *Soldier, Soldier Would You Marry Me?*

A wide smile split her face as she pulled the pins from her fiery red hair, setting it free. The firelight reflected off her freshly combed tresses, causing them to shimmer and sparkle like a crimson halo as she traveled about the circle, dancing lithely and effortlessly, all the while belting out the lively tune.

> *Soldier, soldier, will you marry me,*
> *With your musket, fife and drum?*
> *Oh, how can I marry such a pretty girl as you,*
> *When I have no hat to put on?*

As she sang, she snatched the hat from Jacob's head, dropping it into his lap and ruffling his hair roguishly before she moved on, gliding along the front of the delighted spectators. Many of the Cherokees clapped and stomped their feet in time with the tune, even without understanding the words. As Judith continued prancing around the circle, she deftly grabbed Jacob's green uniform coat from where it hung, draped over the sideboard of one of the carts. She deposited it with a grin in Jacob's lap as she sang the next verse, her voice loud, clear, and melodious.

> *Soldier, soldier, will you marry me,*
> *With your musket, fife and drum?*
> *Oh, how can I marry such a pretty girl as you,*
> *When I have no coat to put on?*

"There it is!" she interjected, quickly stabbing a finger in the direction of the coat before moving along amid hoots and hollers. The next verse drew the most laughter from the crowd and the biggest blush from Jacob as she sang;

> *Soldier, soldier, will you marry me,*
> *With your musket, fife and drum?*
> *Oh, how can I marry such a pretty girl as you,*
> *When I have no pants to put on?*

Reaching out, she playfully pushed Jacob onto his back and gave his pants a playful tug before jumping back with a broad, triumphant smile illuminating her face. All around her, both men and women whooped loudly, teasing Jacob with cries of "He's got a live one!" and "Whose goin' to wear the pants in that family?" Jacob sat through it all, meekly and quietly, unable to look, embarrassed at being the center of attention. His ears glowed like hot irons. Judith continued with unending energy, finishing by wagging a scolding finger in Jacob's face as she trumpeted the last of the tune:

> *Soldier, soldier, will you marry me,*

With your musket, fife and drum?
Well, how can I marry such a pretty girl as you,
With a wife and three kids back at home?

As the last vibrant cords of the song faded, Judith dropped into Jacob's lap. Encircling his massive neck with a freckled arm, she fell back in a spurious swoon. Instinctively, Jacob slipped a muscular arm behind her back, his face genuinely concerned. He was dumbfounded when she opened her eyes and smiled up at him.

"Give her a buss!" someone shouted. Judith pulled herself away from Jacob's supporting arm, giving him a surreptitious kiss as she did so. It was administered so quickly and subtly as she spun from his arms, that many of the people standing around the bonfire did not even noticed it had happened.

But Jacob had.

"If that dumb ox don't get the message after tonight, there's no hope for him," Dobbins whispered into this wife's ear.

Sarah looked back jovially. "Oh, he gets the message, I'm thinking."

Urged on by the crowd, Judith consented to sing one more song to close the festivities. The crowd grew quiet as Judith began the lilting song *Greensleeves*,[16] accompanied by Nat, who lay his bow aside to nimbly pluck the strings with callused fingertips, creating a light, airy melody. As she sang, Judith held Jacob's green uniform jacket cradled in her arm, stroking it plaintively as she crooned the words,

Alas, my love, you do me wrong,
To cast me off discourteously.
For I have loved you well and long,
Delighting in your company.

A hush descended over the guests as the sweet notes of Judith's singing drifted away.

Slowly, by ones and twos, the revelers drifted off. The last group followed the cart across the empty fields towards the barely discernible outline of the village.

* * * *

Early the next morning, virtually every man in the village arrived at the worksite. Each of them carried an ax, saw, or some other building implement. Several brought along horses or wagons. Their wives and daughters trudged along with them, lugging baskets of food to feed the small army of workers. By nightfall, over sixty trees had been felled, notched, and skinned of their bark. They lay scattered haphazardly about the area, ready for use in the morning. Having begun the day already tired after last night's reverie, the entire group of workers headed straight home at the end of the day. There, they dropped immediately into exhausted slumber.

They returned early the next morning. By nightfall the double cabin stood complete except for shingles on the roof, chinking in the walls, doors and shutters, and the chimneys at each end.

Aided by a detachment of eleven, hard-working men, John spent the entire next day using froes and mallets to split shingles from short cedar logs. They added these to the pile already begun by the women and by the time the neighbors departed at sunset, an enormous pile lay stacked and ready for use the following day.

The fourth morning of building arrived cool and crisp. Stretching and yawning broadly, John kicked his blanket off and sat among its folds, watching Grainy and the other women tending to breakfast over an open fire. Inhaling the sharp odor of wood smoke mixed with the smell of frying bacon, his mouth began to water. Off to one side, Roger Weatherford showed the early signs of waking. John managed to stand, despite the protest of muscles grown so stiff from overwork that they forced him to move like an old man. He stretched and moved both arms in wide, circular motions, trying to loosen up the muscles. Grainy, kneeling alongside the fire, looked up and greeted him with a smile. Moving slowly to her side, he bent, groaning with the effort, to kiss her on the crown of her head before limping away to the river to wash the sleep from his face.

He returned fifteen minutes later, refreshed and ready for another day of work. Sergeant Hopkins, Dobbins, and Jacob had arrived during his absence and sat alongside the fire. Dobbins, deep in thought, poked it apathetically with a stick.

"Less you want ashes in your breakfast, you best leave off pokin' that fire," Grainy scolded him.

Dobbins looked up, slightly abashed. He tossed the stick into the coals where it burst into flames. "Sorry ma'am," he said sheepishly. Hopkins chuckled. Everyone was too tired to be offended.

"Morning fellas," John greeted them; he dropped to the ground alongside Jacob.

Judith hovered over the young man like a protective hen, cautioning him to be careful as she handed him a pewter mug of steaming tea, the sides sweating moisture. John exchanged knowing glances with Hopkins and smiled. Hopkins face burst into a gigantic grin. Dobbins muttered something under his breath about six pence,[17] followed by a slight snicker. Judith looked up sharply, frowning in his direction. She spoke no words; her expression was sufficiently hostile to end the tittering of the three men.

They were joined a few minutes later by a tired-looking Roger Weatherford. His face was pale with fatigue; he looked at them through bloodshot eyes rimmed with the color of coal.

"I'm getting a mite too old for this kind of work," he said dryly. "Hope to God this is the last move I'll ever have to make."

Ruth scowled at him. "I hope not, Mr. Weatherford! We'll have one more, soon as you men win this war. I, for one, plan on ending my days in a decent, civilized town." Roger dropped his head. Sergeant Hopkins couldn't resist jumping into the conversation.

"You may not have to wait long for that wish to come true. Everything I hear from back east says that we have the rebels on the run in nearly every colony."

"You've heard news?" John and Roger asked in unison. They looked up in anticipation.

"Some," Hopkins admitted. "You see, we're right on the middle trading path here." He pointed to the ford in the river. "Head down that path on horseback and you'll be in Augusta in four or five days. Traders are always moving through here."

Ruth looked longingly at the trail. "Four or five days," she said soberly and shook her head sadly. "Might as well be four or five years."

"What have you heard, sergeant?" John asked.

"Not much," Hopkins admitted, "which is good news. It seems the rebels are lying low. They've been hurt at Brier Creek and are not so certain now that they backed the right dog in this fight. They're sick of being on the run, but they damned well know that they don't want any more of King George's medicine."

The circle erupted in dry laughter. "That's a good sign. A quiet rebel means they're thinkin'," Hopkins interjected. "If they think long enough, they'll realize that they're being led by nothing more that a pack of opportunist and malcontents. Maybe it'll be over by the time we get back."

"Nah!" Dobbins retorted. "Rebel's don't think. That's why their rebels."

By nightfall, the roof was almost completed. Thanks to the assistance of five very fine Cherokee carpenters, openings had been sawn out on each end to accommodate a pair of fireplaces. Grainy stipulated firmly that her hearth would hold at least a five-foot backlog, or they would never see a decent meal cooked on it.

In front of the cabin, one man sat on the shaving horse rescued from Judith McDougal's home place. Working with a drawknife, he smoothed the planks to be used for making doors and shutters. Two other men were busy with a froe and wooden mallet, splitting boards off a straight-grained poplar log. Each new board was laid alongside the shaving horse to wait its turn at finishing. Before tomorrow evening they would be pegged together, fitted with wooden hinges, and affixed with pegs to the door posts of the double cabin. All of the workers laughed and joked boisterously. They were enjoying their work, taking obvious pride in the results. On the roof, busily engaged in lashing down the cedar shakes, John, Hopkins, and Dobbins progressed steadily.

That night they sat around the fire, smoking their pipes and discussing the final phase of construction.

"Tomorrow," John said, "I'll finish the roof with Roger. If you two are of a mind to, you can hitch up the cart and start bringin' in rocks for the chimney. I figure on goin' up about five feet with stone before finishing it off with logs and mortar." He looked knowingly at the two men, fully realizing the hard work that it would take to pry, load, and transport enough rocks for the task. "I'd do it myself, but I feel that a man should put on his own roof. That ways he won't spend his time blaming anyone else if it leaks on him."

"I'll check with some of the Indians," Hopkins said. "They'll know the best place to find good building stone."

John bobbed his head in Hopkins direction. "I'll be over to help you soon as the last shingle is lashed on."

* * * *

Two days later, the cabin was all but complete. John stopped, hands on hips, to survey their work as he returned from his morning ritual of shaving[18] and face washing in the river, followed by a vigorous scrubbing of his teeth with a bone toothbrush.[19] He carried the toothbrush, carefully wrapped for protection like a cherished heirloom.

The roofline was straight, the doors and shutters were hung, and the chimney was completed. The roof had been finished just in time. John knew instinctively by watching the pattern of the wood smoke that drifted lazily from the chimney that there would be rain sometime today, or tonight. It moved horizontally away from the cabin for only a few feet before dropping to the ground where it lingered to create a fine haze as it drifted off to merge with the trees along the river. He smiled contentedly, watching the flicker of Grainy's movements through the unchinked walls. In a few days the women would mix clay and broom straw together to make a rough mortar that would be used to seal the cabin from the outside air.

Today, the men planned to cut the broom straw and let it cure for a few days before raking it and hauling it to the home site. In the breezeway of the double cabin, John could see Roger Weatherford sitting on a log chair, whetstone singing musically as he put an edge on a pair of sickles that he and John would use to cut the straw. John smiled as he moved under the overhang of the roof.

"Morning Roger," he called to the older man.

Roger paused, looked up from his task, answered simply, "Mornin'."

"Looks like rain," John remarked.

"Feels like it too," Roger agreed without looking up. The whetstone traveled smoothly along the curved edge of the blade with a metallic *zing!* "We best wait to mow that broom straw. It won't do nothing but mildew if we leave it out in the rain." He paused from his work and looked up. "No place to stack it out of the weather. Why don't the two of us drop a few more trees and start laying in a pile of firewood for the womenfolk?"

John pursed his lips while mulling over the idea. "Damn! I reckon you're right." He stretched stiff muscles. "I hate to admit it, but I've grown a might tired of the sound of an ax."

"Me too. If'n you want, we could spend the day peggin' that Jumpin' Colter[20] of Judith's father's together. We'll be needing to make a stump land harrow, too, if you're planning on getting a crop in the ground before heading east to join up with the army."

John nodded. "We'll start right after breakfast. I've had my eye on a downed hickory by the river. It should be seasoned enough to use.

"Hard as a rock, mor'n likely. I prefer working green wood," Roger said sullenly. He was a contrary man by nature.

Chapter 6

Long Swamp Village
Tuesday, March 30, 1779

Grainy, Judith, and Ruth sat in the shade of the breezeway. All three were covered up to their elbows in sticky red clay mixed with dried broom straw. Their skirts, rolled up and pinned at the knees, exposed legs coated as thickly with the semi-dried clay as their arms. Shafts of straw sprouted, needle-like, from their hair, giving them the look of animated scarecrows. Judith rubbed her forehead with the back of her hand, leaving a muddy gash from brow to brow. The other two women chuckled.

Movement caught Judith's eye; she turned to examine its source. "Someone's comin'," she said without enthusiasm. The women straightened with a start, prepared to drop their skirts over exposed shins. It was a group of Indian women approaching. They all relaxed with a sigh and rested their backs against the log walls.

While Judith and Ruth continued to loaf in the shade of the breezeway, Grainy stood and walked into the sunlight to welcome their guests. She shielded her eyes with the back of her hand, studying the approaching visitors. Judith nudged Ruth with her elbow and giggled at Creasy's back, where the tacky chinking between the wall logs had left amber colored stripes across the rear of her simple, one-piece, work gown.

"Why if it isn't Molly and The Forgotten One from Little Chota!" she cried. "And The Traveler!"

The Traveler was the wife of one of the headmen of Long Swamp Village. All three of the Loyalist women had encountered her several times in the past, but since none of the women spoke the other's language, their conversations had been limited to a few courtesies.

"Welcome! Welcome!" Grainy greeted them enthusiastically.

"Come on in out of the sun," Judith said, as she stood and offered her seat to one of the women.

Grainy hugged The Forgotten One and Molly in turn. "What brings you two here?" she asked.

"Thunder's Child and Robin came down for a visit," Molly explained in broken English. "Thunder's Child has a sweetheart here who's a member of the Blue Holly Clan. We came along to serve as matchmakers. And it's a good thing that we did!" Molly grinned. She gestured in the direction of The Traveler. "The Traveler says that the other women in the Village have been meaning to ask you to join them each morning when they go to water, but no one spoke enough English. They've assigned me that task."

"Go to water?" Grainy looked puzzled. Understanding suddenly, she cried, "Oh! You mean the morning bath! Is that what they call it?"

"It's not just a bath, it's a ritual," Molly explained. "We do it every morning just at sunrise."

"Every morning? What about during the wintertime?"

Molly chuckled. "We're not that devout. On the cold days we just break the ice and sprinkle a few drops of water over our face and head."

The Traveler, who had remained standing throughout the exchange, looked around curiously, studying the newly constructed home. She made a few remarks to Molly who translated, saying that the three visitors would be happy to help them finish chinking the cabin. It would be a quick job since only the logs on the back side remained to be done.

Four hours later the women stood side-by-side, appraising their work. The Traveler nodded and spoke to Molly, who interpreted.

"The Traveler says this is a good time to show you where the women go to water." She pointed a muddy finger to the east. "It's downstream. The men always have the upstream side."

"Oh really? That's very chivalrous of them," Judith quipped, "letting the women bathe in their filth."

"It must be that way," Molly told her, "to keep the warriors from being accidentally polluted by a woman's moon blood."

"Moon blood?" Judith looked puzzled. Grainy leaned near and whispered into her ear.

"Oh!" she exclaimed, looking embarrassed. Her face glowed red as Molly patiently explained that a Cherokee Warrior was forbidden all contact with women before preparing for battle, and that should a woman even accidentally contaminate him, she would be responsible for any death or injury that came about as a result of it.

"Well, we mustn't have that, must we?" Grainy laughed at the younger woman's discomfort. Judith grinned back with that stupid grin that people unconsciously display when they feel they've made a fool of themselves.

Ruth Weatherford elected to stay behind to prepare supper for the men, who were exhausting themselves by forcing their homemade plow through a newly cleared field fifty yards downriver.

Grainy and Judith, each supporting Lynn Celia by a hand, walked the half-mile to the women's section of the river. The toddler whined futilely to be carried for most of the way.

Without hesitation, they all leapt in. Pulling their muddy shifts over their heads, they alternately soaked and beat the clothing on the smooth rocks of the Etowah River until they were reasonably clean. After hanging the clothes on nearby branches, Grainy and Judith took turns scouring the red mud from the back of each other's head. The icy water pimpled their skin with goosebumps. Lynn Celia, not in the least enamored by the chilly water, sat on a boulder to one side, squealing like a banshee whenever she was splashed by errant drops.

Later, cleaned of the day's buildup of mud and perspiration, the women sunned themselves on the rocks as they listened to the soothing murmur of the current lapping along the base of their makeshift seats. Lynn Celia, having garnered enough courage to immerse herself in the water, splashed in a shallow pool between the rocks. The Traveler filled the time waiting for their clothing to dry by questioning the two women, through Molly, asking about the English and Americans.

With a slight nod of her head in The Traveler's direction, indicating that the question came directly from her, Molly asked, "What do you think of the Real People?"

"Pardon?" Grainy said, caught off guard by the unexpected question.

Molly smiled and clarified the question. "She wants to know what the white people, where you come from, think of the Cherokees. All we ever see are the traders and soldiers." She frowned. "They don't seem to be good people as a general rule. They don't seem to like Indians either! It's a wonder to us why they even bother to travel to our villages!"

Oh!" Grainy exclaimed, as the understanding of what the other woman was asking dawned on her. "Tell her that my mother was captured and held by the Cherokees when I was a newborn child. She rarely speaks of it, but when she does, she harbors no hatred." She shrugged. "I think it's because no one in our family was killed, and so there is no one to mourn. Mama simply sees it as a fortune of war." Grainy smiled in the Traveler's direction. "You can tell her that I have found no reason to dislike the Cherokees."

Molly allowed her mother and The Traveler time to digest the information. They discussed it with each other at great length before formulating a reply.

Molly turned to Grainy. "They are happy that your mother was returned to you and that there was no blood shed between your family and the Real People. But they do caution you that, like all people, there are good and bad among the Cherokee. They advise that you keep your eyes and ears, and most especially, your minds, open while you visit among us. Just as you

Englishmen fight among yourselves, so do the Real People struggle with each other. We have one faction among us that supports the English in this war, a second that supports the Americans, and a third that wants to remain neutral."

"I see," Grainy said slowly, gathering her thoughts. "Which side do they support?" she inclined her head to indicate the two Cherokee women sitting beside her.

"My mother is for neutrality. The Traveler thinks we should support whichever side is winning."

"That's the King's side," Grainy stated definitively.

Long after their clothing was dried, the five women swapped tales of their experiences in their own worlds. The Cherokee women were aghast at finding out that in the world of the English, men owned everything and women didn't even legally own the clothes on their own backs once they were married. The mouths of both The Traveler and The Forgotten One dropped in shocked silence when Grainy explained that white men could even beat their wives if the wife disobeyed them.

The Traveler patted Grainy on the shoulder with a motherly hand. With Molly acting as interpreter, The Traveler said, "Let me tell you the way it should be." She then explained that in the Cherokee world that Grainy now lived in, the woman owned all property and had sole custody of all children. She was free to divorce her husband at any time. If she did so, it was the husband, not the wife, who must return to his family. She patiently explained that upon marriage Cherokee men moved into, but did not become a true member of the wife's clan, and that his children were considered members of the mother's clan, not the father's. Furthermore, a woman's brothers, not her husband, were expected to train the boys to be men.

"But I have no brother's here," Grainy declared.

"We'll just have to see about that!" The Traveler retorted, incensed at the mistreatment that white women were subjected to from their men. She did not elaborate on the remark, simply stared thoughtfully at the other woman's face for a long moment. She suddenly laughed. "Just watch how Thunder's Child behaves while he courts my niece. You'll see how the women of the Real People handle their men!"

"I can't for the life of me imagine Thunder's Child being bossed around by a woman," Judith interjected.

"Oh, you can't? Why is that?" The Traveler cackled.

Judith hesitated. "Well, for one thing, we were told that he did something very dangerous and heroic to earn his name."

"Is that what he told you?" The Forgotten One hooted.

"That's what Sergeant Hopkins told me when I asked him," Judith said quietly, sensing that she had been the butt of some joke.

"See!" The Traveler laughed. "Just what I was telling you about men!"

"Then he didn't get his name that way?" Judith blurted out, shocked and embarrassed at having been duped.

"No!" All three of Cherokee women split their sides with laughter. Molly, losing her balance, tumbled off of her perch and into the water. She came up laughing so hard that she could hardly catch her breath.

"What's so funny?" Judith asked, as she helped haul her back onto the rock.

Molly, straining to catch her breath, managed to piece out an answer in monosyllables between fits of laughter. "His mother called him that because he was such a mischievous child!" Molly giggled uncontrollably as she spoke, gasping between words for gulps of air. Calming herself she continued. "You see, there are two types of Thunders. The Great Thunder and his two Thunder Boys live in the west. It's their clothing that you catch a glimpse of when you see lightening, or a rainbow. They are kind and helpful and the Cherokee people pray to them. But there are many other, lesser Thunders. They live in the cliffs and mountains, and under waterfalls. These Thunders are full of mischief and cause much trouble and should be avoided. Those are who Thunder's Child was named for, not the three helpful Thunders in the west!"[21]

Red with embarrassment, Judith fumed. "Let's go!" she snapped at Grainy.

When the two women returned to the cabin, Ruth was busy with the evening meal. She didn't look up to acknowledge their return when they deposited Lynn Celia on the cleanly swept and sprinkled floor. Without a word, the two women stripped off their smocks and donned their skirts and petticoats before pitching in with the meal. Ruth stirred about noisily, seeming to generate an unnecessarily large amount of clatter as she worked. Both Grainy and Judith knew that some imagined wrong was festering in her.

"What on earth is the matter with you, Ruth?" Grainy asked, unable to stand the suspense any longer.

"Nothing!" Ruth viciously stirred the stew. She grabbed the crane with an old piece of buckskin that she used as a hot pad and pushed it back over the fire before turning to face the other two women. The coals hissed and popped as some of the broth that had sloshed over the sides of the cast iron pot dripped into the fire.

Judith stood, wide-eyed, beside the table. In her hand she held a wooden trencher, the end of it quivered slightly. Her face had the questioning expression of a person caught completely off guard in an emergency.

"If you must know!" Ruth blurted out. "It's the two of you. It ain't decent! A couple of white women runnin' around naked as jaybirds with these savages! And you a married woman and a mother to boot!" She waved her spoon accusingly in Grainy's direction. "Your husband outta take a hickory switch to you!" She shifted her focus, poking the spoon in Judith's direction. "And you, too, since you don't have a father around to control you." She huffed loudly. "Shameful!" She shook her head and stared at the two miscreants. Grainy and Judith stared at each other in stunned silence. Lynn Celia sat, thumb in mouth, her round eyes missing nothing of the exchange. She suddenly giggled and clapped her hands enthusiastically. Then frowned at the lack of response.

"What?" Grainy managed to blurt out. "We were bathing! What would you have us do? Go about filthy dirty, like a couple of low class Cracker[22] women?"

Ruth pished. "You'll both catch your death of cold! Decent folk don't bathe more'n once a week. 'Tain't good for you!" She shook her head. "Just plain old horse sense if you ask me!"

Both of the startled women stood staring at Ruth's back as they digested this unexpected censure.

"Let's get back to work!" Grainy snapped at Judith. She checked herself, looked apologetically at the other woman, and added, "I'm sorry." The cabin grew eerily quiet as they let the subject die.

John and Roger returned to the cabin well before sunset with a haughty Simpson in tow. The three year old, having ridden perched atop the lead horse all day as the team pulled the wooden plow through the new ground, was convinced that he was largely responsible for any progress that had been made. John and Roger were dog tired; they stood stoop-shouldered as Simpson proudly expounded on his exploits, telling his mother and *Aunt* Judith every detail. John's hair was still damp where the trio had stopped off at the river to wash the sweat and dust from themselves and to wipe down and curry the animals.

"Hard day?" Grainy looked up at John from her kneeling position in front of Simpson, who continued to chatter away.

John dropped onto the puncheon bench alongside the table. He leaned over, elbows resting across his thighs and nodded. "Even with us takin' turns, between fighting with that ole' jump plow and leading the team, I don't believe that I've ever put in a harder day's work in my life! I can't wait to join the Rangers and get some rest." He brightened noticeably and sat up. "By the way! Sergeant Hopkins told me that the bounty for enlisting has increased from 2 to 3 Guineas![23] We could surely use that money."

Grainy's face brightened on hearing the news, then fell as Ruth muttered,

"Mighty cheap payment for a man's life."

Grainy acted as if she had not heard the remark. She stood and smiled down at her husband. "We had some visitors today. The headman's wife, The Traveler, asked us to help in sowing the village fields. She says we'll get a share in the harvest when it comes in."

John laughed. "That would have been a good thing to know before the three of us near killed ourselves on that new land. Right Simpson?" He ruffled the boy's hair affectionately.

The evening meal was eaten largely in silence, the men doing most of the talking. Roger and John, as the adult males in the household, sat in the only two chairs, one stationed at each end of the long puncheon table. Grainy and Judith sat on a long bench along one side, with Simpson nestled snugly between them. Lynn Celia sat contentedly in her mother's lap, sharing her plate.

Ruth sat sullenly on the other side, alone. She cajoled Roger into leaving as soon as the meal was finished, contemptuously leaving the cleanup to Grainy and Judith.

****

As March passed into April, and April turned into May, the refugees continued to shape their new world. Grainy, with Lynn Celia crawling along at her heels, and Judith sweating at her side, helped in the planting of the Cherokee Fields. John and Roger, with the help of Jacob and Simpson, finally managed to wrest an acre from nature and plant their own crop of flax, corn, beans, squash, and pumpkins. Jacob made it a habit of helping around the cabin. He and Judith took frequent walks along the river. As Jacob's shyness receded, he seemed to grow even larger. The only blight on the happiness of the household was Ruth Weatherford, who grew more and more resentful every day. A furious fight between the women finally erupted when Ruth insulted The Traveler one afternoon, threatening her with an iron poker as she stood at the door. Grainy stepped between the two women and confronted Ruth. She was so furious, that as they stood toe-to-toe, screaming like the furies into each other's faces, Grainy resorted to one of the few acts of violence in her life. She gave Ruth a stinging slap across the face, splitting her lip. Wiping the blood from her lip, Ruth studied it for a moment. A murderous look came over her face as she glanced from Grainy, to The Traveler, to Judith. Without another word, she stalked from the room, viciously slamming the door of her cabin behind her.

Grainy looked at Judith; neither spoke. They knew that the pot had finally boiled over.

The next morning, as the women prepared the breakfast, John called repeatedly at the Weatherford's door. Finally, he pulled the latchstring and entered. The place had an empty look about it; an aura of desertion permeated the air.

Suspicious, John went to check on the horses and felt no surprise at finding one of them missing. He returned to the cabin, entered quietly, and plopped into one of the chairs.

"Looks like the Weatherfords have lit out." He stated the news matter-of-factly, as if it was something that had been expected for some time.

"We thought as much," Judith said, as she set the table. "Found a whole five-pound bag of corn meal missing, along with some of the salt pork." She gave a quick, muffled laugh. "It's a good thing that you sleep with your musket over your bed, or they might have taken that too!"

John nodded to himself. "Reckon they've gone to be rebels. I'll let Hopkins know soon as I finish breakfast."

The sergeant was furious. "Why didn't you come to me immediately? Those two are probably twenty miles away by now! God knows the damage they can do if they tell the rebels about us!" He turned to Dobbins who stood half-dressed beside him. "Go! Get Thunder's Child and Robin, see if they'll run them to earth."

Five days later, Thunder's Child returned with the bad news that the Weatherfords had stumbled onto a rebel patrol near the Oconee River, about forty miles west of Heard's Fort.[24] They had headed east with the rebels.

Chapter 7

Long Swamp Village
Monday, May 10, 1779

Judith, her face beautifully framed by a wide-brimmed straw hat, held firmly atop her gathered cap[25] by a strand of red ribbon, strolled hand-in-hand with Jacob. Her suitor strutted alongside her, dressed in his green uniform jacket, freshly washed and pressed by one of the Loyalist women who acted as a laundress for the unattached Rangers. Hands clasped tightly, they swung their arms back and forth in wide sweeping arcs as they made their way along the narrow footpath leading to the double cabin. Judith, unable to take her eyes off of the big soldier, stepped blindly along, trusting him completely to guide her through any dangers. Jacob had asked her to marry him, and she had accepted. Giddy with the suddenness of it all, Judith could only smile like some simple-minded lunatic. When she tried to speak, she cried.

The moment the two lovers stepped into the room, Grainy sensed that something climactic had happened. She grinned expectantly, hands clasped in front of her, waiting. Unable to fully suppress the suspense, she bounced impatiently on the balls of her feet.

"Well?" she asked, her body leaning forward in anticipation.

Grainy's question caused the fragile dam holding Judith's emotions in check to burst. Between sobs of joy, Judith managed to tell her of Jacob's proposal, her acceptance, and their plans for the future.

"Have you set a date?" Grainy asked.

Judith turned to Jacob, silently imploring him to explain their plans.

"You see," Jacob began, "Judith wants to be married by a real minister. As soon as we get one here, we plan on tying the knot."

"Oh! I see." Grainy raised an eyebrow, studying the two with a naughty grin. "What do you two plan on doing 'til then?"

"We're going to be betrothed!" Judith giggled. "We know that it will be hard, but since the men are all leaving tomorrow, we won't be tempted to *jump the broom*[26] before we are legally wed in the eyes of the Lord." She looked up at Jacob, her eyes brimming with adoration. "Jacob says that there's a real

Church of England minister with the British Army. Wouldn't that be grand if he were to wed us?"

Grainy spread her arms wide. Judith fell into them and the two women clung tightly to each other, spontaneously dancing a quick jig of celebration. Grainy checked herself and snapped her fingers.

"You two only have 'til tomorrow! Go on, get out of here and spend some time together." She waved them towards the door. "Shoo! Go on!" She followed them out into the breezeway and watched as they moved away. They seemed to float a few inches above the ground in their happiness.

Grainy dropped onto John's shaving horse. She leaned forward, chin in hands, and smiled wistfully, remembering the day that her own husband had proposed to her. She turned and studied the sleeping form of Lynn Celia through the open door of the cabin. Her tiny daughter lay atop a straw mattress that covered the rude bedstead built into a corner wall of the cabin. The child lay on her back, breathing noisily through an open mouth.

Smiling, Grainy brushed her bare feet through the layer of maple shavings that littered the earthen floor of the breezeway. She picked one up and inhaled the aroma. Only last night, John had used his drawknife to shave this wood by candlelight, shaping a maple post that he would use one day to build her a proper rope bed. With John's departure in the morning, she knew it would be a long wait for that bed. Her vision blurred. She sniffed and wiped away tears with the hem of her apron. Bowing her head, she said a silent prayer that John would return to her. She thought mournfully of the future; only two short days ago she had turned twenty-one. Surely the good Lord would not widow her so young when she had a good, God fearing husband fighting for a king that the Lord himself had chosen. Certainly, she consoled herself, the Lord would protect the soldiers that fought on his side![27]

The leave-taking the next morning had all the somberness of a funeral. John, Jacob, Sergeant Hopkins, Nat, and Dobbins stood beside their mounts. In addition to the five of them, thirty Cherokee warriors from nearby villages, ten Muscogee Creeks who had arrived the previous night from the south, and five runaway Negro slaves who intended to enlist with the British in return for their freedom were packed and ready to ride. Grainy held Lynn Celia on one hip as she hugged and kissed her husband goodbye. In John's arm, Simpson squirmed and fought to get down. The immensity of what was about to take place held less of his attention than did Daniel, the four-year-old son of Sergeant Dobbins. Daniel stood impatiently to one side, fingering his Cherokee blowgun, anxious to be done with all this foolishness so he could escape into the forest and go hunting.

"You make certain to draw the load from that old doglock once a week and reload it, you hear?" John cautioned his wife. "Remember to pour the powder in the measure before you drop it down the barrel."

Grainy looked up, smiling, her eyes wet and red. "I have fired that musket many a time to save my chickens from hungry hawks, husband," she said proudly, desperately wanting his mind to be at ease when he thought of her. She did not want him plagued by any distractions when he came face-to-face with the enemy.

"Please be careful, John!" She hugged him. Stepping away, she forced a smile as she smoothed the capes of his hunting frock and tugged on his blanket roll to make certain that it would not work loose as he traveled. She managed a half-smile as he mounted. The other riders had already begun moving past, eager to be on the trail. John allowed Grainy to walk beside him, hand-in-hand, for only a few paces. With a sad smile, he released her hand and blew her a kiss as he kicked his mount into a trot and rode away. Grainy watched mutely as he grew smaller in the distance. Behind him, only one rider still tarried, Jacob, who found it almost impossible to break away from Judith's embrace. When he finally did manage to force himself to his duty, the sun, which had just broken above the thick tree line to the east, revealed only a few wisps of dust floating above the spot where the riders had melted into the eastern forest.

* * * *

The mixed band of travelers arrived eight days later at Colonel Brown's headquarters in the small German-speaking town of Ebenezer, Georgia. The settlement was located twenty-five miles upriver from Savannah and had been founded in the 1730s by German Lutherans, often referred to as *High Dutch*. Consisting of about twenty houses and a church,[28] it was one of the most prosperous areas of the colony.

Lieutenant Ellis, who had welcomed John at Colonel Waters's Fort in February, met the party of horsemen as they trotted into Ebenezer. "Sergeant Hopkins! No difficulties, I trust?"

"No, sir." Hopkins saluted the officer. "We didn't see a rebel all the way from Long Swamp. You fellas must'a scared the treason completely out of them."

"We can't claim that honor," Ellis replied. "General Provost has moved on Charleston with a portion of our force. Every rebel in the colony is scurrying around like a rat in a corncrib, trying to join up with their General Lincoln and hoping to protect that Olympus of the Carolinas. Meanwhile, we simply cool our heels and take charge of the prisoners that are brought in."

Hopkins inclined his head in John's direction. "Here's a new recruit for you. Brought him all the way from Long Swamp."

The lieutenant studied John's face. "I've seen you before, I'm certain of it."

"Yes, sir," John said. "I was with the party that Sergeant Hopkins brought into Colonel Waters's Fort back in February."

Ellis snapped his fingers. "Ah, yes! I thought so, never forget a face." He looked sharply at Hopkins. "He wants to take the King's Shilling?"

Hopkins nodded. "Which company should I enlist him in?"

"Ours, of course!" Ellis laughed. "What about these other children of Sheba?" He indicated the five escaped slaves, quietly sitting their mounts off to one side and following the conversation with wary eyes.

Two of them, newly arrived Africans that spoke no English, smiled broadly at the officer. It was an evil-looking smile, framing teeth that had been filed into sharp points during puberty. Both faces bore the identical scars of some savage African initiation. The lieutenant raised an eyebrow. "They look as though they'll eat the bloody rebels!" He gave a satisfied nod. "Bring them all along. The law states that an officer of the crown must swear in all new recruits in front of a civilian magistrate. Nuisance! But that's the King's policy." He surveyed John once more. "No weapon?"

"No, sir. I left it with my wife. It was just an old doglock handed down through the family. I trust the King has a better one."

The recruits followed Lieutenant Ellis and Sergeant Hopkins to the civilian magistrate in Ebenezer, where he attested them as a single group. After administering the oath of allegiance, the lieutenant qualified them by carefully instructing them on the articles of war. Sergeant Hopkins smirked behind his hand as the two scar-faced Africans, whose unpronounceable names had been reduced simply to Sambo and Mambo during the journey from Long Swamp, held up their right hands and struggled to pronounce the words that they neither knew nor understood. They stood stiffly, like two militant parrots balanced precariously on a swing, simply repeating what they heard, while one of the other Negroes acted as an extremely inefficient interpreter. For some reason, the lieutenant reasoned that all blacks would be able to somehow understand any language that the others spoke.

These simple procedures completed, Sergeant Hopkins held out his hand. "Welcome to Captain Andrew Johnston's Company of the King's Carolina Rangers, *Private Stokes.*" He emphasized the last two words with a smile. He gave the five black soldiers a quick nod. "My regards to you free men. I am sure that you will prove worthy of the King's largess."

Lieutenant Ellis gave a slight bow. "The King appreciates your sacrifice and your loyalty. I will direct the quartermaster to see to your bounty, minus deductions for some of your equipment. Pay is six pence a day plus a free ration of rum or beer, whichever is available, a gift from the King to his loyal soldiers." He instructed Sergeant Hopkins to take the recruits over to the regimental quartermaster and have them draw uniforms and equipment.

"Yes, sir!" Sergeant Hopkins said, enthusiastically snapping a stiff salute.

John felt a surge of pride as he held out his hands to receive the green regimental coat of the King's Carolina Rangers. He reverently fingered the crimson cuffs and collar. In addition to the coat, he received a waistcoat, a pair of buff-colored trousers, a pair of woolen stockings, leggings, shirt, shoes and buckles, a white stock for his neck, and a black rifleman's hat. The quartermaster informed them that this first issue of clothing and equipment was provided by the King, adding that there were some additional items that would be provided, as needed, by the company's captain, Captain Andrew Johnston. The quartermaster handed each a twist of tobacco, a bar of soap, and cleaning supplies for their belts and accouterments, adding quickly, "The cost of this will be deducted from your pay when it comes due." He motioned for the group to follow him to a side room where he kept the weapons and powder. There, he issued each man a light infantry ax, a shortened Brown Bess musket,[29] flints, cartridge paper and cartridge box, powder, and lead. Noticing the puzzled looks on the faces of the black soldiers, he said, "The Sergeant here will have you instructed on how to properly load and shoot your firelocks."

Sergeant Hopkins waited patiently as the new soldiers donned their uniforms. Once they were dressed, he demonstrated the proper way to wear a pair of double belts across their shoulders to form a white "X" on the center of their chest. On one belt hung a bayonet in a scabbard, across the other shoulder, a braided white rope suspended a tin canteen. The cartridge box, displaying an elegant metal badge containing the King's cipher on its cover, was attached to a waist belt and worn directly over the abdomen. With later experience, most of the soldiers would transfer it to one side, or simply wear it in back.

"Now, for the paymaster!" Hopkins announced while rubbing his hands together hopefully. He ran his eyes slowly around the group that stood in a semi circle. "It's customary for new recruits to buy their sergeant a mug of rum when they receive the King's bounty." He cocked one eye and glared at them with a look that clearly dared one of them to contradict him.

Fully dressed, the six new recruits walked down Ebenezer's dusty street alongside their sergeant. The stiff new shoes of the recruits squeaked as they stepped along and their equipment clattered.

John looked at the sergeant from the corner of his eye. "I feel a might overloaded with all this equipment Sergeant Hopkins. I don't think I could fight with all of this weighing me down, even if the rebels should attack at this very moment."

Hopkins dismissed John's concern with a wave of his hand. "Half of that issue will be stored with the regiment," he said with confidence. "You'll get used to the other half."

Chapter 8

Ebenezer, Georgia
Sunday, September 12, 1779

John sat, his back against the large trunk of a stately water oak, languidly fanning his sweat-soaked face with quick flips of his hat. The small amount of breeze that the effort produced was not as important as the number of gnats that it brushed away. It was nine o'clock in the morning and the pesky insects were already driving him mad. They swarmed by the hundreds, inches away from his face, often flying straight into his eyes, or ears, or nose, sometimes even his mouth. They crawled on his food and followed him everywhere like hounds from hell. There was no escaping them. If the damned things bit like mosquitoes, they'd drive a man to suicide!

Without pausing in his endless battle to disperse the hordes of vermin unmercifully assaulting him, he brushed the crumbs of his breakfast from his shirt, and then occupied himself with studying the condition of his musket. He wiped a greasy smudge of burnt powder from the barrel with his thumb and transferred it to his pants leg. He had fired the musket this morning for only the second time since it had been issued to him three months ago. He would have to clean it today. At least, he rationalized, it would give him something to do. So far, army life had proved brutally boring.

Jacob, who had stood the same guard post with him last night, dozed against the opposite side of the same tree. His shortened French musket looked like a child's toy lying across his massive lap. He breathed quietly and smoothly. His only reaction to the pesky gnats was an occasional quick discharge of breath from one side of his mouth or the other. He had been raised in this area and was used to the pests, if one could ever truly become used to something as disagreeable as a goddamned gnat!

John was amazed at how stoically Jacob reacted to the violent events of this war. A party of rebels, attempting to cross the river in a small dugout from the Carolina side, had surprised the two of them just this morning. The river's heavy mist had cloaked the rebel's careful movements until they had suddenly appeared, like shades crossing the river Styx, twenty yards from the shore. The lead man in the boat had shouted a warning over his shoulder and fired his musket in Jacob's direction. The large caliber ball struck the bank in front of the big man and skipped along the ground, passing within a hair's breadth of the his right leg. Alerted by the shot, John had cocked his musket and moved cautiously in Jacob's direction. The answering boom of Jacob's weapon spurred him onward. He arrived at the riverbank just in time to level his weapon and fire at four shadowy figures in a small boat, tugging furiously at their oars and retreating towards the South Carolina shore. There was a yelp of surprise and pain from someone in the craft. John's musket, loaded with the regulation *Buck and Ball*, a .69 caliber musket ball[30] topped off by three buckshot pellets, abruptly ended whatever mission the four rebels had been attempting to accomplish.

Sergeant Hopkins had appeared seconds later, red-faced and huffing. After being briefed on their encounter with the enemy, he slapped both privates on the back, praising their performance. "I'll see that you two get an extra ration of rum for this!" he bellowed. In this army that was the equivalent of a medal.

Satisfied that it was nothing more than a group of infiltrators coming over to spy on the British positions, no one gave the incident a second thought.

On the far side of the river Private Roger Weatherford, of the South Carolina militia, tended the jagged gouge on his left forearm that had been created by one of John's buckshot pellets. Beside him lay the body of one of his fellow patriots, blood still oozing from a gaping hole torn through his neck from back to front. Roger paused to ponder the whimsy of fate that took one poor fellow's life, based simply on where he happened to be sitting at the time, and then spared the other three for the same simple reason. A hand shook his shoulder; he looked up to see his lieutenant, Andrew Deloach, motion for him to follow. The lieutenant continued on, within a few steps he was swallowed by the fog.

* * * *

Fetching water from the river in an iron pot, John suspended it on a tripod over the remains of last night's fire. He produced a bar of soap, shaved thin slivers from it into the water, and then threw a few pieces of wood onto the hot coals. While they waited for the water to boil, John and Jacob busied themselves with removing the locks and ramrods from their weapons and whittling down twigs with which to plug the touchholes. Once the water began to boil, they took turns dipping a cleaning brush into it and scrubbing the fouling from the outside of the muskets. Then they gave the locks a good scrubbing, rinsing them off by dunking them into the boiling water and swishing them in circles until they were rinsed clean. With touchholes firmly plugged, they leaned the muskets against a nearby fence and carefully filled the barrels with boiling water. Leaving the muskets to soak, they returned their attention to the locks and, with an old scrap of linen, carefully wiped away any moisture that had not yet evaporated. They relied on the heated metal to dry itself. After pouring the oily, black water from the barrel and removing the wooden plugs, they repeatedly scoured the inside of the barrels with patches dipped into hot water. When they were satisfied that all of the fouling had been removed from the barrels, they lay the weapons aside to dry.

After applying a light coat of sweet oil to the barrels and locks, they reassembled the weapons and marched off in search of something to drink and a cool patch of shade to loiter in. Once they located a good out-of-the-way place, they planned to stay put until they were found and given another assignment.

As they dined on cheese and bread, Nat and Private Dobbins, who had just returned from a nighttime foray outside of the lines, plopped onto the ground alongside them. Dobbins triumphantly waved a copy of the *Gazette*, a Whig newspaper, over his head.

"Look what I captured!" he exclaimed with a smile. "Want to hear what the Whigs think of our heroic and loyal soldiers?" He smirked. Everyone present knew exactly how the enemy press villainized them, but they couldn't resist hearing stories about themselves read from a newspaper. Dobbins read the date, July 7, 1779, and remarked that it was, "somewhat old."

He perused the front page and smiled broadly. "It's about General Provost and his invasion into South Carolina. Says here, and I quote, 'that he, the general, has brought into the state a large body of the most infamous banditti and horse thieves that perhaps ever were collected together anywhere.' Must be talking about us." He chuckled, then silently read the next few lines.

He suddenly looked up. "We're not the culprits after all!" he exclaimed proudly.

By this time their small group had grown steadily as other troops and civilians began to gather around to hear the news. Some of them shook their heads solemnly, some smiled and playfully poked their comrades in the ribs; the faces of others were blank masks, betraying neither agreement nor disagreement.

Dobbins continued reading from where he had left off. "Under the direction of McGirth, dignified with the title of colonel, a corps of Indians…" Dobbins stopped reading as laughter trickled through his audience. He looked over at Nat and flashed a quick grin. "Why Nat, you're in here too!" he joked before continuing slowly, "…with Negro and white savages… Now that is us!" He looked around and bellowed loudly before continuing, "And about fifteen hundred of the most savage and disaffected poor people, seduced from the back settlements of this State and North Carolina." He paused once again to administer a verbal jab in the direction of his audience. "That must be you boys," he drawled humorously, grinning like a possum at his own joke.

Their lighthearted revelry came to an abrupt halt as a dispatch rider, whipping a lathered mount viciously with the ends of his reins, thundered past and headed towards Colonel Brown's headquarters. It was obvious to everyone present that something monumental was in the offing. Losing interest in Dobbins's reading of the Whig propaganda, they gathered in a curious knot in front of the headquarters building, waiting for *who knows what?* Moments later, orderlies began to rush helter-skelter from the building and scurry along in the direction of their captain's quarters.

By ones and twos, the regimental captains arrived. Within thirty minutes, everyone in the regiment was aware that a French army had landed a few miles south of Savannah and that the Rangers had been ordered to defend the town. Within two hours, all of the regimental baggage was loaded and by noon they were cantering south in a long, strung-out column, following the west bank of the Savannah River.

It was dark when they arrived at the town. A red-faced British officer rode out to meet them. He was plainly relieved as he greeted Colonel Brown and directed him to begin digging entrenchments along the north side of the city. The Rangers were to hold the extreme right flank of the defensive line; their own right flank would be the Savannah River.[31]

Colonel Brown relayed the orders to his captains, who marched the men straight to their positions. There, they fell out of ranks, stacked their arms, and dropped to the ground. Thoroughly winded by their rapid march, they rested while the officers waited for the engineers to finish laying out the defensive works. To their left, a party of Royal Navy sailors were already constructing a redoubt that was to be armed with guns taken from the British warships riding at anchor in the river.

Early the next morning, the Rangers began the construction of their own redoubt.

"The rebels are such fools," John said, as he hacked away at the soft earth of the riverbank with a mattock.

"Why is that?" Dobbins asked over his shoulder as he flung a shovel full of earth onto the growing redoubt.

"Getting the French involved in this. What do they think will happen if the British are driven out? Why if that ever happens, the French will reclaim Canada, turn against those fools, and conquer the whole of North America. Any half-wit can see that! Why do they think the French are helping them anyway? Out of brotherly love?"

"That's the problem," Dobbins informed him matter-of-factly, "rebels don't think." He reached down and scratched furiously at an itch on his ankle. "I don't know what it is, but something is eating me alive!"

"Me, too!" several men agreed in unison. There seemed to be an epidemic of tiny, itching, red welts on the men's ankles, behind their knees, and around the waistline of their breeches.

One of the black Pioneers, overhearing their conversation, chuckled to himself as he continued to work steadily with a shovel. Dobbins spun to face him.

"You sound like you know what this is, uncle," Dobbins said to the gray-haired old man. "If so, let us know so that we can do something about it. It's fair driving me to distraction!"

"Them's chigger bites," the old man told them. "Some folks call them red bugs. They'll devil the fool out of you." He scratched his leg vigorously to emphasize his discomfort.

"They don't seem to bother you gentlemen of darker tone," Dobbins laughed. "What secret do you use to discourage them, or is white meat just naturally sweeter to them?"

The old man chuckled again. "No sir, we gets them just the same, but we know not to scratch 'em if we can help it. Scratchin' only makes it worse."

"Then what do you do to keep from going daft?" By this time all of the Rangers within earshot had stopped digging and were leaning on their tools, following the conversation with keen interest. Many absentmindedly scratched the inside of their legs with the soles of their shoes.

"What you do is get some lard and paint it on over the bite. It chokes the varmints; they'll go away in a day or two."

"For good?" Dobbins asked hopefully.

The old fellow shook his head and smiled again. "Can't promise you that, sir, but it'll stop them at least until you get them again. Course, the sand fleas and the ticks are still going to nibble on you no matter what, you'll just have to get used to them."

Dobbins returned to his work, his face contorted with frustration. "I just hope that the damned rebels are getting eat up worse than us!" he declared to anyone who would listen. He paused for a moment, thinking to himself, then added, "It wouldn't surprise me none if it was the rebels that set them things on us. And those damned mosquitoes and gnats to boot!"

* * * *

Three days later, on September 15, the French commander, Count Henri d'Estaing, sent a summons of surrender to the outnumbered and ill-prepared defenders of Savannah. General Provost asked for a twenty-four hour truce to consider the request, and the French unexpectedly agreed, giving the defenders more time to continue with their frantic preparations. That evening, a detachment of eight hundred Highlanders from the 71st Regiment of Foot, under the command of Lieutenant Colonel James Maitland, arrived from Beaufort, South Carolina. The Highlanders had performed a heroic march from South Carolina to the banks of the Savannah River, where they had found themselves cut off from the city by French forces. Undaunted, they had maneuvered undetected around the enemy, skulking through the maze of swamps that lined the inland waterway. Once they had appeared on the opposite side of the river from the besieged city, the British Navy wasted no time in ferrying them across. Their arrival had increased the strength of the garrison to about twenty-five hundred men, which now consisted of regiments of British and Loyalist regulars, Loyalist Militia, Hessian mercenaries, and the Royal Navy.

Investing Savannah in a tight ring were somewhere between three-to-four thousand French regulars, with an unknown number of wild-eyed rebel militiamen congregating alongside of them. The rebel ranks continued to swell with every passing day as ever increasing numbers of them converged on the trapped garrison, licking their lips in anticipation, and howling to be in on the kill.

The next morning, Jacob shook John awake before daybreak. "John!" he whispered.

John sat up and rubbed his eyes. In the distance the sounds of digging and chopping, mixed with the croaking of frogs in the swamps and rice fields to their front, provided a raucous symphony of background noises. John took a deep breath. It was the coolest part of the day, just before dawn. He yawned, shook his head.

"I'm going over to see if I can find Judith's brothers. They're with the 71st Highlanders that came in last night. Sergeant Hopkins told me they're over to the left of us," Jacob said, forgetting that everyone in the army was to the left of them since they were positioned on the right flank.

"Have you told the sergeant that you're going?"

"Of course! I'm not that stupid. He said that as long as we get back before our turn at the earthworks comes about, he doesn't mind. Come on!" He gave John's arm a quick tug. "We only have two hours."

"At least let me wash the sleep out of my eyes," John said. He rolled out of his blanket and left it in a tangle alongside those of the other men. No one seemed interested in anything but sleeping and digging.

Slinging their muskets, the two walked casually along the rear of the defensive works. Everywhere they traveled it seemed that an army of red, green, or blue-coated ants scurried about, building up huge mounds of earth. Near the center of the works, they had their first close up look at the Hessian soldiers who had been "rented" to the King of England as mercenary troops. They seemed unusually large men under their tall miter caps. Jacob spoke to one, asking directions, but the only reply was a shrug. None of the German's appeared to speak English with any fluency. Jacob compensated by talking slower and with increased volume in a doomed effort to be understood. The Germans evidently had resorted to the same tactic and before long the exchange sounded more like a shouting match than a friendly exchange of directions. Eventually, when the conversation had risen to a pitch loud enough to be heard many yards away, one of the Scotsmen of the 71st Regiment called to the exasperated Provincials and beckoned for them to come down the line to their position.

The two Rangers found the Highlanders scattered about on the ground. They lay about like dark lumps upon the earth. Those not sleeping were busily engaged in constructing a large battery in the center of the line. The lone sentry behind the earthworks scratched the matted hair under the band of his tam and shook his head.

"Angus and Rory McDougal? Certain I know of the lads. But as to finding them in all of this…" He shrugged and gestured with his hand in the general direction of the encampment, indicating that he was at a loss as to how to locate two men mixed in among that jumbled pile of humanity.

"You're to be their brother-in-law, you say?" He gave Jacob a look of surprised appraisal.

Jacob beamed. "Yes, I am!"

The sentry took a step back to appraise the hulking Provincial. "Aye, Judith picked a grand one for the Cabor toss!" He laughed. Grasping Jacob's hand in a powerful grip, he pumped it up and down with a furious motion.

"Sorry, lad, but it never hurts to be a wee careful in times like these." His whole body seemed to swell with pride as he stood, hands on hips, and announced, "I be Rory McDougal, the brother of your dear Judith!"

He laughed boisterously at the sight of Jacob's mouth falling open and slapped the big man soundly on the shoulder. The unexpected impact of the blow rocked Jacob onto his heels. The Highlander loosed another barrage of raucous laughter. He turned and hailed the sleeping camp, "Arise, Angus McDougal! We have family a visiting!"

A gruff retort reached the three men. One of the dark bundles shifted about, emitting groans and grunts. A head appeared, wrapped in a soiled white bandage, followed slowly by a broad pair of shoulders as the sleeping man rolled into a sitting position, legs kicking animatedly at the tangled blanket. Freed of the constriction, Angus McDougal rose to his feet, looked around at the camp, and belched loudly. "Family you say?" he rasped through a gaping yawn.

"Aye, dear brother, the betrothed of our own dear Judith!"

"Judith! Betrothed? He must be a hell of a mon. Point him out!"

The metallic rasp of a Claymore being sheathed accompanied the shadowy outline of Angus McDougal as he stepped over the prostrate forms of his sleeping companions and trooped across the bivouac. He came to a halt, standing toe-to-toe with Jacob.

Shorter than Jacob by no more than an inch, he peered into the eyes of his future brother-in-law. One eye was swollen shut and a thin trickle of blood seeped from beneath the crude bandage wrapped about his head; it dribbled down his cheek before disappearing into the thorny stubble of week-old whiskers.

"Judith picked herself a big one! Hey Rory?" he bugled. He administered a powerful cuff to Jacob's arm; it struck in the same spot as Rory's. John smiled to himself, wondering how big that bruise would be.

John stepped back defensively when Jacob turned to introduce him to the burly brothers of his future bride. Seeing his skittishness, they roared with laughter as they held out callused hands in welcome.

"Bloody Outlanders!" A disembodied voice reached out to them from the darkness. Both brothers spun around, fists clenched at their sides, surveying the motionless piles with hawk-like stares. All remained quiet. They turned back to face their guests.

"So…" Rory leaned forward, coaxing a response.

"Jacob, Jacob Fenton."

Rory's eyes glittered in the glare of a torch held aloft by a passing soldier. "So, Jacob - Jacob Fenton, tell us about yourself." He guided Jacob by the arm to a pile of freshly squared timbers waiting to be used on the defensive works. The wood was still fragrant and sticky. John remained standing. He placed one foot on the timbers and rested both elbows across his knee.

"Don't mind the sap mon!" Rory bellowed. He plopped down onto the makeshift seat alongside Jacob.[32] "A little bit of a sticky ass never harmed a Highlander!" He bellowed again. John wondered briefly what they had done to make them so happy.

Rory looked towards his brother. "Angus, take a seat, you're still dizzy." He patted the place next to him and watched with concern as Angus lowered himself onto the rough timber.

"We had a slight brush with the rebels the other day at the ferry crossing on the Stono River, up in Carolina somewhere. One of the bleedin' bastards clubbed poor Angus over the head with as fine a rifle as you've ever seen! Pity." Reaching out, Rory gently removed the bandage and surveyed the gash running through Angus's hairline. "Needs stitches I say and Doctor Stapleton wants to put him in the hospital, but Angus don't want to spend the money."[33] Rory shook his head sadly. "Better a dog than a soldier."[34]

John leaned forward and surveyed the injury by torchlight. It was a nasty gash that looked inflamed. He pursed his lips. "Angus, if you'll come to our position at sunup, we can tend to that. It won't cost you anything."

Anger literally shot from Angus's eyes, "We McDougals can pay our own way!"

"I don't doubt that, but as it sits, my wife is alone on the frontier with only your sister to help her look after my young'uns. The least I can do to pay her back is to sew up a hard headed Scotsman." John's smile lent the words the appearance of a friendly jest.

"Much obliged," Rory interjected. "If the sergeant will let us have a bit o' liberty come mornin', I'll bring him over to you."

* * * *

The next morning, stripped to the waist, John, Jacob, Dobbins, and Nat paused to catch their breaths. They had been working up quite a sweat, swinging axes to sharpen stakes and sinking them into the ground in front of their position. Although not effective against infantry attack, they would slow a cavalry charge.

"I'm getting mighty dry," Dobbins remarked to no one in particular. John reached for his canteen; its braided cord was looped over one of the sharpened stakes already firmly embedded in the side of the trench. He frowned at the feel of the hot metal. Although it was still an hour until noon, the sun beat down unmercifully. He took a sip of the lukewarm water, spat it out, and then offered Dobbins a drink.

"Water?" Dobbins asked. "No, thanks, you can catch any number of complaints drinking that foul stuff!" Placing hands on hips, he leaned back and bawled at the top of his voice, "I need rum!"

"And you'll get it, soon as you finish your turn on fatigue detail!" Sergeant Hopkins had a knack for throwing his voice down into the trench as he paced along the top of the redoubt. Loose sand cascaded down the slope under the pressure of his step and showered the four men below.

"Stokes, Fenton. You two come on up, there's a couple of Highlanders from the Seventy-First asking after you."

Tossing their axes triumphantly to the ground, both men mumbled a hurried farewell and scrambled up the forward side of the redoubt. The two Highlanders were Rory and Angus.

John motioned for the two men to follow him to a campsite where some soldier's wives had pitched their tents. It was the one place where any soldier could find a woman to wash his clothes, provide first aid, or tend to any number of other needs. Outside of a large fly tent, pegged opened on one side to form a lean to, he halted. A dark-haired, extremely attractive woman of about thirty sat on a campstool nursing a baby. Another child, about two years old, scampered around on the dirt floor, chasing a small brown puppy. The inside of the tent was hazy with the dust that the child had kicked up. The woman looked up with a bored expression. A few stray strands of dark hair had escaped from beneath the band of her mobcap. She absentmindedly pushed them back behind her ears.

"Mornin' Maggie." John nodded.

"Morning," the woman answered lackadaisically. She leaned over and gently placed the child in a small wooden cradle nestled alongside a fold-out cot. She kept her back to the four men as she tied the front of her blouse,[35] talking to them over her shoulder.

"I was expectin' you sooner."

"My apologies," John said. He looked towards Rory and Angus once she turned to face him. "This is Maggie Shaw. Her husband is in the South Carolina Royalists. She was his apothecary's assistant in Charleston before the war."

Both McDougal brothers bowed courteously, touched their bonnets in salute, and said in unison, "Ma'am."

"Which one is it?" Maggie asked curtly. Her eyes traveled from brother to brother.

John indicated Angus who removed his tam, exposing the crude bandage.

Maggie motioned for Angus to take a seat on the recently vacated campstool. He sat down, an expression of discontent on his face while she bent over him and slowly began to unwind the bandage. Angus flinched a few times, but otherwise remained silent as she gently coaxed the bandage away from the thick scab. She studied the wound with a critical look.

"Has no one seen to this properly?" Concern crept into her voice as she spoke. She shook her head in disapproval.

"We best move outside, away from me babe," she informed Angus. He carried his seat with him and sat it down in the sunshine. Maggie instructed Rory to support his brother by the shoulders as he leaned back. Taking a bottle of rum from a board that served as a shelf, she gently poured it over the wound and softly scrubbed it with a clean piece of linen. After giving it one final rinse with the rum, she handed the bottle to Angus who turned it up thirstily.

While the patient guzzled his painkiller, she fished a long strand of horsehair from a steaming pot suspended on an iron tripod over a small fire. She ran the long strand through her finger appraising its texture, seemed to find it pliable enough, and walked back to the tent, threading it carefully through the eye of a sewing needle as she moved.

"He's got some size to him," she remarked casually. "It's going to take all of you to hold him down." She looked towards the other three men who nodded knowingly. Each of them took a tight grip on a different part of the body—arms, legs, or head—and waited for the operation to begin.

With all three men holding the patient firmly in place, Maggie straddled his chest, quickly pinched the two sides of the wound together, and, amid the howling agony of her patient, tightly stitched them together. Wiping her hands on her apron, she stepped back and surveyed her work proudly.

"As nice a job of sewing as a woman can do on a moving target," she announced proudly, her voice containing the faintest hint of sarcasm. She finished the job by padding the wound with tree moss[36] and tying a fresh bandage over it. With a sour look on her face, she sniffed Angus's old head wrap before tossing it into the fire.

Admonishing Rory to make certain that his brother kept the wound clean and for him to come back every other day for a change of dressing; she dismissed the men with a wave of her hand. Before she could react, Angus grabbed her in a rough bear hug and presented her with a hearty buss on the cheek.

"That's a reward that many another lass has pined for and been denied!" Angus roared as Maggie blushed and waved him away.

"Be gone you rogue, 'fore my good husband returns and runs a foot o' steel through your guts!"

Angus bellowed again and trooped away alongside of his brother. John waited until the two amiable knaves had turned their backs to him and, with a sly wink, quickly tossed a shilling to Maggie. She palmed it easily and tucked it into one of the pockets tied at her waist.

For the next week, John and the Rangers did little but eat, sleep, and improve the defensive works that encircled the beleaguered borough. At intervals, Captain Moncrieff, the Engineering Officer, would stop to inspect the construction. The defensive works, which had begun with only twelve guns, grew steadily as sailors from the warships rigged cannons over the side of the men-of-war anchored in the river and manhandled them into positions ashore. Eventually, the works would be bristling with over one hundred guns.

At the same time that the works grew more defensible, the Rangers, lamenting the loss of the extra money,[37] were pulled from fatigue details and replaced by Pioneer detachments that consisted of runaway slaves who had escaped into the city pursuing the promise of freedom.

John, along with the other members of the regiment, was put through a series of intense bayonet drills by sergeants from the Royal Marines and by Hessian mercenaries, giving directions through interpreters. The Rangers were made acutely aware of the fact that when the main assault of the French and rebels finally came, this weapon would be widely used. Their sergeants drilled them relentlessly until they became experts in its use. The two star students of the training exercises were the African's, Sambo and Mambo, who had clearly mastered the use of the bayonet in the service of some obscure African prince long before they had joined the King's forces. Whenever the two warriors became the subjects of their lively conversations around the fires at night, the Rangers agreed that they had definitely been soldiers, somehow taken prisoner in some forgotten war. John got the distinct impression that the poor bastard, whoever he was, that had purchased these two as slaves, did not live long to enjoy the fruits of their labors.

On the 23rd of September 1779, John and the other Carolina Rangers watched from atop their redoubt as General Lincoln arrived with his army of three thousand rebels. Colonel Brown, standing alongside his men in their positions, studied their arrival with a somber face. He estimated that their arrival had increased the enemy's strength to around seven thousand men, the majority of which were professional soldiers. The British strength was still no more than twenty-five hundred.

Dobbins, watching the procession with a long face, gave voice to a thought that had found its way into the minds of many of the Rangers as they watched the rebels pitch their tents on the opposite side of the marsh, almost directly across from their positions.

"Well boys," he said gloomily, "it looks like we're about to put all those hours of bayonet practice to use. And it looks like it's gonna be right quick."

Shading their eyes from the afternoon sun, many of them easily identified old friends, and even a handful of relatives, among the militiamen who came trudging along at the rear of the rebel column. Some of the Loyalists shouted the names of those they recognized and waved across the open marsh. A few of the rebels returned the greetings, despondently lifting one hand or the other in recognition as they spied their own friends and family standing among the green coated ranks of Rangers. All in all, it was a gloomy day for the men on both sides.

The next day the French began digging parallels in which to approach the British works. The British soldiers watched the drama play out in silence. Often they could hear the commands of the French officers, shouted to the men, as they emplaced their artillery. But overall, the life of the Rangers continued quietly uninterrupted.

Under the supervision of their Marine and Hessian instructors, the Rangers continued to practice forming battle lines, executing the thirty-five steps of the army's musket drill, and carrying out bayonet charges. Even those men who in the past had displayed a pointed apathy towards drilling with their weapons, now participated with deadly seriousness, keenly aware that the use of these skills was imminent.

Chapter 9

Savannah, Georgia
Sunday, October 3, 1779

Perched atop the stump of a freshly downed tree, John looked out over the crowded expanse of the Savannah River. It was brimming with British ships riding listlessly at anchor in the narrow confines of the channel that separated Hutchinson Island from the town. Wearing an old hunting frock and breeches, he felt out of place sitting amid the boisterous hubbub of the busy camp instead of laboring beneath the sweltering sun, digging defensive positions. Jacob and Dobbins sat on the sandy soil next to him, each wearing their extra shirts, along with a pair of overalls that had been issued to them for the summer months. The three men smoked their pipes and chatted idly while they watched Maggie, engaged in the onerous job of washing clothes, slave away on the sandy strip of riverbank below. They had decided that their uniforms, which had accumulated so much filth that they could no longer bear wearing them, needed a good cleaning. Using this pressing need as an excuse to surreptitiously provide Maggie with some much needed extra money, they had asked if they could hire her services. She had immediately agreed but had only bargained for hard money. Preferably white money[38].

Maggie moved about the riverbank scrubbing, beating, and hanging up the clothing at a steady pace. She ignored everything but her work, including Angus, who had flung himself onto the sandy bank of the river alongside of her, where he affected a series of posturing poses designed to impress her with the image of his manly magnificence. He lay, bare-chested, his hands cradling his head as he reclined indolently underfoot, watching Maggie's every move with fervid eyes. His bulging muscles flexed whenever her head turned in his direction. The three Rangers sitting on the riverbank above gave each other amused glances as they watched the primitive mating ritual being played out below.

Tired of waiting for Maggie to notice him, Angus yawned loudly and stretched, long and languidly, showing off his well-muscled physique in an effort to steal her attention away from her work. Ever since he had discovered that Maggie's husband was a short, wiry fellow, he had silently besieged her, continuing to visit her every other day to have his bandages changed, despite the fact that she had declared the gash on his head well on its way to healing.

Maggie couldn't resist toying with the strutting peacock. Grinning to herself, she turned her back and bent over, pretending to be engaged in some pressing problem. She wiggled her hips ever so slightly, smiled covertly, then walked past him to hang another shirt out to dry. After studying him for a moment from the corner of one eye, she addressed him without pausing from her work.

"Looks to me like you need to find a woman to marry up with. You've too much time on your hands."

He turned his head and directed his gaze in her direction as he spoke. "As a matter of fact, I have my eye on a promising prospect this very moment."

"Is that so? Does she live over there?" Maggie indicated a row of slovenly tents located above the bluff a few yards downstream. "The women there are known to be free with their favors."

"There? Why no! She's a decent woman. I wouldn't have anything to do with that bunch of slatterns!" Angus sounded insulted that she would even think such a low thing of him.

"Must be some young girl in town. The only decent women around this encampment are well-married old hens like me, who would *never* be tempted to jump from one chicken coop to another simply on account of one strutting gamecock." She reinforced her position by bending over to check on her sleeping daughter who continued to snooze soundly in her cradle.

Angus frowned, foiled by her logic. If he agreed with Maggie, then he would be admitting that he must stop wasting his time tempting her. On the other hand, if he disagreed with her, he would be insinuating that she was of loose morals. She had him either way! He sullenly decided to retreat and live to court another day. He slowly stretched his six-foot frame, threw back his elbows, and pushed out his chest before clasping his hands together to display his bulging biceps to her.

Without seeming to notice him, the object of this display fished a steaming green coat from the suds in the wash pot. Angus had helped her to break-in the water with wood ash to make the suds; it was his one feeble contribution to the project. She slung the jacket against a smooth log with one fluid motion. The impact dislodged a spray of fine, soapy mist that spewed directly onto Angus's chest. The shocked look on his face caused her to laugh good-naturedly as she beat the offending garment with a flat paddle. Grabbing a second jacket, she repeated the process, casting a furtive glance at Angus's broad, strong back as he lumbered up the bank with a sour expression marring his normally pleasing features. He was clearly in deep thought. She smiled, secretly flattered by the attention. For some strange reason, it made her feel like crying.

After hours of heavy labor, she lugged the bundles of clothing to her tent, where she used a flat iron to carefully press the wrinkles from them. It was nearly dark when she finished.

Spooning rice onto a battered pewter plate, she sat on a folding camp chair and shared the meal with her toddler. When Maggie finished her own supper, she nursed her daughter, crooning softly until the infant drifted off to sleep.

Her day's work at an end, she sat back for her first rest of the day. The oppressive heat of summer was long past; the slight breeze made her drowsy. She rested her head on the back of the chair and immediately dozed off. She jumped, startled, when John and Jacob suddenly appeared to pay for their laundry.

"Sorry if we scared you ma'am," Jacob said apologetically. "We just came to get our uniforms. We can't tell you how much we appreciate your taking care of us like this."

Maggie gasped in surprise when they each produced a shilling to pay her. She knew that it was almost two days wages for them, but they insisted that she take the money, assuring her that a freshly cleaned and pressed uniform was more than a bargain at that price. Noticing a wistful frown that covered her face after she had pocketed their money, John asked her gently if she was feeling well. She smiled one of those sad smiles that is a cross between happiness and heartbreak.

"I was just thinking back to the comfortable home that I shared with my husband in Charleston." Her voice was little more than a whisper. "The ground floor was my husband's apothecary. I kept the shelves so neat and orderly! It made me feel as if I would be happy and safe forever." She paused to wipe away a tear before continuing with her story. "My husband is a good man. Back in '76, he spoke for the King in a tavern. Just one night! I still find it hard to believe that such a simple act brought my world crashing down around my ears. And so quickly! About midnight, a mob of local *Liberty Boys* visited our home. They pulled my husband off his own porch and drug him, kicking and screaming, with a noose around his neck, down to the docks. After they tarred and feathered him, they rode him on a rail out to the end of a pier where they tossed him into the harbor like a sack of garbage." She realized that she was allowing herself to be filled with feelings of rage. She paused to rein in her emotions. "They laughed and hooted as if it were nothing more than an innocent joke! Then they stripped me down and whipped my bare arse with a wooden slat until it was the color of overripe tomatoes! Then they threw me in alongside my poor husband who was as close to death as a body can get and still live. Scarred for life, he is." She sat back and closed her eyes with a sigh. "Thank the good Lord that we had only been married three months and had no children for the fiends to molest!" She stopped to take a deep breath. "I used to be a wealthy, well-dressed woman. Men would open doors for me, they tipped their hats when they passed me on the street." She threw up her hands in defeat. "Now look at me! That love-sick hulk of a Highlander propositions me like a common slattern and people tell me how grand I look for a woman of my age! I'm only twenty-three! I just pray that my husband survives this war. I shudder for my poor little ones if anything happens to him." She surveyed her wash-reddened hands and rubbed them vigorously together as if trying to regain the vaguely remembered softness of youth. She studied them for a moment, then dropped them into her lap, defeated. "We have lost everything! We can't even afford to buy a commission for my husband. He has to serve as a private, while my greatest fear is that I will end up like them." She waved her arm in the general direction of prostitute row.

John stared at the woman, mentally weighing her story against those of a thousand other patriotic Loyalists who had risked everything to support their rightful King. Knowing that there was absolutely nothing that he could say to ease the pain, he simply nodded his head sympathetically.

"One day you will have all of that back," he confidently assured her. "That's why we're here."

She shook her head sadly, utter despair written plainly on her face. "That's what is so fiendish and diabolical about the rebels! They totally humiliate you, so that you'll never be able to hold your head up again. We can never go back! Even when we win, we can't go back! How could I ever walk down the streets of Charleston knowing that every man I pass has seen me humiliated like that?"

Maggie looked up suddenly, surprise and shame written on her face. "My sincerest apologies! I did not mean to burden you so! You must think me daft, babbling on about all of this. It's just that ... that ... I don't know." She began to sob softly to herself. John instinctively reached out and placed a comforting hand on her shoulder. He squeezed it slightly before he turned and trudged away, slump-shouldered, to rejoin his unit. He, like her, knew she was one of thousands. Innocent victims who would never totally recover from this madness.

* * * *

"What the hell?" Dobbins jumped to his feet, startled into alertness by a thunderclap of sound. Not ten yards away, smoke curled from a shallow crater blasted into the ground by the explosion of a fused, eight-inch shell. The men around him began pulling on uniforms and equipment as sand and chunks of earth, thrown into the air by the explosion, rained down on them.

Sergeant Hopkins stood on the top of the redoubt, shouting orders to the milling Rangers below. "That was what we professional soldiers call a ranging shot!" he yelled matter-of-factly. "They'll be more commin'. And soon!"

The men crowded into the bombproof, jamming against each other in their hasty, uncoordinated efforts to take cover. Behind their fortifications the earth erupted in a series of thunderous explosions as French artillery opened en masse on the besieged British city.

Sergeant Hopkins bellowed a warning and raced down the backside of the redoubt, waving the men still standing in the open into the protective shelters. "The bloody French have finally decided to have a real siege!" he called to no one in particular.

To their left, the sailor's battery roared to life, returning fire as French round shot streaked over their heads. The whistling of the projectiles was followed by the unmistakable sounds of splintering wood and crashing masonry as the French shells overshot the defensive works and landed in the town behind them. Around the perimeter of the British defenses, a hundred cannons roared in reply. It was deafening in the redoubts; French and rebel rounds screamed over their heads traveling in one direction, while those fired from the British men-of-war anchored in the river, heading out, crisscrossed them directly overhead. French mortars crews added to the bedlam by dropping high angle explosive rounds directly behind the British fortifications, creating huge craters in the city streets. On top of the redoubt, debris rained down on the exposed defenders like hail in a thunderstorm.

John huddled in the bombproof built into the rear of the Ranger's redoubt. Across from him, Jacob, Dobbins, Nat, and Sergeant Hopkins stared out of the opening, studying the maelstrom outside with great interest. Hopkins unexpectedly laughed, despite the thunderous bombardment that continued to pound them.

"What's so bleeding funny?" Dobbins snapped.

"He is." Hopkins smiled in John's direction. "I was just thinkin'. He's been a Ranger for four months and hasn't done a bloody thing but sit on his ass, take the King's money, and eat the King's food. Well sir, now he's finally going to be a real soldier!" Hopkins roared with laughter as if he had just told the finest joke in the world.

Dobbins rolled his eyes. "And I was just thinkin' how I might stay on with the army after we win this war. Until today, it seemed like a fine, easy way to make a living!"

The bantering of the veterans eased the anxiety of the newer soldiers as they slowly began to realize that, other than the noise, they were virtually immune to the shells bursting outside. So long as they remained hunkered down in the bombproof, their biggest threat was that a cannon ball fired from one of the warships in the river would fall short and tear into the dugout from the rear.

The bombardment continued, unabated, until eleven o'clock that morning, then it abruptly ceased. The Ranger's waited anxiously for the order to man the defenses. The order never came. A profound silence settled over the battlefield. Nat slowly cocked his head to one side like a dog trying to place an unfamiliar sound. He listened intently, the whites of his eyes unnaturally bright in his dirty face. The rattle of drums could be heard faintly, drifting to them from the far end of the defensive lines.

"It's an attack!"

Sergeant Hopkins shook his head. "Hold your horses Nat, someone is beating *The Parley*. Their officers want to negotiate with ours."

"Negotiate what?"

Hopkins shrugged. "Whatever officers negotiate about."

A few minutes later, Colonel Brown squatted at the door of the bombproof. He surveyed the occupants critically, then pointed out John and Jacob.

"You two fellows seem to have the best-kept uniforms. Come with me." He motioned them out of the dugout with a slight movement of his head.

The two soldiers fell out at attention. Colonel Brown nodded to Sergeant Hopkins.

"Very good sergeant, they'll do fine." He motioned towards the two Rangers. "Follow me. And look sharp! I'm ordered to General Provost's Headquarters. You will accompany me and stand by as couriers. Understand?"

"Yes, sir!" Both men snapped to attention and saluted smartly with their muskets. Brown smiled. "Follow me."

They trailed two steps to the rear of the colonel, stepping gingerly around shell craters and piles of rubble that had tumbled into the streets.

John studied the colonel as he walked. He was finely dressed in a well-pressed uniform. Despite the bombardment that he had endured, the only signs that it had left on his person was a slight dusting of sand on his shoulders and in the creases of his hat. He walked with a slight limp, acquired after having had his feet held to a fire by a group of Liberty Boys, back sometime around '75 or so. His crime was having been too vocal in supporting his King. He was a wealthy man and carried himself as such. He walked ramrod straight, left hand clamped firmly on the hilt of his sword, his right arm swinging in march step. When they arrived at headquarters, they found a cluster of officers who seemed intent on the contents of a letter that one of the general's aides was scanning intensely, in preparation for reading it aloud to the assembled leaders. Their faces were somber; some even seemed to be horrified, as if they were hearing something totally unbelievable. A middle-aged, distinguished-looking colonel stood to one side, dressed in a beautifully tailored red uniform coat with royal blue cuffs and facings.

"Good Day, Colonel Cruger," Brown said cordially. "May I ask what the situation is?"

Colonel Cruger cleared his throat. "The general has asked that the French and their rebel allies permit us to load the women and children onto a vessel and sail it down stream under French protection, where it will wait until this business is settled between the two armies. The poor souls are huddled in cellars all about the town and seem to be taking the brunt of the punishment from this bombardment."

"Is there a problem?" Brown asked. "Those gentlemen over there seem somewhat concerned." The two officers moved closer, John and Jacob stepped along behind. A staff officer was in the process of reading the reply to the assembled men. As they neared the group, his words grew clearer.

"The Count D'Estaing in his own name, notified you that you would be personally and alone responsible for the consequences of your obstinacy. The time which you informed him…"

Jacob leaned close to John's ear and whispered, "What are they talking about? Obstinacy?"

John shrugged in reply. He returned his attention to the reader, who was already reading the final lines of the French commander's brief response.

"It is with regret we yield to the austerity of our functions, and we deplore the fate of those persons who will be the victims of your conduct, and the delusion which appears in your mind. We, with respect, etc., etc…" The officer looked up with an incredulous expression.

"Unbelievable, Sir! The damned *dancing masters*[39] refuse safe conduct for the women and children! And blame us for their fate because we dare to decline a summons of surrender? Unbelievable!"

"Barbaric!" One of the officers snarled from the back of the group. The assemblage erupted in a fit of consternation, damning the rebels and their French allies for such a dishonorable stance.

General Provost waved his hands, cautioning the officers loudly. "Be that as it may gentlemen, we have very little time before the bombardment resumes. I want each of the regiments to detail ten men to sweep the area and escort the women and children to the banks of the river." He turned next to address an officer in a Royal Navy uniform.

"Sir, if you will be so kind, please inform your ships that we will need all of their small boats to ferry the women and children across to Hutchinson Island. I am sure that even this Count D'Estaing would not dare bombard them over there!" He waved his finger in a gesture of caution, directed at all of the officers. "Place your men on alert, gentlemen. I think I read a tone of desperation in the good Count's reply." He slowly looked up and surveyed the clouds forming in the sky. "Hurricane season is approaching. Look for an assault at any moment. The French may be anxious to end this quickly in order to get their ships away to safer areas before the storms arrive." He cleared his throat and said the next words loudly and clearly, to be certain all of those assembled could hear. "Make certain that your men know what has transpired here. When the attack does come, we want to make sure that they fight as if there is no tomorrow." He waved the paper in their faces. "This fool will be just the type to order the black flag[40] raised. Dismissed!"

The Rangers mumbled angrily among themselves when John and Jacob relayed the news to them. Ten men, who had wives with the regiment, readily volunteered and raced away to begin the evacuation of the women and children. The remainder of the men were content to sit and enjoy the brief silence as they wolfed down half-cooked rations.

The cannonade recommenced while the sailors were still straining to row their small boats loaded with refugees between the city wharves and a small pier that served the plantation on Hutchinson Island. A few screams for lost children and several moments of anxious shuffling on the docks were the only reactions of the people to the tumultuous sound of cannon fire. The troops, squatting on their haunches behind the defensive works, kicked sand over their fires and quietly moved back into their dugouts and bombproofs.

The bombardment continued, on and off, for days. The Rangers sat in their dugouts passing the time by smoking, or sleeping, or watching Captains Johnston and Wylly, along with their lieutenants, play Whist[41] for hours on end, dealing a frayed deck of cards onto a drumhead table.

On the night of October eighth, Captain Johnston's company was ordered from the bombproof as soon as the enemy's guns had fallen silent. Protected by a wicker basket filled with sand, John surveyed the open rice fields in front of the redoubt, searching for skulking rebels, but expecting to see nothing. Only a bunch of fools would attack across a quagmire such as that.

Bored with inactivity, he allowed his mind to wander, trying to imagine what his wife and children were doing at that very moment back in the cabin at Long Swamp. He could hear laughter, accompanied by the rapid thumping of miniature feet in the overhead loft, and the low hiss of sap boiling from the ends of the logs burning in the fireplace. In his mind's eye he could see the face of his wife, tinted red by the glow of that same fire, her lips compressed into a stern line of concentration as she worked the pedal of her spinning wheel, creating thread for next year's cloth.

Jacob wandered over and stood next to him. The big man leaned forward, elbows resting on the front lip of the redoubt, his musket slung loosely across one shoulder. He puffed idly on a short-stemmed clay pipe, blew the fragrant smoke out onto a stiff, westerly breeze, and watched silently as it was carried away, dissipating over the rice fields. To their left, on the far side of the rice fields, they could clearly see the shadowy forms of rebels as they passed in front of their campfires.

"What do you reckon those fellas over there are thinkin'?" Jacob asked. "I would hate to be in their shoes if the general is right. They'll make fine targets coming across that open ground out there."

Before he could answer, Jacob's head came up, alerted by a slight movement, apparent at intervals along a small wash leading up from the river. The ominous click as he cocked his musket sounded unnaturally loud in the darkness. Instinctively, John's hand went to the hammer of his own weapon. He brought it to full-cock and rested it across the front of the redoubt. Sergeant Hopkins, alerted by the sounds, moved quickly forward. Stepping between them, he peered into the darkness.

"There's someone moving in that gully," Jacob whispered. Even as he spoke, the unmistakable form of a head popped into sight, followed by the clear outlines of a man's shoulders. John raised his musket to his shoulder and braced his elbows on the redoubt. He sighted on the dim outline of the man as he rose smoothly to his feet and crept cautiously towards the redoubt.

"Hold your fire." Sergeant Hopkins hissed. "If it's just one man, it could be one of our spies coming back into the lines. If you see more than one, fire on them." He checked to his left and right to assure himself that the sentries were alert and ready for an attack.

The dark form crept up to the edge of the position. He stopped and called lightly to them.

"Don't shoot! I have important information for your commander."

"Give the watch word," John challenged in a whisper.

The man hesitated. Through cupped hands he answered as loudly as he dared, "I'm a deserter from the Charleston Regiment. I have no watch word."

Hopkins made a snap decision. "You two fix your bayonets and come with me." He said the words over his shoulder as he clambered over the top of the breastwork.

The three men moved cautiously down the face of the redoubt, sliding on the loose earth and creating miniature landslides that moved ahead of them. Lieutenant Ellis, just arrived on his rounds, called down to them in low tones. Hopkins halted and answered softly, before continuing down the slope.

The man was waiting on the far side of a tangled abatis of downed trees that ran along the length of the entire British position. John and Jacob jumped into the dry moat at the base of the redoubt and leveled their bayoneted weapons in his direction, keeping him covered as the sergeant told him to come forward, hands over his head. The man wiggled through the tangled limbs, halting often to free his clothing from persistent snags. He moved towards them in short, jerky spurts, emerging from the obstruction on hands and knees. He stood and immediately raised his hands in surrender before walking with even, unhurried steps up to the edge of the moat.

"Jump down," Hopkins instructed him. The intruder hopped into the ditch. He grunted when he landed, but managed to keep his hands held high. After the deserter relayed his story, Hopkins called gently up the slope to Lieutenant Ellis.

"He's a rebel deserter, sir. Says he has important information."

The lieutenant gave quick directions to one of the sentries to fetch Captain Johnston. He then clambered down the redoubt and jumped into the moat alongside the other men.

"How important is this information?" he asked Hopkins.

"Says that the French and rebels are attacking just before dawn, the whole kit and caboodle of them. Heading right at the Spring Hill redoubt over there." He indicated the next redoubt with his thumb.

Ellis digested this information for a moment. "When?"

"They're supposed to attack at four in the morning."

Ellis estimated that it was about an hour before midnight. He looked at Sergeant Hopkins, who chewed on his lower lip and bobbed his head in a series of shallow nods as he mulled over the information. He stopped suddenly, having made a decision. "Take him up to the redoubt," he said. "There could be something to this story."

Captain Johnston questioned the prisoner only briefly before making his own decision.

"Sergeant Hopkins, you and your two men will escort the prisoner to the general, I will accompany you." Without wasting a moment, he spun on his heels and marched away. The prisoner tramped along at his heels, tightly thronged by the three Rangers.

By three o'clock that morning, every soldier in the British works was standing to, with freshly charged muskets and sharpened flints. From the top of the Ranger's redoubt, John and his companions watched with disbelief as the dark outlines of several hundred rebel troops fought their way through the mire of the rice fields to their front, heading directly for them.

"Surely they don't think this will be successful?" John said, shaking his head.

"That's the trouble, rebels don't think." Dobbins answered him with his low and often voiced opinion of the rebel mentality.

"What a circus," Hopkins said. He looked dubiously at Captain Johnston. "Surely this is a feint, captain."

The captain nodded and smiled. "We'll make it an expensive one." He pointed to the Spring Hill redoubt to their left. "The deserter claims that is their main objective. Every available man—French, Continental, and Militia—is going to assault us right at that point and attempt to break through. They think that the Provincials holding the area won't put up much of a fight against the French regulars. We'll be too awed by their majesty and military bearing." He stood, hands clasped behind his back, studying the situation. "Lieutenant Ellis."

"Yes sir?"

"Once we've beaten back this rabble to our front, I want you to take fifty of our men to the left and fire volleys into the enemy's flank as they attack that redoubt. Can I count on you?"

"Why, yes, sir!" Ellis's voice was enthusiastic. "We've been waiting a long time to even up some old scores with those folks. You can count on us, sir."

Four o'clock came and passed quietly. Across the marsh they could see the enemy troops forming for an assault. Sweaty palms gripped freshly cleaned muskets, hearts thumped in their chest at twice their normal rates. Still nothing broke the stillness of the morning. John stood alongside his comrades, watching the struggling line of enemy infantrymen slog forward through the swamps and rice fields. Thanks to the information gleaned from the deserter, they knew exactly who they were facing - Isaac Huger's Brigade of Charleston militia. They waited, eager for revenge. Watching as the militia continued to fight its way forward through the mud, they could almost feel the shoes being sucked from the feet of the attackers and the cold sweat dripping down their spines.

The first wave of militia scrambled onto the dry ground directly in front of the Ranger's positions where they milled around like a flock of lost sheep. Ignoring their officer's orders to advance, they paused to help friends or family members struggle free of the slush. The Rangers waited, aligned in ranks. Each rank would fire, then retreat to the rear and reload as the next rank moved forward and emptied their muskets into the packed ranks of the enemy. As he waited, John studied the faces of the men who would fight alongside of him. Some displayed grim smiles of satisfaction as they watched former tormentors moving quietly to their deaths. Some had the unmistakable look of fear in their eyes, but the majority looked almost businesslike, as if they were simply waiting to pitch in with a reaping, or a barn raising. No concern, no hurry, just wait for the word to start work. Only today, their work was death.

They watched as the enemy militia formed lines. The white strips of paper that they had affixed to their hats for identification seemed to glow in the morning sun; it's heat was already chasing away the morning fog. The enemy had waited too long, the light had caught them in the open. Most would not survive the day. The rebel officers turned, their swords pointed skyward, ready to give the order to advance.

Any sound that they may have uttered was obliterated as the Loyalist and British fired a volley directly into their ranks. Sailors, dressed in slops, touched slow matches to the cannons emplaced along the redoubt. Jets of flame spewed upward from the touchholes as the main charges ignited, sending hundreds of lead balls tearing through the rebel ranks. The smoke from the guns all but obscured their targets.

John could hear men in the redoubts cheering the carnage as he stepped forward with the second rank and leveled his musket at the back of a fleeing militiaman. He pulled the trigger; the smoke was so thick that he couldn't see the result of his shot, but at this range it was impossible to miss. He sidestepped and moved to the rear. Tearing open a paper cartridge with his teeth, he frantically reloaded.

By the time John rotated back to the firing line, most of the surviving rebels were fleeing across the mud. Without hesitation, he threw his musket to his shoulder and leveled it at the back of a fleeing militiaman. He pulled the trigger, felt the recoil, and smiled with grim satisfaction, contented with having wreaked vengeance on his persecutors. After each rank had fired two volleys, the officers ordered a cease-fire. The artillerymen fired another blast of canister from each gun, unwilling to let any more rebels than absolutely necessary survive to fight another day. Here and there, across the front of the redoubt, Loyalist troops armed with rifles continued to pick off rebels still floundering within range. No one made any attempt to stop them.

The cheering of the men was short-lived. John's rank was ordered at the double-quick to their left. They ran in a single file down the backside of their position and swung around the rear, emerging on the near side of the sailor's battery where Lieutenant Ellis halted them and ordered them into a line. They realized immediately that they were looking directly into the flank of the main enemy advance. The ground behind the advancing

French troops was littered with the dead and dying as the British gunners unrelentingly fired canisters of grape shot into the closely packed ranks. Waves of Loyalist infantrymen rotated between the gaps that separated the guns, volley firing their Long Land muskets virtually into the faces of the enemy.

John took a quick look to either side. Directly to his right were the two Africans, Sambo and Mambo, standing at port arms like ebony statues, their wild eyes blazing with impatience to join in the battle. On his left, Jacob and Dobbins nervously twisted their hands around the stocks of their muskets, appraising the battle through anxious, smoke-reddened eyes. Powder stains blackened their lips and hands. John could taste the sharp tang of black powder in his own mouth.

To their front, the battle raged. The French led the way, several thousand of them, and they dropped like ten pins as they moved forward into the muzzles of the British cannons. Behind them came South Carolina Continentals, supported by more Charleston militiamen. Later, John would be told that the Count D'Estaing had urged his men forward with the shout of "Forward, murder the wretches!" But amid the deafening sounds of the battle, few probably heard him.

The Rangers immediately began to pour volleys directly into the left flank of the attacking French; they continued to blast away throughout the attack. As the French faltered and the rebels, wiggling their way through the wrecked ranks of their allies, renewed the charge, the Rangers shifted their fire onto the South Carolinians. The Count d'Estaing, wounded twice, lay behind a tombstone in the old Jewish cemetery and watched as his men and allies were decimated by the fantastic firepower that was poured onto them from the British works.[42]

John reckoned that he had fired about fifteen rounds before his musket became so fouled that it became useless. He saw one of his companions jam the end of his ramrod against a tree stump to ram home a stuck ball. No one wanted to stop the killing; there was the enemy. Attack! Attack! Attack!

The British and Loyalist regiments defending the redoubt resisted fiercely. Still the attack swept up and over the redoubt several times only to be driven back time and again by the superhuman efforts of the British and Loyalist soldiers. At least three times, the enemy placed his flag on top of the redoubt only to be swept back down into the trenches at the foot of the position by a counterattack of the defenders.

Sensing a rare moment of opportunity, the British commander ordered the reserves forward. The Marines and Grenadiers rolled over the crest of the redoubt and literally leapt onto the rebel and French troops trapped below. Unable to restrain themselves, John and the other Rangers charged with fixed bayonets, screaming like the furies as they melted into the melee, bayoneting the hapless French and rebels in the sides as they engaged the British reserves to their front. Some of the Loyalist laughed as they worked; others went about the task methodically as if they were simply mowing hay on their farms. John caught fleeting glimpses of the two Africans, Sambo and Mambo, cutting their way through the enemy on his right. Their movements were mechanically efficient, like two grim reapers harvesting the pale souls of the enemy. Mambo speared a small French drummer boy with this bayonet. Lifting him completely off the ground, he tossed him kicking and squealing over his shoulder. John heard the hollow thump of the drum as the body crashed to the ground behind him. No one so much as looked back. For one fleeting moment before he turned his attention back to the deadly task before him, John was reminded of Thunder's Child and Robin spearing fish on the banks of the Savannah River.

Broken by the advance of the British reserve, the French and rebel forces grudgingly withdrew. As they neared their own lines, the Chasseurs-Volontaires de Saint-Domingo Regiment moved forward, interposing themselves like human shields between their mauled comrades and the galling fire still pouring from the British positions. The regiment, composed exclusively of free blacks from Haiti, held their ranks perfectly as they traded volleys with the British, absorbing the punishment intended for their French and American comrades. On one flank John noticed a young, ebony faced drummer boy, no more than twelve years old, standing stoically as he tapped out his officer's signals, oblivious to the canister shot and musket balls that whistled past his head or kicked up geysers of sand at his feet.[43]

As the last of the beaten and battered assault troops disappeared behind the forward slopes of the French earthworks, the Chasseurs began their own retreat. Unwilling to turn their faces from the enemy and flee like a beaten rabble, they stepped backwards, slowly, still in ranks, firing steadily as they withdrew from the field. The defenders cheered long and lustily, waving their muskets in both respect and defiance as the last of these brave men disappeared behind the safety of their breastworks. The battle was over.

John dropped to one knee, panting and terrified now that it was over. He looked down, clenching his musket in a vise-like grip as he fought to regain control of his emotions. He felt as if he had temporarily surrendered his body to a total stranger and now fought to regain possession of it. Dimly, he could hear an officer shouting orders to reform. He looked up obediently, conditioned to react instantaneously to the sound, but dropped onto his back utterly exhausted when he realized it was a Royal Marine Lieutenant reforming his men.[44]

The victorious Rangers collapsed at the base of the Sailor's Battery. There they lay amid the lumpy forms of the dead while regaining the strength to march back to their own redoubt. Several of them lifted captured French canteens, made from Chinese Gourds and filled with Brandy, to their parched lips. Their Adams Apples bobbed greedily as they quickly emptied the contents of the containers and flung them aside.

Dobbins, slowly wiping his lips with a dirty sleeve, emitted a slow, sad sigh as he rubbed his thumb across the lock of his musket, clearing away the greasy film of black powder residue. He turned his face, looking directly at John with a resigned expression.

"Fellas," he said as if they had simply concluded some minor business no more serious than musket or bayonet drill. "It's going to take us all day to clean these damned things." He turned away and emptied his captured canteen in a gulp.

Jacob sat with a troubled look on his face. He was not by nature a violent man. A sudden, guilty twinge also pricked John's consciousness; after today, he wondered, *"Am I?"*

When they stumbled back into their own positions they were cheered like heroes. John felt as if the war was as good as won.

* * * *

The Allies resumed their siege, but with a marked decrease in intensity. That evening, as John and the other Rangers sat outside of their dugout, he noticed Maggie struggling towards the river, her baby slung across her back, papoose fashion, as she forced a heavy sack across the sandy earth with a series of yanks and tugs. He immediately moved in her direction, followed by Jacob, to offer his assistance with a task that was obviously beyond her physical capabilities. As they approached, she stopped straining to move the clumsy bundle and dropped listlessly to the ground, sobbing as if her world were at an end. With a slight shock John noticed the familiar shape of the sack's contents. He guessed immediately what it contained.

He knelt beside the grieving woman and gently placed his arms around her shoulders. She melted into him, her sobbing growing more intense and violent.

"When?" he asked, quietly speaking into the top of her head.

"During the attack today. He was wounded in the chest; there was nothing that I could do for him. He died an hour ago."

"And his regiment wouldn't help with this?" John's voice rose in anger at the thought.

She shook her head, rubbing her face across the rough wool of his uniform jacket. "They're too overwhelmed. They were going to throw him into one of the pits that they're piling the other bodies in, but I can't allow that!" Anger caused her to look up. She pulled away and stood wiping her face with the hem of her apron. "I couldn't do that to him. Bury him alongside those rebels! It would fair break my heart to know he must spend eternity in such low company. So…" She shrugged and moved to take a hold on the makeshift shroud.

"We'll get him." The inflection in John's voice made it clear that it was more than an offer. "You just tell us where you want him."

Attracted by the activity outside of their dugout, Dobbins and several of the other Rangers ventured over to satisfy their curiosity. John and Jacob immediately drafted them to help in moving the body and digging the grave. They came along willingly, not one man complained.

When the last shovelful of earth was thrown onto the lonely grave at the top of Savannah Bluff, all of the Rangers drifted away, leaving John and Jacob to comfort the widow. Jacob approached the grieving woman, hesitantly.

"That about does it, ma'am," he said almost apologetically, hat held respectfully over his heart. "As they say in this army, *put to bed with a mattock; tucked in with a spade.*"

Maggie sighed and collapsed next to the grave. Oblivious to the events around her, she refused to return to her tent, waving them away and snapping at them angrily when they tried to persuade her to go. At a loss as to what they should do for the distraught woman, the two men slowly moved away, leaving Maggie sitting cross-legged by the side of the slight mound of earth, her arm around one child, the other in her lap. She rocked to and fro in slow, deliberate motions as she poured out her sorrow, bitterness, and fears in a sea of tears shed over the grave of her husband. Like so many other wives of loyal men who gave their lives in the struggle against the tyranny of the rebels, she was left with nothing. She now found herself widowed in a hostile world—one full of hungry predators, tirelessly on the prowl and ready to pounce without mercy on any unprotected woman.

* * * *

The Allies continued their dilatory siege for a few more days, bickering among themselves and blaming each other for their failures. Finally, using the excuse that the hurricane season was upon them, the French re-embarked their troops and sailed away. By October nineteenth, the rebels had also slinked away in the direction of Ebenezer. There, they crossed into South Carolina and straggled back to Charleston. Despite the overwhelming odds against them, the siege of Savannah had ended in a British victory.

On the first Monday after peace had returned to the town, John was not surprised to see Maggie, a child in one arm and the other clinging to the hem of her skirt, following Angus across the rear of their position. Angus had a sack of Maggie's belongings slung over his shoulder. He was looking down as he walked, absorbed in some inner thought, oblivious to Maggie who stepped carefully along behind him, picking her way through the ankle-deep muck while holding her skirt halfway up to her knees in a valiant attempt to keep the hem from becoming soiled. John could see the semi-liquid mud ooze upward between the toes of her muddy, bare feet as she stepped. She glanced furtively in the direction of the Ranger's redoubt, saw John standing there, and paused briefly. Their eyes locked for one, fleeting moment. Her face seemed sad, resigned to whatever fate had decreed for her. Suddenly she shrugged, her head moved ever so slightly as if to say, "What else can I do?"

Chapter 10

Long Swamp Village
Monday, November 15, 1779

The hollow Thump! thump, Thump! thump, of Grainy's mortar and pestle produced a false echo that spread across the cleared fields that separated the double cabin from the village. The sound seemed to hop playfully back and forth across the open area before disappearing into the low hills to the north. She worked slowly, rhythmically pounding dried kernels of corn into a coarse meal, pausing every now and then to twist a dry, dusty ear between her hands, shaving the kernels from it directly into the mortar. After pounding each portion into the desired consistency, she would stop and lay aside the pestle long enough for Judith to scoop the finely pounded meal into an open mesh basket that she used as a sifter. After shifting the meal into a larger basket, Judith would carry it downwind and use it to winnow the meal by tossing it into the air, relying on the wind to carry away the chaff, as the heavier, edible portion dropped back into the basket.[45] The resulting meal would be mixed with water and used to make a dish that the Cherokees called Sofki. For a better-tasting soup made from the same basic ingredients, the two women would roast the kernels before they began pulverizing them, but that would be the work of another day.

Today was cool. An ever-so-slight chill in the air seemed to energize the people as they went about their daily chores, giving them excess energy that they expended in excess work. Both women toiled easily, but steadily. They wanted to fill a canvas bag with at least five pounds of the meal before the end of the day.

Grainy, sensing some subtle change in the atmosphere, stopped pounding. She looked expectantly in Judith's direction. The other woman had sensed it also. Standing stiffly erect, shading her eyes with her hand, she peered into the glare of the late morning sun.

"What is it, Judith?" Grainy asked.

"It looks like some riders coming in, soldiers with green coats and leading a pack train." She shrugged, puzzled. "Want I should go have a look see? The menfolk may have sent us a letter. We haven't heard from them in six months."

Across the field, Grainy saw Lizzy Hopkins walk out of her door and stand staring in the direction of the visitors. A few moments later Sarah Dobbins joined her. When the two women noticed Judith and Grainy, they waved across the harvested field that separated their cabins and began moving towards their traditional meeting place in the center of the field. Grainy, carrying Lynn Celia on one hip, moved out to meet them. Judith stepped along at her side. A sudden gust of wind caught her unbound tresses and whipped them gently about her face and shoulders like shiny red streamers.

"What you reckon is going on? That looks like a lot of supplies heading in the wrong direction," Lizzy said. She didn't look at the other women as she spoke; her eyes remained fixed on the strange procession. The first two riders guided their mounts down the far bank of the river and into the water of the ford. They disappeared for a moment before rising back into view when they ascended the near bank. They halted, water streaming from their mounts, and looked behind to make sure that the lead packhorses were following them through the river. As they turned back in her direction, Lizzy's breath caught in her throat.

"Why it's William and James!" she shouted gleefully. Her feet began to move forward with a will of their own. After only a few steps, she broke into a slow trot with Sarah Dobbins hard on her heels, their feet kicking up little puffs of dust behind them as they ran. Both women began to wave and call to their husbands; They were fifty yards away when the two men slid from their saddles and scooped their wives into their arms. Hopkins lifted Lizzy clear off the ground in a great bear hug of an embrace and spun her around in a circle, before setting her gently back on the ground.

Behind them, the packhorses continued to splash across the ford. They were running loose, being driven along by a green-coated, ebony-faced Ranger who kept them from straying to the flanks. Grainy took an involuntary step backwards as the Ranger, cantering past, flashed her a quick smile through pointed, razor-sharp teeth. Her hand went to her chest as if to still her heart.

"What a savage-looking man!" she exclaimed to Judith. "I hope that he's on our side!"

Releasing his wife, Sergeant Hopkins shouted at Nat and motioned for him to stop as he followed along at the tail end of the heavily laded packhorses.[46] The Ranger reined in next to him and waited while the other riders thundered past. Judith estimated that there were at least twenty Rangers and over a hundred horses spreading out across the empty field that the four women had just crossed.

"Get Sambo and Mambo to head 'em over to that harvested field in front of John's place. We'll unload the supplies in the spare cabin across from his and then turn the horses loose for the night.

"Yassir!" Nat answered through a cheerful smile. He politely dipped his hat to the two women and spurred his animal ahead.

Grainy's heart jumped at the mention of John's name. She glanced at Judith and saw the same yearning in the young woman's face.

Hopkins laughed and jerked his thumb over his shoulder, pointing back up the trail. "Your two will be along directly," he said. "They're trailing 'bout a quarter mile behind." Giving his wife a long, hard buss, he jumped back in the saddle. Reaching down for her, he took her hand, and she easily spun herself sidesaddle behind him. Grainy and Judith watched them ride away. Dobbins and his wife followed behind.

The two women tried vainly to chase away the dust with their hands as they waited for their men to appear. Chattering excitedly, they moved towards the river in an unconscious effort to hurry the reunion.

Both women felt their hearts leap into their throats when the familiar forms of John and Jacob bounced into sight. A third man rode between them, leading a plodding milk cow by a rope halter; a half-grown heifer followed behind. Grainy clearly heard John's shout as he spied her. He urged his mount forward, whipping its flank with his hat and grinning wildly. Jacob thundered along at his heels waving his hat over his head as a greeting to Judith. The two men splashed across the ford and slid from their saddles. Their mounts, left untended, wandered away after the herd. Grainy burst into tears; laughing, crying, dancing, she showered kisses across John's neck and face while Lynn Celia, crushed between her two excited parents, howled with delight.

"Oh, I thought I would never see you again!" she cried into his face as he bent to kiss her again. They clung together as if they feared losing each other forever. Beside them, Judith and Jacob rocked back and forth, her small, slim form wrapped tightly within his massive arms, her face pressed into his sternum because of his height. Jacob beamed down, admiring the top of her head. He swept her into his arms. They kissed passionately, her feet dangling two feet in the air

Hand-in-hand, both couples followed the other Rangers across the field. Lynn Celia, riding on her father's shoulders, vibrated with happiness. Simpson, who had bounded from the woods like a startled deer at the sight of the returning Rangers, trailed behind like a devoted puppy.

After unloading the pack animals and stuffing several tons of supplies destined for the upper Cherokee towns into the spare cabin, Grainy, John, and their children, joined by Jacob and Judith, sat at the table eating a rare, fine meal. Along with the prized milk cow, John had fetched home a Dutch Oven, which the two women had used to make biscuits. Real biscuits! Formed from finely ground wheat flour they had pilfered from the government supplies stored in the next cabin. Judith had smeared the biscuits with freshly churned butter before placing them on the table wrapped in a linen napkin.

Judith closed her eyes and moaned audibly as she took the first bite of her biscuit.

"It's a real sorrow to me that we could only make such a small amount of butter." She sighed and took a second bite without opening her eyes. "Its been nigh on a year since I had a real, honest–to-goodness biscuit!"

Grainy smiled in her direction. "It's a joy to me that we managed to haul your ma's old butter churn out here with us, otherwise we'd of had no way to churn it today."

"I suppose we should be thankful for small pleasures," Judith murmured. Covering her mouth with a wildly freckled hand, she looked towards Jacob. "How long has it been since you've tasted anything like this?"

"Why we ate like this most every night back with the regiment. It was a common thing to…" He halted abruptly in response to an urgent nudge under the table by John's foot. John gave him a warning look, careful to keep it hidden from the two women.

"Speaking of the army," John interrupted. He waited until both Grainy and Judith were looking towards him before continuing. "I brought something back." He went to the door where his saddlebags were hanging on a wall peg. Flipping up the cover of the leather bag, he rummaged through it for a few moments before producing a travel-stained letter. He returned to the table and held it up.

"For you, Judith," he said with a grin. He handed the precious package to her. She took it, a questioning look on her face.

"It's from your brothers. Jacob and I served alongside them in Savannah. Angus's wife wrote this letter for them."

Judith's mouth dropped. "His wife?" she asked, amazed by the sudden news. She fingered the letter thoughtfully. "And an educated one to boot?"

"Yes, his wife, and an educated one to boot," John parroted her. "It's all in there."

A look of embarrassment clouded Judith's face. She hesitated for a moment before confessing that she could not read, in fact could not even sign her own name.

Grainy quickly took the letter from her and handed it back to John.

"That's nothing, John here can read it for us. Can't you John?" The inflection in her voice made it more of a demand than a request. John took the letter and opened it carefully. Wondering why Grainy, herself, did not volunteer to read the correspondence.

"Wait!" Judith suddenly blurted out. "Let it wait 'til we finish our supper and get cleaned up. I want time to sit back and think on what it says after you finish reading it. They're both well?"

John smiled and nodded. "Very well, the last I saw them."

They returned to their meal. The women of the double cabin had prepared a feast by frontier standards. It consisted of dried peas, boiled and seasoned with salt pork, and cheese melted on toasted bread, all of which were complements of his most Christian Majesty, King George III. Instead of water, they drank tea with a spoonful of sugar, all of which was part of a soldier's daily ration. It was a good, but not a rare meal for the two Rangers, and a welcomed break from the monotonous fare those living on the frontier had been subsisting on. The women and children sat around the table, elbow-to-elbow, devouring the feast at an alarming rate. John and Jacob deliberately ate small portions, claiming that they had eaten an overlarge breakfast and were not hungry.

When they were finished, they sat back, stuffed and smiling. The bare feet of the children tapped out rapid rhythms on the hard-packed dirt floor as they scampered about, playing tag around the feet of their elders. Simpson, due to turn three in a few weeks, halted in front of his father and grinned, then charged back into the fray.

"If you had been here during the harvest, we could have stuffed you to the gills with roasting ears," Grainy told them proudly. " I've never seen such an abundance of corn! The Traveler said it was one of the best harvests that they've had in years."

"I saw that pile of corn in the next cabin when we were unloading the trade goods. Looks like you two have left us quite a chore." John laughed. "I hope we can find the husking pins."[47]

"Don't you fret none, we know right where they are." Grainy grinned triumphantly in his direction. She cocked her head to one side as if an unexpected thought had just struck her. "Before you get to shucking in the morning, how about you two men taking a sickle to the far end of the field and cutting us a mess of that broom corn[48]. We're getting to need new brooms something desperate in this house." Sitting up straight, she smiled broadly. "Now, you men go on outside and have a smoke, we'll call you when we get things cleaned up."

Once the woman's work was done, the men were called back inside. Grainy sat in one of the ladder-back chairs with Lynn Celia reclining contentedly in her lap. The child, mimicking her mother, hugged a cornhusk doll lovingly in her own arms. John sat next to the fire, Angus's letter canted to one side to catch the light. Judith sat sideways on one of the benches, her left arm resting on the table as she listened closely to every word.

When John had finished reading aloud, he carefully refolded the letter before handing it to Judith.

"Thank you." Judith laid the letter on the table beside her. "What's Maggie like?"

John thought for a moment, rubbing his chin as he formulated his answer.

"Like it says, she's a right fine widder woman. Her first husband, the one what was kilt at Savannah, had a store in Charleston where they sold potions and pills and such. She sewed up Angus's head and did our washing to earn extra money. That's about all that I can tell you, 'cept that she has two young'uns, one a suckling babe."

"What does she look like?" Judith asked. John cleared his throat and looked around, seemingly at a loss for words.

Grainy laughed. "Go on John!" She chuckled at his discomfort. "You've got eyes in your head, surely you would recognize the woman if she walked through the front door."

"Well I reckon I would!" John retorted loudly. "It's just that I didn't study on her all that much." He looked towards Jacob. "What's she look like Jacob?"

Jacob smiled broadly, pleased to be included in the family's discussion. "Why she looked right nice!" he informed his betrothed. "She had real shiny dark hair, was about your height and size. Smart too!"

"Was she prettier than me?" Judith snapped, her eyes flared with jealously.

Jacob hesitated, he looked towards John who surreptitiously shook his head, no. Jacob quickly picked up the cue.

"Why no," he informed her proudly. "She looks to be about thirty or so, and she's much too dark complexioned to suit me." He shot a quick look towards John. "She's got children too, I'm thinking that she's missing some teeth. Right John?'

John smiled. "Oh, I'm sure she's missing the two front ones."[49] He looked at Grainy and gave her a quick wink. "Now, if you two women will see the children up to the loft, I think that Mr. Fenton and I will have a look through those packs in the next room over yonder. I'm certain that we have a few small items for you two ladies wrapped up in them somewheres."

When they returned, the women stood open-mouthed as their men presented them with new clothing, fancy beyond their wildest expectations.

Jacob had brought Judith a white chemise and a wine-colored, drawstring skirt of fine linen, along with a long-style bodice, sleeveless and beautifully printed with red stems and flowers.

As Judith squealed and danced with delight, John pulled out his own gifts: a gold-colored French cut bodice with white drawstrings in the front and a dark, drawstring dress printed with tiny gold specks. A ruffled chemise of white cotton completed the ensemble.

As the women admired their new clothing, the two Rangers left the room and returned to proudly present each of them with one last gift: long, woolen, red cloaks.

"I declare! Judith sputtered. "We're going to be the best-dressed women on the frontier!" She leapt into Jacob's arms and rained kisses over every square inch of his astonished face. "Now if'n you'll tell me that you've got a real Church of England preacher in one of those packs there, it would make everything perfect!"

Jacob's face fell. "I reckon I can't tell you that," he said. "Can't get one of them to come this far west for love nor money." He looked sadly into her eyes.

A mischievous grin crept across his face, showing a full set of white teeth. He laughed boisterously before adding, "But one of them Rangers camped outside is... er... was...?" He looked quickly to John for clarification.

"He was a Methodist circuit rider 'til the rebels threatened to stretch his neck if they caught him in their territory again. He's given that up 'til the end of the war, but he's still a preacher. At least when he ain't fightin'," John said proudly .

Jacob looked at Judith with a hopeful, pleading look, "Will he do?"

Judith threw her arms around the big Ranger. "You bet he'll do," she mumbled into his chest.

* * * *

The news of the planned wedding spread like wildfire throughout the village. Immediately after breakfast the next morning, Lizzy Hopkins and Sarah Dobbins came across the old corn field at a fast walk, stepping carefully to avoid the horse apples strewed randomly about the ground by the pack animals that freely roamed the field, chomping on what was left of the harvested stalks. At their knock, Grainy opened the door. They rushed over to Judith, eyeing her as if she were some stranger that they had never seen before.

"What are you planning to wear?" Sarah asked with a concerned face.

When Judith produced the new wardrobe that Jacob had brought her from Savannah, they squealed with delight and envy. Sarah's face grew serious for a moment, as she wondered why James Dobbins had not given her anything like that. For the sake of peace and quiet in the small village,

Grainy decided not to mention her own new gifts.

The three women moved about Judith, squawking like mother hens as they planned her wedding. They worried over every minute detail: What day should it be? Weren't half the Rangers leaving tomorrow? The half with the parson riding with them? Well! They would just have to see about that! Lizzy Hopkins declared that her husband had best listen to reason if he knew what was good for him! What's another day or two? The war was as good as over, wasn't it? The King could do without this handful of Provincials for a few days. Why he would never even miss them!

On and on they planned. Every so often, one of them would look to Judith for agreement on some point or other, asking, "You do want it this way don't you, sugar?" Judith would open her mouth to speak, but it was too late, the next important point was already under discussion.

Grainy caught herself babbling as the excitement took a hold on her. The realization of what was about to take place accelerated her every thought. "What about the Indians?" she asked. More importantly... "What about rum? Would that be wise?" After all, it was a well-known fact that Indians couldn't hold their liquor. As for the soldiers? Well! Half of them were drunks anyway. What would happen if a fight broke out in the middle of the wedding between drunken soldiers, or worse yet, drunken Cherokees?

On and on the planning continued, consuming the entire morning. Lynn Celia sat up in the loft peering down into the mad melee below. It only grew more crowded as the morning wore on. The Traveler arrived along with two Cherokee women that Judith and Grainy routinely went to water with each morning. Even the wives of two of the Rangers from the other detachment that had arrived yesterday made a sudden appearance. They pitched right in. Within ten minutes, any stranger happening along would have thought that the women in the cabin had known each other all of their lives. The only thing certain was that Judith McDougal and Jacob Fenton were destined to have a wedding that would be remembered for quite a spell in Long Swamp Village. It would be a rare one, a mixture of Scottish, Methodist, Frontier, and Cherokee traditions.

Sergeant Hopkins consulted with his counterpart who commanded the other troop of Rangers. Both agreed, amid a verbal beating, administered by both Cherokee and Loyalist women, to give the pack animals three days of rest before the other detachment started into the mountains with the supplies for those towns. Hopkins even agreed that Jacob would not be needed when his own party moved on to Little Chota to deliver their supplies to Blackstone Mullis, newly appointed Ranger Lieutenant and Commissary Officer for the valley towns. He even dispatched a Ranger on a swift animal to deliver an invitation to Sally Chambers, The Forgotten One, and her daughter Molly, despite a firm warning that it was all but impossible for them to return within three days.

The first night's party would be held on the banks of the river beneath the grove of giant oaks that kept the underbrush shaded out and produced a park-like appearance. It was a favorite get together place, especially during hot weather. People began arriving well before sundown to arrange makeshift tables and lay in a plentiful stock of firewood. Every family in the village contributed one lantern and two candles to burn. The lanterns were suspended by cords hung from the trees, so that they could spill their light evenly across the dance area.

Four Rangers were kept busy for several hours building a frame for use during a gander pull that was to take place the following morning. There would be five teams: one from each of the Ranger detachments and one from each of the three clans that inhabited Long Swamp Village. They would each be competing for a prize consisting of a jug of watered down rum. There were already several versions of the expected outcome. Each varied widely, depending on who the prophet was that foretold the future, and was accompanied by a large exchange of bets in the form of everything from hard cash to tobacco.

Teams of hunters were sent out to scour the forest for deer, bear, raccoon, and opossum. Groups of women stood up to their knees in the chilly current of the Etowah River, beating the water with poles and driving their prey through the open end of a vee-shaped fish weir that had been built across the river in ancient times. Baskets after baskets of fish were dumped on the bank by bare-chested Cherokee women; other women stood by, ready to gut and scale the catch and toss them onto grates of green wood where they would be slowly smoked over low fires.

Stepping lightly along the edge of a recently harvested field, John gripped his old doglock musket loosely in his hands, ready to swing it into action at a moment's notice and bring down any quail that he flushed into the open. Roasted quail was Judith's favorite meal, and Grainy was determined that she would have them for her wedding feast. This decided, she had immediately dispatched the two men of her family in search of the elusive quarry.

Simpson followed John two paces to the rear, mimicking every movement that his father made. Although armed with nothing more than a shaved stick, he handled it with as much safety and seriousness as John handled his loaded musket. A sudden flurry of wings rapidly beat the air as a covey of quail exploded from cover. As the birds fanned out directly in front of them, John smoothly swung the long barreled musket to his shoulder and pulled the trigger.

The flintlock erupted, belching smoke and fire; three birds dropped at once, a fourth, wounded, fluttered violently as it sank rapidly to the ground. By force of habit, John immediately dropped the stock of his musket to the ground and began reloading. He finished in less than thirty seconds.

Simpson retrieved the three birds that had fallen directly in front of them. "Can I keep them in my bag, Pa?" he asked hopefully.

"By all means!" John laughed. "Without your help I may have never gotten them in the first place. Let's go check on that wounded bird."

Moving forward, weapon held at the ready, John stepped lightly across the field. As they neared the tree line, a fluttering movement betrayed the hiding place of the wounded bird. It waddled awkwardly, dragging a broken wing on one side. John scooped the bird up and twisted its head off with his fingers.

"Should we try for a few more, or do you think this will make a grand enough meal for your Aunt Judith?"

"Let's get two more," Simpson said, after carefully calculating the number of people who shared his table. John reached out, tousled his son's straw-colored hair, and smiled. "Two more it is."

For the next hour, John instructed Simpson on how to select a hunting blind and then wait patiently, sitting silently and without moving so much as a hand to swat a biting mosquito, until his quarry appeared. Simpson's eyes sparkled as he watched the same covey of quail that they had flushed earlier return to the field and began searching among the stubble for overlooked kernels of corn. John waited until three of them had clustered into a compact group about twenty yards from their blind and then slipped the musket to his shoulder.

He looked at Simpson. "Very slowly, move to my side," he said quietly. Simpson did as he was told. When the move was complete, the youngster was nestled snugly into John's right side, just below his shoulder. He leaned closer and whispered into his son's ear, "Now reach up here and pull the trigger while I aim." Simpson's mouth dropped open in surprise, but he was already too much of a woodsman to make a sound. Careful to keep his head safely to the rear of the touchhole, he inserted both his middle and his index finger inside the trigger guard and gave the stiff trigger a steady pull. The weapon recoiled into John's shoulder. When the smoke cleared, Simpson bounded out into the field and retrieved three more birds. He held up both hands, displaying the trophies.

"We got enough, Pa!" he announced proudly. They started for home.

Simpson, anxious to present their bag to his mother, broke into a run as soon as the cabin came into sight. When he proudly held up the quail for her to admire, Grainy clasped her hands to her cheeks, making much more of a fuss than the feat generally merited. "Come on," she said proudly, "let's get them cleaned."

After slitting open the two birds, Grainy removed the breasts from each carcass, then threw the remains to a group of scavenging dogs sniffing about the cooking area. The dogs immediately pounced on this manna from heaven, snarling and snapping viciously at each other before one of them managed to break free of the melee and race away with his prize firmly clamped between his teeth. After each cleaning, the scene was repeated until only one skinny dog remained. She threw him the last scrap and watched him slink off, casting worried glances to the left and right lest his friends return to share in this rare treat.

By ones and twos other hunters drifted in, empty handed, or with a field-dressed deer swinging on a pole between two swaggering warriors. Rabbits, raccoons, and squirrels were also included in their bags. There would be more than enough to feed the crowd of over three hundred people expected to be attending tonight's gala.

Grainy washed the quails' blood from her hands in a bucket of clean water. Looking at the sky as she toweled the water from her hands, she judged that there was less than two hours before the sun set. It was time to get the bride-to-be, dressed. With a simple inclination of her head, she signaled secretly to Judith, who followed her to the cabin. There, they quickly bundled up some clean clothes and, taking a new bar of soft soap wrapped in an osnaburg[50] cloth, headed inconspicuously for the women's area of the river.

The Traveler met them there, a freshly cleaned and pressed, light blue, lutestring dress in her hand.

"The women of the village send you this." She held it out to Judith with an affectionate smile. "The bride-to-be should be the most beautiful woman tonight. We…" She made a slight arm motion that included both Grainy and herself, "of course, will dress down." She gave an impish smile. "But not too far down!" she cautioned with a quick shake of her finger.

Jacob's jaw literally thudded onto his chest when Judith emerged from the cabin that evening, ready to be escorted to the party. Her hair had been washed and combed until it shone like red ripples covering a sunlit lake, and then pulled back tightly and wound into a bun on the back of her head. Four tiny red curls had been fashioned with a hot iron and left dangling, two to a side, to frame her freckled face. Her lips were bright red, painted with lipstick[51] provided by one of the Ranger's wives who hurriedly explained to the other women, red-faced with embarrassment, that she would never normally buy it herself, but that her husband had found it outside of Savannah in a valise that had been dropped and overlooked during the French withdrawal. He had given it to her as a present, and she hadn't even known what to do with it!

Judith had elected, against the wishes of some of the other women, to leave her eyebrows and lashes their natural red color instead of blackening them with soot collected from the inside of a lantern cover as most of the other women had done. She also declined any flour or cornstarch to whiten her face, explaining simply that, "Jacob loves my red hair and freckles."

Judith's dress alone would have made her stand out among the women of any frontier village, but added to it was an assortment of accessories loaned to her by the other women that made it truly stunning. A beautifully crafted Cherokee necklace of freshwater pearls hung around her neck in three graceful strands, and brightly burnished silver buckles glittered with each step that she took in her highly polished, high-heeled leather shoes, made fashionable with the addition of red heels. Beaten silver bracelets of Spanish manufacture encircled each wrist, others were stacked, unseen, about her slim ankles, three to an ankle as specified by The Traveler so that, "they would rattle together as she walked and danced."

A patriotically colored kerchief of red, white, and blue, the colors of the Union Jack, was draped gracefully over her shoulders and tucked into the bust line of her dress.

She smiled at the stunned expression on Jacob's face. Leaning forward, she administered a long, hard kiss to his left cheek as he stood transfixed like a statue, arm still cocked as an invitation to escort her to the festivities already beginning under the oaks. Slipping her arm demurely through his, she allowed him to lead her away. His face beamed with pure pleasure and sinful pride, completely unaware of the red imprint of Judith's lips adorning his cheek.

Grainy sent Simpson to race ahead and announce that the groom and bride-to-be were on their way. Then, she fell in with the group of other women, who followed the beaming couple a few paces to the rear as escorts and chaperones.

When they arrived, the area below the oaks was packed with laughing, shouting, and smiling people. Over one fire, a trio of Cherokee women turned an entire deer on a spit, basting it every few minutes with a coating of lard and spices to keep the meat moist and tasty. Pots of rabbit and squirrel stews bubbled in cast iron pots, suspended by chains from metal tripods placed over low fires of hickory and oak. Several long tables, hastily formed from empty barrels and pieces of clapboards split from lengths of white oak, were covered with table cloths and piled with apple, peach, and pumpkin pies. Other dishes contained squash, beans, pumpkin, and corn made from recipes found in the unwritten cookbooks carried around in the heads of industrious European and Cherokee cooks scattered throughout the village.

Bowls containing shelled pecans, chinquapins, hickory, and hazelnuts stood among other sumptuous delicacies. Syrups and breads of all types stood ready for everyone's enjoyment. One barrel, that by mutual agreement was not to be opened until the dancing started, contained several gallons of heavily watered rum. Men sat and looked longingly at it, mouths watering, licking their lips in anticipation.

Perched atop stump chairs and puncheon benches, a makeshift orchestra armed with fiddles, dulcimers, drums, whistles, and jugs, tuned up, ready to play all night if necessary. Swarms of children scampered everywhere, underfoot and loud. Babies in makeshift cradles swung from the branches of the stately oaks, others rode round-eyed and curious on their mother's backs. Dogs howled and zigzagged between legs, tripping the unwary who shouted curses at them. It was disorganized chaos, everyone laughed; no one would go away hungry, or unhappy. Weddings, the biggest events on the frontier, had grown to be mighty rare occurrences as the war continued to grind along.

Within a few short hours, everyone either sat on the ground, propped against the trunk of one of the oaks, or lay stretched out on the carpet of newly fallen leaves beneath them. They moved sluggishly, stuffed to the gills with food and drink. Fires, now that their usefulness for cooking was past, were built up in order for them to add their light to the dim glow provided by the dozens of candle lanterns swaying gently in the cool autumn breeze. All was quiet, but it was a false quiet. Everyone knew that the people were simply resting, digesting their meals as they gathered their strength before beginning another round of celebration.

The first mournful strains of a fiddle sounded, followed by the sharp quick notes of a dulcimer and the throbbing beat of a drum. As if commanded by unseen forces, people began to stir. Men moved purposely towards the rum barrel, women shook dust off of their aprons and skirts, smiles appeared everywhere.

As the guests of honor, Jacob and Judith were urged to perform the first dance. They danced a hornpipe[52] to Judith's favorite song, *Over the Hills and Far Away,* after which Judith demanded that her entire wedding party dance a Scottish Reel. The four couples, Jacob and Judith, John and Grainy Stokes, William and Lizzy Hopkins, and James and Sarah Dobbins faced each other in a short line. Grainy and the other bridesmaids tried lightheartedly, but not too seriously, to imitate the footwork of Judith as they each took turns displaying their skills. Soon, everyone was up and dancing. The Rangers and their wives showed the steps of an English Country Dance to their Cherokee allies, then sat back and kept cadence with their hands as the Cherokee couples danced down the line.

As the rum took effect, the dances increased in vigor and rowdiness. Both men and women gamboled about, uninhibited, performing hornpipes, reels, and jigs. Later in the evening, Sambo and Mambo, egged on by the others to demonstrate African music, picked up a drum and patiently demonstrated an African beat to one of the Cherokee drummers. Once he had picked up the cadence, the two African Rangers performed a tribal dance from their homeland. The Cherokees were delighted, clapping their hands, cheering, and urging the sweating dancers on as their dance increased in fury and cadence. The two men danced until they were exhausted, and then collapsed next to the rum barrel. Sergeant Hopkins, who was in charge of distributing the drinks, handed each of them a brimming gourd full of the brew. They sloshed it over their glistening chins and chests as they greedily gulped the liquid down. Temporarily satisfied, they sat back and watched the dancing continue as the Cherokee men and women launched into a mating dance, in honor of the occasion, accompanied by a few brave and lightheaded Rangers and their wives.

The dancing and reverie continued until the last of the rum was poured down thirsty throats and the last dancer had collapsed in utter exhaustion alongside one of the low-burning fires. The snores of the sleepers echoed through the oak grove and carried across to the far bank of the river where it mixed with the steady croaking of frogs and the chirping of katydids and crickets.

* * * *

The next morning, people began to stir beneath the oaks as soon as it was light enough to see. Women comforted crying children as they heated up the leftover food for breakfast. Men stood on wobbly legs and clumped off to the river to throw water over their faces and wash the sour taste of last night from their mouths. Some slept late, retaining what energy they could for the activities of the day.

By mid-morning, the riders began to round up their mounts and rub them down in preparation for the Gander Pull, which was slated to take place when the sun was directly overhead. A gang of energetic boys rounded up six ganders from the village flock, while each of the five teams picked their best rider to champion them. Along each side of a high, three-sided frame, placed in the middle of a narrow raceway, people gathered, forming two lines and chatting boisterously as they waited for the race to begin. Betting began even before one of the judges succeeded in tying the feet of one of the flapping birds to the top rail of the frame. This accomplished, the bird's neck and head received a liberal greasing of lard. Each rider would take a turn racing his mount at top speed along the course and through the framework, pulling the head from the unlucky creature as he passed beneath the bar. There were five teams and six birds, the team with the most heads at the end of the competition would be declared the winner. A gallon of rum was the prize.

The teams drew lots amid an abundance of noise and confusion. The rider for the Blue Holly Clan won the first try. He leaped confidently onto the bareback of his horse and guided it carefully to the starting line, ignoring the verbal jabs thrown at him by the audience as he passed.

Talking ceased abruptly as the judge signaled for the rider to begin. Immediately, the rider lay on with a quirt, urging his magnificent roan stallion into a full gallop. The animal raced along the track at full speed, slowing slightly as he twisted through the tight "S" turn halfway through the course before bounding swiftly ahead and passing through the framework at full speed. A moan escaped from the crowd as the gander, wings flapping wildly, threw its head upward in an attempt to fly just as the warrior reached for it. He missed by a fraction of an inch, actually brushing against the gyrating creature as he hurdled past. A few stray feathers fluttered to the ground in his wake. Cries of outrage and accusations questioning the honesty of the judge were thrown about wildly.

Almost immediately, the second rider, a Ranger from among the new arrivals, thundered down the raceway. Standing in the stirrups, right arm outstretched in front of him, he bore down on the hysterically flapping bird. An instinctive gasp arose from the crowd as the rider rode past, with nothing to show for his effort but a greasy hand. They muttered and shook their heads in disappointment, or relief.

On came the third rider, Sergeant Hopkins, bearing down on the flapping fowl as he dug his heels into his gray mare. Almost effortlessly, he snatched the head free, leaving the headless carcass flapping on the bar. Cheers or boo's arose, depending on which direction the winnings flowed as they changed hands. The next two riders from the Wild Potato and the Wolf Clan each matched Hopkins prowess, cleanly ripping the head from the squawking birds.

All six contestants rendezvoused at the beginning of the course to redraw lots for the second round. Once again the Blue Holly Clan drew first try. Undaunted by his first loss, the rider rumbled smoothly past, snatching the head cleanly off with seeming ease. That left only two more birds. The Wild Potato clan's rider came away with nothing on his second try, leaving the outcome of the match to be decided by one of the two remaining contestants. Sergeant Hopkins had one head, while his Ranger opponent remained pointless. The new Ranger went first, grasped the neck firmly and cleanly, and separated the head without missing a stride.

All eyes immediately swung to the far end of the track, following

Sergeant Hopkins who came on confidently, knees bent, leaning forward in the saddle, arm outstretched as he galloped to certain victory. John watched the sergeant's smile transform into sudden disbelief as his mount stumbled beneath him. The horse lunged forward; a shoe, pulled free of the animal's right front hoof, spiraled high into the air. The sudden movement almost unseated the rider before his mount recovered its footing and limped to a stop at the far end of the track. Red-faced with anger, Hopkins slid out of the saddle and walked back up the racetrack, eyes on the ground, searching for any clue that would point to the cause of the mishap. He located the lost shoe, picked it up, and studied it; it looked good. Disgusted, he flung it away and stood with folded arms, watching with a scowl as the rider from the Wolf clan galloped past to take off the final head, winning with a total of two heads.

A few dilatory fights erupted and some angry words were passed, but, all in all, the losses were taken with good grace. The crowd, suddenly quiet, departed. Exhausted they made their way back into the shade of the oak grove, or to their homes to take an early afternoon nap. There was still more to come. Six of the Cherokee women, frugal as always, swung the headless bodies of the hapless ganders by the legs as they headed back in the direction of the cooking fires.

Ordinarily there would have been another day of celebrations before the wedding, but these nuptials were rushed. The only preacher available would be leaving at first light the next morning. The service would have to be performed today at John and Grainy's cabin, an hour before sundown.

A handful of the Rangers did muster enough brief energy to make a half-hearted attempt at kidnapping the bride and holding her for ransom, but with the giant brute she was marrying keeping a watchful lookout for just such shenanigans, they abandoned the attempt and retreated to their camp. They needed to get a few hours of rest before participating in the shivaree that they had planned for tonight, after the knot had been tied.

Chapter 11

Long Swamp Village
Thursday, November 18, 1779

Andrew Ebey, the Preacher turned Ranger, arrived at John's cabin at six o'clock that afternoon.[53] He was a man of average height and weight with a narrow, pockmarked face. His arrow-straight black hair was combed back from his forehead and tied with a red ribbon into a well-greased queue that dangled freely at the back of his neck. He was not a handsome man by any standards, but when a person looked into his rich blue eyes, they conveyed a kindness and understanding that instantly made anyone feel at ease. He wore a fastidiously clean uniform that someone had obviously spent a great deal of time preparing. When he spoke, his voice was not loud, but it did communicate firmness, mixed with an undertone of morality. John had heard that he was both respected and trusted among his comrades in the Rangers.

Ebey doffed his hat to Grainy, who stood at her husband's elbow.

"Andrew Ebey, Captain Wylly's Company, King's Carolina Rangers, at you service, ma'am." His gesture immediately prompted her into action.

"Reverend Ebey!" she smiled and corrected him. "Tonight, sir, in this home, you are the Revered Ebey." She extended her hand; he took it gently and performed a shallow bow.

"As you wish, ma'am," he said with a simple, lopsided smile.

John offered Ebey one of the ladder-back chairs and waited courteously until he had taken a seat before he sat himself. Grainy magically produced two cups of cool apple cider and brought them on a wooden tray with a bowl of cinnamon and a spoon. John looked at the rare spice with surprise. He said nothing, but cast a questioning look at Grainy. She simply smiled pleasantly.

"Would either of you gentlemen care for a spoonful of cinnamon mixed in with your cider?" she asked. The question was directed more towards the Reverend than her husband.

Ebey looked up with surprise. "Surely!" he said. "Where on earth did you find such a treat?" He licked his lips as he watched Grainy's hands perform smooth stirring motions over the cup.

"It was a gift from a friend. A most unexpected and delicious gift if I may say so."

John wondered what friend of theirs would have access to such a rare commodity, but refrained from asking. He simply gave her his most indulgent smile as Grainy offered him a cup.

The Reverend Ebey took a sip of cider and relaxed against the back of the chair. "Where is the happy couple?"

"Jacob is over at the Hopkins's cabin, Judith is with The Traveler in the village. It's considered bad luck for them to see each other on their wedding day," Grainy said.

Ebey chuckled; this age-old superstition was no news to him. "So I've been told," he murmured, not unkindly.

"The groom should be back within the half hour," Grainy added.

Jacob entered the room with Hopkins a short time later. His somber face caused Grainy's breath to catch in her throat.

"What's happened?" she asked, half dreading some tragedy.

The sergeant patted her on the arm. "There's nothing to be concerned about, Jacob is just a bit overwhelmed at the moment." He took a seat on one of the puncheon benches. Jacob sat beside him, looking down at a golden ring held in the palm of his open hand.

"You know the story of how Jacob came to be a Ranger." Hopkins words were a statement. Everyone in the room, with the exception of the Preacher, knew that story. "After we captured his family's killers, we searched them. I found that…" He thrust his head in the direction of Jacob's hand to indicate the ring. "One of the rebels had taken it off the finger of Jacob's dead mother. I found it hidden on him, and he confessed to his sin before he was brought to justice."

The room grew silent. Grainy looked towards Hopkins, her eyes wide and questioning. He cleared his throat before continuing the story.

"I put it with the other belongings from his family, where it has stayed until today." He reached out and patted Jacob affectionately on the shoulder. "Today, his wedding day, I returned it." He paused for a moment before adding, "I've always half-dreaded this day of opening up old wounds. Even though I never met his mother in life, I'm sure that she would have wanted Jacob to entrust this to her daughter-in-law on her wedding day."

Jacob rubbed his hands over his lips, sniffed, and looked up at the people sitting around him. His eyes were rimmed with red, but tears stubbornly refused to form. He nodded his head, as if to say that he understood and that everything would be fine. Then he slowly rose and left the cabin. Not a word was spoken.

Ebey looked about the room, his face reddened in silent anger. Grainy feared the worst, thinking that they were somehow responsible for his reaction. She breathed a sigh of relief when he went on to explain his sudden display of emotion.

"I am forever reminded of how this unnecessary and immoral war has shattered the lives of so many honest and loyal people such as that fine young man. I understand that the bride's family was also murdered by these so called *Sons of Liberty*." The inflection in his voice made the words sound more like profanity that the name of a group of terrorists. He shook his head. "I know that I am a man of God above all else, but I must confess that it is almighty difficult to pray for the souls of rebels like Sam Adams and his band of Massachusetts malcontents that have stirred up the dregs of society to produce such needless violence. I ask God at times why he does not strike them down!" He looked around, mildly embarrassed by his outburst.

Sergeant Hopkins leaned back, his elbows on the table. "Amen! I couldn't have said it better myself."

He opened his mouth to continue, but Grainy cut him off with a polite, "Gentlemen, this is no night to discuss politics."

By six o'clock that evening, the field and clearings bordering the small cabin were jammed with spectators and well-wishers. Inside, the Reverend Ebey, resplendent in his well-pressed uniform, stood before the fireplace, his Bible in hand.

To his right stood Grainy, the Matron of Honor, and the bride's maids, Lizzy Hopkins, Sarah Dobbins, and The Traveler. To his left stood John, the Best Man, and the ushers, Nat and James Dobbins.

Judith, dressed in the new wardrobe that Jacob had brought from Savannah, was radiantly beautiful. Every eye was on her as she was escorted out of the cabin and into the breezeway. Sergeant Hopkins, also resplendent in his freshly cleaned and pressed uniform, escorted her to the altar in place of her deceased father. He would perform the duty of giving away the bride.

The bride wept quietly throughout the entire ceremony, bursting into open sobs when Jacob solemnly pressed his mother's ring onto her finger. The Reverend Ebey pronounced them "Man and Wife" and Jacob raised her veil and kissed her passionately. He looked up, red-faced with embarrassment, to face the catcalls and applause of the guests.

On signal from one of the guests, the makeshift orchestra, sitting along the outside wall of the cabin, burst into life. Jacob and Judith were rushed from the breezeway into the yard and, once again, danced the first dance before the other guests joined in.

With much disappointment and many remarks about the inefficient use of the King's soldiers, the festivities ended at 9 o'clock. Grainy and John said goodbye, and after surreptitiously pressing a Spanish dollar into the Reverend Ebey's palm, rounded up their children and marched away with the Hopkins, surrendering their cabin to the newlyweds for the night. Jacob waved and beamed after them. He had been excused from duty until the detachment returned from Little Chota.

That night, John lay in Grainy's arms atop a pile of blankets thrown onto the puncheon floor in front of the Hopkins's fire. Beside him, Grainy breathed softly, completely exhausted by the festivities of the past two days. John felt uneasy, something, some slight sound had awakened him. He sat up, listening intently to the quiet, soft sounds of the night and the slow steady breathing of his children.

A shrill scream rent the night, followed by a barrage of gunfire. John jumped to his feet. He grabbed his carbine and checked the priming. As he moved purposefully towards the door, Grainy sat up behind him, groggy with sleep. She looked around, quickly satisfying herself that their two children were still bundled up safely beside her.

Sergeant Hopkins, wearing nothing but his nightshirt, rolled out of his bed and moved quickly to the door of the cabin where he took up a position alongside John, musket in hand. The red flicker of firelight shimmered through a loophole in the front wall of the cabin. Just as he bent to press his eye to the loophole, a long series of hollow Thump! Thump! Thumps, followed by a sound that fell somewhere between the bawling of a newborn calf and the shrieks of a dying horse, floated across the field. Both men looked at each other … they knew that sound! Letting out a relieved sigh, Hopkins pushed the cabin door open and stepped into the moonlit night, musket in hand, followed by John, Grainy, and Lizzy, and last of all, by a wide awake Simpson. Lynn Celia continued to snore.

Across the field, the flashes of muskets were visible a full second before the sounds of their discharges were heard. Torches surrounded the double cabin occupied by the newlyweds. In the bright light of a wildly blazing bonfire, they could see four men working diligently to saw a rosined fence post across a large empty barrel, creating the hellish din that they had instantly recognized.

"I thought that sounded like a horse fiddle!" Hopkins laughed. He turned to the women standing behind him; his face was barely visible in the dark. "I thought the boys would be too tired for a Shivaree! Looks like I was wrong!" Letting out a long catlike wail, he fired his musket into the air.

"That one was for Jacob!" he yelled in the direction of the revelers that were circling the cabin with pots, pans, muskets, drums, or anything else that would scare the pants off of Satan and his imps.

"Give us a shot for Judith, John!" he urged the other man.

"Yes! Do!" Grainy and Lizzy agreed.

"Give us a yell, sergeant!" John shouted. He fired his musket into the air. A long red flame shot from the barrel, accompanied by a second smaller jet of fire that squirted horizontally from the touchhole of the musket.

"Look Pa!" Simpson shouted. He pointed up over their heads. The cloth patch from the musket, ignited by the blast, wafted downward in a steady swinging motion, glowing bright and red as it burned against the night sky. It landed on the ground a few feet in front of them and continued burning until John ground it out with the butt of his musket. Across the field the Shivaree continued. The Hopkins's house turned in for the night.

* * * *

As the calendars were turned from 1779 to 1780, the war began to turn rapidly in favor of the British and Loyalist forces. John and Grainy, along with the other Loyalist families at Long Swamp, began to hope that they would soon be returning to their homes.

These hopes swelled as they began to hear accounts of happenings in the east. In May, Colonel Brown and his force of Rangers moved slowly up the South Carolina side of the Savannah River, intending to reoccupy Augusta. Almost immediately, he began to receive, and accept, offers of surrender from the rebel forces. Somewhere in the area of Silver Bluff, rebel militiamen flooded into his camp, offering to switch sides. They were thanked for their gesture, then paroled, and sent home. John Dooly surrendered his entire regiment and all of its arms a few days later.

In other areas, the news was much the same. At Ninety-Six, John and Grainy's old home, Benjamin Garden's and Robert Middleton's South Carolina regiments surrendered, were paroled, and went home. Even Stephen Heard, at Heard's Fort between Long Swamp and Augusta, asked for the terms of surrender. With their hopes dashed by the decisive defeat of the French at Savannah, many of the rebels thought that it was simply futile pride to continue struggling against the overwhelming might of Great Britain.

Meanwhile, in the main theater of the war, where the regulars and Continentals continued to clash, the news was much the same. In May, Charleston fell to the British. Over 5,000 prisoners and almost 400 pieces of artillery were captured. A few days later, a contingent of Virginia Continentals were caught at a place called the Waxhaws and badly mauled by the British Legion, a unit which was actually composed of Loyalist cavalrymen. One of the few actual Britons in the Legion was their commanding officer, a young and dashing lieutenant colonel named Banastre Tarlton. Although the rebels had been asked to surrender, and had refused, the battle was morphed in the rebel newspapers from a brilliant victory to a massacre of helpless men, and a new term was coined, *Tarlton's Quarter.* Tarlton's Quarter quickly became the battle cry for any rebel unit who wanted an excuse to cut down surrendering troops or helpless Tories throughout the South. Loyalist everywhere shook their heads at the relish with which the lower classes consumed the rebel propaganda without the slightest question. They found it unbelievable that rational men would believe such tales.

By the middle of August, every Loyalist in Long Swamp Village felt that the war was as good as over. Thus it was, that when Sergeant Hopkins received orders to bring his detachment to Augusta, where they would help safeguard and distribute the annual presents to their Creek allies, John confidently kissed a very pregnant Grainy goodbye.

"I should be back within two months," he predicted. He patted her distended stomach gently, almost reverently. She was due to give birth any day now. The Forgotten One, along with her daughter, Molly, and Blackstone's niece, Sally Chambers, had arrived three days earlier and were committed to being on hand to assist in the birth.

Jacob, also certain that he would not be gone long, echoed those same sentiments as he presented an equally pregnant Judith Fenton with a long kiss goodbye. He felt as if his heart would break when he finally threw his leg over his saddle and followed Sergeant Hopkins eastward.

As they passed a guard post outside of Augusta, they were given more good tidings. The sentries jubilantly relayed the news that the main rebel army had been crushed at Camden, in South Carolina, on the sixteenth of August. A British army under General Lord Charles Cornwallis had attacked and scattered a rebel army twice its own size. The rebels had been commanded by their heavily touted Hannibal, General Horatio Gates, *The Hero of Saratoga.*

There was no doubt in the minds of all practical-minded men that the rebellion was, for all intents and purposes, at an end.

Chapter 12

Augusta, Georgia
Wednesday, September 13, 1780

The neatly kept house sat on the outskirts of Augusta, fronting the road that led to the south. John paused to examine it critically before ascending the steps onto the front porch. It was a well-kept, but not affluent looking structure, one that spoke generously about the people that it sheltered. The hard soles of his shoes sounded unusually loud as they stepped across the boards; the only other sound that morning was the song of a solitary bird, perched high up among the twisted limbs of a nearby oak. John took a deep breath, unsure of his welcome, and knocked self-consciously on the front door. While he waited for someone to answer, he nervously fidgeted with the tight-fitting stock that encircled his neck. The curtain in one window made a slight, almost imperceptible movement; behind it he could see a dark pair of eyes appraising him. No doubt the people inside would be nervous. His uniform and the Brown Bess carbine slung across his right shoulder would be greeted with suspicion in many homes around Augusta. Adjusting his collar in nervous anticipation, he knocked again, louder than before. The door opened no more than an inch. John noticed that it creaked as it moved, it sounded grumpy, as if it resented being opened to visitors.

The voice of an older woman lashed out at him through the tiny sliver of doorway. "What do you want?" It was a challenge that snapped like a bullwhip just inches before his face. Startled, he took a step backwards and cleared his throat.

"Is Mrs. Maria Stokes in?" he said in his most cultured voice. "I am her nephew, here to pay my condolences."

The woman's dark eyes looked him over suspiciously, studying every detail, from his neatly styled rifleman's hat to the well-blacked shoes on his feet. He guessed that she must be at least in her seventies, with snow white hair wound into a tight bun on the back of her head where it was partially hidden by the edge of a lacy bonnet. Her narrow, too thin face was a wrinkled map of time. She seemed almost frail; her voice was her strongest feature.

"A Tory is the last thing that Mrs. Maria wants to see right now! You get on with yourself!" She snapped the words through the crack like a sergeant major berating an ignorant new recruit. As she spoke, she attempted to ease the door shut. John's foot shot forward. He smiled down at her, the toe of his shoe was wedged inside the tiny crack, just enough to prevent her from closing the door. He felt a momentary stab of remorse when he saw the fear that this sudden movement had occasioned in her eyes. It was the same fear that he had seen on the faces of people living on isolated frontier farms when he and the other Rangers sprang from a seemingly empty forest to confront them on narrow backwoods paths, or in stump-littered clearings scattered across the frontiers of Georgia and South Carolina.

Her eyes spoke volumes. Who was this uniformed man? A disciplined soldier on a routine patrol, or an irregular guerrilla who would rob, rape, and steal from one side as quickly as he would from the other? He waited for a moment for the shock of his movement to wear off, then removed his hat and said in a calming voice, "Why don't you let her decide if she wants to see her own nephew, Tory or no." He raised his voice only slightly, nevertheless, it clearly conveyed the notion that this was no request.

He removed his foot, expecting the door to instantly slam shut. Instead, the woman stood quietly, weighing the pros and cons of further actions.

"I'll be right back," she said, in a heavily accented voice. She closed the door as she spoke.

When the woman reappeared, she held the door open and gave a quick nod.

"The Missus says she'll see you, sir Tory."

"Thank you." His speech reverted to that of polite society. He handed her his hat, stood waiting as she hung it on a hat tree beside the door, and then followed her to the sitting room. The hard leather soles of his newly issued shoes sounded overly loud on the well-sanded floorboards of the entranceway. Otherwise, the house was as quite as a church at midnight.

An attractive woman in her late fifties with gray-streaked auburn hair tucked neatly into a mobcap, looked up from her chair when they entered the room. A new novel was opened on her lap. She closed the cover slowly, after carefully marking the page with a small white ribbon. John noticed the title, *Evelina,* as she lay it aside. Looking up, she smiled and rose to her feet, then moved across the room in a smooth, graceful walk. She embraced him warmly before stepping back. Holding him at arm's length, she looked him over carefully.

"Welcome, John," she said quietly. She rubbed the tips of her fingers lightly over the black armband that he wore about his left arm as a sign of morning for her deceased husband. A sad twist appeared on the edge of her lips. It was gone in an instant. John noticed that the light in her eyes seemed to fade slightly at the same time.

"I see that you already know of your uncle's death." She slipped her arm through his. Almost absentmindedly, she called for refreshments as she allowed him to escort her across the large, well-apportioned room. When she spoke, her voice was soft, still containing a hint of a Spanish accent, a relic of her early life in St. Augustine before she had eloped to marry John's uncle, Morgan Stokes.

Taking a seat in a leather armchair next to the room's only window, she watched silently as John seated himself on a settee across from her. An ornately carved and heavily polished table separated them.

"To what do I owe this honor?" she asked.

"I saw a rebel casualty list from a battle fought in South Carolina back in May. The words do not yet exist that can convey how very melancholy it made me, to see Uncle Morgan's name on it."

"Then you feel as I do."

"This is the first time that I have had a chance to visit since…" He caught himself, before saying "since the damned rebels burned me out." Instead he ended his sentence with, "since my difficulties over in Ninety-Six."

"We heard of that." She frowned. "Your uncle was furious! As I remember, he mentioned something about *rogues* and *ruffians* hiding behind patriotism as an excuse to run amok."

"Uncle Morgan was a remarkably astute man. I shall miss him mightily. As a matter of fact, my younger brother smuggled his old doglock musket to me on the road outside of Ninety-Six. It fed four families for a week in the wilderness before we were rescued by some of Colonel Brown's men. If you like, I could return it to you the next time that I visit Augusta."

She cocked her head to one side as if listening to a far away sound. "It looks to me as if you are one of Colonel Brown's men," she said, indicating his uniform with a wave of her hand.

He smiled. "Yes, ma'am. I am."

Maria quickly changed the subject. "Your wife … Egrain, if I recall correctly?"

"That is correct."

"How is she? I'm certain that you now have more children than just the one little boy."

John swelled with pride. "Yes, ma'am, I do. I have a daughter, Lynn Celia. I am also quite certain that I have a third child, but have not yet been informed as to the sex or name."

Maria beamed with pleasure. "This family can always use new children!

Where are they that you're unable to visit them?"

John related his story while his aunt sat listening with undisguised interest.

"I cannot explain it, but for some reason God has seen fit to constantly guide this family to the west. Morgan and myself at one time lived in the Creek town of Cussita, over on the Chattahoochee River." She smiled as she recalled old times. "The Indian trade built this house," she said proudly. "Your uncle was well-respected by them, as was his uncle, Titus Stokes, before him. I'll tell you something that you probably don't know." She smiled, and with a wave of her hand vaguely indicated the area to the west of them. "You probably have more than one cousin among those Creek warriors camped out there at Indian Springs." She reached over and gave his hand a gentle pat. "Think about that as you help distribute their presents."

"That assignment will go to another. I am assigned to work with the Cherokees in the valley towns. I rarely have contact with Creeks."

Maria gave him a stern look. "Surely you don't lead them on raids to kill our women and children on the frontier?" The words escaped before she realized what she was saying. She looked embarrassed, stuttered an apology.

John looked insulted for a moment, then laughed loudly. He caught himself and stopped abruptly.

"I am sorry to make light of your accusations Aunt Maria, but I am afraid that rebel propaganda has rather slanted the facts. I personally have never been on a raid with the Cherokees. But last year, when I was stationed down at Ebenezer, I did take custody of a great many prisoners that the Cherokees turned over to Colonel Brown. Even a few that the newspapers had previously printed detailed accounts about, describing their torture and deaths."

He paused to let his words take effect, then continued. "Don't take my word for it. If Colonel Brown was the madman that the journals accuse him of being, why do I constantly see two of the men who held his feet to a fire freely walking the streets of Augusta?" Without waiting for her response he answered his own question. "Because they are on parole and Colonel Brown honors that parole, despite his personal animosity for them. It's the same with most of the other accounts that are inked on the rebel presses. Most of it is pure rubbish!"

Maria flushed, then held up her hands.

"Let us change the subject! Politics is much too volatile of an issue for a family visit. Don't you agree?"

Having made their peace, Maria invited John to stay for supper. When she learned that Captain Johnston had released him from duty until noon of the following day, she insisted that he spend at least one night on a real bed before returning to his company in the morning.

That night, John lay back in his nightshirt, savoring the softness and comfort of a well-tightened bed. Maria had insisted that she and her maid be allowed to drive in new wedges[54] before making the bed with fresh linen. He fell asleep almost instantly.

He was awakened just before dawn by a hand lightly pressed against his shoulder. His eyes popped open, the dark outline of his aunt's maid, Jessica, hovered over him. She held no candle, but the room was illuminated by waving red ribbons of light. For an instant he was back in his old home in Ninety-Six, besieged by a mob.

Sensing that danger lurked near by, when he spoke it was in a whisper. "Something's wrong." It was a flat statement; there was no doubt that it was true. "What is it?"

"Rebels, sir Tory. Lots of them, passing by on the road out front. If they catch you here in that pretty green uniform..." She didn't need to elaborate on his fate under those circumstances. Throwing back the covers, he eased over to the window. Being careful to hide his silhouette by pressing himself flat against the wall, he peered through the edge of the curtain. Jessica was correct. Rebels, several hundred of them, were gliding silently past; the road before them was illuminated by the glow of a few lonely torches. The remainder of the column moved past in darkness, their feet making a steady shuffling noise on the dry roadbed. A sudden knock on the front door caused them to both jump in surprise. The knock slowly mutated into a steady, insistent pounding.

Jessica produced a key from her pocket, opened a chiffonier and motioned for John to enter. He shook his head, no. Taking her by the arm, he hauled her to the door of the room, giving her directions as they moved.

"Act natural, go to the front door and act like you are elated to see rebels. Treat them like long-lost brothers."

"Won't they think that's suspicious?" Although the features of her face where still shrouded in darkness, John could feel the concern written there. His own smile was lost in the dark outline of his face. Leaning towards her, he kissed her quickly on the forehead.

"As a friend of mine is so fond of reminding me, rebels don't think." He applied just enough pressure on her arm to prompt her to action.

In the bedroom, as he quietly pulled on his uniform, John could hear the conversation at the front door. Jessica, and now his aunt, was bubbling over with glee at the return of their brave patriots. John could almost see the vainglorious smiles of the young rebel officer as he basked in the praise of two matrons in distress. It was with some effort that he suppressed a laugh at the absurdity of the situation. Suddenly, his ears caught the sound of a second pair of boots clumping along on the wooden boards of the front porch.

"Sir, there's a fine horse and saddle in the stable." The voice sounded young, probably produced by a rebel soldier no older that his early teens.

"Yes! There is," he heard his aunt readily confess. "It belongs to one of your men who came by last night. He asked to leave it here while he walked towards Augusta. He has not yet returned."

"What was his business?" the officer asked. He had sensed a sudden, dramatic turn to this conversation.

"He didn't say," Maria answered, "but we assumed from his demeanor that he was not interested in being detected by any Tories." Her voice had a conspiratorial edge to it, tinged with a touch of humor.

There was a slight pause, "I see…" John could imagine the indecision in the man. Take the horse and saddle for the use of his own men, and possibly deprive some important spy of a means of escape, or leave it behind, where it may fall into the hands of marauding Tories?

"Are you sure it was one of *our* men?" he asked in hurried, clipped words. Behind him the last of the rebel column was shuffling past.

"Well, he didn't say who he was, but if he had been a Tory, why would he have left his mount here and walked into town in the middle of the night?"

"Yes…" The moment of decision.

"Should I search the house, sir?" The younger voice interjected the question as if the thought had suddenly popped into his head. There was another pause.

"No, we best be leaving, the men are already past. Good morning to you, ma'am, ma'am." John could visualize him courteously dipping his hat to each lady in turn before turning away and hurrying to rejoin the rebel column.

As soon as they were out of sight, John stepped from the bedroom fully dressed, carbine in hand. He tipped his hat politely, and then hurried to the stable, saddled his mount, and walked it out onto the road. In the distance, to the northwest, he could faintly hear the sounds of battle. He guessed it to be somewhere in the neighborhood of the Creek encampment at Indian Springs. Almost simultaneously, more gunfire erupted to the north and northeast. John knew that the firing to the north had to come from the rebels who had passed by his aunt's home only fifteen minutes before. He paused long enough to give his aunt a farewell kiss, before swinging into the saddle and racing towards the sounds of battle.

The detachment of rebels who had passed in the night had veered off to the east, probably to attack Fort Grierson. John headed away from them, towards his company's bivouac. He was within half a mile of the MacKay house when he rode into the rear elements of a company of Rangers, commanded by Colonel Brown, that had sortied out of Fort Grierson. They had been joined by a substantial group of Creek Indians who had retreated from their camp after it had been surprised by a large number of rebels at daybreak. Just as John rode up, the other troops began to dismount and form a skirmish line. He quickly handed his reins to a young man wearing the red coat of the New Jersey Volunteers and looked around for a familiar face. Seeing no one from his own company, he joined the skirmish line with fixed bayonet and waited for the order to advance.

A pair of small cannons stood ready on each flank. The men alongside him cheered when they opened fire on a group of rebels drawn up in battle formation near the home of Robert MacKay. This was where John's company had been bivouacked, guarding the supplies intended for distribution to their Indian allies. He wondered briefly about the fate of his friends as he stood, shoulder to shoulder with these strange men, unknown brothers who wore the same uniform as himself. When the order to advance was given by Colonel Brown, the Rangers moved out at a slow walk, closing on the rebel line behind a steel fence of bayonet points. They halted about twenty yards from the enemy and fired a volley into the ragged rebel ranks that were already showing the early signs of panic. Then, howling like a pack of Satan's imps, they leveled their bayonets and charged. Facing that line of wickedly gleaming steel, many of the rebels scattered like a covey of quail. Others stood their ground, fought fanatically, and died. In only a heartbeat the battle was over. John stood over one of his victims, reloading his musket. Blood oozing down the bayonet dripped onto his hands and made the metal ramrod slippery, slowing the process. Instinctively, he wiped his hands on his pants and continued loading. When he had finished, he glanced down at the dead rebel who lay sprawled on his back, mouth and eyes frozen open, a relic of his life's final surprise. John remembered the rebel's look of disbelief as he had rammed his bayonet through his chest; he had never expected that such a thing would happen to him. Noticing the dead man's fine looking long rifle, John picked it up. He flipped open the pan and found that it was still primed. Quickly stripping the powder horn and hunting bag from the corpse, he slung them over one shoulder, cocked the rifle, and looked for a target. Around him, the other Rangers were busy liberating the weapons and accouterments from other former rebels. Some of them knelt to rest, or took long pulls on their shiny tin canteens.

The Rangers had little time to savor their victory. Within ten minutes more rebels appeared and immediately launched an attack of their own. Outnumbered, Colonel Brown and his men retreated into the stone-sided

MacKay house and barricaded it in preparation for a siege. Inside the haven of the makeshift fort, John found Sergeant Hopkins firing out of one of the front windows. The sergeant slapped John gleefully on his back, exclaiming that he had given him up as either dead or captured.

For over an hour the trapped Rangers traded shots with the enemy, then the fire from the rebels faded away to be replaced by an occasional harassing shot fired from long range. The Rangers took turns firing out of the loopholed shutters of the well-built structure. When not firing, they sat with their backs against the rock wall and rested. Hopkins told John the story of the surprise and capture of most of Captain Johnston's Company that morning, when the rebels had overwhelmed them before they were able to put up any defense at all. Sergeant Hopkins, Nat, and the two Africans had managed to avoid falling into the trap by running to the river, where they took cover along the bank with a handful of Creek warriors. They had managed to fight off the rebels, who, after capturing the Indian stores, showed little interest in pressing the fight. Jacob and Dobbins, along with the other captured Rangers had been marched off under rebel guard about thirty minutes before Colonel Brown arrived with the reinforcements.

The Rangers and Indians trapped inside the stone house lay low until nightfall. Under cover of the night's extreme darkness, they crept outside and began to dig earthworks around the outside the house. The Creeks were not happy at having to fight from inside the crowded house and looked forward to manning the trenches once they were completed.

During the night, the firing continued sporadically. John, using his newly acquired Pennsylvania-made rifle, was stationed by one of the boarded-over windows. He kept a watchful eye for each musket or rifle flash from the rebel lines. When he spied one, he would instantly aim just above the flash and send a .54 caliber rifle ball in reply. Then he would flatten himself against the inside rock wall as the rebels, using the same strategy, splattered musket balls against the sides of the house. He couldn't be sure, but he was fairly certain that he had either killed or wounded at least three of the attackers.

John guessed that it was no more than one o'clock in the morning when a hushed voice called from the darkness at the rear of the house. The voice identified itself as Private John Rockett of Captain Rowarth's company of Rangers. With the muzzles of twenty muskets and rifles following his movements, the man crawled forward until his face appeared at the top of the trenches. He dropped down into their cover with a relieved smile on his face.

Captain Johnston quickly interrogated the man, who claimed to have escaped being captured yesterday by hiding amid the exposed tree roots along the riverbank. Biding his time, he had waited until darkness made it possible for him to move about undetected, and then began crawling towards the trapped Loyalists in the McKay house. The captain listened with interest when Rockett informed him that the river was completely unguarded. If they were planning a break out, that way was wide open, at least for the time being. He also advised the lieutenant that all of the rebels that he had seen were militia, and that most of them had deserted the siege and were roaming about the countryside plundering the Loyalist homes in the area. When asked about the other Rangers, he gave all the information that he knew, which was simply that Fort Grierson and its garrison had been captured.

Armed with this intelligence, Colonel Brown roused every man from his blanket and sent him to the loopholes. Under cover of the brisk exchange of musketry that ensued, one of the officers slipped over the top of the earthworks and crawled away towards the river. Finding it still unguarded, he plunged in. Within minutes, he was safely on the South Carolina side and racing for the British fort at Ninety-Six with a summons for aid.

After thirty minutes of intense gunfire, the fighting subsided. The Rangers, standing a rotating watch, one man watching and two sleeping, continued to trade random shots with the enemy pickets throughout the night.

The next morning dawned, crisp and clear. Slight tendrils of mist escaped from the warm water of the river and rose languidly into the cool morning air. It lingered over the river in silken wisps of smoky, semi-transparent haze that the rays of the early morning sun pierced at random intervals. Birds chattered in the trees. On any other day, such a sunrise would have been greeted with enthusiasm.

Through the loopholes, the Rangers could see the enemy moving around in the trees and behind some hastily erected earthworks they had thrown up overnight. Bare-chested rebels toiled like an army of pale-skinned ants as they continued to improve their positions. One man, no more than seventy-five yards away, kept exposing his head and shoulders as he threw red dirt out of the trench and onto the front slope of his position. John fingered his rifle as he watched the man work, wondering if he should take a pot shot at him, or simply wait.

Neither side seemed particularly interested in firing a shot that may bring on another full-scale engagement. John relaxed and dozed off, resting his head against the cool stonework of the house. He was awakened by a crashing sound that shook the building to its foundations.

When he opened his eyes, dust swirled throughout the room, choking the men who had dropped to the floor when the rebel artillery had begun firing. It coated their backs as it drifted downward. To one side, in the dusty smoke, John could hear a man screaming in agony that his legs were gone. Instinctively he checked himself for wounds, found none, and tried to get lower to the floor. Two more explosive booms from outside the house sounded; the whoosh of solid shot flying past the roof was clearly audible. The wounded man continued to scream somewhere in the rear of the house. Around him, John could hear the low rasping sounds of men sliding through rubble, jockeying for cover as they moved away from the jagged holes that the cannons had blasted through the front of the house. At random intervals, rebel marksmen shot musket and rifle balls through the gaps that ricocheted around the room whining like deadly insects. The screaming in the rear of the house abruptly ended. The house grew silent for only a moment, then another iron ball tore through the wall, removing the painted head of a Creek warrior who had chosen that unlucky moment to sprint through the back door and into the room. The legs of the warrior continued to pump furiously as the headless body raced across the room. It collided with the stone wall and bounced back, dropping heavily to the floor with a meaty splat! The gruesome corpse lay on its back, outstretched arms and legs flailing the air drunkenly for a few brief moments before growing still.

"Well I'll be damned!" one of the red-coated New Jersey Volunteers exclaimed. "Either I'm daft, or that bloody savage just ran across the room without a head!" He looked in wide-eyed wonder at one of his comrades.

"People don't run after their heads are cut off you darned fool!" The other man snapped back at him.

"Chicken's do it all the time," a third man shrewdly observed.

"People ain't chickens!" the second soldier retorted angrily. He looked at the third man sternly. "Don't encourage him, damn you! He's been addled in the head since the rebels whipped him half to death back in Jersey. He's just bloody seeing things!"

"Well, there's the bloody Indian!" the first soldier said angrily. "Where's his head?"

The other man rolled away and faced his loophole again, disdaining to take part is such a ludicrous argument. "Fools!" he muttered to himself.

"All the same, the bloody bastard did it!" the first man squawked. The second soldier nodded in agreement. They continued to lie on the floor. They seemed content to lie quietly amid the rubble, discussing the incident while the cannons roared, and rebel bullets ricocheted throughout the room.

A snippet of their conversation was barely audible above the roar of the struggle going on around them. "I remember the time that…"

John looked to his left. The headless body still lay where it had fallen. He had to force himself not to burst into hysterical laughter at the absurdity of the two soldiers laying there amid the din of battle, calmly discussing the similarities between humans and chickens and calculating the odds of ever again seeing a headless corpse run across someone's parlor. Normal men would have been wordless with terror at a time such as this.

Two more unaimed cannon balls whistled past the house, one sheared a column off the front porch before it skipped away towards the river without causing any further damage. From out of the dusty dimness, Sergeant Hopkins's hand suddenly grabbed John by his coat. He pulled him across the floor and jammed his face to within an inch of his own.

"Take a look out there," Hopkins said, pointing out of the shell hole in the front wall. "You see that gun to the left? Every gun fires high or wide except for that one. Every time it fires, they score a hit. I'm thinking that officer behind it is the only man out there that can lay a gun." He paused, letting the information sink in. "Think you can do it?"

"If it means putting an end to this bloody business, I'll blow his rebel brains out!" John hissed. He rolled onto his stomach, rested the long rifle on the bottom of the hole, took careful aim, and squeezed the trigger.

The rebel officer was squatting behind his gun, focused intently on the process of aiming, when John's ball caught him in the forehead. He jumped to his feet, stumbled backwards a few steps and dropped out of sight.[55]

Hopkins gave John a congratulatory slap on the back. "Now that was some shooting!" he declared loudly. "I'll see that the colonel promotes you to bleeding corporal for that!"

John rolled away from the wall and chanced standing long enough to load the rifle. He dropped down immediately and cautiously peeped through his old loophole. He could see no targets. Sensing an opportunity to sting the rebels, he began to patiently move from loophole to loophole picking off any rebels who dared to expose themselves to man the cannons. Several other Rangers with rifles joined him, picking off the gunners with deadly accuracy until the barrage abruptly ceased. The Rangers smiled and joked with each other, imagining the rebel officers crouched in their trenches futilely attempting to order men up to serve the guns. One foolhardy rebel officer, attempting to inspire his men to greater efforts, jumped from cover and began the slow process of loading the weapon by himself. Two of the Rangers fired together; the man fell across the axle of the gun.

After the guns were silenced, the enemy seemed content to settle back into their original tactics. Throwing up more earthworks, and slowly encircling the beleaguered Loyalists, they waited for thirst, or hunger, to drive them out. John lay to one side of his loophole, eyeing the soldier he had watched that morning work steadily, slowly helping to expand the noose around the necks of the trapped Rangers. John thought that the rebel favored a cousin

of his, which weighed heavily in his decision to not take a shot at him. By
late afternoon, the Rangers were growing thirsty, their water had long since
been exhausted.

Just before sunset, the rebel commander, Elijah Clarke, sent a message
under a flag of truce demanding that they surrender. Captain Johnston
walked out to meet the man, accepted his letter and returned to the house.
The eyes of every man present were on him as he passed the note to Colonel
Brown, who lay on a bloody mattress in the back room. He had been shot
through both thighs, but still remained cocky and ready to fight. He opened
the letter, his hands trembling as he read. With a look of disgust he handed
it to Captain Johnston. Brown looked away while the captain read the note.
He looked up, astonished.

"They want us to surrender? Blast their eyes! The war is almost over
except for this bunch of diehards and they think to threaten his Majesty's
troops into surrender?"

"That's what I say!" Brown agreed vehemently. "Captain, go out there
and warn this rabble that there will be serious consequences for this. We
will defend this post to the last extremity!"

Captain Johnston relayed the message to the flag bearer who marched
haughtily back to his own lines. The Rangers braced for the onslaught they
felt would surely follow their refusal, but it never came. Once again, both
sides settled in, using picks and shovels in place of rifles and muskets to fight
this battle.

"John! Wake up, John!" The voice was urgent. A hand roughly shook
him out of a vivid and blissful dream of Grainy. Temporarily disoriented,
he looked up at the form of Sergeant Hopkins that towered over him. The
sergeant shook him a second time. "Stand to Ranger! There's a lot of men
coming across the river. If it's the enemy, we'll be hard-pressed to fight them
off."

Completely alert by this time, John followed Hopkins out of the back of
the house and dropped into the trenches alongside a disheveled Creek warrior
whose paint was in serious need of a touching up. The face, originally painted
half red and half black was now badly smeared and running together, as if
the man had slept last night with his face rubbing against a pillow. Around
him, other warriors, using small trade mirrors, were busily reapplying their
paint. They didn't seem concerned about the approaching enemy.

The sun was still below the level of the tree tops across the river. John
cocked his musket, favoring its faster rate of fire for this type of fighting,
and rested it across the dirt wall of the hastily constructed trench. His finger
rested loosely on the trigger, waiting for a target. The outlines of men gliding
across the river in canoes were faintly visible. No one could tell if they were

friend or foe.

The canoes moved closer to the shore, disappearing below the level of the riverbank as they grounded on the narrow beach. A moment later, a man's head appeared, a feathered scalplock silhouetted in the morning sun. One of the Creeks, laying belly down on the dirt beside John, rolled lazily onto one elbow, and faced the rear.

"Tciloki,"[56] he said in a low voice to a group of warriors sitting in the bottom of the trench. One of them looked up, nodded, and went back to work reapplying fresh paint. It sounded to John like he had said, "see low key."

John didn't understand the word, but by the tone of the voice and the sudden deflation of tension in the warriors crowded along the earthworks, he knew they must have recognized friends approaching. He looked around for someone to explain. A leathery-faced Ranger, with a two-day growth of thick gray whiskers, sat in the bottom of the trench, tearing on a twist of tobacco with his back molars, his front teeth were all missing.

"What did he say?" John asked when the man looked up, somehow conscious that he was being watched. It was some sixth sense that John had seen several other veterans display in the past. The old Ranger shrugged his shoulders, rested the back of his head against the wall of the trench, and closed his eyes. It was not the type of shrug that conveyed a dearth of knowledge, but one that indicated a complete lack of interest. John turned back towards the river. By now, the new arrivals were climbing stealthily over the top of the bank. Bent at the waist, they loped leisurely towards the besieged garrison, muskets carried loosely in their hands, heads erect, eyes darting here and there, alert for any signs of danger.

A smile appeared on John's dirty face as the first man came close enough to be recognized. Thunder's Child saw him in the same instant. John mouthed a quiet greeting at the warrior, who simply nodded his head in acknowledgment as he jumped into the trench. He looked quickly around, saw Sergeant Hopkins, and called to him, gesturing to the other warriors following behind. At least fifty Cherokees eventually crowded into the trenches. Captain Johnston came to welcome their new allies the instant that he was informed of their arrival.

As the third day of the siege dawned, thirst became a pressing factor. With the exception of a few precious pints of water brought in by the Cherokees the night before, many of the men had been without water for almost two days. Finally, with no word from the relief force, Colonel Brown asked for volunteers. Captain Johnston stepped forward and accepted the job. The remaining men in his company volunteered, to a man, to accompany him. John's face dropped when he was left out of the five member *Forlorn Hope* that the captain selected. Seeing his disappointment, Captain Johnson laid his hand on his shoulder.

"I'll need you and your rifle in here, covering me, more than I need you out there dodging bullets," he said in a kindly fashion.

The six men made their way out to the trenches that lay nearest to the river. They crouched there, waiting for a signal from Sergeant Hopkins who had shimmied into the attic of the MacKay house to spy on the enemy. John was in a position on the second floor, behind a boarded over window; other men, armed with rifles were stationed around the house to pick off any rebel sharpshooters who showed their heads. The remainder of the Loyalists were to use their muskets to keep the rebels occupied while the detail scampered across the open space between the house and the river.

When Hopkins was satisfied that the rebels were off guard, he carefully held a handkerchief out of a vent in the attic and waved it three times. At his signal, Captain Johnston, followed by his five men, jumped over the forward edge of the trench and raced towards the river. They were halfway there before the enemy reacted.

John saw one of the rebels in a blue canvas smock spring out of the trench and lay the barrel of his long rifle over a tree stump. He sighted his rifle on the center of the man's hat and fired. The hat flew off, slapped away by an invisible hand. The rebel dropped his weapon, fell across the stump, and then rolled off to one side, landing spread eagle on the ground. Almost immediately the boards around John erupted into hundreds of flying splinters as rebel marksmen loosed a barrage of round balls at the puff of smoke that betrayed his presence. He felt a bone jarring slap on the inside of his right hand and another against his left knee that caused him to stumble backwards. He landed hard on his rump, his upper torso rolling until the back of his head banged to a stop on the floor. Stunned by the impact, he sat up slowly. Shaking his head to clear away the cobwebs and grunting at the numbness of his hand and leg, he rolled onto his side, checked for wounds, and then sat, straight legged, on the floor. His right hand was numb and showing the early signs of a severe bruise. He tried to clench it into a fist, it obeyed with painful slowness. His fingers felt tight, as if he had spent a day swinging a mattock. He checked the pants leg over his left knee; there was no evidence of blood or a bullet hole. When he reached for the rifle, it came apart in his hands. He sat there, half stunned, and studied if for a moment. The lock had been demolished by at least two rifle balls and the stock had snapped in two, just to the rear of the tang. He looked at the two pieces of the broken weapon with remorse. Searching further, he located evidence of where a third ball had splattered midway up the barrel. Disappointed at losing such a fine rifle, he tossed it to the side.

As he limped painfully down the stairs, he saw two men bringing in a wounded man that he recognized as Captain Johnston. They lay him gently, face down on a cornshuck mattress, where he died quietly a few minutes later. Around his body, men drank sparingly of the much-needed water from the canteens that had cost his life.

Careful to keep his throbbing leg straight, John slid slowly to the floor alongside his carbine that stood propped at an angle beside his loophole. He pulled the weapon into his lap, checked the priming, and lay back, exhausted.

He dozed fitfully; when he awoke the room was eerily silent. There was barely enough light remaining for him to make out the other men crowded along the walls. Sergeant Hopkins was sitting beside him, arms clasped around both knees with his head resting on them. His breathing was slow and steady; John knew he was asleep. On the other side of Sergeant Hopkins, Nat lay on his side snoring lightly, Sambo and Mambo lay beyond him, one on each side of a shell hole blown through the wall of the house. They were both silent. Their eyes were focused on something outside and far away. John wiped the sleep from his eyes and tried to stand. His left knee was so swollen and stiff that he grimaced in pain each time he attempted to put any weight on it. The red-coated Jersey man who had insisted that headless men could not run, laid his Long Land musket aside and supported John by the elbow as he rose laboriously to his feet. John threw his arm around the man's shoulder and attempted to pace back and forth in an effort to loosen up his leg. After a few painful tries he gave up the attempt and, with the soldier's help, slid back to the floor. He felt a slight fever coming on; laying his head against the cool stone wall, he fell asleep almost immediately.

John awoke the next day at noon; the room was the same unearthly quiet. The few men who moved, did so lackadaisically, as if it took every ounce of energy to force their limbs to obey. Without exception, their lips were parched and cracked, their uniforms were filthy, their eyes hollow. John continued to lay propped against the wall, trying to mentally calculate how long they had been besieged. Only four days? It seemed so much longer! He noticed that the cornshuck mattress that had held Captain Johnston's body was now empty, but found that he was too exhausted to ask what had become of him. Unconsciously, he licked his parched lips; the salt made them sting.

A soldier with a wooden bucket entered through the back door of the room, the same door that had cost the Creek warrior his head yesterday … *or was it the day before?* He moved listlessly from man to man, waiting patiently as each took a single chunk of raw pumpkin from the bucket and stuffed it in their mouths. The man shrugged his shoulders after completing his circuit of the room.

"That's all fellas," he said simply. His head dropped onto his chest, as if the last of his energy had just been expended. He drug his feet as he left the room.

The sudden rumble of feet descending the staircase caused the exhausted men to jump to their loopholes. They looked out at an empty world; the rebels in their trenches were not visible. With disinterested shrugs they resumed their former positions. Minutes later the man came back into the room, a sight bounce to his step.

"What news?" he was asked by several of the men at the same time.

"We've just sighted some Redcoats over on the other side of the river. The colonel thinks that it's some of Cruger's scouts with the relief column."

Men, who only moments before looked as if they were on death's doorstep, suddenly felt a surge of adrenaline. All around the room they sat up, curious, a flurry of questions aimed at the speaker flew around the room.

"How many men?"

"What color were the facings on their uniforms?"

"Are you sure it's not some rebel trick?"

"How long before the rest of the column gets here?"

The man threw up his hands in surrender. "You boys know as much as I do. All I know is that there's some mighty good looking Redcoats on the other side of the river." He turned and disappeared up the stairs.

The room, so silent only moments before, hummed like a beehive as the men discussed this news and tried to make some sense out of it. Everyone had an opinion about when the siege would be lifted. Two hours, by the end of the day, tonight, tomorrow?

The sun set that evening with no sign of the relief forces. The burst of hope and energy from the afternoon had faded, the men slowly settled back to wait. The night passed slowly with only occasional exchanges of gunfire. Most of this was done purely out of boredom.

Just before daylight on the fifth day of the siege, the men began to stir once more. John leaned forward and gently felt his knee through his pants leg. It seemed swollen to twice its normal size. He rubbed it gingerly in an effort to bring the swelling down.

"They're here!" The sudden shout from the back of the house startled him; he looked up as a wild cheering arose from the trenches nearest the river. One of the officers stepped into the room and commanded the men to begin firing on the rebels. The relief force needed cover as they waded across the river ford and ascended Hawk's Gully.[57] John managed, with Sergeant Hopkins helping hand, to struggle to his feet. Keeping his weight on his good leg, he leaned his shoulder against the wall for support and fired unaimed shots in the general direction of the rebel works. It seemed as if only a few minutes had passed when they received the order to fix bayonets and charge the rebels. John looked around frantically for something to use as a crutch. He pointed to a Long Land musket lying unused on the floor and called to Nat to hand it to him just as the order to charge came. Nat thrust the weapon into John's hand before disappearing through the front door of the house.

John waited until the others had cleared the room before limping with the aid of his makeshift crutch onto the front porch. He watched as the green-coated Rangers, joined by the red-coated soldiers of Colonel Cruger's troops, stormed up and over the rebel works. It was all over in less than five minutes. The siege was broken and the remnants of the rebels were fleeing pell-mell away from Augusta.

No one was as yet aware of it, but the revolution in the South was taking a dangerous turn. A few short weeks later, at a place on the border of the Carolina colonies called King's Mountain, a group of 800 Loyalist militia, along with a company of Major Patrick Ferguson's New York and New Jersey Loyalists, were surrounded and decimated by rebel militia from Georgia, the Carolinas, and Virginia. Major Ferguson, the only soldier on the field of battle who was actually English, was killed, along with over one hundred of his men. The remainder were either wounded or captured. The wounded were left to die on the mountain when the prisoners were marched into the North Carolina backcountry. There, the rebels hanged several of the prisoners after local militiamen got drunk and pointed them out, denouncing them as thieves and murderers.

The rebel victory at King's Mountain delayed the invasion of the main British Army under Lord Cornwallis. Emboldened by the victory, hundreds of rebels renounced their sworn paroles and swarmed out to resume the fight.

While all of these events were taking place on distant fields of battle, Sergeant Hopkins and his small band of men were detailed to serve with Colonel Thomas Waters in the Ceded Lands to the north of Augusta. Their job was to round up these parole violators and bring them to justice.

Chapter 13

The Ceded Lands
Friday, November 17, 1780

John dismounted cautiously. Holding onto the pommel of his saddle with one hand, he dropped his foot carefully onto the sandy soil, wincing slightly as he slowly applied weight to the injured leg. The pain, such as it was, was trifling, fading with each passing day. His knee had shrunk to its normal size and only a faint, yellow stain remained as a reminder of the huge bruise that had originally stretched from six inches below his swollen kneecap to mid-thigh above it. Limping slightly, he led his mount to the edge of the river, where he stood holding the reins loosely as it lapped water from the gentle current.

The morning air was hot, heavy with humidity. He could feel its weight on his shoulders, it weighed him down, sapped his energy. Sweat tickled his sides and ribs as it wiggled down the insides of his heavy shirt. He removed his hat and wiped his forehead with a dirty shirtsleeve.

Behind him, he could hear the other men dismounting and speaking together in hushed tones. They had been patrolling the Ceded Lands for over two weeks, seeking out rebels who had broken their paroles by once again taking up arms against their King. Colonel Waters had been supplied with a list of these criminals; he kept it in a hunting bag at his side.

The patrol operated with the mechanical efficiency of a well-drilled unit. After sniffing out its quarry with merciless persistence, it would swoop down on isolated farms, holding the occupants at gunpoint while the colonel checked the name of some hapless rebel against those written on the list of the condemned. John couldn't help but feel a touch of sympathy for the poor, sweating prisoners each time one was trussed up and led away to face a military tribunal in Augusta, Savannah, or Ninety-Six. Time and again, he had heard the prisoners spout the same sad story as they sat dejectedly in their saddles, their mounts being led by one of the Rangers. They all claimed to have given their paroles in good faith, only to have Elijah Clarke and his men materialize outside of their homes a few months ago demanding that they join them in their raid against the British outpost at Augusta. Clarke had bluntly given them only two choices: either honor their paroles, in which case they would immediately be stood against the wall of their own cabins and executed, or violate their paroles by joining the rebels and risk being hung by the British if they were caught. Well, they were caught, abandoned after Clarke had been chased out of Augusta by the Rangers and their reinforcements from Ninety-Six—left alone to face the flighty whims of that fickle harlot, fate.

John rubbed his hand affectionately over his mount's shoulder; he had grown fond of the white mare since she had been assigned to him at the end of the siege. The rebels had captured the animal he had ridden from Long Swamp on the first day of the battle. After their defeat it had vanished into the wilderness with them.

Sergeant Hopkins, Thunder's Child, Nat, Sambo, and Mambo pulled their mounts on line beside his and dismounted stiffly. While the animals drank their fill, the men stood like a line of silent statues, gazing over the smooth surface of the Savannah. Stray shafts of early morning sunlight penetrated the thick foliage overhead, skipping along the surface of the river and causing it to glimmer brightly enough in places to dazzle their vision. The hot, sticky air was filled with the mellifluous sounds of the current's watery song.

"I wonder what Jacob and Dobbins are doin' right now." Hopkins spoke without looking up. It gave the impression that he was speaking to the river instead of to the other men.

"I don't know, lucky bastards!" John said. He was thinking of the two men who were probably back in Long Swamp Village at this exact moment, living an easy existence while they waited on word of their exchange. With the approach of the garrison from Ninety-Six, Clarke had delayed only long enough to issue paroles to all of the captured Rangers before following his men back into their forest sanctuary. Many Loyalist had been surprised at this humane gesture from their normally ruthless adversary.

Hopkins gave a dry chuckle. "It almost makes me wish that I had surrendered along with them! What about you, *Corporal Bentley Jonathan Stokes*?" He used John's full name and newly acquired title when he spoke; his tone made it sound like some chronic affliction.

John thought for a moment. "If I had," he said slowly, "I would still be a poorly paid private soldier, instead of a wealthy corporal." He grinned. "With our luck, if we had surrendered, they would have hung us all."

"That's probably just what they would have done," Hopkins agreed.

Colonel Waters motioned for the sergeant to join him, abruptly halting their conversation. Hopkins trotted over to join his commander and a Loyalist militia lieutenant standing at the edge of the trail. They conferred briefly.

Hopkins returned and spoke to Thunder's Child in Cherokee. The warrior asked a few short questions before mounting and plunging across the shallow ford of the river. On the far bank he melted into the thick underbrush on the South Carolina shore. The rest of the patrol cast about for a place to relax, they would not be moving until he returned.

* * * *

It was two hours before the scout splashed back onto the Georgia side of the river. He dismounted quickly and conversed in hushed tones with the leaders of the patrol. John watched the three men with great interest as they argued hotly with each other. Thunder's Child and the lieutenant took turns speaking, each gesturing towards a different side of the river as they spoke. Both were clearly trying to press their opinions on Colonel Waters. The colonel rubbed his chin thoughtfully and nodded his head as he listened attentively to each man. Having heard enough, he held up his hand, asked a few more questions, and called for the men to assemble. They stood in a semicircle as he knelt in the sand and used a short stick to outline his plan. "There's a paroled rebel officer living about two miles up river from here on the South Carolina side. He's listed as having taken part in the siege at Augusta in September, and at the battle on King's Mountain last month. We're going to bring him in and turn him over to Colonel Brown for trial. I want you five," he indicated Sergeant Hopkins and the four green-jacketed Rangers standing beside him, "to circle around to the north of the farm. Five of your militiamen will circle to the right and come in from the east." He looked up, speaking directly to the militia lieutenant. "I will come straight up from the south. The two Cherokees will stay on this side of the river. When Sergeant Hopkins and his Rangers are ready, he will signal us by blowing three sharp notes on his signal whistle. All of us, with the exception of the Indians, will converge simultaneously on the farmstead." He looked up. "Any questions?" A pause. "Let's mount up."

* * * *

The Rangers followed Sergeant Hopkins single file through the relatively open forest to the east of the farm. Slipping unnoticed along the tree line they halted, sitting their mounts casually as the sergeant scanned the area for signs of danger. Their target was working the field that lay between them and the cabin. A young boy, no more than fourteen, probably the man's son, walked in front of the lone ox, leading it along the furrows. The field was sectioned off with a split rail fence that zigzagged along the shoulder of a well-used wagon trail that cut through the middle of the farm. Farther on, a thin curl of smoke escaped from the top of a log chimney. It dropped quickly towards the earth and drifted lazily over the stump-littered clearing before intermingling with the trunks of a large oak grove lining the cleared area to the south. A thin woman, wearing a light blue bonnet and a linsey-woolsey gown, was bent over a wooden washtub in the front yard, scrubbing clothes with a vicious intensity. Her arms were covered in foamy suds up to the elbows. A small girl child chased a cavorting puppy around the woman's legs as she worked. John felt a sudden surge of homesickness. He could imagine himself and Grainy working together in a tranquil setting such as this, once the war ended.

They waited until the team of oxen reached the end of the furrow alongside the cabin. While the man was distracted with turning the team, Hopkins raised his wooden signal whistle to his lips and blew three shrill notes. From three sides of the clearing, the drumbeat of iron shoes shattered the tranquility of the morning. John followed Hopkins along the narrow trail beside the split rail fence, guiding his white mare with one hand and holding his carbine at an angle with the other. They closed rapidly on the homestead.

Expecting a quick, bloodless capture, they were caught off guard when the man turned and bounded for the cabin. Grabbing a musket that stood propped against the wall, he turned and leveled the weapon in their direction. All five Rangers fired together. The rebel, struck three times, collapsed against the log wall.

The ox, standing between the antagonists, was hit in the middle of its spine by a low shot. Its hind legs crumpled. The wounded animal bellowed plaintively as it pawed the ground with its front legs in a futile attempt to pull itself erect.

The scene erupted into pandemonium, the painful bellowing of the mortally wounded ox mingled with the hysterical screams of the woman and the cries of her small daughter to fill the air. For one instant, John thought the boy was going to lunge for his father's musket. Instead, he stood rooted in shock, with his mouth hanging open and tears streaming down his face.

The rest of Colonel Waters's party thundered up seconds later, weapons were held at the ready. The colonel dismounted and, purely out of habit, tipped his hat respectfully to the woman. Without a word, he moved past her and stood over the dead man, studying his face. He nodded, satisfied that the right man had been taken. He grabbed the dead man's musket and fired it into the oxen's head. The bellowing ceased. He studied the musket, rubbing his finger over the markings on the lock.

"French Charleville. Almost brand new," he mused aloud. He handed the weapon to the lieutenant and mounted quickly, already prepared to move on. The woman's harsh curses arrested him.

"What am I to do now?" she bawled through her tears. "Me out here with no man and two young'uns?" She marched over to the side of his horse and stared defiantly. It almost appeared as if she were daring him to shoot her. The colonel looked down at her. His face was a mask; it was impossible to guess his thoughts. He had simply experienced too much sorrow to let it openly affect him.

"Ma'am," he said, "I deeply regret this event. However, your husband did violate his parole, and he did attempt to fire on my men. What would you have me do?" He reined his mount around and cantered away without a backward glance. The militia lieutenant paused to look one more time at the scene. The woman recognized him as a one-time neighbor and jumped to his side. Grabbing his leg, she cursed him roundly.

John, watching the exchange, could see by the haunted look in her eyes that she had lived with the dread of this moment for many years, but had been totally unprepared for its consequences. He caught himself staring, unable to force himself to look away.

The woman noticed John's pitying look. She stopped talking and peered at him intently, as if attempting to memorize his features. Her tears stopped abruptly, a hardened, hating expression possessed her face as she returned her attention to the Loyalist officer and continued to rave.

"What's a woman to do?" she cried in a fury. "Bury my husband while all that ox meat spoils, or butcher the ox and feed my children while my husband spoils? It's a sorry choice you godless Tories have forced on a good woman in this heat!"

John felt a sudden anger at the sad plight that the dead man's ill-conceived choices had left for his family. He would never understand misguided people such as these who were ready to turn the entire world on end, based solely on the propaganda spread by the transparent and malignant rebel press. No wonder Colonel Waters just rode away. Kindness and reason was wasted on people such as these!

The militia lieutenant, tiring of her tirade, pushed her roughly away from him with his foot and cantered after the patrol. John and the other Rangers followed. Behind him the woman dropped to the ground and pummeled it with her hands, all the while screaming vile curses at their backs.

* * * *

That night, John sat staring into the fire as it died to a red glow. He was silent, thinking on the events of the day. Across from him, barely visible in the dim light, he could see the forms of two rebels they had taken that afternoon as the patrol made its way back towards Colonel Waters's Fort. He felt no sympathy for them. They were hard, heartless men, who had been accused of murdering several Loyalist families along the Broad River in Georgia, including the parents of Judith McDougal. They were the worst kind of rebels, those who fought not for some vague and misguided idea, but for the loot they could gain by plundering the farms of helpless men and women. Before the war, many of them would have been branded outlaws by both sides. Now, with the services of murderers and plunders in high demand, they were called *Patriots,* and at times, *Loyalist partisans.* The name shifted with their allegiance. He glanced at Sergeant Hopkins who sat with his back against a nearby tree. Sambo and Mambo were rolled in their blankets asleep. Nat, musket in hand, guarded the two prisoners. John turned back without speaking to stare into the fire.

"Are you troubled, Corporal Stokes?" Hopkins asked quietly. He tapped his pipe against the sole of his shoe, dislodging any ashes clinging to the inside of the bowl.

John turned to look in his direction. "I was just thinking about how the rebel papers will account for the incident at that farm today.

Hopkins loosed a short, humorless laugh. "You've been around long enough to know that!" Pretending to follow the lines of an imaginary newspaper with his finger, he simulated reading the printed words. "*Savage Tories, aided by bloodthirsty savages, shoot down an unarmed farmer in his field, while his sick wife and ten hungry children look on!*"

"And every rebel in the country will take it as gospel without the slightest care as to the truth of the matter!" John shook his head and gave a sigh.

Hopkins looked pensively at the fire before he proceeded. "I don't think that I've ever told you this story, but I was in Boston ten years ago when the so-called *Boston Massacre* took place." He looked past the fire wistfully for a moment before he went on. "My brother had a trading brig that he sailed up and down the coast, and I accompanied him from time to time. My first wife was still alive at the time, and I took my youngest son along with me so he could see the world." He looked over at the two prisoners who were sleeping fitfully and made a careless gesture in their direction. "The boy is on that side now," he admitted sourly. Reaching inside his jacket he retrieved a tobacco pouch. Using his thumb he began to tamp a pinch of it into the bowl. "Well, we were walking the streets of Boston that night, it was snowing, and James was only nine. He wanted to walk in it, you know what a novelty snow is to children raised down south. We heard this commotion at the customs house and went to see what the ruckus was all about. There was a mob of the lowest sort of people who you could ever imagine bedeviling the sentries, just causing trouble. Drunk, most of 'em. All of a sudden one of the mob yells 'Fire!' at the top of his lungs, trying to wake the neighborhood. You know how the townsfolk dread a fire. They'll pour out into the streets at the slightest hint of it, not to mention what they'll do when some fool shouts it out in the middle of the night like that." He smiled as he reminisced, but it was a smile that lacked warmth. Thrusting the end of a small twig into the glowing embers, he waited for it to burst into flame and then carefully lit his pipe. He tossed the twig onto the coals where it smoldered for a moment before dissolving into ash. The whites of Hopkins eyes shone brightly in the temporary glare.

"To make a long story short, one of the soldiers must have thought that his officer had shouted 'fire', so he fired into the crowd. Then the rest of the detail fired." He smirked, his shoulders jerked with a suppressed laugh. "That was the end of it. The mob of folks who had flowed out of their houses at the word *fire*, wanted nothing to do with a street full of harbor trash. They melted away. A good thing too! I was fearing for the safety of my son at that moment, wondering what would happen if a riot started and us caught up there in the middle of those damned Yankees!" He looked at John with a knowing smile. "Thanks to the Boston newspapers, they have been transformed from harbor trash to bloody heroes! You have to give the rebels credit, they know how to turn any story to their use. Always have."

He jerked his head towards the dark outline of Colonel Waters's tent. "That's why he left the Indians on this side of the river today. Didn't want to be accused of having turned them loose to scalp defenseless women and children. 'Course, that's going to be printed anyway."

"What about those two?" John asked, indicating the two prisoners.

"They'll be hung, most likely, and lamented as fallen heroes. We're doing them a favor actually. If they live through the war, they'll just end up as common banditti and border trash. But as soon as they hang, they'll be heroes of the bloody Revolution!"

"A lost Revolution, let's hope," John prophesied.

"That's the one idea that motivates men such as Adams and Washington more than anything else. They know that history is written by the winners. If we lose, they're heroes with children and towns named in their honor, but if they *lose* … they're just a bunch of damned traitors. They've too much pride to allow that to happen without being killed first."

"You've heard what they're saying about Colonel Brown?" Both men jumped, mildly startled by the voice. They both rose respectfully.

"Good evening, Colonel Waters," Hopkins greeted the officer.

Waters indicated for them to resume their seats and sat alongside of them. He was in a talkative mood tonight. Other than the sentries, they were the only three still awake.

"What are they saying, sir?" Hopkins asked when they were all settled down.

"That Colonel Brown had thirteen rebels hanged from the staircase of the house you men defended in Augusta."

"What?" Both men were startled by the accusation. "He was shot through both legs. I don't think hanging people was his priority at the time." Hopkins was always quick to defend his commander.

"They're saying that he had some of his men carry him out on a stretcher so that he could sit in the parlor of the house and watch as each of those thirteen men were pushed from the stairwell. After they were dead, the rebels claim that the bodies were given to the Indians to scalp and mutilate."

"What men?"

"Can't say. One name that seems to stand out in my mind is Henry Duke. That's how I know that it can't be true. He was hung by Colonel Cruger for violating his parole, not by Brown at the White House."[58]

"I don't believe it either!" Hopkins interjected. "We were there. We would have seen it. 'Sides, Colonel Brown is always cautioning us to make sure that the Cherokees follow the rules of war. He would not countenance any such thing as turning over prisoners for torture."

Waters shook his head. "Be that as it may, stories such as this are being circulated, and they are always believed. Isn't it ironic that there were thirteen men supposedly hung? How apt, one for each colony in revolt! We must be on our guard at all times. Incidents like the one today are unavoidable if we are to vigorously enforce the Disqualifying Act;[59] but you can be certain that they will be used against us to recruit a whole new rebel army. That's why I have asked that we be allowed to make a sweep through the upper reaches of Georgia and South Carolina, to destroy their spirit before they can reform any farther. That damn debacle at King's Mountain will make them think they're winning the war if we don't act immediately to quell their spirit."

Signaling for them to keep their seats, he rose and stretched.

"Time to be turning in," he said through a wide yawn. He looked down at John, before adding, "By the way, my warmest congratulations on the promotion, corporal. I remember you coming to my fort after the rebels burned you out. You have a wife as I recall. I hope she is well."

"Yes, sir. And we've have a new son since then." John was clearly flattered that the colonel remembered him.

Waters nodded. "Good night." He moved slowly back to his tent, slumped shouldered, like an old man.

Chapter 14
Waters's Fort
Tuesday, Dec. 19, 1780

A slight frost dusted the interior of Colonel Waters's Fort, a fragile relic of last night's frigid weather that would evaporate at the first gentle touch of the morning sun. John mounted his white mare and waited silently, just inside the front gate, for the order to march. Using only slight pressure from his knees to communicate his wishes to the animal, he held her steady while he flipped open the pan of his carbine and checked that the priming was dry. Satisfied, he flipped the frizzen shut with a metallic snap and laid the weapon across the pommel of his saddle. He glanced, grim-faced and gloomy, at Jacob and Dobbins, who had rejoined the Rangers only last week, after having been exchanged for two rebel prisoners three weeks before. Both men looked back without speaking; neither seemed particularly pleased about being a part of this upcoming mission. They turned to watch Sergeant Hopkins approach, the frozen ground crunching beneath the newly shod hooves of his horse. The three black Rangers and their two Cherokee scouts followed behind him, the creak of saddle leather and the blowing of their horses the only other sounds in the half-light of early morning. When Thunder's Child and Robin passed their little group, they flashed quick grins in the Ranger's direction. They were silently pleased that the British commanders had finally seen what they had known all along, that the settlers on the frontier were a vulnerable and necessary target in this war of attrition.

To the east, the main armies maneuvered for advantage: the British in the hopes that they could lure the rebels into a major battle where they could be destroyed with a single stroke; the rebels avoiding any major confrontation, knowing that by simply surviving, they were winning the war of patience. Reports of skirmishes across the backcountry continually reached the Rangers at their isolated post. As the weeks passed, the frequency of the encounters steadily increased.

Jacob and Dobbins had ridden into the fort a week ago with a message from Colonel Brown who was still recuperating from his wounds in Augusta.

The message instructed the Rangers at the fort to accompany Colonel Waters on a sweep through the backcountry, burning and foraging as they went. This mission would accomplish two highly important objectives for the cause of both the British and Loyalist in the South.

The raid would keep rebels serving in the frontier militias tied down, either chasing the raiders, or staying at home to protect their families and property. Livestock and food the Rangers captured would be used to maintain their main army as it attempted to smash the rebels regrouping under their new commander, General Nathaniel Greene. Greene had been personally selected by Mr. Washington and sent south to take command of the rebel's southern army, all but shattered at Camden last year.

The plan made perfect sense; still John felt ill at ease, not liking the idea of burning the homes of other men and leaving families to starve unless their menfolk carried them to the safety of the rebel army, where they would be a constant drain on the scant supplies available to them.

Hopkins reined in next to the three men, his face set, betraying no emotion. Clearly, he did not like the idea any more than they did. Of the seven Rangers, only Sambo and Mambo seemed eager to go. They smiled, broad smiles that displayed their savagely filed teeth. They sat ramrod straight on the backs of their horses, proud of their newly acquired horsemanship. Mambo looked at John, nodded, and said something to Sambo in their native language, his words condensed into a soft cloud of frozen breath that swirled about his face as he spoke. Both laughed and chattered together, clearly elated at the prospect of coming battles.

"What'd they say, Nat?" Dobbins asked.

Nat shrugged and busied himself with preening his uniform. He straightened his stock, holding his head high and proud. Beside one of the log cabins built into the side of the fort, a young mulatto girl, newly arrived from a plantation on the Ashley River, smiled provocatively at him. She blew a kiss in his direction before bending over to tend to a fire beneath a scalding pot. Four headless chickens, destined for the table, lay on a chopping block beside her.

John couldn't suppress a smile, happy that Nat had found in Ester a woman willing to share her life with him. The two had *jumped the broom* three days ago and she had immediately moved into the cabin that housed Nat and the other black Rangers at the fort.

Colonel Waters appeared a few minutes later, swung into the saddle, and thundered out of the gate, heading towards the rebel settlements and their outlying farms. He gave them no farther instructions; they all knew what was expected of them. John decided, after studying the colonel's departing back, that he did not care for this business any more than most of the other men did. But, as they had all convinced themselves, it had to be done.

Four days later, on the banks of the Saluda River, they were joined by two bands of Loyalist irregulars. The first were under the command of William Cunningham, a notorious Tory raider who the Patriots called *Bloody Bill*. Cunningham had once been a Patriot during the early days of the war. Like Daniel McGirth, he had deserted to Florida and joined the British cause after being flogged by one of his officers for some trivial offense.

Cunningham rode into camp followed by sixty lean, hard-eyed partisans. Their entire demeanor was one of businessmen on an important errand. He sat his mount expertly. Bending slightly, he held his hand out to Colonel Waters, who looked up to him from the ground.

"Pleased to join you, colonel," Cunningham said. "We came as soon as we received Colonel Brown's summons. I take it that my men are the first to reinforce you?" He spoke quickly, like a man with little time and important appointments in the near future. His mouth remained a straight slash across his lower face, his eyes bored into those of his superior officer. He emitted an aura of deadly efficiency. Cold hostility.

The colonel shook his hand warmly as he smiled into that unsmiling countenance glaring down at him. "We're to forage everything that the enemy has and burn what we can't take with us," Waters said. "Have your men dismount and get some rest. We're still waiting for Colonel McGirth and his men to show. Meanwhile, come on over to the fire and have a bite to eat."

John and the other Rangers watched Cunningham's men with a mixture of appreciation and apprehension. They wore no uniform; however, by some unspoken consensus, they seemed to have settled on a green hunting frock with doeskin leggings or buff-colored trousers. Hats were as varied as their owners. Many wore tricorns, others wore hats with wide round brims, and still others had tacked theirs up on one side with a pin or thread. The only uniform item on their headgear were red cockades or ribbons. Shoes varied as much as the hats, ranging from bare feet, to moccasins, to leather shoes sporting expensive silver buckles. Without exception, they were well-armed, many with rifles decorated with ornate patchboxes. Those armed with muskets had shortened the barrels and double-shotted them with buckshot for use in the thick brush of the southern forests.

Recognizing Hopkins and John as non-commissioned officers, three of the raiders detached themselves from the knot of milling men and walked over to their fire. Each held out a hand in greeting. John was surprised at their precise and formal language as they introduced themselves. Hopkins offered them a seat and a swig of rum.

"Your men look like they've been busy," Hopkins observed. One of the men, the leader of the group, dusted off the front of his frock. He gave them a smile that completely lacked warmth. "That we have. Had to stop a few times on the way up to hang some rebels. Right boys?" He looked around at the other two, who smiled slyly as they nodded. "Yep, captured ole John Towles and two of his cattle rustlers down river a ways. They had over thirty head of cattle plundered from the Loyalist families in the area." He winked at the Rangers. "We won't be bothered by him again."

"Hanged 'em." Hopkins words were a statement; the fate of captured plunderers was a foregone conclusion. The same would happen to them if they fell into rebel hands.

"Wasn't them men doing what we're set to do?" Nat asked, hesitantly.

"No!" Hopkins barked with a laugh. "A damned rebel is a looter; King's men like us are foragers. There's a sight of difference between the two."

Nat shook his head mournfully. "I sure hope someone explains that to the rebels 'fore we run into 'em."

"Don't worry about any rebels around here," the partisan assured him. "We've made a clean sweep of them in this area."

"I hope so. But who are we supposed to get our forage from if there's no rebels around?" Hopkins interjected.

"Don't worry about that. North of here, they're thick as fleas."

The assembled men rose to their feet as the approaching rumble of many mounted men drifted to them from the south. A slight tremor of the ground heralded their coming before they broke from the cover of the trees and moved into the encampment, traveling four abreast.

"It's McGirth!" someone shouted to ease the apprehension of the men. They all stood, hands tightly gripping rifles and muskets, ready if needs be, to defend themselves from any approaching enemy. Gradually, they sank back to their seats, or grounded their muskets, watching the approach of their allies. With the arrival of this contingent, their numbers now swelled to over two-hundred-fifty men.

McGirth rode over to Colonel Waters and Captain Cunningham, throwing them a casual salute despite his role as an irregular leader. His men were dressed much like those of Cunningham's. Their faces betrayed their readiness to deal out whatever punishment they were capable of to the enemies of the Crown.

Colonel Waters waved Sergeant Hopkins and John over to join the three officers. As the only members of an established military unit, they would add a slight touch of legitimacy to this foray.

John extended his hand to the rescuer of his children.

"Colonel McGirth!" he said with a genuine smile. "I can't express my gratitude for your repatriating my children last year. If I can ever do anything…"

McGirth dismissed the accolade. "It was an honor for me to be of service to a fellow servant of the Crown," he said, modestly. John was startled when the colonel actually blushed, embarrassed by the praise.

Colonel Waters nodded appreciatively, then introduced the two Rangers to the newly arrived partisan leaders. He outlined his plan, carefully considering any advice, or recommendation from the other men. Unrolling a crudely drawn map, he staked it out on the ground with stones and produced a brass inkstand containing a tin canister of ink and two quill pens from his saddlebags. With them, he inked in changes suggested by the two partisan leaders and redrew the location of well-stocked farms and plantations.

The conference continued until late afternoon, when it was decided to wait until the next morning before moving to the nearest objective. Waters, always cautious, sent the Cherokees to scout in all directions before he allowed his men to stand down for a good night's rest. He cautioned them not to waste this opportunity; it would be their last chance to rest for quite a while.

That night, John, along with Sergeant Hopkins, Jacob, and Dobbins, sat around a crackling fire, sipping rum with a group of Cunningham's men who regaled them with stories of their exploits that stretched across the South, from Savannah to the North Carolina border. The Rangers expressed surprise that there were any rebels left in the two colonies after the partisans had cut their bloody swath through them.

When John and the other Rangers were pressed for stories of their own experiences, the other men seemed disappointed when the Rangers admitted that they could tell of no Indian massacres, or fiendish tortures of prisoners that they had witnessed. A groan of disappointment escaped many of them when Sergeant Hopkins expressed his own doubt as to the truth of the story circulating about Colonel Brown hanging thirteen prisoners from the staircase of the White House in Augusta. Clearly these men reveled in the death and destruction of rebels of all sex and ages. As the rum took effect, they began to tell of how and why they became partisans. John, having heard similar stories from virtually every Loyalist that he had ever served with, was particularly struck by the story of one man who told of the shooting of his two-year-old son by some Liberty Boys. They had taken to shooting randomly through the sides of his home after drinking heavily at a local tavern. One night, he had been sitting quietly with his wife and children when a shot rang out. The ball came through a shutter and struck the child in the head, killing him instantly. Overwhelmed with grief, he had run onto his front porch seeking revenge. Outside, a crowd set upon him, beating him unmercifully. The local Sheriff had accused him of recklessness in the

death of the child for refusing to leave when the local Committee of Safety
had ordered him out. He was jailed and his property confiscated; his wife
and children were turned out into the street with nothing but the clothes
on their backs while he was confined on a schooner in Charleston Harbor.
He never knew what became of them. He had spent months searching for
them after being freed when the British occupied Charleston six months
later. His story was interrupted several times by a hacking cough that he had
developed while a prisoner. He looked frail, but his companions vouched
for his tenacity in riding with them and his zeal in punishing any rebels that
fell into his hands.

* * * *

The next morning, the avenging Loyalist thundered down on their first
victim, an unprotected rebel farm. There, they found a woman left alone
with four small children while her husband served with the rebel army as a
militiaman. The harvest this year had been abundant, and the raiders loaded
the farm's cart with corn, pumpkins, squash, and dried beans. Chickens
flapped their wings and squawked in harsh protest as the raiders tied their
feet to the sideboards with strips of homespun ripped from spare clothing
the woman had painstakingly manufactured by hand during the few spare
moments of her existence. All of the livestock—a milk cow with a month-
old calf chasing behind it, two small pigs that were being fattened for next
year's slaughter, and three freshly sheared sheep—were herded together and
driven to the east along with the herd of cattle taken the day before by
Cunningham's men.

John, along with the Rangers and Cherokee scouts, galloped in advance
of the small army. Behind them, twin plumes of smoke sprouted from the
house and barn. It rose straight into the cloudless sky for hundreds of feet,
a warning to all of the other rebel families in the area that the long-dreaded
day of destruction was at hand.

"I wish they hadn't burned those people's homes," Hopkins remarked
off handedly to John as they rode, knee to knee, along a narrow path.

"Nor do I," John agreed quietly. He remembered the feeling of total loss
when his own home had been burned almost two years ago.

Hopkins gave him a searching look, guessing his thoughts. "It's not that
I lament the loss to that woman back there, they would do the same to
us. *Have done*, I should say. I was thinking as a soldier. Those clouds are a
warning to every rebel in the area. They'll be hiding their cattle and food
now. I hate to think of the methods that Cunningham's men will use to get
these poor fools to divulge their hiding places."

John silently absorbed this information for a few moments, deciding he
would use that argument with the officers to keep the torch from being

applied at the next farm.

The next farm proved to be a large, well-apportioned plantation. The Cherokees raced ahead, rounding up the slaves in the fields while the Rangers continued on to the main house. John and Sergeant Hopkins gave the other Rangers instructions to check the area while they mounted the steps. They were confronted by the sounds of excited murmurs and soft sobbing noises from behind the barred door.

Hopkins battered on the door with the butt of his musket. "Open up in the name of the King!" He looked quickly at John, smiled, and shrugged noncommittally. "I couldn't think of anything else to say," he said, in answer to John's questioning look.

He pounded again, more urgently this time, and repeated the summons. "Ma'am, we know you're in there. Open up before I have my men batter down this door!"

A moment later the door opened, just a crack. A bright blue eye appraised them before the door swung open. A pretty, very pregnant woman of no more than seventeen stood in the doorway. She seemed to breathe a sigh of relief when she saw that they wore uniforms.

"Thank God!" she exclaimed. "I thought you were some of the trash that plunders the area under the guise of Royal troops." She suddenly smiled; it was a smile more of relief than of happiness or welcome.

Hopkins removed his hat respectfully. "I hate to be the bearer of ill news, but that trash, as you call them, are not far behind. For your own safety, I would advise that you and the other women make no hostile acts towards them. We are here to forage for supplies for the main army. My men and I will do what we can to save your home, but we promise nothing." He stepped forward, forcing her to move to one side as he entered the foyer.

"Corporal Stokes!" Nat called. He sat his mount at the edge of the porch. "What you want me to do with these black folks? Enlist 'em, or round 'em up?"

"Separate any that want to enlist, and we'll send them on to the main army with the livestock," John said. "Turn the rest over to Colonel Waters."

Nat gave a quick nod and galloped back towards the fields where a cluster of slaves stood, surrounded by the garishly painted Cherokee scouts and the Rangers.

John entered the main house. Inside, he found the young woman who had met them at the door sitting amid a trio of frightened children. They looked much too old to be the offspring of the pregnant woman. He asked her where their mother was.

"She died last year. I am my husband's second wife."

"Where is your husband now?"

"He's gone east, on business."

"Business with the rebel army?"

"Certainly not! He's still honoring his parole from Charleston."

Both of them looked up as Sergeant Hopkins stepped back into the room from a door at the rear of the house. He paused to survey the contents.

"They're alone," he said to John. "Ma'am." He gave the woman a quick bob of his head, then exited onto the front porch with John at his heels. From the west, the first faint rumbling of approaching cavalry reached them. A few moments later the riders popped out of the tree line. With a whoop, they spurred their mounts forward, eager to get an early pick of the plunder. Behind them, other riders emerged from the trees, spied the wealthy-looking estate, and spurred their mounts ahead in a race for the main house.

The men wasted no time on formalities. With the efficiency born of practice, they stripped the farm and in less than an hour had two of the owner's wagons piled high with food. A third wagon, reserved for their own personal plunder, was stacked with pewter and silverware.

A scream erupted from inside the main house. John rushed up the steps, followed closely by Dobbins and Hopkins. Inside, two of the irregulars had the young mistress of the house held against the wall, a third man, his hand already inside the neckline of her gown suddenly pulled it downward, shredding it from top to bottom.

"Hold it!" John shouted as he entered the room. Hopkins and Dobbins flanked him with carbines in their hands.

"Don't get your dander up soldier!" The man exposed tobacco stained teeth when he laughed. "We're not going to harm the little lady." Before either of the Rangers could react, he yanked a knife from a sheath at his waist and slit a homespun sack tied around the woman's waist. Silver and gold coins, intermixed with continental and British currency, spilled onto the floor at her feet.

"Now, I wish that my Missus would give birth to children such as these!" the man exclaimed as he bent to retrieve one of the large gold coins. He held it up to admire it. "As I live and die! A Spanish piece of eight." He flipped it to John who caught it. John stood looking at it, feeling like a goat. *Duped by a pretty face!*

The partisans pushed the woman, now wearing nothing but her thin shift, to one side and began going through the pile of loot on the floor. One of them unfolded a piece of paper. John watched his lips move as he read it to himself. The man suddenly looked up, a twinkle in his eye.

"Looks like we got us a bloody spy!" he announced triumphantly. "You boys get this sacked up while I take this damn rebel over to the colonel. And don't forget my share!"

Still wearing nothing but her shift, the woman was half dragged across the front yard of the house to where the three commanders were conferring. Colonel Waters looked up, a frown on his face at the sight of the disheveled woman.

"What's this?"

"Sorry, sir," the militiaman said with a quick salute. "I've caught us a rebel spy." He held the papers out as proof. The colonel took the papers and perused them for only a moment. He held them out to the other two officers without taking his eyes off the woman. He surveyed her intently, his lower lip thrust forward in thought.

"This is a hanging offense young lady!" he informed her curtly. "Do you have anything to say for yourself?"

She spit in his face. "Go to Hell, you damned Tory bastard!"

The militiaman cuffed her solidly on the back of her head. She stumbled forward against the colonel's chest, regained her balance, then stepped back, eyes blazing with defiance.

Waters casually removed a handkerchief from a pocket inside his waistcoat. He carefully wiped his face clean with it, all the while holding his anger admirably in check.

"Young lady," he addressed her in a strained voice. "If I were even half the devil incarnate that your people paint me as, you would be dancing a jig from a limb of that oak tree over yonder this very moment." He carefully refolded the handkerchief and replaced it in his pocket. "What is your name?

The young woman met his hostile stare without blinking. She refused to speak.

"I know her colonel." One of the militiamen stepped forward. "She's Dicey Langston, from over Traveler's Rest way." He waved his hand in that general direction. "Her whole family's nothing but a bunch of damned rebels."

Waters turned to Cunningham and McGirth. "Gentlemen, what are you're thoughts on this subject?"

"The law's clear, she should hang," Cunningham snapped. He didn't see any sense in wasting time mincing words when the punishment was obvious.

Waters looked towards McGirth who nodded his agreement.

"Captain Cunningham is quite correct." He held up his index finger, thinking to himself before adding. "But I've no stomach for hanging a woman."

"I have!" Cunningham interjected.

"And she does deserve to hang," McGirth observed. "But since we are sending these supplies to the main army anyway, why not send her along and let our most gracious General, Lord Cornwallis, deal with her?"

"Why waste the time?" Cunningham said. "The damned rebels will call it a lynching no matter what we do! I say leave her kicking when we depart this place and have an end to it." He huffed and turned away dismissing the subject with a wave of his hand. "Do as you wish, it's no skin off my nose."

Waters looked to McGirth for guidance, not wanting to offend either of the partisan leaders.

"I say truss her up and send her to Cornwallis," McGirth said. "No sense in letting a spy cause problems between us. I don't care how pretty she is."[60]

Clearly relieved, Waters ordered the militiaman to return the woman to the house.

"Guard her well," he cautioned, "and give her some clothes to put on. But make sure there are no weapons concealed in them before you do."

Looking towards the militiaman who had identified Dicey and who was now standing off to one side leaning on his musket, he added, "You go with the drovers, make certain that she gets to Lord Cornwallis in one piece."

John stood to one side and watched sullenly as the young woman was led back into the house. "I can't believe how easily she pulled the wool over our eyes!" he complained to Hopkins, who shook his head and with a smirk said, "Like my pa always said, 'live and learn'."

Their duties ended, John and the rest of the Rangers mounted and rode ahead, leaving the remainder of the troops to follow with the slow-moving wagons and livestock. Behind them, the sky remained clear. Colonel Waters, too, had been concerned about signaling their position to the rebels each time they left a farmstead. On the porch of the house, the three abandoned children stared forlornly after the departing soldiers. The childlike faith that their absent parents would return for them was evident on each face. Childish faith not withstanding, Colonel McGirth had selected one of the elderly slave women to be left behind to tend to them until their parents returned. The owner's name did not appear on Colonel Waters's list. It was a hopeful sign for their future.

For the next six days they foraged their way across upper South Carolina, stripping farms of all available supplies, and executing parole violators and spies. Occasionally, they would put a dwelling to the torch, but more often they were left, stripped as bare as Mother Hubbard's Cupboard. It was a clear invitation for the rebels to replant and restock, so the King's army could be fed again from next year's harvest.

* * * *

By John's reckoning, it was Saturday, December 30, 1780. Tomorrow would see the end of the old year. He made a mental calculation to remember to mark its passing in some way. The men of the raiding party had spent the morning herding cattle and loading supplies onto wagons confiscated from two farms that local sympathizers had led them to. The rebel families watched sullenly as a year of hard work vanished before their eyes like a handful of dust thrown into the face of an angry wind. Shortly before noon, John and the other Rangers, preceding the column as skirmishers, halted in the yard of a small abandoned settlement to await the arrival of the main column. They found a well brimming with clear, fresh water, and an open pasture that stretched for over a hundred yards in any direction around the buildings. It would be a good place for the men to rest and eat their noon meal. The Cherokees had continued on to make certain that no rebel troops were laying in ambush ahead of them. Dismounting, John tied his reins to the hitching post in front of the store.

"Anyone know the name of this place?" he asked after giving the sturdy log structure a cursory inspection.

"It's called Hammond's Store," Hopkins said. "I saw the colonel mark it on his map this morning. Cunningham mentioned that it was a good place to lay over."

Hopkins dismounted stiffly. When his feet touched the ground, he winced and rubbed his lower back with both hands before slowly straightening with a groan. "I'm getting a might old for this much riding," he lamented. "Every joint in my body is stiff!" He looked around and located Dobbins, who stood to one side, smiling at his discomfort. "Check out the blacksmith shop! We may be able to have some of the horses shod. I noticed more than one limping along in the past few days."

Dobbins returned a few minutes later with the news that the entire settlement was deserted. Satisfied as to the safety of the area, they all sat in the shade of a large oak and lit their pipes. When the remainder of the raiders came into view, they were as dirty and exhausted looking as the Rangers. Two weeks of constant campaigning was rapidly wearing them down. They sat their horses listlessly, slump shouldered, and with bloodshot eyes.

Colonel Waters slid from his lathered mount and stared at the small cluster of buildings. "Looks like a good place to rest. Have you checked the area?"

"Yes, sir," Sergeant Hopkins assured him. "I've sent out men to the north and south and the Cherokees are riding out to the west. Your rear guard can tell us about the east."

The colonel nodded slowly.

"Good. We'll camp here until tomorrow. Have you checked out the smithy?"

Hopkins inclined his head in the direction of the building. "Yes, sir. No one in sight, but the tools and pig iron are there. I'm sure we have a few smiths among us who can re-shoe any mounts that need it."

Colonel McGirth and Captain Cunningham rode in thirty minutes later. Cunningham looked as tired as the men, but McGirth seemed ready to ride on. Having spent the last four years almost constantly in the saddle, he had become inured to the hardships. Still, an almost inaudible grunt escaped him as his feet touched the ground. He patted the Gray Goose affectionately on the neck before leading her to the trough, waiting for her to drink her fill before taking a long draught from his own Japanned[61] canteen. Wiping his lips, he looked around at the other men.

"I reckon you're planning on staying here for awhile, hey Thomas?" He used the colonel's Christian name, something that he rarely did.

"At least 'til tomorrow, maybe longer." He threw his head towards the east, where the herd of confiscated cattle was wandering untended about the clearing. "We'll send some men down to Ninety-Six with that livestock. That'll speed us up when we get started again."

McGirth jammed the cork stopper onto the spout of his canteen and hooked the corded strap over his saddle pommel. He remained silent for a moment, as if confused by the colonel's words.

"Should we stay put that long? The rebels have to be out looking for us. After all the damage that we've done…"

"Let 'em find us," Cunningham volunteered. "That's what Cornwallis wants isn't it? A fight?"

"But not here," Waters corrected him. He turned his attention to McGirth. "The men and animals need rest. We have a good well here and a blacksmith shop to boot. I'm thinkin' that any time spent here will be well worth it when we resume the march. Do you suspect trouble with the rebels?"

"No, but they're a slippery bunch. I do bow to your orders, however, and agree that a good rest is needed for the command." He looked at Sergeant Hopkins. "Have you scouted the area?"

"Yes, sir, I have men out everywhere except behind us, where you were. If you're satisfied that it's clear back there, I can guarantee that the men on the other three sides will warn us of any danger."

McGirth pointed to the store. "Let's make that our headquarters." He barked a string of quick orders to his lieutenants and sergeants, then led Gray Goose into the shade and stripped off her saddle. He began to curry her, talking to her as if she were a human instead of a horse.

Around the clearing militiamen began to imitate their commanders. Soon the entire command was lounging beside hastily lighted fires and preparing their midday meal. Some of the men spread their blankets under shade trees and took a nap. The herd of animals, dispersed casually around the buildings, cropped at the winter brown grass. Hopkins looked around with a dissatisfied expression on his face. He shook his head.

"I don't like this, John. I don't see the first sentry out to the east. I think I'll mention it to the colonel." He started across the yard, but was halted by the arrival of the Rangers returning from the north and south. The Cherokees were still out scouting to the west. Jacob and Nat sat their mounts between Hopkins and the store, waiting as the sergeant moved in their direction. Looking down at his superior, Jacob wiped sweat from his forehead with a linen rag. He removed his hat and wiped the rag through his matted hair, then quickly brushed the brim clean of dust and popped it back onto his head. "Not a soul in sight to the north," he said. "No tracks of any kind. When they skedaddled out of here, they didn't go that-a-way." Hopkins turned his attention to the two African Rangers who waited patiently to one side. They told him in halting English the same story. Hopkins glared at Nat.

"You sure you don't speak their gibberish?"

"I'm sure, sir. I can speak some Bantu that I picked up back in St. Augustine, but what their speakin', ain't it."

Hopkins gave him a doubtful look. "Ride over to the west side of this cleared area and set us up a camp. Looks like we'll be staying here 'til tomorrow." He turned to John and told him to go also. "I'll be over as soon as I speak to the colonel."

Thirty minutes later, the five Rangers sat beside a small fire, waiting for the water to boil in a battered copper pot. Their horses stood shoulder to shoulder on a picket line, saddles and blankets piled by their heads, ready for instant use. Hopkins guided his mount across the open area, heading towards them at a slow walk. His shoulders slumped with fatigue, red-rimmed eyes looked with disapproval across the disorderly camp. The men lay about, arms stacked at odd angles, completely unprepared for defense of any kind. He only hoped that the pickets would give ample warning if an enemy approached. He dismounted morosely and led his animal to the picket line.

From the east, the muffled report of a musket floated across the campsite. The Rangers sprang to their feet, heads turned towards the sound. Across the camp from them a line of mounted men in white jackets burst from the tree line. On each flank of the uniformed dragoons, several hundred rebel militia debouched from the woods in long wavering lines. The line slid to a halt and fired a volley into the startled ranks of the Loyalists who milled about the clearing in open-mouthed astonishment. At least thirty men dropped to the ground. Those nearest the rebel line immediately held their hands high in surrender. A rebel trumpet sounded, the notes drifting softly through the still air. Sabers flashed in the sunshine, dragoons spurred their chargers ahead with the cry of *"Tarlton's Quarter!"* barely heard at that distance.

The dragoons crashed into the ranks of the surrendered Loyalist. Hacking viciously with their sabers, they cut a bloody swath through the helpless men.

John spied Colonel McGirth. Hidden from the view of the rebels by the blacksmith shop as he raced towards the Rangers on the back of the Gray Goose. He was using his reins as a whip to urge the already fleet animal to greater speed. Behind him, Colonel Waters and Captain Cunningham raced to the north. Every Loyalist recognized the makings of a massacre; there would be no surrender for a defeated foe today.[62]

The Rangers reacted instinctively. Racing to their mounts they sprang onto bare backs and plunged into the tree line, crashing through the underbrush, ignoring the thorns and branches that whipped their faces and legs. Putting as much distance as possible between themselves and the rebel murderers was their only thought. To their rear, the rebels continued to shoot and hack at the unarmed men who raced helter-skelter in panicked flight.

John guided his mount through a narrow opening between two huge oak trees, almost coming unseated when the mare leapt a steep-sided gully hidden on the far side. She stumbled forward a few steps before regaining her footing, then raced on, emerging onto a well-traveled path leading to the west. John held onto her mane with a vise-like grip as the animal raced down the path at breakneck speed, almost colliding with Thunder's Child who was leading the group of Cherokee scouts back towards Hammond's Store. With tremendous effort, John managed to halt the excited mare alongside Thunder's Child. He pointed behind him and frantically shouted one of the few Cherokee words that he knew: "Tso tsi da na wa!" "Enemy!"[63]

When the warriors simply stared at him, he repeated the warning. Behind him, he could hear the rumbling of approaching riders. He steeled himself for a fight, then breathed a sigh of relief when he recognized Colonel McGirth and ten of his men racing towards them.

McGirth slowed, shouted a quick warning to the Cherokees, then raced away. John and the Cherokees followed him without hesitation.

John estimated that they had covered at least seven or eight miles before the partisans to his front slackened their pace. The inside of his breeches was soaked with lather from his straining mount. He knew that she wouldn't be able to continue moving at this pace much longer. They slowed their animals to a walk but didn't dare stop to rest, even for a few brief moments. Each time they stopped to listen, they could hear the drumming of hoof beats to their rear. Friends or foes? No one wanted to chance being caught by those white-coated dragoons and their flashing sabers. They continued their retreat, prodding their jaded mounts forward, seeking the safety that only distance could bring them. Late in the afternoon, John was finally able to bring his mount alongside Colonel McGirth.

"Where're we heading, colonel?" he asked. McGirth looked over at him and smiled when he recognized John.

"To the fort at Ninety-Six. It's only fifteen more miles, and most of that is through Loyalist country. I think that we'll make it safely. We'll be there tonight."

"How many do you think escaped back there?"

"If they all struck out like we did, without waiting too long, at least half, I would think."

John was stunned. Half! That meant that over 125 men had been lost. He rode on in silence.

Ten miles from Ninety-Six they were overtaken by Sergeant Hopkins and the other Rangers. They had lost no men, only equipment. Of the six Rangers, only Sergeant Hopkins still rode with a saddle. John almost wept when he recognized his comrades; the feeling that they had been lost had been weighing heavily on his mind as he rode along. Feeling secure at last, Colonel McGirth ordered the men to dismount and walk their horses for the next mile. Many of the animals were played out, and several were beginning to falter. Everyone complied willingly with the order. No one wanted to be stranded afoot and at the mercy of rebels with the sanctuary of a British fort so near at hand.

The dispirited party reached the safety of the fort an hour before the sun set. They immediately reported to Colonel Cruger, detailing the catastrophe. Little by little, in ones and twos, other survivors trickled in throughout the night. By morning, Colonel Waters and Captain Cunningham straggled in with four tired men. When the final count was completed two days later, only 60 survivors of the original 250 men were accounted for. It was January 1, 1781, a dismal beginning for a New Year.

Seventeen days later, at a place not far to the north called Hannah's Cowpens, a rebel army crushed Colonel Tarlton's British legion. When John and the other Rangers at Augusta heard the news of the defeat, they felt morose, fearing for the first time that their world may truly be starting to unravel.

Chapter 15

Augusta, Georgia
Tuesday, April 10, 1781

John followed Ranger Captain Alexander Wylly[64] through the gates of Fort Galphin.[65] The six Rangers from Long Swamp had been transferred to Captain Wylly's company after they had straggled back into Augusta following the debacle at Hammond's store. Now they were ordered to escort that officer to a council being held at Little Chota. Riding up the Middle Cherokee Trading Path, they would stop at Long Swamp for one night before moving northeast to attend the council.

It had been eight months since John had last seen Grainy and the children; he wondered what his newest son, Daniel, already seven months old, would look like. Would he come to this stranger who was his father? Or would he cry out and shy away when he reached out for him?

Riding directly behind the captain, John studied the officer he had known since the siege of Savannah. He remembered watching him and his fellow officers while away the hours of bombardments, playing games of Whist inside their bombproof. The captain was a middle-aged man about the same age as Hopkins. He had served in the Georgia Rangers, a provincial corps that patrolled the frontiers of the province before the war had broken out. Like Colonel Brown, the captain had remained loyal to the Crown when the rebellion had begun. He seemed a capable, even-tempered man who took his job seriously, along with the knowledge that if this war was lost, he lost everything that he had spent a lifetime building.

John looked constantly to his right and left as he rode, always wary now of ambush. Behind him, the other Rangers drove a herd of heavily laden packhorses along the narrow trail. All of the animals were piled with presents destined for the chiefs and warriors who were expected to attend the council at Little Chota. He turned in his saddle to check on Jacob, who, with a jaunty attitude, prodded the animals along. He had already seen his new son and had sired another, which Judith said would arrive sometime in August of this year. Their eyes met; Jacob grinned, his teeth unusually brilliant behind the dusty mask of his face. John took a deep breath, exhaled it briskly, and smiled to himself. He would not miss the world they were leaving behind.

That night, as they sat around the fire savoring a meal of venison, the discussion turned to the military and political situation in the southern colonies. Every day seemed to herald some new catastrophe for the British forces. Battles were fought with the rebels, and won, only to be followed by a withdrawal back into the safety of Charleston or Savannah. Post after post was abandoned by the British and their Loyalist allies; they simply lacked the manpower to garrison them. Only Augusta and Ninety-Six still remained in British hands, two lonely symbols of the King's declining power in the backcountry.[66]

"Do you still feel confident that we're winning this war?" Dobbins asked the captain. It was the most important question on everyone's mind.

The captain sat back, seeming to digest the question along with his meal. He looked up at the stars overhead, which shined like a brilliantly luminous tapestry woven onto the cloudless sky. With a sigh, he looked down and studied Dobbins for some time before answering.

"I do," he said. He gave the men time to think about this answer before continuing. "The rebels are slowly taking control of the hinterland, that's true. We've all heard about the abandoning of the posts across South Carolina. But what do the rebels gain by that if we still hold the ports and control the sea lanes?" He paused to give them time to form a mental map in their minds. "What would happen if we simply pulled back to the coast and let them wither on the vine? No trade, no money, no *anything* coming to them from the outside. It doesn't take much imagination to know that they wouldn't last a year without outside contact." He reached inside his shirt and pulled out a small leather pouch. Carefully loosening the drawstring, he produced an ornately carved scrimshaw pipe. Without getting up, he reached into his saddlebag and fished out a bag of tobacco. He filled his own pipe, then offered some to the other men who politely declined. They all had their own; no Ranger would ride into the wilderness unprepared. They watched him light his pipe and take a few meditative puffs. Across from him, Hopkins and Dobbins filled their own pipes. Wylly exhaled a fragrant puff of tobacco smoke, then looked directly at John.

"What are your thoughts on the subject, corporal?" John was somewhat taken aback, unused to officers asking his opinion. He cleared his throat and looked nervously for encouragement from the other Rangers. They kept their eyes fixed on him, waiting to see what kind of an answer he would come up with. He shrugged noncommittally.

"I don't rightly know. All I can say is that I've been a Ranger for just over two years. In that time I've only been in one fight that we lost, Hammond's

Store. It seems queer to me that we continue to whip the rebels at almost every turn, and still we sit here asking if we're losing."

Wylly laughed like a schoolmaster who had led a student to a difficult conclusion.

"There you have it! It's a clear case of win the battles, but lose the war!"

John's mouth dropped. "Surely you don't think that we're actually losing?" The idea was too preposterous for him to grasp.

Wylly shook his head. "I don't know. But we're only seeing a small part of the strategy being played out around us. Up in the northern colonies, they fight hardly at all. On the sea, England reigns supreme, and Canada is still firmly in England's grasp. Even here in the south, the rebels have only managed a few minor victories in some isolated backwoods pastures. I feel we will triumph in the end, but I still rely on the old axiom, *Hope for the best, plan for the worst.* That's the best answer that I can give you."

John lay awake long after the other men were snoring. The thought that there was even a slight chance of England being defeated gnawed at his guts like a ravenous wolf. What if it *was* to come about? What would happen to him? To his family? Everything they had worked for would be lost forever. Where would they go? What would they do?

* * * *

Grainy was kneeling in front of the hearth with her back to the door when John stepped into their cabin and called her name. Startled, she jumped to her feet and spun to face him. As she leapt into his arms with an elated shout, tears flowed in rivulets down her cheeks. Unheeded in his crib, nine-month-old Daniel wailed, upset by the cries of his mother. John felt his knees start to buckle as she guided him to the well-used bench alongside their table. They sat together, entwined in each other arms, oblivious to the world. Through the open door of the cabin, Simpson and Lynn Celia burst into the room and bounded onto the bench beside their father. Their eyes looked up into his face with the unabashed adoration usually reserved for only the greatest of men. He hugged and kissed them both, repeatedly. He gave Grainy's hand a tender squeeze.

"Isn't it time that you introduced me to my new son?"

She led him to the crib where the red-faced and squalling child leered angrily out at his violated world. He quieted instantly at his mother's touch. She picked the infant up and held him cradled in one arm, her other arm she draped around her husband's waist, unwilling to part from his touch. The child nestled the side of his head against her neck, studying the strange, scruffy man with unblinking blue eyes. His thumb went automatically to his mouth. John saw his hands tighten, tiny fingers twisting into Grainy's blouse for a more secure hold when he reached for him.

"Now, now, darlin'," she cooed to the child. "It's time you met your Da. Go on now." She handed him to John, gently disengaging his fingers one at a time to free herself from his tiny clutches. He looked up at John, face contorted as if they had forced a sour crabapple into his mouth, and burst out bawling fiercely. With the most doleful look imaginable, he reached out pleadingly to his mother, whimpering pitifully. He wailed even louder when she refused to take him. Looking at John's face, Grainy suddenly burst out laughing.

"Don't take it so hard, John!" she said. "After all, he's never seen you before. When he gets used to you, he'll love you as much as these other two angels do. Just give him some time."

The two older children, unable to restrain themselves, jumped from the bench and latched onto his legs. John managed to sit, patiently watching his wife as she prepared their noon meal. Each of his legs remained firmly imprisoned by tiny arms while the baby continued crying woefully on his lap. Across the breezeway he could hear the feminine laughter of Judith, together with the lower tones of Jacob's voice, and the delighted squeals of their son as Jacob playfully tossed him in the air.

That night as they lay in each others arms, John related his adventures to Grainy while she filled him in on the day-to-day activities of her life. She held on to him with such fierce passion when he told her he must leave in the morning, that he thought she might refuse to be parted from him again. As the night grew quieter, they could hear faint sounds drifting across the breezeway from Judith and Jacob's cabin.

Grainy snickered quietly and whispered into John's ear. "They fairly drove me wild! Carrying on like that while Jacob was on parole. And you so far away!"

"This war won't last forever," he said hopefully. "Then we'll never be apart again." He kissed her and lay back, absentmindedly stroking her dark tresses as she lay beside him, her head resting lightly on his chest and her leg thrown across his body, unconsciously attempting to trap him forever in this gentler, more peaceful side of their lives. He felt the warm moistness of a tear drop onto his chest.

"What's wrong, Grainy?"

She propped herself up on one elbow and looked sadly into his face. "What happens to us if we lose this war?"

The suddenness of the question caught John by surprise, he hesitated, unsure of his answer. He took in a deep breath and held it for only a moment before exhaling sharply. "Life will go on, I suppose."

"I know now how an orphan must feel," Grainy said. "It seems as if my whole life has been erased." Her mouth twisted, revealing an inner anguish.

"I loved our old life with a passion! Kissing you goodbye in the morning and seeing you off to the mill, then lying in your arms every night, safe and secure. It was a comforting thing to know that you were right there, at hand, someone I could turn to, someone to help solve any problem. My parents and friends all lived just a stone's throw down the road, just where they had always lived. I could visit them any time. If I needed someone to ride into town with me, or someone to just sit and sip tea in the afternoon when I was feeling a little blue, someone was always there. And I knew exactly who that someone would be, the people that I had known all of my life. But now!" She shook her head as the tears increased, sliding down her cheeks in fast flowing rivulets. "My whole world is gone! The people that I knew are either dead or scattered to the ends of the Earth - just like us."

She paused and looked away, studying the rough-hewn logs of the cabin's walls. "I have a confession to make." She inhaled sharply and wiped at her tears before continuing, "I am frightened to death! What will become of me if anything happens to you? I have no one in the entire world except for you and the handful of people left in my life. I couldn't live like that woman in Savannah, the one that married Judith's brother. Going from man to man, hoping each will be as good as the last, but knowing that he won't, always struggling to feed the children and having to rely on the generosity of strangers." She sniffed and shook her head morosely from side to side. "Cast adrift in a sea of strangers," she murmured.

Her voice sounded far away, heavy with melancholy. She looked around wistfully at the cabin, not really seeing it. "I want a family again! Brothers, sisters, mother, father, aunts, uncles, cousins—nieces and nephews that I can watch grow. I want the peace of mind that being a part of something like that gives a person. Until this happened, I had never been more that twenty miles from home; now I'm at the ends of the earth. I feel so lost! Will we ever find our way home?" She dropped her head onto his chest. "I know this will sound selfish, but I think that it's the women who suffer in this war." She placed her fingers lightly on his lips to still his response. "When a man dies, his troubles are over. It's the woman he leaves behind who has the hardest job, the job full of tears, and worry, and despair. Why can't it be like it was before this ungodly war started? Why did the rebels have to completely destroy my world in order to build one of their own?" She pounded on his chest in frustration. "What have I ever done to deserve this? All I want … is to go home!" She tilted her head and looked deeply into his eyes, a lonely, longing look. "Promise me that one day you'll take me home. Please! I need a dream to cling to, just like everyone else."

Long after she'd fallen asleep, he lay there, her questions ringing in his mind as her shallow breaths feathered the fine hair on his chest. His thoughts wandered fitfully. He wondered just when this war would be over, and what would its outcome be? Would they ever, truly, go home?

Chapter 16

Little Chota, Nacoochee Valley
Thursday, April 26,1781

John stood respectfully along the outer wall of the council house, alongside the other Rangers, all of whom were immaculately dressed in new green jackets issued to them from the stores of Fort Grierson for just this occasion. Their necks were wrapped with spotless white stocks; highly polished, buckled shoes adorned their feet. Their entire countenance was designed to impress the assembled Cherokees with the wealth and power of Great Britain.

In front of them, Lieutenant Wylly sat facing a collection of angry Cherokee headmen. Sergeant Hopkins, serving as interpreter, sat on one side, newly commissioned Lieutenant Blackstone Mullis sat on the other. The negotiations were not going well for the British. Like John, the Cherokees were coming to realize that their world was quickly unraveling. Only yesterday, Wylly had received a message from Colonel Brown warning that the large numbers of rebels roaming about in the neighborhood of Augusta were growing bolder by the day, and that he may well stand in need of Indian allies at any moment. When the headmen began to invent excuses for not rushing to the aid of the English King, Wylly reminded them that there was a large store of provisions sitting in the storehouse at Fort Grierson. Provisions that were earmarked for them, provisions that the Cherokees were in desperate need of if they were to defend themselves against the depredations of American raiders pouring into their lands from the north, east, and west.

But the Cherokees were in no mood to be bought off. Several of the chiefs attending the council openly accused Colonel Brown of leading them to destruction. Rebels from Kentucky, led by John Sevier, had destroyed over a dozen Cherokee towns. The people of those villages were still scattered throughout the mountains and valleys to the north and northwest, starving, searching for safer places to rebuild their homes. Chief Tassel openly confessed that he had sent peace emissaries to the Americans, while another headman, the Terrapin, scowled at the Rangers and accused them of being the cause of all of the vast troubles now besetting his nation. The Ranger officer harangued them for hours, reminding them of how the English King had kept the American squatters from crossing the mountains into their hunting lands with his Proclamation of 1763. He also warned them that if the British were forced to leave the land, the Cherokees would be alone, fighting against an ever-increasing tide of settlers who, if not for the war, would already be leveling the forest and chasing away the game. The American's had nothing but contempt for the tribes—Cherokee, Creek, Chickasaw, Choctaw, Seminole, or Shawnee. All Indians were seen as obstructions to the westward flow of land-hungry settlers. How long would the Cherokee remain in these mountains? Without the British and their Loyalist allies they would be slowly forced westward by treaty after treaty until, one day, they would stand with their toes in the western ocean, looking over their shoulder at the land that had once been theirs. What would become of them then?

The lieutenant raised his voice in one final expulsion of frustration. Were they blind, or just simply so browbeaten by the Americans that they refused to see the truth?

The Terrapin jumped to his feet. "Fight the Americans if you must! But I swear to you, here and now, if your actions bring anymore sorrow to the Cherokee people, I will hand you over to them!" He spun angrily on his heels and stalked into the darkness. As if waiting for this signal, the council evaporated without any clear indication of what aid could be expected from the Cherokees.

Frustrated, but still confident, Wylly confided his plans for the immediate future to the Rangers. He ordered John and Jacob to return to Long Swamp with the two Africans. Hopkins, along with Dobbins and Nat, were told to prepare to follow him northward, where he would continue his efforts to rally the Cherokees living in the Overhill towns and encourage them to send support to Colonel Brown and the English King.

* * * *

John and Jacob spent an idyllic interlude with their wives and families at Long Swamp. John reveled in the planting of the fields. Working side-by-side with Grainy, he forgot his concerns for their future as they planted squash, beans, corn, flax, and pumpkins. All of his spare time was spent shaping new boards with which to build the bed that he had begun the year before. The only duty that was required of him as a soldier was to issue stores from the King's supplies to needy Indians and meticulously record their dispersal in Sergeant Hopkins's ledger.

On the evening of May twentieth, Nat appeared at the door of the double cabin. He handed a sealed letter to John. "Orders from Captain Wylly," was his only explanation.

While John sat in the breezeway, Grainy led Nat into the cabin and ladled a hearty helping of stew onto a wooden trencher. He ate quickly and silently, shoveling the food into his mouth as if he feared it would evaporate if left exposed on the plate too long. He washed down his meal with a mug of hot buttered rum. After wiping the foam from his lips, he described his travels with Captain Wylly and Sergeant Hopkins, telling of their trek through the high mountains to the north and of a short skirmish between the Rangers and a party of rebel hunters from the Watuga settlements. "I already know what that says." He pointed to the letter.

John nodded. "He's not having much luck. The Cherokees are as tired of this war as we are."

Grainy looked at him with concern. "It's as bad as you say then?"

John nodded. He had never expressed his doubts openly to his men, yet everyone knew that he was beginning to lose faith in winning this war any time soon ... as were they. Hearing a knock on the door, John rose and opened it. Sambo and Mambo stood outside in the breezeway. They looked around, spotted Nat, and stepped into the room. Seley Smith, leading her daughter by the hand, followed them in. She had returned with them from Little Chota, after *jumping the broom* with Sambo. The expressions on their faces looked strained, as if they expected bad news. The men asked questions in broken English mixed with their native dialect, which Seley interpreted as closely as she could, into the King's English. They all breathed a sigh of relief when they were told that, other than the reluctance of some of the Cherokee to join them, all was well.

For the next week, life in the settlement returned to its normal, easy-flowing rhythm. John and the other Rangers hunted and fished in the mornings, then grabbed hoes and cultivated the fields in the evenings. While they worked in the fields, the women prepared supper. They often looked towards the trail leading to the east as if expecting a pale rider to appear. When that dreaded visitor never came, they slowly shed the habit, living in the moment, happy, contented.

During the heat of the afternoon, John followed Grainy and the children to their swimming hole on the Etowah River, where they bathed in the cool water beneath the stately oaks. Slowly, as John returned to his old self, confidence in their future returned. They made plans for their return to Ninety-Six after the war was won.

One sultry afternoon, lying side-by-side on a large boulder in the river, Grainy finagled a promise from John that their new home would contain a large bathtub. She confided in him that after almost two years of living among the Cherokee and taking daily baths in the river, she would never again feel completely refreshed without one. John laughed, reminding her of the old and widely accepted notion that bathing strips away the protective body oils and contributes to disease. Grainy turned onto her side and raised herself to one elbow to see over the baby, who lay sleeping contentedly between them.

"You don't really believe that, do you?" she asked him seriously. "Just look around at the Indians. They all seem much healthier than the people in the towns back east."

"I've seen plenty of sick Indians. Who's to say?"

Grainy sat up, a pout forming on her lips. "All I can say is that this is one family that is going to stay washed if I have anything to say about it! Let's head back to the cabin, it's almost time for me to start cooking those fat little rabbits that you brought in this morning."

They ambled towards their home, hand-in-hand, with Daniel snoring drunkenly on his father's shoulder. The other two children, laughing and cavorting, followed happily in their footsteps.

John suddenly stopped. "Now who could that be?" he thought aloud. Handing Daniel to Grainy, he hurried across the yard to confront the rider who sat in the shade behind the cabin. The man saw him coming, rose slowly to his feet, and waited, holding the reins of his mount loosely in his hand. He wore a hunting frock and Indian leggings over linen trousers.

"Corporal Stokes?" he asked when John came close enough.

John nodded. "Yes."

The man extended his hand. "I'm Scott Roquemore, a militiaman from north of Augusta. I have an urgent message for the commander of this post. The Indians told me that's you."

John smiled. He had never thought of himself as commander of anything, but in the absence of the captain and sergeant the honor had devolved onto him. He smiled. "I guess that's right."

"Good." The man removed his hat, swept sweaty red hair back from his face, and pulled a damp message from inside the crown. He handed it to John.

"Bad news. Augusta is under siege, again."

John slipped his finger beneath the wax seal and flipped the letter open. He read it quickly.

"Please, go on in. My wife will fix you a bite to eat," John said. He refolded the paper neatly and patted Roquemore's horse. "Mind if I borrow this animal for a few minutes? I need to round up my men, and you look like you're ridden out."

After a slight hesitation, the militiaman acquiesced. John felt sympathy for the hard choice that he had asked the young man to make. A man's horse, was a man's horse after all. Often his life depended on its condition. It was rarely loaned out to anyone.

John returned within thirty minutes. He tossed his hat onto their bed, then sat to eat.

"He tells me that it's bad news," Grainy said with a slight movement of her head to indicate their visitor. John nodded as he continued to chew. He finished eating in silence, finishing off his meal by wiping the pewter plate clean of gravy with a biscuit from Grainy's Dutch Oven. He took a long drink of fresh milk to wash down the meal, then slammed the wooden cup onto the tabletop. Daniel jumped, startled at the sound, and began to cry. Casting her husband a rare, hostile look, Grainy moved to comfort the child. John combed his hair back with his fingers.

"I'm sorry. I'm losing patience with the damned rebels! They just keep stirring up trouble." He looked at his wife apologetically, then turned his attention to their guest.

"Please accept my apologies for that unwarranted outburst."

Their young visitor nodded. John looked at Grainy. "The rebels have laid siege to Augusta—again! I'll be leaving first thing in the morning. I've already sent Nat around to tell the warriors to prepare for a quick journey." He gave his wife a questioning look. "Any idea where Jacob and Judith are?"

"Probably in the village, at The Traveler's. Their baby has been fussy with the croup lately."

John nodded. The Traveler was a member of the Blue Holly Clan, the keepers of children's medicine. It was a logical place for them to go in the absence of any British doctors.

"I'll send Simpson over to get him," Grainy volunteered. She walked out into the breezeway and called to her son. The four year old came bounding out of the trees that lined the riverbank behind the cabin. He rushed off, strutting like a tom turkey at having been assigned such an important mission.

"We'll be leaving the first thing tomorrow," John said as soon as the other Rangers had assembled. "We're to take as many of the Cherokees as we can get to the aid of Colonel Brown." He shook his head dejectedly. "They've already been under siege for five days. I just hope that we're not too late to help!" He threw up his hands and shook his head, the gesture clearly indicated how little he respected the rebels' judgment.

A long silence permeated the room. The message weighed heavily on all of them. Here they had been, enjoying their families while their comrades fought and died, and waited on them to come to their aid. It was a guilty feeling that no one enjoyed. Jacob shook his head and looked at the floor.

John dispatched Robin to guide Jacob, backed up by the warlike visages of Sambo and Mambo, to locate Dragging Canoe, the famous war leader of the Cherokee's anti-American, Chickamauga faction. Dragging Canoe had sent aid to the British during the first siege a year ago. Colonel Brown's message beseeched him to do so once again.

Nat was sent galloping to the north to apprise Captain Wylly of the situation and inform him that John would be heading to Augusta with twenty warriors, all that were available and willing from Long Swamp Village.

Chapter 17

Outside Augusta, Georgia
Thursday, May 27, 1781

John led his mount forward. The hooves of the horse, muffled by strips of buckskin, made soft, almost inaudible noises in the loose, sandy soil of the Augusta hills. To his rear, the Cherokees glided like feathered wraiths through the night. They were now so near to the enemy that even the mosquitoes, feeding voraciously on the exposed skin of their necks and hands, were ignored. The sound of a single slap was certain to betray them. It would be sunup in less than an hour. Musket and rifle fire, accompanied by the angry shouts of men, erupted directly ahead of them. The flashes of the weapons lit the sky like heat lightning, the discharges sounded like distant thunder.

Thunder's Child paused just below the crest of a low hill and signaled to the others to remain where they were. Handing his reins to John, he moved forward and crouched behind a large holly bush. Using its dark shadow for concealment, he studied the battlefield below for several minutes before he turned and motioned for John to join him.

John dismounted and ran stoop shouldered up the hill, dropping to the ground alongside Thunder's Child. The warrior stabbed his finger to the east where the muzzle flashes from a hundred weapons flickered in the half-light of early morning.

Below them, they could make out the rebel trenches that pinned Fort Cornwallis against the Savannah River. As they watched, the gates swung open and, with shouts of defiance, the garrison sallied out. The early morning sun, now barely visible above the eastern horizon, glinted sharply off the Ranger's bayonets as they charged across the open ground.

The rebels fired a ragged volley before jumping from their trenches and rushing forward to meet them. The two sides came together with a crash at the forward edge of the trenches; within seconds, the battled degenerated into a savage, hand-to-hand melee. Rebels swung the stocks of their muskets and rifles against the oncoming Loyalists who parried the blows and thrust back with deadly results.

Thunder's Child nudged John with his elbow and pointed downhill. As they watched, a Ranger mounted on a sleek bay raced through the ragged lines of men. The animal jumped the empty rebel trenches with ease and raced up the hillside, heading directly towards them. Two rebels turned and gave chase on foot. John pulled his musket to full cock and raised it to his shoulder. Thunder's Child stilled him with a touch of his hand and a shake of his head.

As the Ranger neared the crest of the hill, one of the rebels threw his musket to his shoulder and fired. The horse stumbled forward onto its knees, unseating the rider who sailed over its head. He landed face down on the sandy soil. Almost immediately, the Ranger pushed himself to his feet and continued running uphill with an awkward, stumbling gait. As he lurched past John and Thunder's Child's position, the second rebel fired. The ball struck the Ranger high in the back with a dull thunk! His shoulders arched as his feet continued to propel him forward for a few halting steps before he tripped and fell to the ground.

Behind him the two rebels continued forward, the first one loading his French-made musket as he ran. They scrambled past John and Thunder's Child without seeing them. Thunder's Child, waiting until the second rebel had moved past, leapt from his hiding place and onto the man's back, riding him to the ground before dispatching him with a single blow of his tomahawk. The other man, sensing the danger, spun around defensively as John leveled his musket and fired, killing him instantly.

John bounded through the gray swirl of powder smoke that hung in the still air and knelt by the wounded Ranger. The man was laying on his side, breathing fitfully, struggling for breath. It was obvious that he was dying. Despite his pain, when he saw John's uniform, his blue-tinted lips drew back in a smile, exposing bloody teeth. He tapped the front of his jacket, indicating that he wanted John to retrieve its contents. John pulled a sealed envelope from a small pocket sewn to the inside of the garment and held it up. The Ranger smiled, and struggled to speak even as he coughed up blood in ever increasing amounts. "To Colonel Cruger, Ninety-Six," he gasped. "It's up to you now, Ranger."

John looked at Thunder's Child and held up the letter.

"I'm taking this to Ninety-Six, understand?" The warrior nodded and John continued, "You take your warriors over the hill and join the battle. Tell Colonel Brown that one of his Rangers is taking his message to Colonel Cruger."

The warrior nodded again and signaled for John to go.

He rode north, putting as much distance between himself and the rebel army as possible before crossing the Savannah River and heading east.

Early on the morning of May 29, 1781, John neared the British-held fort at Ninety-Six, South Carolina. A few miles outside the town, he came to a small farmhouse with a single lantern burning in the window. Unsure of the local situation, he lay in hiding, spying on the inhabitants for over an hour while deciding on his next move. There were two women in the house, of that much he was certain, but they were strangers to him. He had hoped to see someone he knew to be a Tory sympathizer before taking the risk of exposing himself. Over to the east, a series of brilliant flashes lit the sky, followed a few seconds later by a succession of large explosions as an artillery duel erupted between the besieged Loyalists in the Star Fort at Ninety-Six and the besieging rebel army of General Nathaniel Greene.

Drawn by the sounds of the bombardment, the two women in the farmhouse stepped onto the front porch and stood staring at the flashes. From their conversation, John guessed they had menfolk in the Star Fort. He breathed a sigh of relief at encountering two Tory women.

They saw John as soon as he emerged from the trees, leading his jaded white mare across the dusty yard. Startled, the women retreated towards the door of the house before recognizing his uniform. They stopped and faced him.

The older of the two women was the first to speak. "This is not a healthy place for a King's man to be seen in the light of day," she said flatly. "But God must surely be looking out for you, young man." She introduced herself as Mrs. Ann DeLancey Cruger, the wife of the commander of the Loyalist forces in Ninety-Six. Gesturing towards the other woman, she identified her as simply Mrs. Greene, the wife of Major Greene, another Loyalist officer.

John removed his hat, holding it over his heart. He gave his name and regiment. After giving the two women time to absorb this information, he asked them about the situation at Ninety-Six.

Mrs. Cruger motioned him into the cabin, and then looked towards Mrs. Greene. "Would you mind taking the young man's horse to the stable?" she asked with an unmistakably northern accent.

John entered the small structure and, after waiting for Mrs. Cruger to take a seat, seated himself. He rose respectfully when Mrs. Greene returned from the stable.

"Are you familiar with Ninety-Six?" Mrs. Cruger asked. When John told her that he had lived no more that five miles away for most of his life, she smiled broadly. "Good! Here is the situation. We hold Holmes Fort to the west of town, you probably remember it as Williamson's Fort. We also hold the town, along with the Star Fort to the east of the town. Trenches connect both of the forts to the main town. Our people can move freely along them, but they're covered over and mighty shallow, so they must crawl through

them with great effort. The rebels are digging trenches to the north—
traverses I believe they're termed in military language—but elsewhere they
are spread out thin. Some of our black Pioneers have been able to slip in
and out of their ring fairly easily at night. If you're determined to get into
the fort, you can most likely slip in from the south side. When you leave the
wood line, make your way northward, across the open area to the vicinity of
the old town jail. Its been converted into a blockhouse. That's the way most
of our men get in there." She sat back, spine straight, and slapped her thigh
through her petticoats. "That's about the size of it. Now! As for you. This is
definitely not a safe place to linger. The rebel commander, General Greene,
has found out that we are staying here. He was kind enough to send a note
yesterday afternoon promising to leave us unmolested. He also promised to
post a guard sometime today to ensure our safety. You are from the area, is
there any place that you can hide until nightfall?"

John thought for a moment. Time was definitely a factor. At every outside
sound, the three plotters looked up, holding their breath until they were
certain the rebel guards were not approaching.

He looked at the concerned faces of the two women. "Do you think that
it would be safe to leave my mare here?"

"I believe so," Mrs. Cruger said after thinking a moment. "Why?"

"I will be much less conspicuous afoot, and I have grown somewhat
attached to her. I would be sorry to turn her loose and leave her for the first
rebel that comes along."

"Certainly. Leave her here. There's no way for the rebels to know how
long we've had her. What will you do?"

"I think that it would be best if you remained innocently ignorant of my
whereabouts. Suffice it to say, I intend to be inside Ninety-Six well before
this time tomorrow."

* * * *

Stealing through the wooded area south of the town, John used every
trick of woods craft that he had learned in his two years of service with the
Rangers. He took up his position midway between the Island Ford Road,
which ran past him on the right, and the ravine containing Spring Branch
on his left.

Lying just inside the tree line, relying on the shade and underbrush to
conceal him, he spent the day watching unobtrusively as the rebels threw
shovel full after shovel full of rich red dirt out of their burrows and onto
the ground in front of their trenches. A perpetual fog of red dust swirled
over their heads as they worked. Ever hour or so, a red-coated Loyalist,
using a long rifle, would shoot from between a screen of logs thrown up
along the top of the Star Fort's earthen walls. Often, the shot was followed

by indignant shouts from the rebel trenches as another sapper was killed or wounded. Rebel marksmen retaliated by returning fire and, for a few brief minutes, a battle raged at long range between the antagonists. Then the area briefly returned to a period of relative quiet, until another shot rang out and the whole deadly drama was repeated.

John dozed off and on, conserving his strength for the night. Each time a rider galloped along the roads to the east or west of him, he awoke and studied the situation until he was sure there was no danger before drifting off again into a light slumber. He judged it to be two in the morning when he began the slow, painstaking process of crawling across the open area that separated him from the questionable safety of the fort.

Periodically, one side or the other released a rocket that streaked skyward. Exploding with a dull thump, it briefly illuminated the area between the two armies with a flickering glow. Whenever that happened, John rolled into a ball, hoping to appear as nothing more than one stump among many in the shadowy night. Foot-by-foot, he eased himself forward, using his elbows to pull himself along. His face, blackened with a combination of grease and soot, felt hot and oily; the smell of the rancid combination assailed his senses. It took him three hours to cover the one-mile stretch of open area.

Having reached the stockade, he lay against the base of its wall, panting quietly, listening to the steady tramp of the sentries as they methodically made their way along the walkway above. The ominous sound of a musket being drawn to full cock startled him. Should he lie still, or cry out that he was a friend? His dilemma was solved when a voice hailed him softly from above.

"I don't know who you are, but we've been watching you for the past half hour. If you're a friend, now would be a most opportune time to give the watchword."

Panic seized him, he hadn't reckoned on that. He mentally chastised himself, of course they would ask that! Taking a deep breath, he looked up at the dark outlines spread along the top of the wall. The light of the stars behind them illuminated their silhouettes. John could make out four men, two with muskets aimed downward. He guessed the other two were the Sergeant and the Officer of the Guard.

John whispered to the phantoms hovering above him. "I'm a corporal of the King's Carolina Rangers, with an urgent message to Colonel Cruger, from Colonel Brown, besieged at Augusta." John held his breath. He could clearly hear two of the men discussing his fate in muted tones.

"We might as well let him work his way around the base of the stockade, to the capoiner[67] sir," he heard the sergeant say. There was a pause, then the same voice muttered, "One man under our guns can't do us any harm. If he is a spy, we can deal with him once we get him under cover."

John held his breath, awaiting his uncertain fate. He closed his eyes and took a deep breath to settle his nerves.

"Very well, sergeant," he heard the officer say. "Bring him to me as soon as he is secured."

"Yes, sir."

John's face broke into an involuntary grin. The sergeant leaned over the wall and began to speak. The sound of a rocket shooting skyward from the rebel works to the north interrupted him. "Duck!" he hissed quickly. All of the sentries disappeared behind the wall.

John lay still, barely daring to breathe as the rocket exploded, illuminating the night with a brilliant flash. Darkness returned. The soldiers' heads popped back into view at the top of the wall.

A disembodied voice floated to him through the log walls. "Crawl along the base of the wall to your left, until you come to the communication trench. I'll meet you there."

John almost jumped. The speaker had been standing directly behind him on the other side of the wall, no more than a foot away. Without speaking, he began to move. The sergeant followed his progress from inside the safety of the walls, speaking to him periodically, pumping him for information, or giving him warnings.

No more rockets were fired, although once a rebel musket barked defiantly in the night. John could hear the large caliber ball skipping along the ground towards him. It struck him violently on the back of his right thigh before it embedded itself in the log wall behind him with a loud whack! He let out a groan and rubbed the back of his leg through his trousers. The fabric felt torn. The sergeant waited, listening for a few moments.

"Are you hit?" he asked quietly.

"On the back of the leg, but it's not serious. Just feels like I've been kicked by a mule."

"I don't think they'll fire again. Probably didn't see you, either. Just the luck of fools that they hit anything," the sergeant whispered through the small spaces between the logs. "Most likely no more that a drunken rebel. A body would think that the bloody bastards had never fired a weapon before, the way they waste their powder shooting at nothing. That one will be tellin' his wife when he gets back home about how he assaulted the fort single-handedly. 'Course, that will be after he tucks his tail between his legs and slinks away like a beaten dog." The sergeant's voice sounded totally unconcerned as if he were on parade, not besieged by a thousand screaming rebels in a lonely frontier fort. "Come! Come! Let's hurry along now before a sober Yankee Doodle spots you!" he quipped energetically.

John smiled to himself, he already liked this sergeant.

* * * *

Colonel Cruger shook John's hand warmly after he finished reading Colonel Brown's dispatch. The colonel looked intensely into his eyes before he spoke. "I'm sorry that we can't send any aid to your commander. But, as you see, we are a bit preoccupied ourselves at the present time.

"Yes, sir," John agreed.

"In the meantime." He looked towards the red-coated sergeant standing just inside the door. "Take this man to the hospital and have his wound seen to."

The sergeant saluted stiffly and tapped John on his shoulder. John followed him out the door.

"We use the old Smith house for a hospital. It's just down the street a ways," the sergeant said. "I'll drop you off there and be on my way. By the bye, I'm Sergeant Grant Van Riper of Major Drummond's Company, New Jersey Volunteers. 'Course, the major is not with us at the moment, so Lieutenant Jenkins, him what you heard talking with me on the wall, is in command."

"Pleased to meet you Sergeant Van Riper," John said. "And thank the lieutenant when you see him for not having me shot."

The sergeant laughed, a short, ha! "My pleasure. By the bye, the men call me Sergeant Rip. Kind of speeds things up, you see?" Rip stopped and motioned towards a door. "This is where the hospital is. I'll go in and see that they treat you right. After that, you can stay here for tonight. I'll come by and pick you up tomorrow and introduce you to the other men in the company."

"Then, I'm not leaving any time soon?"

"No need to risk it. The colonel has already sent two messages to Colonel Brown, asking for *his* assistance. I'm sure your people already know anything that you could tell them."

"I would prefer to return to my own regiment." John felt his face flush.

"Now don't go gettin' your dander up!" Rip cautioned him. "If you're so all fired up to get out of here, you can talk to Lieutenant Jenkins in the mornin'."

John felt the anger flow out of him. He had no wish to stay angry with the sergeant.

"My apologies," he stammered.

They were met at the door by a harried orderly who ushered John to a table in a dark side-room. "Now you just crawl up on that table. Take off your jacket if you've a mind," he said, "and use it as a pillow. I'll send someone over to dress that wound in a few minutes."

John lay on the table; it felt surprisingly comfortable. He drifted off to sleep as he waited. His mind came awake slowly, conscious of someone's hands gently examining the wound. He looked over his shoulder; a soft feminine voice spoke to him.

"You just lay still for a few moments. I'll have you fixed up in no time." The woman's words were punctuated by a sharp pain.

"There! The ball barely grazed you, but it left a tiny splinter in the wound. You'll be fine!"

John jumped when she rubbed a rum-soaked rag across the open wound.

"That wasn't so bad, was it?" she asked, with a slight touch of humor in her voice. She bound the wound with a strip of linen cloth. When she finished, Sergeant Rip helped him to sit up and John looked into the face of his doctor for the first time. He recoiled with a start; his eyes widened in surprise.

"Maggie!" he exclaimed in wonder.

Maggie looked at him and smiled broadly. "Well if it isn't my old friend from Savannah! What kind of luck is this? Every time I get caught up in one of these blasted sieges, you turn up!" She laughed.

"I take it that you two know each other," Rip cut in.

"We met during the siege of Savannah two years ago," John said. He looked at Maggie, whose face, although drawn and tired, still retained the physical allure that had attracted Angus McDougal.

"Are Angus and Rory here?" he asked.

Maggie's face fell, transformed from gaiety to sadness in an instant. "Poor Angus. He fell last month at the battle around Guilford Courthouse. Rory begged me to stay and let him care for me, but I've just about had enough of armies." She looked around at the stale-smelling room. "Not that you can tell it just now!" She looked at him more seriously. "Even my babe is gone, taken by the smallpox a year ago."

"What about the other child?"

"Four years old now. He's out on one of the farms around here. I sent him off with a Loyalist woman just before the siege started."

"And yourself?"

"As you see me, more lines and wrinkles, but the same sorry specimen that you knew in Savannah."

"That sorry specimen in Savannah swept many a soldier off of his feet, as I recall."

"Soldiers are all fools, poor devils! And they drink!" She laughed. "Now, the good sergeant here tells me that you're to stay here for what's left of the night. Come with me. I'll find you a bed."

* * * *

Sergeant Rip arrived early the next morning. John was already awake and ready to move. He had eaten a Spartan breakfast and brushed his coat as best he could. Water, being the Achilles heel of the garrison, was much too precious to waste on washing. They left the hospital and crawled through the communication trench to the Star Fort, where John's request that he be allowed to return to his regiment, was flatly denied.

"I'm sorry," Lieutenant Jenkins told him, "but we simply can't afford to waste any men roaming the countryside. All available fighting men are needed here."

That settled, Sergeant Rip took him to the section of the fort held by the New Jersey Volunteers. John, as a corporal, was put in charge of three Loyalist soldiers, all privates from New Jersey. He laughed out loud when he recognized the three men who had fought alongside him during the first siege of Augusta. Extending his hand in greeting, he asked if they had seen any headless Indians running around lately. All three of the men erupted into loud guffaws. They said that they remembered him well and bragged to Sergeant Rip on his performance under fire.

The unofficial leader of his small group was a good-natured brawler with the unlikely name of Garbrant Garbrant. He was a giant of a man from Trenton, as was his brother, Peter Garbrant. The third member of the trio was slim, but feisty, Zebulon Cockifer. Zeb was the owner of one of the finest Pennsylvania rifles that John had ever seen. He was deadly accurate with it and took pleasure in taking well-aimed shots at the rebel sappers sweating in the trenches to their front. He was a ruthless man who, if possible, always aimed for the hips of his victims. His saying was, "A dead man's dead, but a wounded rebel needs carin' for." This was a new idea to John, but he had to agree that it did make a ruthless kind of sense. Zeb's only complaint was that with the rebels tucked down in the bottom of their trenches, he usually had nothing more than a head to draw a bead on. It troubled him when he couldn't make a rebel suffer. He did draw some pleasure by shooting the rebels who were, with great effort, attempting to build a Maham Tower just to the north of them. When it was complete, rebel marksmen would be able to shoot into the Star Fort from above. Zeb had sent more than one of the workers spiraling to the ground.

Both Garbrants were armed with the standard issue Long Land, Brown Bess. They preferred them to rifles because of the bayonet lug. They claimed that the New Jersey Volunteers were famous for their bayonet work and were eager to display their skill whenever the damned rebels quit *playing in the mud*, as they termed it, and decided to storm the fort.

John's group was assigned a small section of the fort's earthen wall to defend. They took turns, two watching while the other two rested. Of course, the Garbrants didn't consider themselves properly rested until they had taken advantage of at least one of their fellow soldiers in a *friendly* game of cards. John quickly came to realize that the other sergeants and corporals had taken this opportunity to pawn their most incorrigible men off onto an unsuspecting stranger. After reflection on this epiphany, he decided that when the Yankee Doodles did finally decide to make their move, these incorrigibles would be the best men of the lot to back him up. He smiled to himself, thinking of what a deadly combination he would command if only Mambo and Sambo were here.

For the next three days, life in the Star Fort continued with its deadly routine. Then, on June third, the rebels finished construction of their Maham Tower. From the top of the thirty-foot structure, riflemen set about picking off any red-coated Loyalist that dared to show his head above the parapet. Zeb managed to trade a few ineffectual shots with them, but without sufficient time to aim, he scored only one hit. The remainder of the time, the garrison hunkered down and kept their heads low.

Colonel Cruger had only three small cannons at the fort. In a desperate gamble, he ordered his inexperienced artillery men to heat the balls red hot and try to set the dreaded tower ablaze. As there was no oven in the Star Fort, John and his three men volunteered to heat the shot by baking them in the coals of several campfires built closely against the inside of the earthen wall. Letting the balls cook until they glowed, the gunners carried them to the small fieldpieces using a set of large tongs and dropped them down the barrels on top of heavy leather pads that had been inserted to keep the power from igniting prematurely. The moment they were ready, the artillerymen pushed the guns over the rim of the fort, took quick aim, and fired before jumping back behind the protective parapet. The cannons were yanked back down using chains previously attached to their tongues. In this way, the brave men who manned them were exposed for as little time as possible.

For the next twelve hours, the determined defenders continued their futile attempts to set the tower ablaze. From the far tree line, the rebel artillery answered back. Slowly, one by one, the small three-pounders were put out of action by the superior firepower of the rebel guns. By the next morning, all of the Loyalist cannons were silent. The tower, built of green logs, grinned down at them and stubbornly refused to burn.

That night, John and the other members of the New Jersey Volunteers, along with the troops of DeLancey's New York Brigade, formed a line and began passing sand bags up to a detail of stouthearted volunteers. Despite the constant sniping of the rebel marksmen in the tower, by the next morning they had managed to add three feet of height to the northern wall. Still, the rebels in the tower continued to sweep the interior of the fort with their deadly rifle fire. The officers conferred, and then ordered the militia and Pioneers to begin constructing a sixteen-foot-high wall across the inside of the fort. While the work inside the fort continued, the regular troops kept the rebels pinned down by peppering the front of the tower with heavy loads of buckshot, fired at regular intervals through loopholes in the sandbags.

Once the interior wall was completed, the defenders were able to move about inside the fort with some freedom, but one moment of inattention, or one inadvertent misstep, provoked an immediate response from the rebel marksmen.

Early one evening, John was visited by Sergeant Rip. The sergeant had been keeping an eye on John's group and was well pleased with what he had seen. "There is just one thing, however," he said. "I have noticed that each time we show ourselves to the enemy, they have a tendency to direct an inordinate amount of lead in your direction."

"You have?" John answered with a hint of surprise in his voice. "I had thought that it was just my imagination."

"No, I'm sorry to say, it's not." The sergeant held out a new uniform coat. It displayed the markings of the New Jersey Volunteers, red with royal blue cuffs and facings. "Here, put this on." Smiling at John's questioning look, he went on to explain. "You stand out like a sore thumb in that green uniform. You're the only regular soldier not wearing His Majesty's red coat. That's why they aim at you so often. I can hear them calling their shots now, *'That one in the green is mine!'*" He laughed knowingly.

John took an involuntary step backwards. "You're probably right sergeant. Still, I would feel like a deserter removing this uniform when my regiment is still fighting in Augusta."

Rip gave him a friendly smile. "I'm not asking you to throw your uniform away, just wear this one until the siege lifts." He held the jacket out. "For your own protection." When John continued to hesitate, he added offhandedly, "Don't force me to make this an order."

Reluctantly, John removed his familiar green tunic and donned the red and royal blue of the New Jersey Volunteers. Sergeant Rip held out his hand. "I'll leave your old jacket in the care of Miss Maggie, at the hospital. If that's agreeable to you."

Feeling as if he were betraying an old friend, John handed over his jacket. "I'll be wantin' that back as soon as this siege ends."

"I don't doubt that." The sergeant gave the jacket a shake. "You know where it'll be. By the way, those buff-colored breeches will still make you a target where everyone else is wearing white. Just shove your head over the wall and keep the important parts under cover."

The instant the sergeant departed, the men in John's group were on their feet, saluting him repeatedly and addressing him as your lordship and Sir John. The Garbrant brothers gave him a congratulatory slap on the back that almost knocked the wind out of him. After regaining his breath, John struck a haughty attitude and surveyed them arrogantly. "Back to work, you buggers!" he snapped at the rowdy group. "And give me a call when the tea and crumpets are ready!" He smiled as they returned to their duties. Looking down at the famous red jacket of the British Army that he now wore, he had to admit that he did feel a slight flush of pride at wearing it.

* * * *

That evening, the rebels resorted to another tactic. Several of their men crept through the ravine in which Spring Branch flowed and shot fire arrows over the walls of the stockade in an attempt to set the roofs of the buildings afire. From his post at the Star Fort, John watched the flaming arrows streak upward in a high arc before plunging downward onto the roofs of the houses. Wherever the arrows struck, they looked like small campfires burning with men and women scurrying around them, their bodies briefly outlined by the glow before the flames were extinguished, or the arrows were plucked from the shingles and tossed onto the dirt below. Once on the ground, a hundred feet stomped them into oblivion. Bright flashes of musket fire erupted from the walkways of the town's stockade as the sentries fired across the open ground and into the gully, hoping to hit one of the attackers whenever they appeared above the lip of the ravine. John's attention was diverted from the battle by a dark form moving along the base of the wall. He recognized Sergeant Rip's stocky outline immediately. John held his hand up to indicate his position.

"Get your men ready for a sortie," the sergeant barked. "Meet us over there in fifteen minutes." He jabbed his finger at the spot where a group of soldiers were already converging.

John and his men were ready in less than five minutes. Sergeant Rip smiled when he recognized them approaching in the darkness. He turned and said something in a low voice to Lieutenant Jenkins, and then looked back. His eyes were invisible in the black outline of his face, but John could feel them boring into him as he leaned on his musket, waiting for instructions.

Lieutenant Jenkins held up his pocket watch and canted it to one side to make out its face in the red glow of a distant fire. Behind him, the rebel bowmen had at last succeeded in igniting a wagon canvas with their arrows. It burned intensely for a few minutes, sending red flames and sparks trailing high into the night sky. The lieutenant stood, silently looking from man to man, mechanically winding his watch. When the last group of men arrived, he dropped the watch into a waistcoat pocket.

"We're making a sortie against the enemy trenches while they are distracted." He pointed to the west. "They're enjoying the fireworks over at the town. Follow me and your sergeants, we are going to disrupt their fatigue details with our bayonets. Don't shoot until we are discovered! When I blow three sharp notes on my signal whistle, we will fall back to the fort. Bring as many of their tools and equipment with us as you can carry. Destroy what's left. Any questions?"

"Prisoners?" someone asked.

"No prisoners," he answered promptly. "We've no room or water for them."

The men were divided into three groups. Lieutenant Jenkins would lead the first group, which would fall on the nearest trenches with their bayonets. The second group, commanded by a Sergeant Stagg, would move to the right of the first group once contact with the enemy had been made. Several of these men carried buckets of oil and tinderboxes to be used to burn the Maham Tower and any other items they could use to pile against it and set ablaze. John's group, led by Sergeant Van Riper, would keep the riflemen in the tower pinned down and counterattack any relief forces that started forward against them.

The company continued to wait. Periodically, the lieutenant would look to the east, awaiting the signal to attack. He said not a word. A signal whistle shrilled in the distance, the lieutenant straightened and motioned for the men who were kneeling around him to stand.

"Come along, lads," he said in little more than a whisper. "It's time to pay Mr. Greene a visit."

The soft tread of boots on the bare earth was the only sound they made as they moved forward. Only essential equipment had been brought along. Each man carried a cartridge box, his bayoneted weapon, and his ax. Tonight's work was strictly death. Ahead of them, they heard the shouts of rebels, surprised to find themselves face to face with British steel. Groans and screams rent the night as the first wave disappeared into the rebel trenches. Sergeant Rip formed his detachment into a firing line and bellowed the order to fire. Their muzzle blasts lit the night, musket balls slammed against the upper logs of the tower like hailstones. John could hear the men to his right and left loading rapidly. The metallic scraping of ramrods being withdrawn from barrels, accompanied by the loud clicks of hammers being drawn to full cock, sounded like some discordant symphony from Hell. Cocking his musket, he threw it to his shoulder, sighted on the tower, well above the heads of the Loyalist soldiers who were trying desperately to ignite the lower logs, and pulled the trigger. Almost before the sound of his shot died away, he was tearing a paper cartridge with his teeth. Other men worked frantically around him, he could feel the two Garbrants to his left and Zeb to his right loading as quickly as possible. He knew exactly what they were doing without looking at them. It seemed as if one or two of the muskets in their firing line were constantly being discharged as the men, each reloading at slightly different paces, fired their weapons at will.

A loud, "Ump!" alerted John that the soldier standing to the right of Zeb had been struck by a rebel ball. The soldier made no other sound, just turned and stumbled towards the rear, his right hand clasped tightly to his chest, his musket still firmly clutched in his left hand. John felt Zeb move to the right, closing the ranks. He sidestepped with him. To their left the entire line shifted instinctively inward, closing the gap.

The battle ended as suddenly as it began. Before John realized that he had fired eleven rounds at the enemy, he heard the three short blasts of the lieutenant's whistle. Sergeant Van Riper's line began backing slowly to the fort, firing steadily over the heads of their comrades as they climbed out of the devastated trenches and stumbled to the rear, encumbered by all manner of captured rebel equipment. Their muskets where slung over their shoulders; the tips of the bayonets protruding above their heads were dark, dripping with blood. Bullets whistled past them in the night and large caliber musket balls, fired at long range, skipped along the ground. The soldiers ignored them. Some of the men passing through their firing line were actually laughing, reveling in the deadly joke they had just played on the Yankee Doodles, giddy with having lived through it. Others looked as if they had eaten tainted meat. Lieutenant Jenkins, sword in hand, marched stiffly back to the fort, refusing to be hurried, openly displaying his complete contempt for the angry rebels howling unseen in the night. Behind them, the tower smoldered sullenly, its green wood refusing to burst into flame.

Throughout it all, John wanted desperately to shout '*hurry up!*' as they moved slowly back to the fort. He expected at any moment to feel the bite of one of the lead mosquitoes buzzing past his ears. His knees almost buckled when they finally regained the cover of the Star Fort. He sank to one knee and bent forward, taking deep breaths while collecting his thoughts and fighting to bring his frayed nerves under control.

"Are you hit, corporal?" Zeb touched his shoulder lightly. John shook his head without looking up.

"It's a funny thing," John said, his head bowed, "but I never thought of being killed the whole time we were fighting out there. Now that it's over, it frightens me to death, thinking about what would have become of my family if I had died."

Zeb shook his head in agreement. "It's a strange thing all right. I often feel the same way after a close call. It don't bother me none at the time, but it preys on me later. Churns my insides to mush."

John spit. Using his musket as a crutch, he pushed himself to his feet and slung the weapon over his shoulder.

"Thinking 'bout it won't help none. Let's get back to our position. Them damned rebels are likely to do anything after this."

In the days that followed, the other companies made sorties against the rebel lines. John and his three men settled in to wait out the enemy. Occasionally, Zeb would glimpse a target, throw his rifle to his shoulder, sight quickly, and hurry a careless rebel along to his meeting with St. Peter.

* * * *

June 8, 1781, day nineteen of the siege dawned hot and clear. Every defender dreaded the heat of the coming day. On the far western horizon, clouds were gathering, but no one expected them to produce rain. How they all wished for it! John looked up at the summit of the earthen wall above him. The two Garbrants were lying on their sides, facing each other with their heads just below the top of the protective sandbags. Periodically, Peter raised an old, battered hat on a stick; within seconds two or three rifle balls would zoom in from the rebel lines. Lowering the hat, he carefully examined it, and then raised a second stick with a dirty rag tied around it and slowly waved it back and forth, the number of oscillations signaling the number of new holes that had appeared in the hat. All along the wall the other soldiers watched with deadly interest, money-changing hands after each round of firing. John spied Lieutenant Jenkins sitting against the base of the wall, shaded by a makeshift awning. He had a folding desk perched atop his lap and was busy scribbling in his journal with a *porta crayon*[68]. Periodically, he looked upward, counted the rotations of the rag-wrapped stick, and shook his head. Bored, John sauntered over to speak with the officer.

"It's quiet this morning, sir," John said. "Would you have any objections to my visiting the hospital?"

"Are you ill?" Jenkins asked without looking up from his writing.

"No sir. I'm fine. They told me when they dressed this scratch on the back of my leg to come by after a few days. I haven't had an opportunity as of late."

The lieutenant looked up from his writing. "Oh! Corporal Stokes. Certainly, go ahead. Inform Sergeant Van Riper before you leave. And be back quickly, one never knows when these rebels will begin acting up."

Taking a step backwards, John threw the officer a stiff salute, spun about smartly, and marched off to inform Sergeant Rip of his errand.

John entered the makeshift hospital. He stood to one side of the door, out of the way of the busy orderlies scurrying about the room, and looked up through the missing roof into the blue sky overhead. In the brightly-lit interior, he had no trouble locating Maggie. She was working diligently, bent over the soldier who had been wounded in the chest during the last sortie. Methodically, Maggie removed the old dressing and threw it into a bucket of soiled linen. She gently prodded the wound with bloody fingertips.

"The bruising is yellowing, and the scab seems to be solid. That's a good sign," she murmured to herself as she worked. "I think you'll mend fine. The ball didn't penetrate the lung, just lodged itself in a rib." She paused and looked into the patient's face. "Have you always had such luck?" she asked him with a smile.

He groaned as she pressed a new dressing in place. "I don't feel lucky ma'am. It hurts something fierce."

"That's just the shock to the skin. It'll fade quick enough."

Her task completed, she turned to leave, almost colliding with John who was standing silently to one side, watching over her shoulder as she worked.

"Well good day to you, corporal!" she said lightheartedly. "To what do I owe this honor?" John followed her as she walked across the room to a cloth covered table. She carefully wiped down the instruments laid out in a line on top of it, inspecting each one critically before returning it to a box of surgical instruments beside her.

"You told me to come by to have my wound checked on. Here I am."

"To be sure. Come over here and lay face down on the table. I'll take a quick look at it. No sense in bothering the doctor."

John did as he was told. He lay quietly while Maggie removed the dirty bandage and tossed it into a nearby hamper. She prodded the wound gently and quickly pronounced it almost healed.

"It's a wonder it didn't fester with all this dirt in the bandages," she commented dryly as she wiped it clean. "I think it will be fine to leave it open to the air, provided you stop wallowing around in the dirt like a pig!" She shook her head and made a ticking sound with her tongue against the roof of her mouth.

"It don't look like there's much chance of that any time soon." he replied, slightly piqued at her tone. He let out a huff. "How have you been?" he asked, having grown tired of waiting for her to inquire about him.

"Well enough," she replied. They both remained quiet, unsure of what to say next.

"That's good," John said, breaking the awkward silence. Unable to think of anything else to add, he said slowly, "Thank you. I'll be getting back to my post now."

He hopped from the table onto the floor and shouldered his musket.

"Would you mind if I walked with you a ways?" Maggie asked as he moved towards the door. "I need some fresh air." She grinned playfully and looked up at the bare rafters. "As you can see, we have an abundance of sunshine!"

John grinned sheepishly. "Come on. I was hoping that I could talk to you for awhile. It gets mighty droll being around nothing but strangers, day in and day out.

"I can empathize with that! I haven't been around anyone that I really know for almost three years!"

John held the door for her as she stepped out of the building and into a beautiful June morning. Despite the warm day, Maggie had thrown a shawl around her shoulders; she held it clasped tightly with one hand as they walked.

"Have you been in any danger?" She laughed suddenly at the absurdity of the question, then added a quick, "Other than being besieged by a swarm of angry rebels intent on murdering all of us in our beds, I mean."

John jerked his thumb over his shoulder in the direction of the hospital. "I was with that patient you were tending to when he was wounded a few days ago. But since then, my existence has remained fairly mundane. The same for you, I hope?"

"Other than the fire arrows. I suppose you've noticed that Colonel Cruger has ordered all of the roofs in the town removed.

"Well, I may have noticed some slight change to the town since the last time that I visited." They both laughed. The other people in the streets stared at their outburst with questioning looks. They ignored them. It felt strange to be laughing in their present predicament, but it was refreshing.

They walked slowly along, John answering questions about Judith, the sister-in-law that Maggie had never met, and her child. Maggie studied him for a moment.

"What is it?" John asked. It was very similar to the way Grainy looked at him when she was about to ask him for something that he may not approve of.

Maggie shrugged her shoulders. "Nothing, just thinking." They approached the entrance to the communication trench in silence.

John said, mainly to himself, "I'm not looking forward to that crawl. It's mighty hard on the knees."

Maggie opened her mouth to speak, then shut it. She turned slightly and held her head at an angle trying to pick out a new sound. It was faintly audible. John listened with her. All along the stockade walls the sentries anxiously studied the road that led to Augusta.

"That's drums. Military drums!" John said.

They both scampered to the nearest ladder and quickly ascended onto the walkway above, where they joined the sentries who peered curiously to the west. Other soldiers were climbing up and shimmying around them on the way to their posts. Down below, the women in the town began to step out of their doors, wondering what was happening. One of them, a well-rounded housewife, waddled over to the base of the wall and shouted up at John.

"What is it corporal? More rebels, or some of our men?"

"Can't tell yet, but it's military of some type."

The rumble of the drums grew steadily louder. The soldiers lining the walls craned their necks to get a glimpse of whatever group was moving their way. Was it deliverance, or more enemies?

John looked quickly at Maggie. "You best get down. There's liable to be shooting at any time."

Maggie shook her head saucily. "When there is, I'll go down! You just make sure your powder's dry."

John shrugged, defeated in his attempt at chivalry. He turned back to the sound of the drums, but not before flipping his frizzen forward and checking the priming in the pan.

"It's rebels!" one of the soldiers shouted; he pointed to a rider emerging from the trees. He was wearing a blue and buff uniform. A collective groan of disappointment escaped from the Loyalists.

"Wait, look!" another shouted. "What's that flag they're flying? Why, it's reversed!"

John's heart leapt to his throat as the breeze caught the regimental flag of the King's Carolina Rangers, reversed on its staff and carried behind the drummers. It was an insulting gesture. Tears threatened to seep from the corners of his eyes as he saw the column of men appear, marching four abreast. They were wearing green uniform jackets with red collars and cuffs, the uniform of the Rangers! John's knees weakened, he reached out, holding onto the sharpened point of one of the logs to steady himself. Along the wall everyone stood, staring in silence as rank after rank of prisoners emerged into the open. They drug their feet wearily after the long march from Augusta. Suddenly, John turned to Maggie.

"Where is my uniform coat?" he asked quickly.

"Down there." She pointed to the hospital.

"Go get it, I've got to let them know that not all of us are taken!"

Maggie scurried down the ladder and raced to the hospital. She was back within minutes, carrying John's coat in her hand. He quickly stripped off his red coat, donned the Ranger uniform, and jumped onto the top of the parapet. Several of the soldiers reached out and held his legs, steadying him as he raised both arms and bellowed at the top of his voice.

"Rangers…!"

He waved his hands over his head to gain their attention. One of the men saw him, poked the man in line beside him, and pointed in the direction of the stockade. The other Rangers slowly turned their heads. Recognizing him as one of their own, they swept off their hats and gave a loud whoop of greeting. Feet that only a moment before had been dragging in despair suddenly came to life. Their steps grew stronger, even jaunty as they continued to yell and wave their hats in encouragement to the defenders of Ninety-Six. The guards spurred their horses up and down the line of prisoners, yelling harsh epitaphs and beating the cheering soldiers with the flats of their swords.

"What a damned dastardly thing to do!" a voice behind him snapped.

John looked down. Colonel Cruger had ascended to the wall and stood looking out at the procession. His face was stern, he was not pleased with the spectacle that the rebels were putting on.

"If they think that this is going to dishearten us, they have another thing coming!" He looked up at John. "Corporal! You had better jump down behind this wall, things are going to get ugly here in just a few moments." He waited until John was under cover, then, noticing Maggie for the first time, spoke sternly to her, "Young lady, remove yourself immediately! This is going to be no place for a woman."

Maggie gave him her best scowl and made a point of hesitating for a moment, just to let him know that she was highly displeased with his decision but was willing to voluntarily obey his orders. Without speaking, she clambered down the ladder and hurried back in the direction of the hospital.

Colonel Cruger waited until she was safely away from the walls. Then he shouted down the line of incensed soldiers. "You men with rifles!" he bellowed. "An extra ration of rum for every one of those rebel guards you can pick off before they get out of range!"

Grinning like possums, the soldiers armed with rifles jumped to obey. A few defiant shots rang out. The rebel guards, who had earlier been content to display the prisoners as they leisurely rode along, suddenly whipped the column to life and hurried them out of range. A sigh went up all along the line when the firing finally ceased. Hampered by the need to be careful, lest they hit one of their own men, the riflemen had not been able to pick off a single rebel.

"Damn!" Colonel Cruger muttered in disgust before turning away from the scene and retreating down the ladder.

John continued to stare after the column of captured soldiers long after they had disappeared behind the rebel encampment to the north. He had strained to make out the faces of the men as they passed, but at that range they tended to blend into one. He suddenly felt totally alone in the world.[69]

To make matters worse, rebel troops, both militia and Continentals, freed by the capitulation of Augusta, began to arrive. The defenders watched silently as more and more enemy troops were amassed against them.

Late that afternoon, John's company was given a warning to be ready to sortie out against the enemy entrenchments as soon as the sun set. The officers calculated that the rebels would not expect the defenders to launch offensive operations against an enemy that had just been strengthened by reinforcements.

Once again they would attack in three sections, John's section would be the first. They were to clear the trenches with their bayonets while a second group destroyed any enemy equipment they could lay their hands on. The third group, under Lieutenant Jenkins, would stand by to engage any enemy troops attempting a counterattack.

The plan worked to perfection. Caught completely off guard by the bold move, the rebel sappers were routed with little trouble. The Loyalists hounded them for only a short distance before breaking off their pursuit. During the melee, John noticed one well-dressed officer shouting in heavily accented English to the fleeing men. The officer tried valiantly to halt the fleeing troops, but sensing the futility of his efforts, he turned to go. John threw his musket to his shoulder and fired without aiming, sending his load of *buck and ball* chasing the blue-coated target. Dirt flew up in small geysers to the left of the running man as the scattered shot struck all around him. The man jumped as if he had been stung by a bee and clapped his right hand to his hip. He disappeared around the next angle of the trench holding his rear and limping badly.[70] The two Garbrants, who had been following John closely, howled with delight.

"I guess he's carrying a load of buckshot in his ass!" Peter shouted. He gave John a powerful slap on the back that seemed almost as loud as John's musket blast. As they turned to go, Peter noticed a tunnel off to their left. Garbrant fired his musket into the opening before John bent to look inside. He looked up quickly and pointed to a torch thrust into the bank behind Peter.

"Hand me that!" he shouted over the din of battle. Other Loyalist troops continued to move past them, pausing occasionally to fire over the rear edge of the trench.

"Reload this." John handed the carbine that he still carried to Peter. "Those Long Lands of yours are too long to take in there with me."

"You're not crawling into that tunnel!" Garbrant exclaimed. "There could be a hundred rebels in there with shovels and mattocks just waiting to crush you skull."

John pointed in the direction of the Star Fort. "This is leading straight to the fort, there must be a reason for it. Let's find out what it is." He reached for the carbine that Peter had reloaded. Holding it in one hand, and the torch in the other, he disappeared into the opening.

He crawled slowly along the tunnel, cautiously looking to the left and right, wary of an ambush in such tight quarters. From the mouth of the tunnel he could hear the Garbrants shouting for him to hurry, he kept moving forward but encountered no trapped rebels. After crawling at least fifty feet, he stopped. There was still no end to the tunnel. *It must go almost to the wall of the Star Fort!* John thought. Slowly, he backed out, painfully aware that his time was limited. The sounds of the battle increased steadily as he neared the mouth of the tunnel.

"Goddamn!" Garbrant shouted as soon as his head reemerged from the opening, "The lieutenant blew that bloody whistle almost a full minute ago. Let's get the hell outta here before we're trapped!" A rebel volley, fired from no more than twenty yards away, sent a flurry of musket balls over the top of the trench. "Goddamn!" Garbrant repeated.

The two brothers reached down, each grabbed an arm as they bodily drew him into the open and began running, towing him along as he fought to regain his footing. Ignoring his protests, they galloped through the deserted trench. Musket balls, fired from both the Loyalists in the Star Fort and the rebels behind them, crisscrossed each other overhead. John's feet drug in the dirt until he managed to shake off his two eager rescuers. Together, the three of them hopped out onto the level ground between the last traverse and the safety of the Star Fort. They rolled to their feet and raced ahead. Overtaking Lieutenant Jenkins's detail just short of the fort's moat, they raced past them, not stopping until they were safely behind the protective walls. The rebels, back in their trenches, continued to fire volleys as the last of the raiders scrambled to safety.

"You damned heathens like to have scared the life out of me!" Zeb shouted down from atop the earthen wall. He had been left behind to pick off rebels with well-aimed shots of his deadly rifle. "I thought that the three of you were dead!"

"You wish, you cheatin' bugger!" Garbrant shook his fist up at him. "You'll not get out of payin' your debts so bloody easy!" Both men roared with laughter. Zeb patted his rifle affectionately. "Don't you worry, Ole Patty here will earn us more than enough once this fightin' ends and I can get back to work with her." John looked questioningly at Garbrant, who grinned.

"Ole Zeb there cleans these backwoods bumpkins out of everything they've got in shootin' contests. They think city folks can't shoot." A soldier on the walls above Zeb suddenly fell back and rolled to the bottom of the embankment. He came to a stop at Garbrant's feet. The man tried to push himself up onto his knees, but with a groan sank slowly back to the ground. Garbrant felt the pulse in the man's neck. He stood and shook his head. "Deader than a door nail," he told John. Another rebel volley kicked up dirt along the upper walls of the fort.

After Zeb and the Garbrants headed back to their positions, John went in search of Lieutenant Jenkins. He found him bent over a crudely drawn map of the rebel entrenchments, reporting to Colonel Cruger on the success of the raid. John stood quietly to one side, waiting to be recognized. They talked on for what seemed an eternity before the colonel spied John and stopped in mid-sentence.

"Corporal, you look as though you have something important on your mind. Do you require our attention?" John moved into the circle of light created by four flickering lanterns that held down the corners of the map.

"I remember you!" Cruger's eyes lit with recognition. "You're one of Colonel Brown's Rangers. I didn't recognize you at first in that red coat."

John saluted smartly. "Yes, sir. I have some information that may be important."

"By all means, share it with us."

John quickly told of finding the tunnel in the enemy trenches and of what he had discovered during his short inspection.

"Am I to understand that you crawled into the tunnel, alone, with a battle raging around you?"

"Not exactly alone, sir," John corrected him. "Two of my men were guarding the entrance."

"Nevertheless, it was a brave act." Cruger cut his eyes at Lieutenant Jenkins. "He's one of your men now?"

"Yes, sir. He is attached to me for the duration of the siege."

"Lucky for us. Now, show me on the map here where this tunnel is located."

"Then you think it may be important?" The question slipped out before John could stop himself.

The colonel laughed. "Very important! I would bet a hundred pounds that those buggers are digging a mine. They have plans to stuff it full of powder and blow us all to Kingdom Come. Your information may well have saved us from disaster." He clapped John on the shoulder. "What can I give you for a reward?"

John thought for a moment, then quickly replied that a double ration of rum for his men would be considered payment in full. The colonel looked at him, puzzled by the strange request. He had expected more. Lieutenant Jenkins leaned close and whispered something in his ear.

"Ah, I see." He nodded his head in understanding and turned to one of his orderlies.

"See to it that this request is fulfilled immediately."

* * * *

"As I live and breathe!" Garbrant exclaimed in happy surprise when John returned and presented them with the colonel's reward. He slapped Peter on the back.

"What'd I tell you? The man has the luck of the Irish. And he's not even Irish!"

Zeb deserted his post at the mere mention of rum. He came sliding down the hill like a hound dog on the scent of a coon, his mouth opened as wide as his eyes. John handed the jug over and climbed to the top of the wall, leaving the three men arguing over the best way to go about drinking spirits.

"I say we just pass the jug around amongst us and take turns turning it up 'til it runs dry," Garbrant suggested. He held the jug in his lap, two handed, caressing it like a lost child.

"That's the best idea that I've heard," Peter agreed wholeheartedly. "I'll go first." He reached out, but Garbrant hugged the jug to his chest like a protective parent. His mouth dropped open creating a perfect 'O'. He looked like a fish after a juicy worm.

"What? We need to make sure that the first man what turns it up don't suck the bottom out of the damn thing! I'm the only trustworthy one of the bunch, I should go first." He looked pleadingly in Zeb's direction, casting about for an ally.

"Like hell you'll go first. I'm the smallest, I take smaller drinks than you two Huguenot oxen," Zeb argued. Both Garbrants cut him off with a wave of their hands.

"What do we look like Zeb, a couple of wet-nosed kids? Why, you'd drink piss out of a dirty boot if someone told you it was rum!"

"That's a might harsh, Garbrant!" Zeb jumped to his feet, he was getting his dander up, feeling his oats. Wild oats that needed to be watered!

"I'm with you Zeb!" Peter shouted, suddenly turning on Garbrant. The other man thrust out his lower lip, glaring at his traitorous sibling.

"Why you treacherous whelp!" Garbrant bellowed in disbelief. "I can't believe my ears! My own brother! And they say blood is thicker than water!"

"Damn right it is! But it ain't thicker that rum! I'm not about to sit here and let you drain that jug before I get a chance to wrap my lips around it. I'm plum parched out!"

"Let's wrestle for it!" Garbrant suggested suddenly.

Peter jumped to his feet, stripping his tunic off in the blink of an eye.

John scrambled down the embankment. "Hold up there fellas!" he cried just in time to prevent a brawl. "Give me that rum, and empty your canteens. I'll ration it out.

"That's an idea!" Zeb shouted. "Why with all this hostility, we might have broken the jug!"

"It wasn't ever in danger." Garbrant scowled at the smaller man. "I don't understand these two, corporal. Don't I always look out for them?" He seemed genuinely affronted that the other two men would doubt his sincerity.

* * * *

That night, the fort's defenders conducted another sortie against the rebel lines. Totally surprised by the bold move, the rebel sappers, who had just returned with new equipment, dropped their tools and fled precipitously back down the trenches towards the relative safety of their secondary lines. John lay on his belly and watched the attack through a loophole in the sandbags. One company of red-coated infantrymen hounded the rebels back to the far wood line, while a large detachment of Pioneers used the abandoned rebel tools to fill in the captured trenches.

At one point the attackers collided with a detail of rebel artillerymen in a secondary trench. The rebels, who were in the process of laboriously dragging a battery of four small cannons into positions nearer to the Star Fort, fled in surprise, abandoning the guns.

After routing their fellow colonials, the Loyalist troops milled around the abandoned field pieces, unable to decide what to do with their prizes. With nothing to spike them with, nor the time to remove them, the cannons posed a dilemma for their captors. Unable to think of anything else to do, they simply dismounted the guns by knocking off their wheels and then left them to be buried, along with the other captured equipment, by the Pioneers.

The assault seemed to go on forever. Along the far wood line, rebel troops were massing for a counterattack. The red-coated company of Loyalists lining the rear of the captured trenches poured a steady stream of fire in their direction. From time-to-time, a man on one side or the other would drop to the ground like a rag doll. Despite the deadly seriousness of the panorama on the plain below, the scene had a morbid beauty about it. The flashes of the rebel cannons, almost half a mile to the rear, silently lit up circular patches of trees in dark silhouette long before the sound of their reports reached him. Muskets belched long tongues of flame that dropped arcs of glowing sparks to the ground. Rockets spread their red glare over the scene in interlocking red trails before impacting amongst the attackers. The white crossbelts of the troops stood out in stark relief to their red coats that looked black in the distance. Musket barrels, sanded until they were shiny enough for a man to see his reflection, caught the multitude of lights and gleamed as they reflected it back into the night sky.

The shrill piping of signal whistles precipitated a general retreat. The first troops to make it back to the protection of the Star Fort were the Pioneer's, their ebony faces shiny with sweat as they lugged all manner of captured equipment with them: spades, mattocks, axes, crowbars, sponge rammers, hammers, hatchets, even a keg of nails. They dropped their burdens to the ground behind the traverse that bisected the fort's inner grounds. Breathing heavily, they laughed, their white teeth shining in the glow of cooking fires and candlelight.

As the infantry regained the safety of the fort, they scrambled up the bank and dropped flat, peering curiously over the sandbags like children waiting for a fireworks display. Thirty seconds later, with a dull thump, the entire fort seemed to leap upward a few inches beneath them. Outside, in the smooth plain that separated the fort from the forward rebel trenches, the ground suddenly collapsed, forming a smooth-sided ditch pointing like a finger directly at them. John smiled. The mine that had cost the rebels so much time and energy to build, had been destroyed.

* * * *

Three days later, Hugh Aikens, a local farmer, made a mad dash across the open spaces separating the two armies. He brought the welcome news that Francis, Lord Rawdon, was marching to their relief with two thousand regular troops who had recently disembarked at Charleston. They were reported to have already marched beyond Orangeburg. The defenders cheered wildly. With relief now definitely on the move, they felt as if they could hold out as long as necessary. The loyalist militia breathed a collective sigh of relief; a most uncertain and painful future awaited them if they ever found themselves at the mercy of their former neighbors over in the rebel lines.

A few days later, they experienced their first major setback when the rebels took up positions from which their guns could fire directly into Holmes Fort, the small stockade located on the west side of the town. Colonel Cruger knew that it would be useless to defend it. He ordered it abandoned and the garrison withdrawn.

Rebel guns could now sweep the ravine through which Spring Branch, the town's only supply of water, flowed. Thirst, the unseen enemy that had always stalked them, now became a major concern.

Some of the most brave and loyal troops among the besieged garrison were the black ex-slaves that had enlisted in either the Pioneer Battalions[71], or in the line companies. Like the Loyalist militia, these men were well aware of the fate that would befall them if the army they served was defeated. They often took great risks to ensure the eventual victory of the British forces.[72]

One of these risks was crawling naked through the dark night to fill canteens from Spring Branch. This work required enormous patience and nerves of steel. It was extremely dangerous because each night the rebels randomly strafed the ravine from end to end with blasts of grape shot from their cannons. Anyone unfortunate enough to be in the ravine when this occurred was almost sure to be seriously wounded or killed. Despite the enormous risks, the dark-skinned warriors continued to hazard the trip night after night. Their valor enabled the Loyalist garrison of Ninety-Six to hold out during the long days of waiting for the relief force to arrive.

Chapter 18

Ninety-Six, South Carolina
Sunday, June 17, 1781

The days of waiting for Lord Rawdon to appear passed slowly. With their black tricorns shading sunburned faces, the defenders of Ninety-Six watched the enemy through the loopholes of their sandbagged sanctuary. Dry tongues licked cracked, peeling lips. The earth, baked by an unshielded sun that hovered stubbornly overhead, was so dry that what movement there was inside the Star Fort produced clouds of semitransparent haze that hovered within the confines of the walls, choking the garrison.

To the north, rebel sappers worked doggedly in shifts, pushing their assault trenches closer. From time-to-time, Zeb, with a slight curl to his bleeding lips, eased his rifle to his shoulder. Taking care not to let the muzzle protrude beyond the edge of his loophole, he took careful aim at some careless dirt digger, pulled the trigger, and immediately rolled to one side to avoid being struck by the return fire of rebel marksmen skulking about in the Maham Tower. Giving John a satisfied nod, he would lay back in a semi-reposed position to await his next chance, comforted for the time being, by the thought that there was now one less rebel sharing the world with him.

On John's other side, the two Garbrants somehow managed to snooze, despite the savage heat bearing down on them. Garbrant, who had been snoring steadily for a good fifteen minutes, suddenly sat up coughing and spitting. He hacked a few times until he had managed to accumulate enough saliva to spit, thought about the scarcity of water for a moment, then swallowed instead. He looked at John and Zeb who were staring at him with amused interest.

"Damned flies!" He yawned and stretched stiffly. He wiped the sweat from his forehead with the cuff of his jacket and looked around at the scene of dejection below. Men were crowded together in tight clusters, greedily hoarding every available scrap of shade in the fort; there were few patches available to them. He turned his head to look at John.

"Where in tarnation is that woman friend of yours? I could sure use a good swig of cool water right about now!" He looked impatiently towards the covered trench, took a deep breath, and exhaled noisily to demonstrate his impatience with the timing of the opposite sex.

Maggie had made a habit of visiting the Star Fort each day after finishing her duties at the hospital. She always appeared with a canteen of tepid water as her excuse for coming. Actually, they had all guessed that she was simply lonely and the only person in the fort not a complete stranger was John. Garbrant naturally pooh-poohed the idea, insisting that her visits were intended strictly for him.

Some time later, Maggie emerged from the covered trench. She arched her back as she stood stiffly erect, massaging the aching muscles caused by the hundred yards of maneuvering on hands and knees through the dark and cramped tunnel. She brushed her dirty hands on the front of her apron and adjusted her mobcap, pushing the stray strands of hair that had escaped from beneath it back into the confines of the band before moving towards John's position. The eyes of several soldiers followed her as she stepped along the base of the wall. A few ribald invitations, that she pretended not to hear, were called down to her by the defenders manning the sandbags above.

Garbrant rubbed the back of his hammer-like fist while he eyed the loudest of the hecklers. "I never could abide a man showing disrespect for a lady!" he growled to himself.

Peter, who lay beside him, chuckled. "What about that tavern maid back in Trenton?" He laughed. "You remember, the one whose pa chased you so hard that you joined the bleeding army?"

"Pshaw!" Garbrant dismissed the idea offhandedly. "That's completely different, and I would thank you to not mention that in front of strangers!"

"John and Zeb aren't strangers!"

Garbrant turned to Peter and shushed him loudly. "And just what do you call all of these heroes sprawled on the ground like a bunch of, of … whatever it is that sprawls on the ground like that!" He waved his open hand in the direction of the milling soldiers crowding the parade ground below. It seemed a perfect imitation of Moses parting the Red Sea. "Anyway, this isn't a proper subject to be discussing in front of a lady!"

Peter rolled his eyes and lay back, cradling the back of his head in both hands. He looked up into the cloudless sky. "I wish it would rain."

To their right, Zeb's head jerked up, his fingers tightening around the stock of his rifle. Peering through the loophole at some target that had inadvertently presented itself, he began to slide the weapon to his shoulder. Garbrant rolled his big eyes in Zeb's direction.

"Now don't go making them damned rebels angry just when Miss Maggie gets here!" He gave Zeb a cautionary leer.

Zeb let the rifle slide back through his hands and onto the ground. "They moved anyways," he said, so that Garbrant would know that he hadn't passed up a shot at a rebel solely on account of some silly whim of his.

Maggie reached the base of the wall below them and smiled upward. Garbrant waved to her and called down a greeting.

Peter, still laying on his back and staring at the sky, took a deep breath and closed his eyes. "You three go on down, I'll stay up here and keep an eye on those rebels down there. But mind you save me a swallow or two!"

The other three men half-walked, half-slid down the interior of the wall, raising a maelstrom of dust that followed them like red mist as they descended to the floor of the fort.

Maggie guided the cord of the tin canteen over her head and held it out to John. Before he could reach for it, she disappeared into Garbrant's treelike arms as he embraced her in a crushing bear hug meant to be a sign of welcome.

"Why I thought that you'd never come!" he bellowed. When he opened his arms she jumped back, scowling. After wiping the wrinkles from her clothing and repairing her disheveled hair, she complained to John.

"Corporal Stokes! Can't you control this hairy beast before he crushes the life out of some innocent woman?"

"Maggie!" Garbrant gave her a genuine look of despair. "Ain't you glad to see me?"

Maggie tossed her head defiantly, refusing to reply. She turned to face Zeb instead. "Why don't you use that rifle that everyone's always bragging about to put this brute out of his misery?" Despite the humor in her eyes, her voice was harsh, demanding.

Zeb grinned, his face flushed in embarrassment.

"You've got to forgive this here sorry specimen of a man!" Garbrant quipped. "He ain't a ladies man like me." He gave the blushing Zeb a look of disdain and reached up to straighten his stock. Because of the heat, the other men had long ago removed theirs.

"He means I ain't a lady, ma'am, like him," Zeb responded dryly.

Garbrant refused to give merit to the other man's words by reacting to them. He took a swig of the precious fluid and thrust the canteen in Zeb's direction.

"Here! You little June bug. Take a swig and get back to your post. Poor ole Peter's all but overwhelmed by the responsibility of guarding his majesty's fort all by his lonesome. Just look at the poor soul up there!"

Zeb rolled his eyes upward to where Peter lay stretched out peacefully on the ground. They could faintly hear his snores above the hustle and bustle of the cramped fort. He looked back in Garbrant's direction and shook his head, but remained silent.

"I believe he's had a sunstroke up there," Zeb remarked sardonically. He took a long pull and handed the canteen to John. John took a sip and handed it back.

"You two run this on up to Peter before he does get the sunstroke," John said. His words sounded flat, almost like an order.

Garbrant sighed; he rolled his eyes to demonstrate to Maggie how vexing John's arbitrary moods of authority were to him. He took the canteen, slipped the cord over his shoulder, and tipped his hat politely. "Ma'am."

John watched the two men clamber up the wall, their footing uncertain as the dry earth gave way beneath their feet. The tin canteen swung loosely against Garbrant's back, emitting brilliant pinpricks of light as it reflected the rays of the late afternoon sun.

He turned to Maggie. "How are things with you, Maggie?"

She sank to the ground. Flaring her skirt around her, she kept her legs discretely folded beneath their protective covering. John sat next to her, waiting for her answer.

"Fine! Fine!" She nodded her head. "You?"

"Hot." He motioned up the wall with his head to the three bickering soldiers. "And noisy."

She smiled, displaying perfectly formed white teeth, a rarity in a woman halfway to thirty. John unconsciously compared her to Grainy, caught himself, and forced his thoughts into another direction.

"What are your plans? I mean, after the siege is broken?" he asked.

She looked at him as if this were some eccentric idea, too unlikely to be taken seriously.

"It will end soon, Lord Rawdon can't be far away," John reminded her.

She looked at her hands clasped tightly in her lap. Her lower lip quivered for an instant. When she looked up, her eyes were moist.

"Have I upset you?" he asked, genuinely contrite.

She looked down and shook her head "No, it's just that I don't know what I'll do when this is over." Her face was contorted with a mixture of emotions, the least of which was despair. "I've no one left in the world but my son. I have a confession to make. I sometimes dread the end of this siege."

"Why?"

"Because I'm only useful while it lasts. Once it ends, I must take my son and find some way to live. Most of the options that come to mind are quite unsavory."

John studied her for a moment. "Have you ever considered the frontier? I'm certain your sister-in-law, Judith, would be happy to take you in. With your knowledge of medicine, you would be a valuable asset to our little village."

She smiled at him, one of those kind smiles that people generally reserve for the simple-minded. "I'm afraid that I wouldn't look well in buckskin," she teased him. "No, my future lies in some large city." She lay back onto the soft earth, closed her eyes, and relaxed as she spoke, visualizing her perfect future. "My dreams are to have a home again, a real home where I can raise my children, with a husband who comes home every night without smelling of blood and black powder. I hate to admit it, but I was a spoiled woman before all of this madness began." She blew her breath out between pursed lips. "This can't last forever." Wistfully, she turned her head and opened her eyes, studying his reaction. "Does that sound treasonable? Wanting the war to end, not really caring anymore who wins?"

John smiled down at her. "Well, I for one hope that you achieve those modest goals. After *we* win this war."

"What about you?" she asked. Her voice was barely above a whisper.

"My dreams are the same. Come back here to Ninety-Six, rebuild my life, and spend the rest of my days coming home to my wife and children at the end of each day." He paused to flash her a playful smile. "And I won't be smelling of blood and black powder either!"

Maggie smiled, the sad smile of the depressed. "It's too bad you're already taken," she said unexpectedly. When she realized what she had blurted out, she flushed. "Oh my, it's late! I must get back to the hospital. The doctor will be frantic if he finds me missing." She jumped to her feet as if suddenly aware of an urgent appointment.

Garbrant vaulted down the embankment the instant she appeared to be ending her visit. He volunteered immediately to escort her back to the opening of the covered way, *just to make sure that she wasn't molested.*

John returned to his post atop the wall. Along with the other two soldiers, he stared down from the wall, grinning at the unmatched pair as they made their way in the direction of the traverse. The big Huguenot swaggered by Maggie's side like a peacock, keeping a wary eye out for anyone who dared to venture too near to his charge.

* * * *

The night passed peacefully. The steady sounds of digging coming from the rebel trenches lulled John to sleep. He lay on one side, his filthy uniform jacket rolled into a pillow under his head, his musket cradled in his arms. All around the earthen walls of the Star Fort, men slept on their arms. In their exhausted slumbers they created a scandalous symphony, composed of every conceivable noise that a human body is capable of producing.

Garbrant sat with his back against the protective pile of sandbags, his head slowly turning on his thick neck like a vulture in search of some foul smelling meat. He scrutinized the interior of the fort disdainfully. Satisfied that he had spied what he had been searching for, he gave the sleeping Peter a jab that displaced the smaller man a few inches across the ground.

"Peter! You awake?" he asked loudly enough for his voice to be heard clearly in the rebel trenches. Peter mumbled a reply that might have meant anything. Satisfied that he had a sympathetic ear, Garbrant mused loudly. "Just listen to those buggers!" he complained. "Soldiers are the worst sort of scum! A body would think that none of them ever had a mother the way they carry on. I tell you, it's enough to turn your stomach. I'm mighty glad that Miss Maggie isn't here to witness this! Don't you think so?"

When no reply was readily forthcoming, he prodded the other man again. "You still awake?"

Peter mumbled another muddled reply that seemed to satisfy Garbrant of the veracity of his argument.

He nodded his head, a quick jerk of a nod, and grunted to display his satisfaction with Peter's judgment. "You're damned right!" He congratulated the sleeping man with a stinging slap on his back. Peter coughed, a hacking, choking thing that caused him to roll onto his side and prop himself up on one elbow. He gagged for a moment still coughing forcefully, dislodged whatever had stuck in his throat, spit, then with a groan, settled back onto the ground.

Garbrant turned his attention to Zeb who sat next to his loophole, performing his duty as sentry for the small knot of men. He stared, glassy eyed, into the night, his inner thoughts focused on some image from the past, or future.

"Bug musta crawled down his throat," Garbrant rationalized. Zeb remained silent. Garbrant pushed himself away from the wall and stretched out on the ground, his head resting on a loose sandbag. "Let me know if there's any emergencies," he said to the silent sentry. Within moments he began to produce a steady roar of ungodly sounding snores that all but smothered the noises emanating from the rest of the fort's occupants.

Far to the north a cannon fired, producing a brilliant flash of light that ballooned in the semi-darkness of the early morning. Seconds later, the shell impacted the wall of the Star Fort directly beneath John's position. He sat up as the delayed report of the gun sounded. Almost immediately a second shell flew over the wall, burying itself in the face of the traverse behind him.

Down below, Lieutenant Jenkins was on his feet shouting orders, hurrying men up the dusty slope into their positions behind the loopholes, and demanding that cartridges be brought forward into the lines. A momentary lull followed the impacts of the first scattered shells, fired simply to range the guns. An eerie calm descended over the battlefield. Thirty seconds later, every rebel field piece fired a simultaneous broadside.

"Get ready men!" someone cautioned in a confident voice. "This could be what we've been waiting for." John looked over his shoulder to see Sergeant Van Riper kneeling behind him, peering cautiously out at the plain below. Smiling broadly, he glanced at John and nodded his head. His confidence was infectious. John felt ready to handle anything that the rebels could throw at them.

Behind him, on the far side of the traverse that slashed across the floor of the fort, he could see the swarthy faces of the Pioneer Troops, standing by with spears, spades, axes—anything that came readily to hand. He felt sorry for any rebel who found himself face to face with those murderous bastards.

To keep from exposing themselves to the enemy's fire, John and the two Garbrants lay on their sides next to their loopholes and cautiously peered through them at an angle. They lay there patiently waiting for the rebels to pour out of their trenches and roll up the hill like a blue-coated wave of death in an attempt to overwhelm the fort's defenders. Along the walls to either side, their fellow Loyalists waited grimly, holding muskets loaded with buckshot and sixty-nine caliber balls in sweaty hands. Their bayonets were already fixed. Everyone on both sides of this battle was well aware that the outcome of this struggle would ultimately be decided face-to-face, with cold, pointed steel. The Loyalists were confident in their ability to use these weapons. Not one of them had ever seen rebels, particularly militia, withstand a disciplined bayonet charge.

In John's group, only Zeb was actively participating in the battle. Watching through his loophole, he methodically picked out his targets among the rebel marksmen stationed inside the Maham Tower. Once the smoke of a rifle had betrayed the exact location of a loophole, he laid his sights on the slender opening and waited, finger resting lightly on the trigger, until he saw the muzzle of the weapon protrude for the next shot. Then he fired slightly above the barrel. Using this simple method, he steadily picked off rebel marksmen in the most remarkable display of marksmanship that John had ever witnessed.

For over four hours the cannons thundered. The defenders lay quietly under cover, praying that it would continue. Each of them was well aware that a major attack would be launched against them the minute that the balls stopped flying. As it was, the artillery was doing little damage. That would all change when they came face-to-face with the first wave of rebel fanatics screaming up the steep forward slope of the Star Fort.

The red-coated soldiers looked at each other and shook their heads. Those rebels who would come first had to know that, barring a miracle, this would be their final hour. Still they would come, willingly sacrificing themselves for an idea that many of them couldn't clearly express and didn't fully understand. Most of the Loyalist troops awaiting their inevitable charge did not admire them. They simply thought of them as weak-minded puppets whose emotions had been manipulated by unscrupulous and unprincipled men lusting for power. What exactly were they fighting for anyway? Freedom? When, as Englishmen, had they ever *not* been free?

* * * *

Judging the hour by the sun, John guessed that it was almost noon. To their front, rebel troops had begun to fire aimed volleys upward at the defenders who remained huddled behind their protective sandbags. A whistle sounded, signaling the enemy to advance. With a cheer, they poured over the rim of the nearest trenches. Many of the men charged forward carrying nothing but wickerwork fascines for use in filling in a pathway across the fort's moat. Ignoring the steady stream of musket balls buzzing around them, John and his comrades fired volley after volley, down onto the heads of the enemy troops swarming at the foot of the earthen wall. Rebels, armed with nothing more than shovels, began to throw desperate spadefulls of red earth over the top of the wicker work fascines that their comrades had piled in the moat, while others, armed with axes, crawled from the ditch onto the lower slopes of the Star Fort. Ignoring the horrendous fire tearing through their ranks from above, they hacked viciously at the base of the sharpen stakes embedded in the fort's wall, cutting a pathway for the assault troops in the second wave. Above them the Loyalist infantry rotated in sections, firing volley after endless volley. Each of the sections stepped up to the sandbags, thrust their weapons over the wall and fired almost point blank into the ant-like mass of rebels in the ditch below. Their weapons emptied, they side-stepped smartly to allow room for the next rotation to take their place as they made their way to the rear, where they immediately begin to reload. By the time they had rammed a fresh charge down the barrels of their muskets, another section was already pulling the hammers of their weapons to full cock and preparing to step up to the wall in a never ending cycle of destruction aimed directly at the rebels below.

As John stepped forward on his third rotation, he was almost struck in the face by a long-handled hook thrust up from below. The hook dropped sharply down the length of his body and dug into the sandbag directly in front of him. Holding his fire, he leaned forward far enough to see a rebel's face, blue eyes wide in terror, staring up at him. The man's white knuckled hands grasped the handle of the hook with desperate urgency. John saw the man's shoulder muscles tense in preparation for yanking the sandbags from the wall, an act that would expose the defenders to the muskets and rifles of the rebels below. Without hesitating, he shouldered his musket, pointed it directly at the upturned face, and pulled the trigger. He sidestepped before the smoke cleared and dropped back below the protective level of sandbags. He didn't see his enemy die, but knew that he couldn't have missed at that range. As he bit the end from a paper cartridge, he glanced towards the top of the parapet and saw that the hook was still embedded in the sandbag. He made a mental note to pull it into the fort on his next rotation.

Fully absorbed in the heat of the battle, John jumped, startled, when Sergeant Rip suddenly clapped his hand onto his shoulder.

"Listen closely!" Rip bellowed in order to be heard above the din of the raging struggle. "We are sending out two flanking parties! They're going to circle around through the fort's trench and attack the rebels on both flanks! Do you understand?" He waited for John to nod his head before continuing. "When they attack, our company is to jump the wall and go at them from above with the bayonet. Understand?" John nodded again and Rip moved on to repeat the message to Sergeant Skidmore's platoon, fighting desperately on the left. To his right, Sergeant Stagg was already relaying the message to his own men. Tight lipped, the men looked at him through wild eyes and nodded. They shrugged their shoulders, both frightened and eager at the same time.

On signal, the Loyalist garrison sprang to their feet and jumped the wall of sandbags. Yelling like banshees, they charged into the faces of the rebel forces below while the flanking parties hammered them on both flanks. Men from New York, New Jersey, and South Carolina, wearing the red uniform of King George III, clashed murderously with their cousins from Virginia, Maryland, Delaware, and the Carolinas wearing the blue uniform of the rebel Congress. It was a savage, hand-to-hand affair. No quarter was expected, or given.

A wild-eyed, young rebel lunged at John, slashing at him with the tip of his bayonet. He missed, but the heavy barrel of his musket struck John's bayonet solidly, snapping it off at the lug. John jumped back, reversed his own musket, and using it like a truncheon, shattered the stock over the head of his attacker. The man dropped to the ground, mortally stunned. Temporarily without a weapon, John frantically wrenched the French-made musket from the clutching fingers of the dying man just in time to turn its bayonet on an onrushing rebel, impaling him a millisecond before being skewered himself. He yanked the bloody bayonet free of the man's chest and used the butt to push him to one side before moving forward to confront another enemy. On his right, the Garbrants employed their bayonets with reckless abandon, forcing their antagonists back towards the fort's dry moat with powerful and well-aimed thrusts. Ahead of them, some of the rebels began taking halting steps backwards, hesitant to face certain death at the hands of the grim-faced Loyalists advancing steadily towards them. Some of them, already teetering on the edge of the moat, were forced backwards by their retreating comrades, and, with arms spinning wildly in a desperate attempt to retain balance, disappeared over the edge of the moat. Under the deadly pressure of the three-pronged bayonet charge, the rebel lines broke. They fled, leaving the front of the fort littered with their dead and wounded.

The dull thumping of the regimental drums, sounding the recall from inside the fort, was barely audible over the tumult in the bottom of the moat. Packed into the confined space between the narrow dirt walls, John found himself wedged shoulder-to-shoulder with a hundred other shouting and milling troops in the bottom of the trench. The battle had transformed it into a charnel house littered with the bodies of rebel and Loyalist alike. The limbs of the dead and the grasping hands of the wounded entangled the legs of the survivors, tripping them as they fought their way clear of the hellish scene. Men kicked heartlessly at the hands of the wounded, or yanked their feet free of their frantic, grasping fingers, unable to take the time to lend assistance. The next wave of attackers could appear at the top of the trench at any moment. If that happened, they would all be slaughtered. Everyone had the same thought: get clear of this tangle of bodies as quickly as possible, and then race back to the relative safety of the Star Fort.

Breaking free of the melee, John turned and trotted along the floor the trench. He had managed to move only few yards when a broken musket wedged across the bottom of the narrow opening tripped him. He hit the ground hard and slid to a stop. Before he could fight his way back to his feet, the men following behind him literally pounded him into the dry dirt as they raced over him. A foot landed directly between his shoulder blades, knocking the wind from him as he fought to raise himself to his knees. Choking and gasping, he tried to rise again just as another group of men rumbled over him, their heavy boots punishing him severely. Dazed, he vaguely felt a powerful hand reach down from above and grab him beneath one arm.

"We seem to be making a habit of this, corporal!" Garbrant's ugly face grinned at him. The two Garbrants had thrown a human wall across the narrow trench to temporarily divert the flow of humanity around them, protecting him long enough for him to stagger to his feet. Behind them, the next wave of fleeing troops piled into their backs, their increasing weight pushing them forward. With John on his feet, the three men flattened themselves against the walls of the trench and allowed the bulk of the other men to flow past unimpeded. Then they followed them towards the safety of the Star Fort. John noticed that Peter, running ahead of him, had a bloody wound just above his left shoulder blade. He yelled to him as they ran, asking if he was seriously injured.

"It's just a scratch!" Peter yelled back, although he grimaced with pain. "One of the bloody buggers mistook me for a sandbag and tried to pull me down the outside of the wall with one of those damned hooks of theirs!" He waited until he had taken a few breaths, then added hastily, "If Garbrant hadn't grabbed me in time, they would have landed me like a bleeding fish!"

The enemy made no attempt to stop the Loyalists from reentering the fort. For the remainder of the day, John and the other defenders lay behind the protective wall of sandbags, awaiting a renewal of the attack. With the coming of night they held their posts, one man sleeping, one awake.

The next attack never came. Throughout the day, the Loyalist troops noticed a marked decline in the activity in the rebel trenches to their front. Catching only an occasional glimpse of their foes as they scurried back and forth through their works, the defenders began to fear that some ploy was being played out beyond their vision amongst the trees to the north. The only hostile action by the rebels was when an occasional shot from the Maham Tower sent a man tumbling down the inside wall of the fort. Zeb, or one of the other riflemen, would fire back in retaliation.

Far across the open fields, rebels could be seen milling around their camps and tending to cook fires, but not one was digging. What was this?

Darkness fell; an ominous silence descended on the Star Fort. No muskets barked, no cannons boomed, no rebels screamed threats at the weary defenders. Depending on their temperament, Loyalist soldiers prayed, or slept, or kept watch through the loopholes with unblinking eyes, wary of a sudden rush by their besiegers. Those without faith, gambled. Just before daybreak, Sergeant Rip nudged John awake with his booted foot.

"Something going on?" John sat up, rubbing sleep from his eyes.

"Something's already gone on," Rip replied. He stood straight-backed, hands on his hips, looking out across the rebel entrenchments while he spoke. He seemed to be searching for something out there, something hidden by the darkness. "Take a look out there at the rebel camp," he said knowingly.

Noticing for the first time that the sergeant was standing erect, in full view of the rebel riflemen in the Maham Tower, John advised him to get down behind the cover of the sandbags. Rip only shook his head.

"No need, they're all gone, every last one of 'em."

"I hope you're right," John said, expecting to hear the crack of a rifle at any moment.

Sergeant Riper was correct. Dawn revealed deserted trenches. The abandoned Maham Tower frowned down at them, the familiar outline of the rebel tents in their four widely spaced camps had disappeared, vanished. A quick sweep of the area by a company of mounted Loyalist militia reported that the rebels were heading north, towards the Saluda River, in full retreat. A rider mounted on a fast horse was dispatched immediately to the southeast. Lord Rawdon had to be drawing near; it was the only explanation for the enemy's bizarre behavior.

The beleaguered garrison greeted Lord Rawdon's advancing columns as if they were a legion of angles sent to prepare the way for the Second Coming. Waving hats, firing salutes with their muskets, shouting, and gesturing with upraised arms—doing anything conceivable to demonstrate their joy at being delivered from a cruel and vindictive enemy, they welcomed the relief column.

The relieving force looked as if they had been besieged themselves. The soldiers, fresh off of the transports from Ireland, had been pushed to the limit of endurance, marching under the blistering Carolina sun, still wearing their heavy woolen uniforms. Some had succumbed to sunstroke in the harsh, unfamiliar climate. Others wearily plodded on, mechanically placing one foot in front of the other. They simply followed the man marching to their front.

"Well it's about time that we had some actual Britishers here!" Garbrant remarked as he watched the files of troops pass below them. "It seems mighty queer to me. Here we are, a bunch of Americans backed by England, fighting to hold a British fort against another bunch of Americans, backed by France, fighting to take it away." He thought for a moment, then asked Sergeant Rip standing to one side, "Is there anybody in this damned fort that isn't a Colonial?"

Rip thought for a moment, then said, "There is one officer that was born in England, but other that that, now that you mention it, this fight was more of a family feud than a battle."

Colonel Cruger greeted Lord Rawdon with great enthusiasm. The two men clasped hands like long-lost brothers. They immediately retired to Colonel Cruger's roofless quarters where they stayed for several hours before reemerging.

Their decision was that Lord Rawdon would leave a thousand infantrymen and a hundred cavalrymen at Ninety-Six. With the remainder of the troops, he would chase the retreating rebels across Carolina and into the arms of General Charles, Lord Cornwallis, crushing them between the two armies.

The gallant defenders of Ninety-Six, outnumbered three to one, had withstood the longest siege of the American Revolution, successfully defending the only remaining British outpost in the interior of the southern colonies. It was with shocked dismay that they were informed of Lord Rawdon's order to Colonel Cruger: destroy the fort and town, then abandon it. Orders to that effect, which had been dispatched to them well before the arrival of the rebel army, had been intercepted en route to them. They shook their heads in disbelief. If not for that one small incident, there would have never been a siege at Ninety-Six, South Carolina.

* * * *

John, Zeb, and Garbrant walked to the hospital to visit Peter after their company was dismissed. Their steps were unhurried as they ambled over the open plain between the Star Fort and the town. Beside them was the roof of the covered way, through which they had been forced to crawl on hands and knees during the thirty days of the siege. Its protection was no longer needed now that they could walk in the open without danger of being fired on by rebel marksmen.

Zeb was the first one to broach the subject that both he and Garbrant had wondered about.

"What are your plans now that the siege is lifted?" he asked John. It was one of those lazy, unhurried questions that required no immediate answer.

John stopped, he looked back towards the Star Fort, both hands on his hips. The Pioneer troops were busy tossing the bodies of dead rebels into the trenches near the northern face of the wall. He wondered briefly if their attackers had known when they were digging those approaches that they were actually digging their own graves. He took a deep breath and exhaled it completely before he spoke.

"Go back to Long Swamp Village and make a new life with my family. Out of the reach of these damned rebels!" his voice cracked with suppressed emotions. He shook his head. "Who would have ever thought it? In less than a year, every British outpost in the backcountry is lost. Ninety-Six is to be destroyed. Hell! The Rangers *are* destroyed!" He looked longingly in the direction of the roofless buildings inside the town and took another deep breath. "Once Ninety-Six is destroyed and evacuated, everything that I've fought for: my home, my future, justice for the wrongs I've endured, is gone forever." He looked sternly at Zeb. "Can you imagine what kind of a place this will be when the rebels control it? Any man that disagrees with them will be whipped or hanged! English liberty will be gone forever, replaced by the arbitrary justice of their Committees of Safety. No, Zeb, I for one cannot abide to live where I am not free." He seemed to come to some inner decision. "I'm going back to Long Swamp Village. Unless God himself intervenes, it would appear that my war is at an end."

"What are you talking about, John?" Garbrant exclaimed. "We've won every battle that we've ever fought against that rebel trash! Always outnumbered too, I might add! We're just falling back to the coast to regroup. We'll cut off shipping to these bumpkins and this rebellion will shrivel on the vine." He nodded his head. "Should have done that long ago. You can't coddle rebels, they ain't normal!"

John smiled. "Rebels don't think." As he said it, he wondered briefly if Dobbins was still alive. He felt a sudden overwhelming dread that some evil had befallen his wife and children back in Long Swamp. He made a quick mental decision. Thrusting out his hand, he shook each of theirs warmly.

"You have been two of the most steadfast comrades a man could wish for. I will not forget you."

"What are you getting at John?" Garbrant asked, his eyebrows knitting together in anticipation of John's reply.

"I'm going to inform Sergeant Rip that I will be leaving at first light in the morning. I couldn't stand to watch Ninety-Six be destroyed. I'll pick up my mount from Mrs. Cruger and be on my way."

Both Zeb and Garbrant looked ill. They had not expected such a sudden turn of events. Garbrant recovered first. With a great smile he clapped John on the shoulder.

"This calls for a drink!" he announced loudly. "If we can find one."

John talked to Sergeant Riper and Lieutenant Jenkins that afternoon. Hiding his doubts about the future of the war, he simply explained that as a Ranger, it was his duty to man his post until relieved or transferred. Also, any Rangers that had escaped falling into the hands of the rebels would have made for the Indian towns where they could regroup to fight another day. Lieutenant Jenkins agreed to discuss the matter with Colonel Cruger at the earliest possible moment. He assured him that it would be later that evening, or failing that, in the morning.

True to his word, he sent written orders to John at reveille the next morning. They were signed by Colonel Cruger's aide, directing him to return to his posting in the Cherokee country. There, he was to report to the senior officer at that post. He also included an authorization for John to draw any past due pay from the regimental paymaster who would, in turn, be reimbursed by the Carolina Rangers as some future date. As a gesture of appreciation, he was authorized to draw a new coat from the regimental stores. Clearly, Colonel Cruger wished to show his appreciation for John's contribution to the successful outcome of the siege.

John carefully rolled his orders and inserted them into a small copper cylinder to protect them from the weather. He slipped that into the meager pack of belongings behind his saddle. After drawing his pay and his new coat, a heavy woolen one for winter use, he went in search of Zeb and the two Garbrants. He found them loitering about the hospital. Zeb was sitting alongside Peter's cot, engaged in an animated discussion with the wounded man. Garbrant was following Maggie and attempting to ingratiate himself into her good graces by assisting her in any way possible. The look on Maggie's face plainly told that, despite all of his good intentions, he was generally making a nuisance of himself. Having already been apprised of John's intentions by Garbrant, she disappeared into another room and reappeared a moment later with his green uniform in her hand. It was freshly cleaned and pressed. He wondered as he watched her cross the room if she had stayed awake last night to clean it. She held the coat out to him, then leaned forward to give him a farewell hug. After patting him affectionately on his back, she held him at arm's length, studying his face intently. A painful smiled twisted the corner of her lip. Her eyes glistened with tears. She nodded once, unable to speak, and turned away to resume her duties.

John sat alongside Peter, while Zeb finished his tale. He took each of them by the hand once again.

"I'll miss you, you giant brute!" he exclaimed, craning his head to look at the great bear of a man.

"You know where to find us," Garbrant responded. "Just find the New Jersey Volunteers and we'll all be there with them." John nodded, turned away from the men who had become almost like brothers to him over the past thirty days, and walked out of their lives forever.

Chapter 19

Middle Cherokee Path
Saturday, June 30, 1781

John halted the white mare on the east bank of the Chattahoochee River. Something on the far bank, back in the bushes, caught his eye, something that seemed oddly out of place. His sixth sense nagged at him, warning him of danger. After having traveled through territory populated by gangs of rebel marauders and terrified Tory families, abandoned to their fate by the withdrawal of the British forces, he found himself ruled by caution, forever wary of an ambush. He would lie for hours spying on a cabin, waiting to discover the political leanings of its occupants before approaching it to ask for food or directions. He wanted no truck with rebels, or with their families who would not think twice about shooting him down in cold blood. In this area, devoid of laws, Loyalists were thought little better than Indians; both could be shot down for sport, without fear of repercussions from the rebel authorities.

Checking the priming in the captured Charleville musket, he drew the hammer back to full cock, and motioned for the three men behind him to spread out along the riverbank. The men were Loyalists from the Ceded Lands who had grasped at the unexpected opportunity of escaping from their precarious existence by following John into exile. They had brought their families with them, along with as many meager possessions as they were able to stuff into their saddlebags, or carry strapped to their backs in makeshift packs. All of the men were marked for retribution, having served in the Loyalist militia during the sieges at Augusta.

After their defeat, the Loyalists had been paroled to their homes without arms, at the mercy of their rancorous rebel neighbors. Now, armed with nothing more than axes and knives, they prepared to meet whatever danger lurked on the far side of the river. Their wives and children huddled together behind them, thoroughly traumatized by their treatment at the hands of the rebels.

Through the trees that lined the opposite shore, John caught a glimpse of reflected sunlight, his body tensed. He lay the long-barreled musket horizontally across his saddle, balancing it on the tops of his thighs.

Through cupped hands, he called the Cherokee word for friend, "O gi na li I,"[73] across the water. A figure emerged into sight. Pushing aside the thick underbrush, the man led his mount out onto the sandbar that lined the far shore, grounded his musket, and stood on the bare sand, peering across the water that separated them. John smiled for the first time in two weeks and breathed a sigh of relief. He motioned for the other men to relax. The man wore the green coat of the King's Rangers; it was Sergeant Hopkins!

Recognizing John as the leader of the shabby group, five more Rangers stepped into the open. They were all there: Hopkins, Jacob, Dobbins, Nat, Sambo, and Mambo.

With a loud whoop! they threw their legs over their saddles and plunged their mounts into the water. They pounded towards him, spray flying as their horses cut a narrow path through the shallow water of the ford.

"We thought you were dead or captivated with the rest of them poor bastards at Augusta!" Hopkins exclaimed as he reached for John's hand.

"I've been trapped with Colonel Cruger's troops in Ninety-Six for over a month," John told them. "We held the rebels off for thirty days, then the British up and ordered it abandoned!"

"What?" Hopkins blurted out.

"Its been burned and abandoned. With every other post held by the rebels, the British said they couldn't support it, stuck out there like an island in a sea of sedition." John spit. "Lord Rawdon's words, not mine."

A look of serious concern crept into Hopkins eyes. "Then we're alone?"

John nodded. "All alone. There isn't a British post left standing in Carolina except for those around Charleston."

The other Rangers crowded around, mumbling quietly to each other, troubled by the news.

John looked at them and knew exactly what they were feeling. He took each of them by the hand and shook it warmly. "What are all of you doing out here?" he asked.

"Captain Wylly keeps two of us guarding this here river crossing all the time, lest the rebels try to sneak up on us," Jacob told him. "If we see them coming, we're to light a big pile of brush back yonder as a signal." He waved his hand to indicate the far side of the river. "Nat and me were here all of last week, but you caught Mambo and Sambo about to relieve us. Half an hour later and you wouldn't have had anyone to greet you except these two heathens." He looked towards the two Africans and laughed. They smiled, exposing those wicked teeth.

"What's the news from the settlements?" Jacob asked.

John told them what he knew. When he finished, feeling guilty about being the cause of such long and distraught faces, he quickly added some positive news. "The news isn't all bad. Lord Rawdon landed in Charleston with a new army fresh from Ireland. With him to aid Lord Cornwallis, they may be able to trap the main rebel army between them and get things under control again. Hearsay is, that they are going to block all shipping into the ports and starve the rebels into submission."

"Starve? Wait 'til you get back to Long Swamp!" Dobbins disagreed. "Why the fields there are going to be so fruitful this year that we won't have enough room to store it all! If we're that well off, the rebels are too."

"Not if we go after them, burn their crops, run off their livestock." Hopkins said it as if it were a real possibility.

"What? And bring them down on our heads?" Dobbins looked at Hopkins as if he had lost his mind. "Look around sergeant, there are only six of us left!"

Hopkins dismissed Dobbins's skepticism with a curt wave of his hand. "There're more of us scattered around the Indian towns." He indicated the three men who had sat silently throughout the exchange. "Here's three more right here. Not to mention all the Cherokee and Creek warriors that would follow us. You're just back from the settlements John, what do you think?"

John looked slowly from man to man, hesitant to voice his real feelings. He considered the options, weighing each carefully. Once he reached a decision, he looked straight into the sergeant's eyes.

"I think you're both right. If we give up, we've lost everything. There is no middle ground in this business. But Dobbins does have a point. With nothing else to distract them, the rebels would descend on us like a plague of locust if we started attacking the settlements." He gave them time to ponder this information before continuing. "If you want to know what I think, then it is this. We keep a watch on their movements and we wait." He held up his hand as Hopkins opened his mouth to speak. "Hold on sergeant, hear me out. I am just saying that we should do nothing until we hear from Colonel Brown or whoever is in command of this area now. If we ride off half-cocked to attack the rebels and stir them up, who knows what will happen?"

Hopkins leaned forward, resting his forearms on his saddle, and studied John's face before his gaze moved on to sweep across the faces of the three refugees. He nodded thoughtfully.

"We'll go that route for the time being," he agreed. "No sense in stirring up that hornet's nest without someone to help us out."

John could almost feel the tension flowing out of the three refugees. Dobbins and Jacob also looked as if they had just dodged a bullet. No one wanted to do anything that may start the fighting again, especially now that it seemed futile to do so. On the other hand, no one was quite ready to admit defeat and wash their hands of everything that their lives stood for.

Leaving the two Africans to secure the crossing, the others returned to Long Swamp where John received a hero's welcome from Grainy and his two older children. John tried to mask the disappointment that crept into his face when the baby, Daniel, greeted him like a stranger once again.

Grainy immediately sent Simpson, now almost five years old, into the loft to search for a sack of finely pounded corn meal while she and Judith stoked up the fire in her outdoor bake oven. Chattering gaily, the two women set about preparing a welcome home supper for the returning Ranger. As they worked, they constantly issued orders to the other members of the household. Three-year-old Lynn Celia was drafted as baby sitter for Daniel and for Judith's son, William. Simpson was put to work splitting kindling and hauling firewood, and Jacob was dispatched with his musket to bring in some fresh meat. John was allowed to rest and was fawned over shamelessly by both women.

As word of John's return spread throughout the village, old friends began to drift by, stopping to welcome him home and ask him questions about the topic foremost in everyone's mind: what about the war? Grainy and Judith were kept busy, preparing supper for John, and at the same time, feeding bowls of hasty pudding mixed with cream to the guests.

A yelp from the direction of the far wood line announced Jacob's return from hunting as he swaggered towards the cabin, holding his musket carelessly across one shoulder. In his hand were two wild turkeys he had flushed from along the banks of the river. He grinned boyishly at his wife as he dropped the two headless fowls into a pot of steaming water, suspended by a tripod over a small fire.

"Will those do?" he asked, proudly giving Judith a quick buss on her cheek. He gave her lightly rounding belly a clandestine caress at the same time.

"Where's John?" His eyes swept across the clearing, stopping on Grainy. She dusted flour from her hands and inclined her head towards the cabin.

"Inside, with Daniel."

Jacob found John sitting in his high-backed chair with his youngest son jumping playfully on his lap. Like a three-year-old adult, Lynn Celia sat proudly in the spare chair with Jacob's sleeping son in her lap. Jacob sank onto one of the puncheon benches and leaned back against the kitchen table, resting his elbows on top of it.

"It's good to see you again, John. We had just about given up hope. After you left for Augusta it took us a sight of time to get a relief force together. Dragging Canoe and his Chickamaugas came once Dobbins found them, but by the time we reached the Chattahoochee we got the word that Augusta had already fallen. The Indians just turned around and marched back home." He shrugged. "Can't blame them."

John nodded, trying at the same time to calm his young son, who seemed to possess unlimited energy when it came to jumping on adult laps.

"I wondered what had happened to ya'll when I saw the Rangers marched past Ninety-Six. Does anybody know how many were killed?"

"We know that Colonel Brown has been paroled and sent to Savannah. The Cherokees went with him. I don't suppose that you've heard about Colonel Grierson?"

"The refugees told me that he was murdered after he surrendered. Some of the other Rangers were too."

Jacob leaned forward and sat looking at the floor, hands clasped together, elbows resting on his knees. "He was a good man," he mused aloud. "We can most likely expect the same, if they ever come for us."

The thought disturbed John. He let Daniel slip to the floor. The child immediately began to crawl around the room on all fours, inquisitively inspecting everything within his reach. John watched him quietly with a sad smile. He kept his thoughts to himself.

"Let's just hope that never happens. If we stay close, and don't do anything to gain their attention, we should be fine. As they say, out of sight, out of mind."

Jacob walked across the room and lifted the Charleville[74] carefully from its pegs above the door. He examined it closely. Flipping the frizzen open, he studied the odd angle of its placement, then held it to his shoulder, testing its balance.

"This is a fine weapon," he said, "and that carved cheek piece on the stock lets you get your eye right behind the barrel." He dropped the butt of the musket to the floor and examined the mouth of the barrel. "What caliber?"

"Sixty-nine."

Jacob nodded. "That's good. You can carry more shots with the same weight of lead as we do."

"It's a fine weapon. I just hope that putting meat on the table will be the only thing that I'll ever use it for again.

Jacob carefully replaced the musket on its pegs.

"Let's both hope so."

That evening, the two families sat down to a feast lovingly prepared by the women of the double cabin. A Turkey, basted and stuffed with nuts, mashed sweet potatoes and herbs, had been slow roasted in the outdoor oven and was served along with freshly made biscuits, generously topped with melted butter, churned fresh that morning. The sack of meal that Simpson had retrieved from the loft had been turned into delicious johnnycakes that were served with whole sweet potatoes, slow baked in their skins until they were tender and moist. All of this was washed down by milk, cider, water, rum, or small beer and followed by a dessert of delicious apple pie made from last year's dried apples. John ate ravenously, unable to stop himself after a month of half starving in Ninety-Six.

Stuffed to the gills, John pushed away from the table and lit his pipe, drawing on it slowly. With closed eyes, he blew the smoke upward as he savored the tobacco's smoky flavor. "I had almost forgotten how good food can be. Thank you ladies." He removed the pipe from his lips and smiled at them.

Judith, reaching over to pat her husband affectionately on the knee, smiled back. "We owe it all to Jacob here. Without the outdoor oven that he made, we would have had to cook indoors over the fire place." She looked towards Grainy. "I don't think that we could have stood the heat, do you?"

Grainy looked with a smile towards her husband. She reached out and gently caressed his shoulder. "I would have stood it for you," she assured him tenderly. "Now! If you men will step outside into the breezeway, we women will get this mess cleaned up. Take the boys with you."

She looked sternly at Lynn Celia, who was attempting to make herself small on the bench across from her. "And you stay and help young lady. We females have to stick together, don't we?"

Lynn Celia gave her a snaggle-toothed smile. Her small frame seemed to swell with pride at being included as a woman, even if it was for the purpose of work.

John looked at Grainy as he stood. "If it's all right with you two, I think we'll just mosey over to Sergeant Hopkins's for a spell, " he said quietly. "I need to walk off this supper, so's I can sleep tonight." He gave Grainy a sly wink; it was intercepted by Judith who nudged her friend playfully in the ribs. Grainy suddenly pretended to be engaged in a flurry of important activity as a feeble ploy to hide her blushing face. Judith, more bold that her mentor, laughed heartily. With a rakish grin she called to the children over her shoulder. "Lynn Celia! Simpson! You two will be sleeping on our side of the cabin tonight!"

The first week home crept past contentedly. John and the other Rangers lent a hand helping the three new families erect their cabins along the banks of Long Swamp Creek about a mile to the north of the village. They built their homes in a small cluster, loopholed and situated near enough together so that each cabin could use its musket to sweep its neighbor's walls clear of any enemy in the event of an attack. Having lived on the frontier all their lives, they still had the inbred dread of Indians, and couldn't bring themselves to settle too near to them. The Cherokees in the village sensed this animosity almost instantly, and made it a point to steer clear of the newcomers. Never a man to pass up an opportunity, Hopkins immediately enrolled them in the Loyalist militia, armed each of them with a well-used musket from the King's stores, and assigned them the duty of guarding the northern approach to the village.

The following Sunday John shouldered his old doglock and, accompanied by Jacob and Simpson, went in search of a herd of hogs roaming on the south bank of the river. John loaned Jacob his Charleville for the day and he, in turn, allowed Simpson to proudly lug his battered carbine along, just in case it was needed.

Chestnut trees, which grew in profound abundance across the river, were the perfect food for the herd of hogs that had been intentionally released into the wild[75] by the Cherokees and Rangers. By keeping the river as a buffer, it prevented the hogs from rooting in the fields and destroying the crops.

On the village's side of the river, young boys, armed with bows and arrows, were given the duty of keeping the fields cleared of the large deer population that had expanded to such an extent that they were becoming a nuisance. If left unchecked, they could destroy an entire field of beans, corn, and squash almost overnight. The men of the village had already began formulating plans for a concentrated hunt, designed to both thin the herd and provide an ample supply of smoked and dried meat for the coming winter. That hunt would take place in the Fall, after the weather had cooled.

The three hunters stripped off their clothes and held them in bundles over their heads as they waded the river. The two men wore loose fitting hunting frocks, having left their uniforms at home for the women to clean when they returned from berrying.

Climbing onto the far bank, they used their hands to wipe as much water as they could from themselves. Then, pulling their clothing on over moist skin, they checked the priming in their muskets. Jacob emptied the powder from his pan onto the ground and wiped it clean with the hem of his hunting frock before replacing it with fresh powder. When he was ready, they moved forward single file, with John leading the way. No more than a hundred yards from the river, they came onto a large hog wallow. The churned earth was still damp and the smell of swine tainted the air. John pulled his musket to full cock. Unconsciously, his hand stroked the tomahawk in his belt, ensuring that it would easily slide free if needed. They spread out, moving forward three abreast. Simpson was in the center and a few paces behind the two adults. All three walked stoop shouldered, the muzzles of their flintlocks canted in the direction of travel, their carefully placed feet moving ahead slowly and quietly. Overhead, the wind slipped along the tops of the trees in long sustained gusts, its approach mimicked the sound of approaching rain as it stirred the upper leaves of the giant chestnuts. As the rush of air subsided, the sound would subside along with it, leaving the earth silent for a few fleeting moments before the cycle repeated itself. It seemed as if the earth were breathing.

Underfoot, the ground was carpeted with chestnuts. Squirrels skittered noisily here and there, engaged in a frantic race to gather their own supply of the meaty nuts and store them before the sows, trailed by their litters of piglets, devoured them completely.

John stopped and held up one hand. Musket at the ready, he eased forward, parting the branches of a thick holly with the barrel of his weapon. On the far side of the bush, he spied a brood sow and a half dozen, half-grown piglets. He motioned to Simpson and Jacob, who moved silently to his side. They held their fire while John lined his musket up on the sow and pulled the trigger.

Boom!

The forest exploded with sound. Birds took flight, squawking belligerently, squirrels and pigs scattered helter-skelter among the trunks of the trees. Across the river, in the village, a dog began to bark insistently. When the smoke dissipated, the sow lay dead on the ground, shot cleanly through one eye.

Jacob moved forward. Extending his weapon with both hands, he prodded the carcass. When he was certain that it was dead, he dropped the butt to the ground.

"She'll weigh a good ten stone,"[76] John said proudly. He turned to Simpson. "Hand me the gambrelle[77] and that rope out of your pack. Lets get her hoisted up and butchered, so we can get her back across the river 'fore dark."

With his hunting knife, John pierced the hind legs of the sow and inserted the hooks of the gambrelle into the incisions. The contraption held the legs spread apart. Tying the rope to the eye of the metal bar, the three men hoisted the hog free of the ground, leaving its head dangling no more than a foot in the air. Jacob slit the jugular and they stood back, allowing the blood to drain onto the ground before slitting the belly from crotch to throat. The entrails unraveled onto the ground at their feet.

"I hate to leave those chitterlings to the wolves and foxes," Jacob remarked over his shoulder as he worked.

"Me too," John agreed, "but just the meat will be about all that we can handle between the three of us. We'll come back in a few days with the horses and bag us a couple of whole ones."

Flies and gnats, attracted by the gore, buzzed by the hundreds in dark clouds around their faces and bloody hands as they worked to carve the swine into manageable chucks. When the chore was completed, Jacob shouldered one entire side of the meat and headed for the river, followed by John carrying the other half of the carcass. Semi-coagulated blood oozed from the freshly butchered meat and dripped onto the backs of their hunting frocks, staining them black. Simpson proudly trotted at their heels with the carbine slung over his shoulder and a long musket in each hand.

Back at the cabin, the two men cut the meat into hams, bacon slabs, and ribs. The bacon, hams, and shoulders were hung in a small, ten-by-ten-foot smokehouse that Jacob and Dobbins had built to the rear of the cabin while on parole. They would kindle a slow fire of hickory in the middle of the tightly chinked room and keep it burning for a week. By then the meat would be completely smoked, and show the pleasing pink color that made it appetizing. Had it been wintertime, the easier method of curing would have been used: immersing the hams in salty water for a week and then hanging them from the rooftree of the cabin, tied securely in an osnaburg sack and left to cure for several months.

After kindling a fire in the smoke house, they threw the two slabs of ribs onto a framework of green poles laid over a hickory fire that had been allowed to burn down to hot coals. The ribs would be carefully roasted over the glowing embers, flavored by the oily smoke, until the meat began to separate from the bones. Then it would be forked onto a wooden trencher and served as the main course for supper.

Grainy and Judith returned from berrying with their infants strapped to their backs papoose style. Lynn Celia trotted along beside them, her mouth and fingers stained purple with the juice of blackberries. Both women smiled when they smelled the roasting ribs.

"It looks like you had luck on the hunt today," Grainy said. She removed Daniel from her back and transferred him to Judith's care. "If you'll watch the babes, I'll bake some cornbread and turn these berries into a custard for tonight." That said, she turned her full attention to John. She smiled pleasantly. "Would you please fetch me some wood for the oven?"

* * * *

Over the next two weeks, life at Long Swamp slowly slipped back into a predictable routine. Each day the women would rise, and after going to water, they would assemble to check on the progress of their fields. The men would hunt, taking only enough game to satisfy their immediate needs. In the heat of summer, the meat would spoil rapidly if a hunter overkilled.

Just a few days into August, as they two families were gathered around the table finishing their evening meal, Judith announced that the Cherokees planned to begin celebrating the Green Corn ceremony the next day.

Grainy, seeing the blank look on John's face, explained. "We've forgotten that you've never been in the village when the Green Corn Ceremony was celebrated. But surely you've heard of it?"

"Some kind of a harvest festival, or so I've heard."

Judith jumped into the conversation with the intention of helping Grainy explain the significance of the event. "You've heard of the Martinmas Fair that we Scots celebrate? It's very similar to that. It even has some of the same rituals. Isn't that strange?"

"With all of the Highlanders living in the Cherokee towns, it's no wonder. The Indians probably picked up some of their customs."

"I don't think so. The Traveler tells us that the Cherokees have always observed the festival. I've been told that all of the other tribes do, too."

"You say it will be held tomorrow?"

"Yes. Seven days ago a runner came through and gave us the date. He also took an ear of corn from the fields of the Blue Holly Clan."

"Just one ear?"

"That's all. There's some significance to it, but I'll have to ask The Traveler to explain it. I really don't know much about the different parts of the ritual."

* * * *

The next morning the entire village, Cherokees and Loyalists alike, rose earlier than the sun. All of the fires in the village were extinguished. At the double cabin, Grainy swept the ashes from the fireplace into a bucket, which she emptied into the ash pit behind the cabin where they would be used for making lye soap in the spring. Once the fireplace was swept clean, she laid the beginnings of a new fire, starting with spongy dry punk, taken from a rotten log so dry that it took only a few sparks to ignite it. Over this she placed several pieces of lighter, taken from the rich, sap-filled stumps of downed pines.[78] Finally, she laid some twigs and topped all of this off with pieces of split cedar. After the ceremony had been held in the village council house, a new ceremonial fire would be kindled and runners would visit each home in the settlement. They would rekindle the fires in every hearth using torches lighted from that one sacred flame. Old weapons, plates, and tools were either repaired or discarded. Criminals, who had violated the laws of the Cherokees, would be pardoned, unhappy marriages could be annulled. The slate was wiped clean, a new world had begun.

But first, before all of this took place, everyone in the village—men, women, and children—assembled in the communal fields and began the harvesting of the corn or Selu, as the Cherokee called it, in honor of the mythical woman who was slain to bring it into the world. The harvesting was more of a festival than work. Bag after bag was filled with the juicy ears of green corn and brought in. When enough had been harvested for the feast that night, it was shucked and cooked as soon as the fires had been relighted. Sacrifices consisting of a deer tongue and kernels taken from seven different ears of corn, all taken from a field of a different clan, were burned in the ceremonial fire, along with a sprinkling of sacred tobacco.

After a prayer by the village headman, the women entered with enough food to feed all of the people in the village. Laughter filled the Council House. John, along with Jacob, Dobbins, and Hopkins, gorged himself until he was sure that his stomach would burst. Across the room he could see Sambo and Mambo, looking more like Cherokees in black paint than members of one of King George's regiments, engaged in crude banter with some of their neighbors. A few of the new families of Loyalist refugees also came, but many did not. The Cherokees did not seem to miss them, nor did they seem offended by their absence. John hoped that this benevolent attitude would continue as more and more white families fled to the frontier to seek the protection of the few remaining troops of the King

* * * *

In November, they received news that literally stunned the entire village. After having chased the rebel army out of the Carolinas and into Virginia, General, Lord Cornwallis, had been trapped in a small town on the coast, named Yorktown. On October 19, 1781, after a twenty-day siege, an entire British army had surrendered. John was speechless when he heard the news. Taking his old doglock musket, he crossed the river to hunt and reflect on the news alone. He felt the uncontrollable need to ponder his future. It was almost too bizarre to be true! Less than seven months ago the rebel cause was, for all practical purposes, lost in the South. Then, by some terrible twist of fate, his whole world had come crashing down around his ears. When he had left Ninety-Six, he had felt that the cause was in serious trouble, but this! He hadn't prepared himself for this! Who in their right mind would have thought that it would ever come to this? He roamed through the thick forest in stunned disbelief, oblivious to the game scurrying about him. What would he do now? Where would he go with his family? They couldn't stay here forever, and going back to the rebel held areas after having served in the King's Rangers for the past two years was definitely out of the question. If he wasn't hung outright, what future would he have? No land, no home—no hope. Suddenly, finding himself miles away from home, with the sun already settling, he roused himself enough to kindle a fire and scrape together a bed of leaves for the night. He wondered briefly how Grainy and the others were taking the news. He suddenly regretted leaving without saying a word to anyone. They, too, would need something solid to cling to as their world dissolved into a fog that would soon be blown away by the winds of time.

With the fire burning brightly to keep curious animals at bay, he sat with his back against the base of a tall oak, staring into the flames. His mind was completely unsettled, alternating between total numbness one moment and then filled with racing thoughts of *what if?* the next.

He sat there all night, feeding wood into the fire and watching it being slowly consumed by the flames. It was as if he was watching his own past, once so bright, being transformed into nothingness.

He dozed off sometime during the night. Opening his eyes on a new day already half consumed by father time, he loitered long enough to kick dirt over the remains of last night's fire before beginning the trek back to Long Swamp. He had no idea of what to do.

When he pushed open the door of his cabin that evening Grainy ran to him, clutching him with desperate ferocity. She cried openly, as completely devastated by the news as John had been. He looked around the cabin, seeing it as if in a daze. He could hear his wife's words, but they seemed to be an echo, coming from far away. The efforts of his children to gain his attention left him exhausted. Suddenly he comprehended a few short words directed at him by Judith.

"What are we going to do?" Judith asked him. For the first time he became aware that Jacob was absent. He asked about him.

"They're all over at the Hopkins cabin, trying to figure out what to do," she said. "No one seems to know. Do we stay put, or do we join what's left of the British army in Savannah? No one seems to know." She twisted her hands uncertainly.

No one seems to know, those words summed up the situation in a nutshell. John rose from his chair and headed towards the door.

"I'll be back as soon as I find out anything," he mumbled to no one in particular. He left his musket laying across the table where he had dropped it when he had returned.

Judith picked it up and flipped the frizzen forward. "It's not even loaded." Dropping the weapon onto the table, she began to weep quietly. "For God's sake, what do we do?"

As John approached the Hopkins's cabin, he could hear a sound like the buzzing of a disturbed beehive. Horses were tied to trees all about the area, the atmosphere seemed disturbed, tense. Inside, all of the Rangers, and the majority of the Loyalists in the area, were crowded around the single room. They sat on chairs and tables and with their backs propped against the log walls. Jugs of rum passed freely from hand to hand; many of them looked drunk. Sergeant Hopkins rolled his red eyes in John's direction without rising from his prized rocking chair. He slammed his open palm onto the table, producing a stinging clap! The blow upset a pair of wooden cups sitting on the edge; they toppled to the puncheon floor, spilling their contents in dark puddles.

"About time that you decided to join our little council of war!" he bellowed. He pushed an empty bench with his foot. "Have a seat corporal and help us decide on our course of action," he said before adding the omnipresent, *"No one seems to know what to do."*

John removed his battered hat and hung it on a peg by the door. He crossed the small room slowly, stepping over the outstretched legs of men too far gone to notice. Noticing Lizzy Hopkins sitting up on the edge of the loft with her bare feet dangling in the air, he tipped his head politely. She scowled down disapprovingly at the assemblage below, then dropped the sewing she was working on into her sewing box and clambered down the ladder.

"I think I'll walk over to see Grainy," she announced with a frown. Hopkins glared vacantly in her direction and nodded slowly.

"Good idea. Maybe you women can come up with something." His gazed traveled around the lethargic forms in the room. "We men damned sure can't!" He turned up his mug, emptying it in a long, sustained pull, then banged it noisily on the table.

"Fetch me another 'fore ye leave!" He pushed the mug in Lizzy's direction. She glared at him, then, red-faced, stalked across the room and disappeared into the lean-to, which John had helped add onto the rear of the cabin. She grabbed another jug of rum from the King's stores that were cached there and returned, pausing to pour his mug brimming full. Angrily throwing a shawl around her head and shoulders, she beat a quick retreat through the cabin's door.

Hopkins returned his attention to John. He caressed the jug like a loose woman. "Take a swig or two, Johnny. It sets well in a man's belly when times are bad. Like now." He gave John a long hard stare. "I'm thinkin' that we should lead the Cherokees against the frontier. The war isn't over you know, just Lord Cornwallis's war. There's still British armies in St. Augustine, Savannah, Charleston, Wilmington, New York … Canada." He clicked the locations off on his fingers as he recited the list. "Not to mention us."

John gave him a dubious look. "Come now sergeant, if we gathered every Ranger, from every Cherokee and Creek town in the Indian territories, I doubt that we would have a hundred men. Probably less. What could we do with so few men?"

"Don't forget that we would have at least a thousand warriors with us."

He swiped the back of a grubby hand across his lips. "Between us we could do the rebels a lot of damage."

John let his gaze wander across the table to Jacob and Dobbins, who sat quietly nursing their own cups of rum. Dobbins was staring blankly across the room, his unblinking eyes focused on some slight imperfection displayed by one of the wall logs. Jacob, who had been folded over the tabletop, resting his head in his arms, looked up with vacuous eyes. His face clearly expressed disbelief in the sergeant's idea. He remained silent, but his eyes wandered to John, waiting for him to dissuade Hopkins from this course of action.

John took a long pull from the jug. "We need a hot poker and some butter for this stuff," he said, licking his lips. "Put some kick in it."

"We need to put some kick into rebel pants is what we need!" Hopkins blurted out. "If we don't, mark my words, they'll descend on us like a plague. No siree! We best put the fear of God into them, make them think twice before they come west looking for us."

"What makes you think that they'll come looking for us?"

"They have to."

This new turn of conversation had roused Dobbins from his lethargy; he abruptly took a fresh interest in the topic. Leaning forward, elbows on the table, he surveyed them through bloodshot eyes. When he spoke, his speech was slurred, slow, heavy with the strong smell of rum. "Rebels don't think much, but when they do..." He shook his head; even without finishing the sentence the meanings of his words were obvious. He cleared his throat, looked lazily around at the floor for a place to spit, then swallowed, and took another long drink. "Rebels are fanatics, at least as far as their politics goes. You see, they preach freedom, but the freedom that they espouse is for them alone, not you. You're free to think your own way only so long as you agree with them. Those who don't, must be whipped into submission, or exterminated. They see the disaster that our tolerance for the views of others has reaped for us, and they don't intend on being hacked by the other edge of that same sword." He shook his head before adding softly, "I tell you this, a man who believes he is the only one who is right—that is a dangerous man. They'll never be able to put their minds at ease knowing that there are men out here who disagree with them, men they can't bend to their will. The thought that we might, one day, exercise our freedom to change the world back to what it was, will gnaw at their insides like a rat in a corn crib. Mark my words! Now that they have won this war, those who agitated the most for change will suddenly find themselves called on by God to preserve the status quo. Once that happens, we will have become the radicals, the threat. They'll worry themselves half to death until they convince themselves that we are too much of a danger to their way of life, that we're enemies of their freedom. Then…" He shrugged his shoulders. "They will put an end to us poor misguided bastards once and for all."

"Then you think we should carry on the fight?" Hopkins asked, hopeful that he had found an ally.

"Hell no!" Dobbins sputtered. "That would only make them come for us sooner. I say wait until we have orders to back us up before we make any moves. We're completely cut off out here. For all we know, Charleston and Savannah may already have been taken. I'm just as distressed as you are about this news, but if we run of half-cocked…"

Hopkins banged the side of his fist on the table a few times. "It just don't sit right with me, sitting here and doin' nothing. I just wish…" He stopped, shook his head. A look of defeat hung heavily about him.

"Like my old Pa used to say, be careful what you wish for," Dobbins said quietly.

Chapter 20

Etowah River
Tuesday, New Years Day, 1782

From his position beneath the large, winter-naked limbs of a gigantic red oak, John had a clear view of the Etowah River and the goings on along both of its banks. Resting his shoulder against the rough bark, he grounded his musket and studied the far shore. Behind him, the women and children of the village congregated with knives and hatchets in hand, eager to begin their job of butchering whatever meat the hunters provided. They stood quietly, arms at their sides, faces turned to the north, studying a thin pall of smoke that rose above the canopy of the tall trees. The smoke marked the progress of a crescent of fire set by the hunters to flush the trapped game in the direction of the river.

At the bottom of the low bank, the prows of several canoes jutted out from a sandbar. The men in them chatted idly as they waited to push out into the current at the first sight of the panic-stricken animals plunging into the river. Their job was to catch their quarry while they were still struggling in the water and dispatch them with quick blows of their tomahawks, or if possible, simply reach from the canoe and push the head beneath the water until it drowned.[79]

John and a handful of other men waited atop the riverbank, ready to use their muskets on any animals that managed to escape onto their side of the river. Farther back in the woods, the young boys of the village waited, eagerly bouncing on the balls of their feet with pent-up energy and suppressed excitement. They would bag the smaller game that managed to slip past the hunters. This was to be the final and largest hunt of the season. They hoped it would provide enough meat to feed the entire village throughout the coming winter.

The panicked sounds of many feet shuffling through dry leaves drew nearer. The larger males, deer and Wapiti, intermixed with a few fleet-footed black bears, were the first to appear. Some of the animals, surprised by the presence of the hunters, hesitated and tried to turn back, only to be herded along by the intense heat of the approaching flames. Others leapt into the water without hesitation and attempted to make it to the dubious safety of the far shore. The canoes shot out into the current, men paddling furiously to overtake particular animals, shouting and gesturing wildly as they closed in for their kills.

John, startled by the sudden appearance of a rare woods bison, shouldered his musket. The muzzle of his weapon followed the animal as it drew closer. He fired the moment that its front legs touched the solid earth of the riverbed. The ball struck the animal squarely on the crown of its head and ricocheted off the thick skull. It whined away into the trees on the far side of the river, producing a series of hammering sounds as it careened from tree trunk to tree trunk.

While John frantically reloaded, the animal emerged from the river, scattering the startled hunters. Jacob stepped from behind a tree, swung his musket to his shoulder, and fired. The ball struck the bison behind the right shoulder with a solid thunk! The animal, seemingly unaffected by the wound, bellowed defiance at its tormentors and charged forward. Women scrambled for cover, snatching children from the ground and flinging them across their shoulders like sacks of cornmeal as they fled.

Swinging his freshly loaded musket at his side, John chased the rampaging bison away from the riverbank, silently praying that the massive creature would not seriously injured anyone. His legs churned wildly; ahead he could see wild-eyed women and squalling children scurrying out of the animal's path.

His heart leapt into his throat when he recognized the very pregnant form of Judith Fenton scrambling to reach safety. She led Lynn Celia by the hand, literally dragging the child along the ground in her hurried flight to escape as the enraged animal thundered down on her. John couldn't tell if it was his shout, or Jacob's, that caught Judith's attention. She glanced over her shoulder with desperate eyes, watching as the animal, its shaggy head lowered, bore down on her. Realizing that she would never make it to safety, she mustered the strength to hoist Lynn Celia into both hands and throw her to one side, out of the path of the charging bison. The child landed spread-eagle beside the trunk of a large oak. A puff of dust sprouted around her as she slid on her stomach, clutching at the earth with tiny hands. Almost before she came to a complete halt, a dusky hand reached from behind the tree and snatched her to safety.

Judith, thrown off balance, stumbled forward and fell, landing on her stomach, her arms breaking her fall. She made one desperate attempt to rise before the huge animal rumbled over her. Planting one of its massive feet squarely between her shoulder blades, it crushed her to the ground, before thundering through the final ring of women and children.

With an almost inhuman wail, Jacob threw his musket aside and raced headlong for his wife. She lay on the ground, unmoving. He pulled her into his lap, begging her to speak, demanding that she be unhurt. Her eyes rolled upward to meet his, a slight smile formed at the corner of her lips as they formed soft words, spoken and immediately lost as they were carried away by the wind.

Jacob, tears streaming down his face, leaned nearer. "Yes, my love?"

"A Kiss?"

Jacob pressed his lips to hers with a desperate intensity. Judith smiled up at him.

"You... always could... take... my breath... away..." she panted. There was a sigh as her spirit fled, then silence. It was their last good-bye; Judith was gone.

Gasping for breath, John raced to the tree that had shielded Lynn Celia from harm. He dropped to one knee as he gathered the child into his arms and hugged her to his chest. He thanked God for sparing her life, while behind him Jacob's wails echoed through the woods. The young Cherokee girl who had saved Lynn Celia held out her hand, assuming responsibility for her safety, and motioned for John to go to his friend.

Jacob sat on the ground, holding Judith's lifeless body in his arms. He looked up and wailed his sorrow to the heavens. John knelt beside him and place his hand lightly on one shoulder. Judith's face seemed serene in death; the great unknown had held no terror for her. A tear trickled down his cheek. He quickly wiped it away as Grainy and Lizzy Dobbins knelt in the leaves beside the body. Their faces were masks of stunned disbelief. Grainy clasped Judith's lifeless hand between hers. She held it to her cheek, studying the face of her dearest friend through tears that threatened to blind her, memorizing for the last time the features that would soon be lost to her forever.

A ring of concerned faces surrounded the sad drama. Over their lamenting, a barely discernible volley of shots rang out in the distance as the hunters finally brought the rampage of the wounded beast to an end.

One of the Cherokee women cried out and pointed to a slight movement beneath Judith's skirt. She dropped to her knees, held the material up, reached carefully beneath, and withdrew a struggling baby girl. The last act of Judith's short life had been the creation of another human being.

Grainy immediately took charge of the infant. Clasping it protectively, she took it to the river and wiped it clean. The child began to wail, a strong, hearty cry that assured everyone present that it was a completely healthy infant. Spotting one of the newly arrived refugees from the Ceded Lands with an infant in her arms, Grainy confronted her.

"You have enough milk for two," she stated flatly. "Feed this child while I see to its mother." She thrust the newborn gently, but firmly into the woman's arms.

* * * *

Judith was buried the next day at noon, in a hastily built coffin of cedar. Jacob vehemently prohibited burying her in a simple shroud; he would have no dirt thrown into her face. He sat alone beside the grave that day, refusing the food Grainy offered him. When he spoke, it was in monosyllables, any movements he attempted were slow and lethargic. He retreated into himself. He desired nothing but to be alone. As night fell, he continued to refuse food or comfort. John took a blanket to him and wrapped it around his shoulders. The temperature was falling rapidly, it was destined to be a cold night.

For the next several hours both Grainy and John took turns, stepping out into the breezeway of the double cabin to check on him as the night grew darker. When it grew too dark to see, John set a cup of warmed cider next to him and draped another blanket over his shoulders. Towards midnight, John banked the fire and went to bed. When they woke in the morning, Jacob was gone.

A pall hung over the entire village. Judith had been one of those rare individuals who was a friend to everyone. The eyes of Loyalist and Cherokee alike would brighten at the merest sight of her. She never turned away a person in need, never shirked her fair share of work.

A week later, Jacob reappeared, tired and trail worn. When asked where he had been, he simply grunted, "Nowhere." It was a mystery to everyone, and would remain one. Jacob had grudgingly made his peace with God and returned to be both father and mother to his grieving son and infant daughter.

After Jacob returned from the river, cleaned and freshly shaven, Grainy laid the newborn gently in his arms. "I hired a widowed Loyalist woman as a wet nurse for little Judith," she told him. "I took the liberty of naming her Judith. I hope that you don't mind."

Jacob choked back a sob, and nodded his head. He held the child up, inspecting her features. "She'll be the image of her mama," he spoke his thoughts aloud. The child began to gurgle, she clutched his index finger with a tiny hand. He rested his daughter in the crook of his arm and reached out to his son, who stood with a thumb thrust into his mouth, patiently eyeing his father. Drawing the boy to his side, Jacob rested his cheek on the child's tousled hair.

"It's just me and you, Daniel," he whispered, "just you, and me, and little Judith."

* * * *

One week later, the Loyalist population of Long Swamp more than tripled in a single day when Colonel Waters arrived, accompanied by over a hundred Loyalist men, women, and children. Embolden bands of rebel irregulars, backed up by the militia and a smattering of Continentals, had forced the abandonment of Waters's Fort and precipitated a general migration of the King's people still living in the Ceded Lands. The people represented at least twelve families, along with a goodly number of single men who had been marked for execution by the rebel government now sitting in Ebenezer. Confiscated Tory property was being sold to fund the rebel government in lieu of taxes; no loyal family was safe from depredations.

Among those displaced faces from Waters's Fort, Grainy and John located their old friends, Matthew and Rebecca Nowland, the couple who had sheltered them back in 1778, when they were, themselves, refugees. Now happy to return the favor, they helped them carry their belongings to the double cabin where Jacob turned over his side of the cabin to them. Another family of old friends, James and Jenny Brooks, who had given shelter to the Weatherfords at the same time, also moved into that side of the cabin. Jacob and his widowed wet-nurse moved in with John and Grainy.

In the hustle and bustle of raising shelters for the newcomers and searching out food supplies, the war was all but forgotten. Even Colonel Waters worked from sunup to sundown like the Moses of old, helping his people settle in the Promised Land.

In the second week of February, Thunder's Child and Robin returned to the village. They brought a message with them from Savannah, sealed by Colonel Brown and addressed to Colonel Waters. The colonel called a meeting of all of the Rangers in Long Swamp. They were to congregate at the Hopkins's cabin just after sunset. He also summoned any of the refugees who wished to join the militia.

That evening, John, accompanied by the other men of the double cabin, walked through the harvested fields, heading to the meeting with Colonel Waters. The yellowed stalks of last year's harvest, beaten down by wind, rain, and animals, crunched and crackled beneath their feet. A thin wisp of dust trailed in their wake.

"What do you think the colonel wants us for?" Matt Nowland asked whimsically. He chewed on a long shaft of broomstraw as they walked.

"Whatever it is, it bodes ill for us," Jacob replied. All three men turned to look at the speaker, the sound of Jacob's voice had become a rare occurrence. Heads down, they continued on. No one replied to Jacob and he didn't speak again.

A group of women, including Sarah Hopkins and Lizzy Dobbins, passed them in the dark, heading in the opposite direction. The women fretted quietly among themselves, complaining about the coarse jokes and salacious behavior of the half-drunken throng of men they had left behind.

Sarah cast a quick glance at the small knot of men and bobbed her head. Her face, hidden by the darkness, said, "Evening," before she returned her attention to the other women. The greeting lacked warmth, was given strictly out of habit.

"Evening," all three men responded as they politely tipped their hats.

The two groups continued in silence, following opposite courses. The steady hum of male voices grew louder as they approached the Hopkins's cabin.

John was surprised by the number of men milling around on the hard packed clay of the Hopkins's yard. All told, he estimated that at least forty men had answered the call, many of them wearing the patched and faded green jackets of the King's Rangers. Twenty Rangers who had been conducting raids out of Waters's old fort had accompanied him to Long Swamp. Fifteen of the newly arrived refugees, ranging in age from fifteen to fifty, had also reported to be sworn into the militia, which until now had been composed of the handful of families settled to the north of the village. Jugs of rum provided by the colonel were passing freely from hand to hand among the laughing recruits. John mused to himself that those jugs would, in all likelihood, be the only pay that many of them ever received. The four men pushed through the milling crowd that blocked the door of the cabin. As they stepped into the dimly lighted interior, Sergeant Hopkins clapped his hand roughly on John's shoulder.

"Here's the corporal, Sir!" he shouted to be heard over the hullabaloo inside the cabin.

Colonel Waters looked up from a sheet of paper. He smiled with recognition and dropped the letter onto the Hopkins's table. Advancing across the room he extended his hand. "A pleasure to see you again." He inclined his head slightly, John returned the gesture.

"John, here, can write a fair hand," Hopkins told the colonel proudly.

"Good, then I am assigning you the task of enrolling these men in the militia." He pointed to the puncheon table in the middle of the room. "Sit him down there," he told Hopkins, pointing to the table. "Make sure that he is well-supplied with foolscap[80] and ample writing supplies." Without waiting for a reply he moved on, greeting other new arrivals like long lost friends.

John settled himself onto the rude bench behind the table, freshly sharpened quill in hand, a stoneware inkwell and sander sitting to one side. As each man stepped forward, he stated his name, and, taking the offered pen, signed the militia list. If unable to write, a man simply indicated his willingness to join by inscribing his mark. John then wrote his name for him beside it, along with the notation, "his mark." After every few names, John paused to sand the ink before somberly continuing the ritual.[81]

Once all twelve men had been added to the muster list, Colonel Waters read them the articles of war directly from a copy that he kept specifically for this purpose. When this was done, Gilbert Grant, a King's Justice of the Peace who had accompanied the refugees, and who had also inscribed his name on the list, attested the document to make it legal.

This formality complete, the colonel instructed the men to gather in the front of the cabin. He stood in the open doorway, illuminated by the light of several candle lanterns. His gaze traveled across the forms of the forty men sitting cross-legged or leaning on the muzzles of their muskets, appraising them silently. They waited in silence, wondering what he would say. Many of the older ones were keenly aware that their futures could very well rest on the next words spoken by this man.

"Men," he began, waving the letter from Colonel Brown before him as a symbol of his authority. "I've received orders from Colonel Brown in Savannah. He has instructed me to send as many raiding parties of Indians and militia against the frontier as possible. He further instructs me that each of these parties will be led by members of the King's Rangers. They will rotate that duty amongst themselves. As for the militia…" He paused to give them time to focus their attention on his upcoming words. "You will be divided into parties of ten men. Each of these parties will also be led by one of the Rangers. Your job will be to patrol the frontier and alert us of any encroachments by rebel parties. If possible, you will engage and destroy them." He paused, waiting as quiet murmurs passed from man to man. He smiled and added quietly, "These, of course, are my orders, passed on to you. They are to be obeyed. Are there any questions?"

One of the new arrivals rose to his feet. He removed his battered hat, holding it in both hands before him, and spoke in a quiet, almost apologetic voice.

"With all due respect colonel, with the war all but over, is it wise to stir up the rebels with these raids? What good purpose will it possibly serve?"

Colonel Waters bowed in the man's direction. "The war's not lost. We still have armies in Savannah, Charleston, New York, and several other places throughout the colonies. Don't think for an instant that we cannot turn this business back to our advantage. Why just look at what the rebels have done in just nine months! Surely, his Majesties forces can duplicate that feat with the proper efforts."

As usual, the men were divided into three camps: those who wanted to prosecute the war to the last extremity, those who wanted to admit defeat and begin building a new life immediately, and those who thought it wise to sit idly by and wait to see which way the wind ultimately ended up blowing. Then there was the fourth, silent camp, that had secretly decided to desert and join the rebels at the very first opportunity. Colonel Waters quickly reminded everyone that the choice was not up to them. They were all soldiers of the Crown, duly and lawfully enlisted and bound by oath to follow the orders of their superiors. On this note, the meeting was adjourned. Every able-bodied man was to muster at Sergeant Hopkins's cabin at noon tomorrow with his weapon. After they had been inspected, they would be given their assignments.

John and Jacob were assigned to accompany Sergeant Hopkins and a raiding party composed of warriors from Long Swamp, Little Chota, and Tugaloo Old Town. Riders had already been dispatched to those towns with the message that all warriors would rendezvous in seven days at the Chopped Oak,[82] between Little Chota and Tugaloo Old Town. There, they would plan their strategy and break into smaller parties before moving on the frontier settlements. Other Rangers received similar assignments and departed to carry out raids along the frontier from Georgia to Virginia. The British had every intention of keeping the pressure on the rebels, never allowing them to totally regroup and organize their newly conquered territory.

John and his group arrived at the Chopped Oak six days later; the warriors from the other towns were absent. Climbing from his saddle and dropping heavily to the ground, Hopkins ordered the other men to dismount and prepare camp.

"We'll wait here for no more than two days before we push on," he informed John and Jacob. "In the meantime, get as much rest as you can, you'll need it."

That evening, John and Jacob, finishing the last of their supper, sat with their backs against the scarred trunk of the ancient oak and watched the sunset in the western sky. The twenty-five warriors from Long Swamp lay scattered haphazardly about the campsite, their attitudes indifferent. They made no attempt to hide themselves, feeling they were safe from attack this far inside their own country. Many of them passed the time gambling, others smoked, a few slept. Hopkins separated himself from a group of warriors and approached the two Rangers. He settled cross-legged onto the ground, facing them.

"We'll leave here the day after tomorrow and travel down the Savannah, staying on the Georgia side of the river. We'll bypass everything until we get to the Broad River, then swing back around and forage our way back home. My plan is to strip the countryside clean, kill any men that resist and take any women and children who look healthy enough to stand the ordeal as captives. We'll hold them to exchange for our own people. The rest we'll hold as hostages, or ransom. Any questions?"

"What about those women not able to travel?" John asked.

"Leave them; the rebels can tend to them later." He studied John's face. "You haven't been with us on one of these expeditions where the Indians outnumber us. It can get savage real quick. This will make your ride with Waters and McGirth seem tame if the Indians get out of hand. Keep an eye on them. Their rules of war are different from ours, but we need them. If it comes down to a choice between offending them or sacrificing the life of some rebel to keep them happy, don't interfere. Without their help, we don't stand a chance of dealing with these rebels." Noting the hesitant look on John's face, Hopkins looked toward Jacob. "Am I correct?"

Jacob nodded. He had seen many things that were best forgotten during the past year as the war steadily degenerated into a savage civil war. The men who had cast their lot with the Rangers had found out to their own grief that old friends make the most vindictive and cruel enemies.

Hopkins rose to go. He patted John reassuringly on the shoulder. "Don't worry none. Unless the rebels start something, the Cherokees are honorable fighters."

At noon the next day, twelve warriors from Little Chota came trotting their warhorses into camp. They whooped excitedly and waved the new muskets that had been issued to them from the King's stores as an incentive to join the expedition. Four hours later, a similar party arrived from Tugaloo Old Town.

* * * *

The raiding party departed at first light. The warriors were groggy after spending the night working themselves into a frenzy, dancing and chanting under the Chopped Oak and mimicking the horrors that they intended to bestow on any hapless rebels that fell into their hands. The Rangers led the procession. Muskets, carried horizontally across their saddles, bounced to the rhythm of their mounts as they snaked down the narrow trail past Toccoa Falls and struck out for the Savannah. By late afternoon, they had moved far down river and penetrated the outer edges of rebel territory. That night, they made a cold camp, posting double sentries around its perimeter.

Before the first faint streaks of dawn appeared in the eastern sky, they rolled out of their blankets and into the chill of a March morning. After a breakfast of dried meat, they continued moving south, bypassing unsuspecting cabins, mentally marking their locations as they slipped past them in the trees. The isolated families, unaware of their passing, continued to work their farms and fields, ignorant of the fact that they had been marked and were now destined for destruction.

After three days of riding, the war party made a final camp fifteen miles north of Augusta. Parties of rebel militia had passed them several times in the past two days heading east at a fast trot, always east, where other groups of Rangers and Cherokees were already at work. Hopkins sat beside Thunder's Child, talking to him in a lighthearted tone; the success of their raid seemed to be foreordained. Hopkins let out a short laugh; Thunder's Child flashed a rare smile.

Jacob nudged John, who sat on the ground beside him, and indicated the two men. "They seem to be confident about this business, but somehow it just doesn't seem right, burning the homes of these folks. It doesn't seem fair."

"What doesn't seem fair?" John lay back, hands clasped behind his head. He looked up at the sky, painted red by the setting sun.

"That the people who started this war never have to suffer for it. They sit in the Rebel Congress up there in Philadelphia, talking about rights and justice, while the innocent people who have nothing to gain do all the fighting and dying." He lay back alongside John. Resting his head on the ground, he folded his arms across his chest. "What do you think will happen to us when this war is over?"

John had thought about that question many times before. "We'll go back to our homes and rebuild, start over again," he said. "It will be just like the past few years never happened."

"I don't think that we can ever go back to the way that it was. For one thing, half of the people that we know will be gone. Either killed, or run away." He shook his head, grinding the dry grass into his already matted hair. "Nope, that life has slipped through our fingers. It's gone forever."

Jacob waited for an answer. The only sound was John's steady, shallow breathing. Jacob smiled, covered his face with his hat and drifted off. Tomorrow promised to be a busy day.

The next morning the war party broke into three groups and headed north. Each would advance five miles apart from the other, confiscating and burning as it went. Prisoners were to be herded along as fast as possible, those not able to keep up were to be left behind. Those were Sergeant Hopkins *official* orders.

John's group started north along their original route. Paralleling the river, they came upon cabin after cabin of terrified settlers. Most of the Cherokees sprinted ahead, leaving John to follow behind with a small group who checked the area to make sure that the destruction was complete after the warriors moved on. Each burning farm he passed depressed him deeply, a feeling of wanton destruction had descended over the raiding party, several times he happened on the scalped and mutilated bodies of men, sometimes women, who had resisted the tide of destiny and paid the ultimate price.

The three groups converged at a prearranged rendezvous just before sunset. John's party arrived first and spread out, acting as sentries around the perimeter of the camp in the unlikely event that they were being pursued by rebel militia. John hadn't forgotten the lessons learned at Hammond's Store.

Sergeant Hopkins's party rode in thirty minutes later, herding a forlorn group of captives before it. John counted eight women, many clutching children to them as they stumbled into the camp. Matted, tangled hair framed dusty faces streaked by tears and sweat; their bare feet looked bruised and battered. They moved listlessly, devoid of hope, living with the terror that at any moment they could be set upon by the ring of painted warriors that prodded them along at gunpoint. John noticed one young woman with her arms tied behind her back and a pole thrust through them at the elbows. Her face was blackened, smeared with oily paint by a vindictive warrior. Everyone present knew the meaning of the blackened face, her fate had already been decided. She would die a slow, horrible death, unless some kind-hearted Cherokees stepped forward to adopt her into their family. The woman looked around, her eyes shone feverishly behind the black mask, giving her the appearance of an owl. She bared her teeth in a snarl, spitting curses at the warrior who led her forward with a noose around her neck. Having endured enough of her insults, the warrior gave the rope a vicious tug, pulling her forward and off balance. She stumbled and, unable to break her fall with her bound hands, crashed face first into the ground. The warrior stopped and glared down at her from the back of his horse. As she struggled to regain her footing, she spit blood and dirt from her battered lips.

John asked Hopkins what the woman's crime was.

"Being a damned rebel!" Hopkins retorted angrily. "She doesn't know when to keep her mouth shut!" He shook his head, disgusted by the woman's lack of sense. "We caught her in a cabin alone. She barricaded herself and fought it out with us, even wounded one of the Cherokees with an ax when he broke down the door. I tried to be civil with her, but this was the thanks that I got!" He motioned toward the woman. "I tell you, we'll be damned for this in every rebel newspaper once the word gets out. My detachment hasn't had to harm a single person; their men are all away chasing Indians." He laughed. "Poor fools! Now this hardheaded woman has agitated the Cherokees so much that they're going to burn her. Probably tonight, if she doesn't learn to mind her tongue!"

Jacob's wing of the expedition arrived after dark. Working through the area the farthest from the river, they had destroyed the fewest cabins. Only four prisoners had been taken. These all rode behind their captors in relative comfort. Jacob looked agitated as he rode up to the other two Rangers.

"Slim pickings," Hopkins observed.

Jacob bobbed his head. "We had four militiamen cornered in a gully about four miles back of here, but I couldn't get the Indians to flush them out. Damn it! They're probably already half way to Augusta! We'll have that damned Wizard Owl,[83] on our tail pretty soon!"

"Let him come," Hopkins said matter-of-factly. "We'll take care of him if he shows his face around here."

The sound of a scuffle breaking out drew their attention to a knot of Cherokees. The warriors were milling angrily around the captives. The black-faced woman had spit into the face of one of the headmen. He hovered over her, tomahawk poised to strike, but the warrior who had claimed her as his captive would not allow it. The two warriors argued hotly; it threatened to quickly turn violent. Sergeant Hopkins rushed to defuse a situation that could escalate to the point of splitting the war party. He stood between the two antagonists, trying desperately to mediate the situation. The three men exchanged heated words, arms flung here and there to emphasize some important point. The voices subsided slowly. John and Jacob began to relax. They could tell by the tone of the conversation that some compromise was being worked out. Hopkins kept looking from one warrior to the other, asking short, pointed questions, that they nodded their heads in agreement to.

Having resolved the issue to the satisfaction of both parties, He detached himself from the duo and walked back to where John and Jacob waited. He shook his head. "That was close! I thought for a moment that we were going to be fighting each other."

Jacob laughed, a relieved laugh now that the tension of the moment had dissipated. "What was the decision?"

"A poor one for that woman. She'll be tortured in both villages before they burn her. That way both of the warriors will be avenged for her insults." A slight shudder ran up his spine. "I just glad that I won't have to witness it."

"We can't allow that!" Jacob's face turned red in anger. He was clearly horrified by the decision.

Hopkins placed his hand lightly on the bigger man's shoulder. He looked into his eyes as he spoke to make sure that John understood what he was about to say. "We are in no position to *not* allow it, understand?"

Both John and Jacob slept fitfully that night.

* * * *

John and his party crawled forward, their movements hidden by the night as they snaked through the scattered tree trunks, closing in on the unsuspecting cabin that sat like a lonely sentinel guarding the outer reaches of a far-flung frontier. All about them, crickets and other night creatures fell silent at their approach, as if sensing the tragedy that was to come.

The one-roomed structure sat alone in the middle of a tiny clearing, surrounded by a sea of trees. A faint, silvery moon glowed softly, illuminating the open area and allowing the attackers to glimpse the first coils of smoke as they drifted from the throat of the stick-and-mud chimney. John could visualize the woman inside, stirring the banked coals to life, laying the makings of a new fire over them, readying the ingredients of a poor breakfast while waiting for the flames to come to life. Behind her, sleepy-faced children would be rolled tightly in their blankets, savoring those last cherished minutes of warmth before duty rousted them from their beds and sent them scurrying out to face another day of chores. There would be no chores today.

John and Thunder's Child stepped lightly to the door, the latchstring was in, they looked at each other, John nodded. Quietly, he placed his hands on both sides of the doorframe and used his booted foot to kick the door open. As the door swung inward, he saw a very rotund and matronly looking woman turn toward him. She was holding a wooden bowl of corn meal in her hands; it dropped to the floor. The contents rose like a mushroom under the impact before settling back into the bowl. She screamed and her hands started toward her face. They froze halfway and began to quiver in fear as Thunder's Child and John crowded into the cramped room. The woman sank to her knees and continued to wail pitifully, her own cries of terror mixing with those of her terrified children. Startled by the wailing of their mother, the children boiled from beneath their patchwork quilts like a litter of puppies and bolted instinctively to her side, congregating behind her, using her rounded body like a human shield, confident of her protection.

"For God's sake, woman! Be quiet!" John barked the command into the woman's upturned face. He was more than a little unnerved by her terrified screams. Looking at the hideously painted face of Thunder's Child, he understood what the woman must feel. He knelt beside her and reached out to comfort her. She shrank back, with the same startled look that people display when they unexpectedly encounter a snake in the grass.

"We are not going to harm you," he told her, trying to control his voice in an effort to calm the hysterical woman. The woman increased her howling.

"E lo we hi!"[84] Thunder's Child leapt forward as he barked the word at the woman. He stopped, holding his hideously painted face inches away from hers. The woman's screams ended as abruptly as if an invisible hand had reached out and choked them off. The warrior looked up at John and smiled. Then he stood, and assuming a dignified posture, pointed forcefully towards the door, "Do ye hi!" He snapped the Cherokee word for outside, into the woman's upturned face. Startled, she hesitated; he repeated the command. Reaching down and pulling her to her feet, he gave her a slight shove in the direction of the open door. Hesitant at first, the woman moved towards the opening with small, uncertain steps, her four children tagging along behind her like ducklings. When she realized that no one was going to stop her, she broke into a run and disappeared into the darkness outside.

The clearing around the cabin was alive with painted warriors herding any animals they could find together and lighting torches as they prepared to burn the cabin and the small barn behind it. The woman's plump legs, energized by the sight of the savage raiders, propelled her forward with greater speed than seemed possible for a person of her stature. Despite her weight, she coaxed amazing speed from her overworked legs as she raced across the clearing, her children dutifully following in her wake. Some of the warriors stopped and shouted encouragement as she ran past. They laughed as the woman's legs pumped furiously, laboring to drive her to the safety of the forest. No one interfered with her. They turned back to their work, methodically stripping the poor farm of anything of value before putting what was left to the torch.

By the time the raiding party had returned to the Chopped Oak, they had over thirty-five prisoners, most of them children, and a hundred head of livestock. Not one raider had been killed or seriously injured, and over thirty rebel farms had been destroyed. The raid was a great success; they had deprived the rebel army of tons of desperately needed food.

* * * *

The raids continued throughout the spring, their frequency subsiding as the planting time rolled around. Then, they increased again, reaching their height in May and June. At the end of July they received word that the British had evacuated Savannah. Disheartened, they discontinued the forays completely.

Despite repeated urgings to continue the fight from British General Alexander Leslie, whose forces still controlled Charleston, the Rangers knew that the end was at hand.

"Why should people continue to die, just to give the peace commissioners a bargaining chip in their negotiations?" John and the other Rangers asked each other as they rationalized their unwillingness to continue leading raids against the frontier settlements. When their officers ordered them onward, they threw up their hands in resignation and led the raids, but mysteriously could locate no rebels to harass. With the celebration of the Green Corn ceremony in September, the raids stopped completely as the Cherokees elected to stay at home and enjoy their harvest. When the headmen were urged by Colonel Waters to dispatch warriors with his Rangers, they politely shook their heads and went about their own business.

The Cherokees were slowly beginning to change their attitudes about the presence of the Loyalist in their towns. It was a subtle shift, but noticeable to the Rangers and their families. Invitations to join in dances ceased, as did the friendly, drop by visits of old friends. The presence of the Loyalists was generally becoming viewed as a necessary evil, since Colonel Brown was still sporadically sending them supplies from St. Augustine via the Creek country. Even so, every Ranger and Loyalist knew that it would take only one major catastrophe to turn the entire Cherokee nation against them.

News of that catastrophe filtered through the stunned Cherokee nation and exploded on the men at Long Swamp Village one bright Sunday morning in September of 1782.

Chapter 21

Long Swamp Village
Sunday, September 26, 1782

Few of the English celebrated the Ripe Corn ceremony with the Cherokees that year, the exceptions being the six Rangers who had been garrisoning Long Swamp for the past few years. John and Grainy had taken part, along with the other Rangers, but the atmosphere had been subdued. With the exception of The Traveler and her immediate household, few words were exchanged with them. Mildly uncomfortable, they had all departed slightly depressed, sensing that an unhappy change would soon be occurring in their lives. Sambo, Mambo, and Nat, along with their families, were the exceptions. They seemed to be accepted as permanent inhabitants, perhaps because, unlike the white Rangers, they truly had no place to retreat to, no family to fall back on. They had found their new home; there would be no moving on for them.

Two days later, a rider raced into town on a lathered animal that looked ready to collapse at any moment. He slid from the saddle and took a long pull from his canteen before blurting out his message to the excited crowd that had gathered around him in anticipation of some dreaded and dire news.

"Pickens and Clarke are ridin' against us!" he exclaimed between gulps of air. "They crossed the Savannah from Long Canes and attacked Tugaloo Old Town last week. They burned it to the ground!"

Disbelief registered on many faces, others simply nodded their heads. They had long expected some form of retaliation for their raids on the border settlements.

The messenger continued, "When I left yesterday, they were moving towards Little Chota. The men there have already sent their women and children to safety on the other side of the mountains, but some of them are coming here. They'll need every warrior that we have to help them turn the Americans back." He paused for a moment, and looked around. "If they destroy all of the crops that we have stored for the winter…" His voice trailed off. There was no need to tell them what they already knew.

After conferring hurriedly with the headmen, Sergeant Hopkins raced away to muster his Rangers. They would leave tomorrow, Cherokees, Rangers, and militia to head off this invasion of their land.

* * * *

Twelve days later, the six Rangers, accompanied by Colonel Waters, sat their mounts atop a steep-sided hill on the south bank of the Chattahoochee River. They watched as the rebel columns moved into the Nacoochee Valley and fanned out across the harvested fields.

The Cherokees had retreated before the oncoming Americans. Twice they had fired on the advancing column, slowing its movement for a few hours before falling back, biding their time and waiting until there were enough men gathered to resist this invasion. They had watched with impotent rage as the soldiers, commanded by General Andrew Pickens and Colonel Elijah Clarke, burned town after town. Tugaloo Old Town, Tussee, Estatoe, Soquee all lay in ashes, their carefully stored crops destroyed. With the destruction of each town, the Cherokees had grown more surly and hostile to the presence of the Loyalists living among them. More than once, John had overheard them blaming this destruction on the Rangers, forgetting the part their own warriors played in bringing about this invasion.

Colonel Waters twisted in his saddle and looked down at the trail leading to the southwest. Just past the ford in the river he had concealed his thirty loyal militiamen, along with the warriors from Little Chota and Long Swamp. He turned to face his men and once again reiterated his plan to ensure that every man understood exactly what he was to do.

"Once they get to the village, we'll ride to the ford and let them see us. Act surprised as hell! Fire off a few shots to needle them, then wheel your mounts around and run like the devil himself is after you! Make it look like you're panicked. After you clear the far end of the ambush, turn about and engage any of the enemy that pursues you. With them caught from three sides, we should be able to deliver them a sting they won't soon forget. Any questions?"

All of the Rangers nodded, they had seen this trick used repeatedly against rebel militia. For some unexplained reason, even after losing countless men to this transparent ploy, a handful of rebels simply couldn't resist thundering after a group of Loyalists when they spotted them. If the fleeing group consisted of Indians, or blacks—well, that was a foregone conclusion—the whole damned army would race after them. Unfortunately, Colonel Waters didn't have enough men to handle a whole army; he would have to be satisfied with whatever he could get.

Descending to the trail, they found Blackstone patiently waiting for them. He smiled affably.

"Afternoon," Blackstone said in his quiet voice. He reached inside his coat and produced a Cherokee amulet that he extended to John. "The Forgotten One asked me to give you this. She claims that it will protect you from harm."

John took the talisman and slipped the leather thong over his neck and tucked it securely inside his shirt.

"Obliged." He nodded his head in Blackstone's direction. "A man can't have enough luck in times like these."

Blackstone smiled. "I've gotten my people started toward Long Swamp, figured to make myself useful with you gentlemen, if you don't have any objections."

Waters nodded. "You stay with me. We'll wait for these four men at the far end of the ambush." Leaving Hopkins, Dobbins, John, and Jacob to play their parts, the remainder of the Rangers trotted southward on the heels of the two officers. The four men sat their mounts silently, giving the others time to get to their positions. Hopkins reached into his saddlebag and pulled out a twist of tobacco. He took a bite and offered it to the others; they all shook their heads, preferring to smoke instead.

"All right men," Hopkins said through the chaw in his cheek, "let's get this shindig started."

The men cantered along the trail, making as much noise as possible without being too transparent in their actions. They halted at the edge of the river, staring as if surprised at the swarming group of militia. John hoisted his Charleville to his shoulder and fired at the nearest knot of men. One of them yelped and spun around. He stood staring across the open ground in their direction, dumfounded that he had been signaled out to die for the cause of liberty. He fell forward, his body straight, like a toppling tree and crashed onto his face. Dust swirled outward. The men with him looked up. One of them pointed across the river towards the knot of Rangers milling on the far side.

While John reloaded, the other three Rangers discharged their muskets into the militiamen. Another rebel dropped to the ground. The Rangers wasted no time in taking to their heels and racing pell-mell down the trail to the south. A dozen militiamen followed them, hallooing like hunters whose dogs had sighted their quarry. The rebel officers shouted after them, damning them as fools and ordering them back to the ranks. All but four of the pursuers reined in, turning back reluctantly after casting envious eyes on the backs of their galloping comrades. They were certain they had been cheated of great sport.

The Rangers led their quarry on the fool's errand for a quarter of a mile before abruptly turning on them. The lead rider reined his mount in hard;

it reared on hind legs, sliding a few feet before coming to a complete stop. The rider's eyes widened, suddenly aware that he had led his men into a trap. Before they could turn, a volley of arrows flew into them. Cherokees flooded onto the trail, grabbing the reins and roughly pulling the men from their saddles. They hit the ground, stunned, only to be finished off by tomahawks and war clubs.

Having killed silently, the ambushers returned to their positions and settled in to wait. Not hearing musket fire would unnerve the other militiamen. Someone would eventually muster enough courage to come in search of the dead men. They picked off two more victims before the other soldiers gave up their attempts at rescue.

From the hills across the Chattahoochee, the Rangers and Cherokees watched the methodical destruction of Little Chota. Smoke covered the valley in a low-lying haze, dyed red by the setting sun. After sunset, glowing coals outlined the destroyed cabins and sheds of the village. Of all the buildings in Little Chota, only Blackstone's Commissary and blacksmith shop remained standing the next morning.

Strong detachments of rebel soldiers were dispatched to search the surrounding areas for any caches of food or livestock. When found, these were quickly destroyed, or brought back into the village, where they were quickly consumed by the rebel army. Bands of soldiers who remained in the village attacked the ancient mound with picks and shovels, searching for any valuables interred in the graves of the ancients. Other groups rode up and down the river for miles, searching out hidden cabins or villages.

For four days the rebels lingered in the desecrated valley. On the morning of October thirteenth, they set the commissary and blacksmith shop afire and assembled for the march. They splashed across the ford, cautiously heading south, wary of an ambush. Behind them, twin plumes of black smoke rose like headstones above the site of Little Chota's charred remains.

Two days later, John, with the aid of Thunder's Child and Jacob, was able to pick off a rebel officer who strayed too far ahead of the advancing column. Rifling through the dead man's belongings, he found a large, brass spyglass that he stuffed hurriedly into his hunting pouch while Thunder's Child removed the scalp with a liquid plop! Alerted by approaching hoof beats, the three men gathered up the dead man's weapons, which included a finely made rifle, and raced off into the thickets lining the sides of the trail. They left their victim laying face down in the middle of the trail as a warning to the others. The rebels stopped alongside the body, cursing loudly as they dismounted to inspect the dead man. One of them shouldered his rifle and fired an ineffectual shot into the forest before turning his attention to his fallen comrade. The rebels had grown much too savvy to follow Rangers and

Indians blindly through the forest, even to avenge the death of a friend.

Using hit and run tactics, the handful of Rangers and Cherokee warriors managed to slow the enemy's advance to a snail's pace. They found that just a few scattered shots would cause the invaders to come to a complete halt for hours at a time, while their scouts probed ahead, ensuring that it was safe to move the army forward. The Cherokees called them old women and cowards, but the Rangers quietly disagreed. This group of men had no intention of failing in their mission. They were prepared to move as slowly and safely as possible to ensure the outcome they desired: the total destruction of the Rangers along with their Cherokee allies.

On the fourteenth, John sat on a steep mountainside, studying the rebel army through his captured spyglass. Jacob sat next to him, using his hat to fan the multitude of insects that descended on friend and foe alike. A hundred feet below, the invaders were cautiously fording Yahoola Creek.[85] John snapped the instrument shut and shook his head.

"That bastard!"

"Who?" Jacob asked.

John handed the spyglass to him and pointed down the slope. "Look right there on the far side of the creek and tell me what you see."

Jacob studied the scene but shook his head without taking his eye from the instrument. "What?"

"Watch the man in the butternut hunting frock, the one that's talking to General Pickens."

Jacob studied the man intently. When he turned to gesture across the creek, Jacob dropped the glass and turned to stare at John. "I didn't believe that a man could sink so low!" He shook his head in disbelief.

"But he has. I can't believe it myself. Roger Weatherford is leading them right to our door. And after we took him in! Why I have a good mind to take a shot at him with this rifle!"

"Now, don't go getting hasty!" Jacob cautioned him. "If they see us up here, we'll be lucky to make it over the crest of this hill without getting plugged."

John blew through his lips in exasperation. "I know, it just seems so low down and traitorous to my way of thinking!"

Moving slowly and keeping under cover, they crept up to the crest of the steep hill. John lay on his stomach, scanning the invading army with the spyglass, but his quarry had moved on. He collapsed the instrument with an angry snap and took careful aim with his newly captured rifle. He fired into a group of axmen who struggled to clear the tangled limbs forming an abatis across the narrow trail below. One of the men yelped and grabbed his foot, hopping around like he had stepped on a nail. A rifle-toting sentry looked in John's direction and fired a reply up the side of the mountain, aiming for the smoke that betrayed John's position. John heard the ball strike wood behind him as he mounted his mare and urged her downhill, away from the rebel army.

The two Rangers emerged onto a well-beaten path and followed it to the southwest for several miles. There, they found their own camp. Rangers and Cherokee alike were sprawled on the ground, snatching a few moments of sleep before returning to harass and spy on the enemy.

Slowing his mount to a walk, Jacob waited until John pulled alongside. He indicated the men about the campsite with a slight nod of his head and said in a low voice, "Have you noticed that there are fewer Cherokees with us every day?"

John nodded. The two continued to the far side of camp where they dismounted and tied their animals to a picket line stretched between two large trees. As they stripped their saddles and dumped them on the ground, John looked around to make sure that no one was near enough to overhear their conversation.

"How long do you calculate it'll be before we're fighting alone?"

"When they burn Long Swamp. I've noticed that our warriors are the only ones who seem to be sticking with us. Those from the towns already destroyed are deserting every day."

* * * *

That evening, Colonel Waters called a meeting of the Rangers and militiamen. Sitting in a semicircle, their faces tinted red by the fire, they followed the officer's words with interest.

"Men," he began, "it has become obvious that the destruction of our town is simply a matter of time. Therefore, I am dispatching all of the militia to Long Swamp where they will immediately escort the women and children, along with all the supplies that they can carry, down into the Creek country. Hopefully, the rebels will not be so bold as to follow them there." He paused to scan the line of faces staring up at him. His gaze steadied on Sergeant Hopkins. "That will leave the burden of forestalling the enemy for as long as we can to you Rangers." He made a gesture to indicate the Rangers grouped alongside him. "I want the militia to leave here at first light, and I want them to leave Long Swamp the next morning."

Waters seemed tired, discouraged, as was every other Ranger. There was not a man among them who didn't know that their time was at an end. That fickle whore, fate, had eloped with the enemy.

John spent the night composing a letter to Grainy:

September 18, 1782

My dearest wife and oldest friend,

I pen these few feeble lines using borrowed foolscap and ink. My mind is flooded by far too many sentiments to adequately express them in such a short space. Only know that it is with a heavy heart that I must inform you of our failure to halt the enemy, who is even now drawing nearer to our home with the intention of totally destroying it.

Colonel Waters will dispatch the militia in the morning to escort our families to safety. I have entrusted you to the care of our old friends Matthew Nowland and James Brooks. They have assured me that you will be in the best possible hands until we are reunited in the future. I have assured Jacob that his two children will likewise find safety and shelter in your gentle and capable arms. I know that I waste time informing you of your responsibility for those poor motherless children, but Jacob is very distraught and his mind would not be laid to rest unless I included it in these passages.

I have acquired a brass spyglass that I use to watch the enemy from the mountainsides as they advance through the obstacles that we thrust into their path. I have seen several of our old neighbors among them. I spied your brother, Richard, among the enemy ranks. I must admit that I was filled with the greatest nostalgia for the old days when I first laid eyes on his familiar face. I remembered us as children. Do you recall the time that we stole the apple pie that Mrs. Wilson had baked for the parson and then were caught in the act of devouring it by that esteemed servant of God himself? Richard and I swore that you were innocent of the crime and steeled ourselves to take all of the punishment. Even then, at only nine years of age, I loved you more than myself. I think that I felt your punishment more keenly than mine when you confessed along with us, unwilling to let me suffer without sharing in my fate. I wish that God in his mercy would reach down from heaven and whisk us back to that very moment, in order that we may relive our entire lives together. I would change not one moment of it. But I digress, and must move on to more pressing issues.

Do not be anxious for me. The rebels avoid any attempt we make to draw them into a battle. They seem content to simply destroy towns and food supplies in the hopes that starvation will thin our ranks during the coming winter. I am convinced that once Long Swamp falls, our small band will be scattered to the four winds like the Israelites of old. Once that happens, you must surely know that the Rangers from Long Swamp will allow nothing to keep us from being reunited with our families in a safer and better place. They talk of Canada as a haven for us.

The words do not exist to adequately express my love for you, therefore I will not insult the muses by endeavoring to do so. I close now. I will dream of you tonight and every night until we are once again reunited.

Your loving and devoted husband,
BJS.

John carefully folded the page and sealed it with Colonel Waters's borrowed seal. Not trusting himself to speak without betraying emotions better left unexpressed, he simply handed the letter to Matthew Nowland and pulled his blankets around him to sleep.

Three days later, a rider appeared with the welcome news that their families were safely on their way south, accompanied by almost six hundred Cherokee refugees whose only hope for survival during the coming winter were the British supplies promised to them by Colonel Waters.

The Rangers held their final council of war that evening. They would fight one last battle, make one final attempt to divert destiny.

They rose early the next morning and filed into positions selected by Colonel Waters the evening before. The path of the rebels would lead them through one last defile in the high, steep-sided hills before they moved into the more gently sloping country to the southwest.

Rangers and Cherokees alike flitted through the trees on the hillside, jockeying for the best fields of fire as the sounds of the approaching column increased. Fingers gripped the stocks of muskets, anxiously twisting back and forth in nervous anticipation as the moment of battle drew near. Through the trees, the frocks of the enemy riflemen could be seen moving slowly and cautiously. There was a slight hesitation, barely discernible, in the advancing scouts. These were no fools; some sixth sense warned them of impending danger. They moved fluidly from the trail into the protective cover of the trees on each side. A turkey gobble sounded. All along the hillside the warriors began to desert their positions and flow back over the crest of the hill, knowing that they had been spotted by the sharp-eyed frontiersmen below. John and the other Rangers held their positions, watching their allies evaporate like mist on a hot summer morning. By ones and twos, the Rangers themselves began to melt away. They would not risk a fight against such overwhelming odds. No one was eager to be the last man killed in a lost cause.

The Rangers and warriors from Long Swamp soon found themselves deserted. From the far side of the hill, they could hear the plaintive notes of Colonel Waters signal whistle recalling them. Reluctant to let the invaders enter their town without some sort of a fight, the more determined warriors opened fire. John and the six Rangers from Long Swamp joined in, firing as fast as they could load, determined to slow the advancing rebels for a few more hours.

Down below, the rebels returned fire from the shelter of the trees. Taking careful aim with their rifles they picked out targets along the hillside above. Their return fire was deadly accurate. Within minutes, two of the Cherokee warriors tumbled limply down the hillside.

John picked out one of the rebels below and marked his progress through the trees. He recognized the stocky form of Lieutenant Andrew DeLoach, the notorious Loyalist hater from Ninety-Six, who had three years earlier burned his home and driven him into exile. Despite the extreme range, John took two well-aimed shots at the man, chipping the bark off of the tree he stood behind on the second try. DeLoach jumped back behind its cover. John carefully reloaded the rifle. He laid it across a rock to steady it, and waited. DeLoach, undaunted, sprinted from tree to tree, working his way closer. John followed him, patiently timing the man's movements. He squeezed the trigger, felt the stock of the weapon recoil against his cheek. DeLoach fell forward, rolled, and immediately jumped to his feet and disappeared behind another large tree.

"Damn!" John cursed himself for missing. When a hand descended on his shoulder. He jumped in surprise and turned to see Sergeant Hopkins grinning alongside him.

"If you haven't noticed, we're about the only ones left up here. Look." He pointed uphill, where the struggling figures of Rangers, intermixed with warriors, clambered upward and disappeared over the crest. "Come on, let's get!" Giving John's arm a slight tug, he turned and began moving cautiously through the rocks and trees.

John, breathing heavily, scrambled upward behind him. With the cuff of his jacket, he wiped the sweat from his forehead. It seemed to pour from him like a river, trickling down to sting his eyes. Once he reached the crest, he turned to take one last look at the rebels below. Near the base of the hill, he could see some of the bolder ones stripping the bodies of the dead Cherokees, taking weapons, clothing, and scalps as trophies to display at home.

* * * *

Colonel Waters admitted the hopelessness of further resistance and retreated with his remaining men. He issued orders for the Rangers from Long Swamp to remain behind and search the village, destroying any useful stores that had to be abandoned. By depriving the rebels of badly needed provisions, he hoped to force them to turn back, thus saving other Cherokee villages from destruction.

The Long Swamp Rangers bid a somber farewell to Thunder's Child and Robin who would depart with Colonel Waters as a part of the rear guard. John, Jacob, Hopkins, Dobbins, and Nat were left behind under the command of Blackstone to carry out the destruction.

Both Sambo and Mambo, along with Seley and Ester, had disappeared during the night, striking out northward into the mountains with a group of Cherokees who had given up the fight. Hopkins found their green uniform jackets that morning, hanging on pegs outside the door of their cabin as a symbol of their resignations. No one blamed them; no one spoke an unkind word. They would be remembered as steadfast solders and fierce fighters. Hopkins sat quietly on his horse as the door of the cabin opened and Nat stepped out, still wearing his threadbare uniform jacket.

"Why didn't you go, Nat? I noticed that your woman went with them."

Nat smiled up at him. "I'll see them soon enough. Thought that I would stay around long enough to see this business through." Hopkins gave him a sad smile. He steered his mount toward the village.

They transferred everything useable to the council house and stuffed it with dry grasses that could be easily ignited before they left in the morning. The exhausted men went about the chore leisurely, feeling no sense of urgency. The rebels were still fifteen miles away and moving slowly, expecting another ambush before reaching the village.

With the last of the stores piled against the inside walls of the building, they stood and surveyed their work. Hopkins wiped the dust from his hands as he looked towards Nat and Dobbins,

"You two ride out toward those rebels, no more'n a mile mind you! And keep an eye out for them. If they get too close, ride like hell and give us the word. We'll fire this and head out after the column." He gave Blackstone a slight smile. "With your permission, of course, lieutenant."

"My thoughts exactly," Blackstone retorted lightly. "The rest of us may as well get what little rest there is."

John followed Jacob to the double cabin, where he helped him remove Judith's headstone and cart it to the river where it disappeared with a splash beneath the water. Next they obscured the grave, leaving the ground looking as if a grave had never existed. They both knew of the rebels penchant for desecrating the graves of the Indians. Jacob could not abide the though of his wife being disturbed in her final rest.

They spent the night in the double cabin, walking through it, running their hands nostalgically over the tool marks in the logs that they and the other Rangers had shaped and fitted into place. The memories overwhelmed them. Unable to sleep, they kindled a fire and sat reminiscing the entire night. They looked at each other, startled, the next morning when Hopkins called to them from outside. Gathering their gear, they left the cabin for the final time, pausing to give it one last look before closing the door and pushing the latchstring back through its opening. John wondered if Grainy had left with such reluctance when she had gone.

Having finished a breakfast prepared from the food baskets that they would shortly be committing to the flames, the Rangers sat with their backs against the outside wall of the council house. They lit their pipes and puffed on them leisurely. The rebels would not arrive until tomorrow, there was no hurry. Tomorrow morning, before heading south to rejoin the Rangers, they would watch the rebels from the far side of the river to determine if they would turn back, or continue the pursuit of Colonel Waters and his refugee column. There was little hope of their turning back.

Suddenly, they were on their feet. The sound of many approaching riders, heading in from the west, grew louder by the second. Each man grabbed his weapon and mounted, prepared to fly at a moment's notice if the approaching men proved to be enemies.

Sergeant Hopkins lowered his weapon, holding it loosely across his saddle as the riders burst into view from the far wood line to the west. A slight smile graced one corner of his lips. "They're Cherokees," he observed, more than a little relief evident in his voice. "It's about time!"

At least two hundred warriors galloped across the village fields, churning the withered stalks of harvested corn into the ground. Hopkins raised his hand and gave them a friendly wave, smiling broadly. The other Rangers relaxed, exchanging relieved glances with each other.

As the riders drew near enough for their features to be recognizable, Hopkins frowned slightly. He turned in the saddle, speaking over his shoulder to the other men. "This is strange. That's the Terrapin leading them. He's one of their pro-American chiefs."

The warriors flowed through the empty streets of the village and swirled around the six Rangers like an angry flood. Their faces were hard and unsmiling as they milled alongside the Rangers so closely that their knees touched. The Terrapin scowled at Hopkins; he looked angry, ready to fight. He flashed a quick signal to the warriors, who immediately swarmed over the Rangers, pulling them from their saddles and slamming them savagely to the ground. John, spitting blood and dirt, tried to rise, but a warrior knelt over him with a knee planted firmly between his shoulder blades. His hands were yanked behind his back and tied. He could hear Hopkins shouting at the top of his lungs, cursing the treachery of these warriors. Then, all six of the men were pulled roughly to their feet.

"What the hell's the meaning of this?" Hopkins shouted harshly, his eyes glowing with anger. Blood dripped from his chin. "Damn you, the King will hear about this!"

The Terrapin, seated atop a fine looking stallion, looked down disdainfully at the angry Ranger. He did not snarl or smile. His face remained stoic as he spoke, but his eyes blazed with anger. "Your king is gone!" he said viciously. "Don't try to threaten me with his revenge. He has been overturned by the Americans. We speak of him no more." He paused as he fought to keep his prancing steed under control. The Terrapin stabbed a finger in Hopkins direction. "I told you that if you and your pack of liars[86] ever caused my nation to suffer, that I would kill you! Look around you!" He threw his arm up angrily, indicating the deserted village. "Look what you have brought on us! Twelve villages destroyed!" He yanked his tomahawk from his belt and brandished it over Hopkins head. "I should kill you now, but you are more useful alive." He jerked his head towards the western horizon. "Take them away!"

Dropping nooses around their necks, the Cherokees dragged them across the fields at a trot, treating them as they would prisoners of war, no longer as allies. They led them to their camp and tied them securely, back to back, against narrow trees.

"Just what are you planning on doing with us?" Hopkins called to a vaguely familiar warrior in the Cherokee tongue. The warrior gave him a stern look and shrugged his shoulders. "It's for the Terrapin to decide. He goes now to parley with Pickens and Clarke."

John's heart sank. They were all well-aware of the fate awaiting them at the hands of the rebels. Anxious glances traveled from man to man. Hopkins tried to ease their fears. "I hope that they give us to Pickens, he's an honorable man. But Clarke? There's no telling what that fanatic will do! He treats this war like a religious crusade. He's always been like that, even when we was boys."

"You know him?" John asked. This could be a positive point.

"Yep, grew up with him. He's married to one of my cousins."

"Well, mayhap there's some hope for us," John said hopefully.

Hopkins let out a short, barking laugh. "Don't lay any bets on it. We don't get along very well. He's death on King's men, relatives or not. The best that we can hope for is a long term in some rebel prison. And that is only if we are given to Pickens. I hate that it ended like this for you boys, betrayed by our own people."

John thought about his words for a moment before answering. "What else can they do when you get right down to it? They're only trying to salvage as much good as they can out of a hopeless situation. They probably look on it as being us, who deserted them."

"No matter what happens tomorrow, at least our people will know that we put up a good fight and stood to our duty to the bitter end," Jacob said stoically.

Hopkins let an unintentional snort escape; it demonstrated his disagreement with Jacob's opinion.

"You don't think so?" Jacob looked puzzled.

"Jacob, son, we are the losers in this war. The vanquished have no friends, or champions. We will be forgotten or vilified in every history. I doubt that the world will even take note of our passing."

"I prefer to think that they will give us our due as loyal and steadfast servants of our lawful king," Dobbins interjected.

Hopkins gave the speaker a dubious look, started to reply, then fell silent. He saw no harm in letting them put their minds at ease. If letting them believe that the morality of their cause would be acknowledged by future generations, so be it.

It was dark when The Terrapin and his emissaries returned to the camp. He slid from his horse and stalked angrily over to confront the captives. He squatted in front of Hopkins.

"Tomorrow we will turn you over to the Americans as proof that we have turned our faces away from the lies of the English King." A look of uncontrolled rage contorted his features for a fleeting moment. He took a deep breath before continuing, "We Cherokees will be forced to sign a new treaty with them tomorrow. A treaty giving them all of our lands south of the Savannah River and east of the Chattahoochee!" He thrust his finger into Hopkins face. "This was your doing! And theirs!" Making a motion with his hand as if he were throwing away a broken tool, he jumped to his feet, and stalked away.

Chapter 22

Long Swamp Village
Tuesday, October 22, 1782

The next morning, the six captives were marched through the empty village. It swarmed with rebel militiamen under the command of Colonel Clarke. Smoke was already beginning to curl from between the shingles and from under the doors of the buildings. In places it lay close to the ground, obscuring the distant line of trees. They were led to the grove of oaks alongside the river. Jacob looked around, remembering the night, only three short years before, when he and Judith had been the centerpiece of a grand party honoring their imminent marriage under these very trees. His face was pale, dreading what the immediate future held in store for them.

Colonel Clarke was seated among his officers. They stood as the prisoners were pushed forward.

"Who claims command of this pack of renegades?" Clarke snapped the question impatiently and smiled as if expecting no one to volunteer. His eyebrow arched in surprise when Blackstone stepped forward to claim that honor.

"I am Lieutenant Blackstone Mullis, King's Carolina Rangers, Commissary to the Cherokee valley towns. As the ranking officer present, I am in temporary command of these men."

A few disparaging looks passed openly from man to man among the rebel officers. Blackstone noticed it and his face flushed.

"I should not have to remind you of the rules of war concerning the treatment of uniformed combatants," Blackstone said, but there was little hope in his voice.

The colonel walked slowly along the line of Rangers, inspecting them as if they were on parade. He halted abruptly in front of Nat.

"What's this?" he asked in mock surprise. "You've put your slave in uniform, Lieutenant Mullis?"

"That man is a soldier of the King," Blackstone snapped.

The colonel pivoted and walked slowly along the line of prisoners. He stopped in front of Blackstone and leaned forward until their noses almost touched.

"One of your men, you say?"

"Yes, sir, he is."

"Looks like a slave to me." Clarke turned to his officers. "What is the penalty for arming escaped slaves?" he asked with a knowing smile.

"Hanging!"

John noticed that some of the officers did not smile; it gave him a slim thread of hope to cling to.

Clarke nodded; he turned and gestured to a squad of soldiers waiting to the side. "Hang these two!" He pointed an accusing finger at Blackstone and Nat. "One is an escaped slave bearing arms and the other is a Tory renegade who has confessed to his crime."

The men moved forward. They already had a short length of rope tied into a noose at each end.

"We only got three ropes," one of the men said holding up the ropes for inspection.

"I don't think the *lieutenant* here will mind sharing his final ride with one of his men," Clarke said. He emphasized the title *lieutenant* sarcastically, he was not an easy man to like.

Without ceremony, the rebels wrestled the condemned men onto the back of a horse. Positioning them back to back, they led the animal forward and halted it beneath a stout limb. A militiaman scrambled up and out onto the limb where he twisted the short length of rope around it several times until he had the length of each noose adjusted to his satisfaction. He dangled the nooses with one hand, nursing them carefully over the heads of the two Rangers, then gave the rope a firm tug to tighten the knot. Blackstone rolled his head to one side, casting an apologetic look to the Rangers still awaiting their fate. Clarke nodded, a soldier slapped the horse on the rump and the lives of Blackstone and Nat ended, their bodies dangling back to back in the shade of the stately oak. John felt his knees threaten to buckle; the suddenness of the act had stunned him. The feeling was quickly replaced by an inner rage that he kept carefully concealed.

"Now who's in charge?" Clarke asked with a morbid smile.

When Sergeant Hopkins stepped forward, one of the onlookers poked a dirty finger in his direction. "I seen that man before, leading Indians against the settlers on the Savannah! And that fella with him, he was there too!"

"Do you wish to confess?" Clarke asked.

"I'll confess to nothing but serving my King."

Clarke turned to the officers behind him. "What is the penalty for arming Indians and inciting them to violence against the law abiding citizens of Georgia?"

"Death! Hanging!" several of them chanted in a murderous chorus.

Clarke nodded in agreement and pointed out his next two victims. "Hang them as well," he said to his squad of executioners.

Hopkins looked down at Colonel Clarke as the noose was slipped over his head. "You're going to hang prisoners of war out of hand? We've done nothing to deserve this and the war is as good as over."

Clarke jabbed an accusing finger in the direction of the ten Cherokee witnesses sitting stoically to one side.

"You're their example! If it weren't for you and your Tory trash, they would have sat peacefully aside during this war."

"Don't insult me! You know as well as I do that they're doomed. At least with us they stood a chance of surviving in their own land!" Hopkins saw that argument was getting him nowhere, so he tried a different tack. "At least parole my men. They have been honorable and faithful soldiers throughout this nasty affair." Hopkins motioned with his head towards John and Jacob, who stood side-by-side, waiting their turn to ride into eternity. "Damn it Elijah! They're only common privates, with wives and children depending on them. If General Pickens were here he wouldn't stand for this madness!" He looked hopefully at his former neighbor. "There's no reason to cause any more pain than is necessary at this late date. Is there?" It was a slight voice, containing a slight plea.

Clarke reached out and snatched the Forgotten One's amulet from John's neck. He shook it in the sergeant's face, and then threw it violently to the ground. "They're nothing but a bunch of renegade whites, just like you!" He exhaled an exasperated breath. His hawk-like features fixed themselves on his old playmate. "Damn you! General Pickens isn't here! I am in command!" He pounded a fist into his open palm. "Can't you damned Tories understand that we are trying to give birth to a new nation here?" Clarke lifted his gaze and studied the two bodies swaying gently in the wind. He grimaced slightly. "There is always pain in a birthing," he said softly.

"A damned poor midwife you'd make!" Hopkins retorted angrily. "I pity the poor trollop you minister to. You'd throw out her other children in order to bring a total stranger into the world." His voice cracked slightly as he added, "Do you think that the Yankee Congress up in Philadelphia really gives a damn about you? I wonder, what will you do, when the monster that you've help to create has grown hungry enough to devour even you?"

Clarke did not answer; he simply nodded to the militiaman holding the reins. The soldier calmly walked the horse forward and the two men slipped, one after another, from the rump of the animal. They each bounced once when they reached the end of their rope. Their bodies, back-to-back, rotated slowly to the left a quarter of a turn where they came to their permanent rest. Their faces were ghastly; eyes bulged from their sockets, their tongues protruded from gaping mouths. Dobbins's left leg kicked twice and dropped limply, his quick wit stilled forever. *Rebels don't think!* John dropped his head. The utter finality of the act released an inner anguish beyond belief. It welled up in him, threatening to explode; he felt himself sway, lightheaded. Nothing that he could do would ever undo this simple act, performed with such casual thoughtlessness in the single blink of an eye. They had been like brothers to him, now they were gone forever. He stood stock still, disbelief written on his face. His gaze traveled over the faces of the militiamen who made up the death squad, and paused to look upon a face that he remembered well - Andrew DeLoach.

DeLoach returned the stare as he advanced with an almost jovial step. John thought, *he's enjoying this.* DeLoach wore the knot of a lieutenant on one shoulder. John was surprised that he hadn't noticed him earlier.

"Get them other two up!" DeLoach snapped. It took four men to hoist Jacob onto the bare back of the animal. John was thrust roughly behind him; the two men who had lived life so closely would greet death back-to-back. DeLoach looked up smugly. He turned to Clarke.

"We're runnin' out of limbs, sir." He seemed pleased with his attempt at humor.

"Use that one!" the colonel barked. He pointed to a smaller limb on the other side of the tree. It was obvious that despite his ill temper, the death of his old boyhood playmate weighed heavily on his soul. The fate of the last two men did not concern him, they were strangers, troublesome insects that he would swat and instantly forget. He was ready to be done with this business.

"It's a mighty small limb, think it'll hold?" one of the executioners asked. He looked up, mentally gauging the strength.

"If it doesn't, we'll find another one. Get on with it!" Clarke turned his horse and rode over to where the Cherokees sat witnessing the power of the new American nation. He guided his horse to the end of the line where he sat alongside them, watching, silent and hollow eyed.

"Use a limb on that tree." Jacob inclined his head to indicate a giant oak near the top of the riverbank. "It looks like its got some good limbs."

John said nothing, recognizing the tree as the oak that Jacob had carved his and Judith's initials into the day after they were married.

"The damned Tory sure has an eye for hanging limbs. Probably hoisted many a brave fellow off the ground in his own time," DeLoach said. Several of the soldiers chuckled at the jest

Two men stepped forward and led the animal to Jacob's tree. The two friends sat facing in opposite directions, their backs rubbing in rhythm with the steps of their mount. One of the rebels clambered out onto the limb of the big oak and looped a rope containing another double noose around the limb several times before dropping it down on top of the doomed men. The noose struck John on the shoulder with a solid thump, slid off, and then swung idly at his side, bumping against his ribs. Leaning from his perch, the hangman wrapped one arm around the limb and stretched with the other to wiggle a noose over the head of each man.

"Look up, damn it!" the man hissed at Jacob, whose eyes were fixed on the arrow-pierced heart containing the initials of Judith and himself. Jacob jumped, startled by the sudden outburst. When he looked up, the noose slid easily over his head and came to rest on his broad shoulders. The rough rope chafed the tender skin of his neck. He shuttered as a silent sob escaped his lips.

"Stop your crying and take it like a man, you Tory son of a bitch!" the militiaman holding the reins snapped cruelly. A malicious smile spread across his face. "You can't stand a dose of your own medicine?"

Off to one side, out of John's view, some of the other rebels laughed.

"Hang the bloody coward!" someone yelled.

With a great effort, John was able to twist his neck around just enough so that he could see the speaker.

"You rebel son-of-a-bitch!" he hissed at the man. "If you think this man is a coward, why don't you cut his hands loose, and face him like a man?"

"Not a coward?" the man spit disdainfully onto the ground. "Look at him! He's crying like a baby. Probably knows that he's going to burn in hell! Just payment I call it, for all of the good patriots that he's robbed and killed!" More snickers and catcalls sounded from the soldiers.

"At ease!" Clarke snapped. "Act like soldiers." The men jumped, a measure of civility returned.

"I'm sorry," Jacob managed to gasp over his shoulder. "I'm just so mortal sad! Who'll love my children when I'm gone?" He sniffed; John felt his shoulder spasm again.

"Be damned to you and your bastards!" DeLoach shouted. "I'm tired of this Tory blather!"

Without warning, he slapped the flank of the animal. Startled, the mare bolted forward, tumbling the militiaman at her head to the ground as it pulled free and leapt away. Unrestrained, it raced from the oak grove and out across the clearing, past the surprised faces of the rebel officers.

John and Jacob plunged downward. The green limb of the oak, much too springy to be an effective gallows, gave under the sudden weight of the two men. Their feet almost brushed the ground before the limb rebounded and lifted them upward. They bobbed beneath the branch like a pair of morbid puppets. The springiness of the limb had prevented their necks from snapping, now they kicked and struggled as they fought against their bonds, struggling for one last breath of the crisp fall air. The pressure on their throats began to force their tongues slowly from their mouths; their eyes bulged hideously as their own weight slowly strangled them.

John's lungs felt as if they would literally burst through his chest; his feet kicked wildly, instinctively searching for a foothold as he bobbed beneath the limb of the oak. Behind him, he unconsciously felt Jacob's feet pounding against his calves as he kicked futilely against fate. Somehow, in response to the violent gyrations, John's body twisted, he turned slowly in a half circle until he was facing into Jacob's broad back. He was only vaguely aware of the scratchy feel of Jacob's woolen coat rubbing across one cheek. How he pined for one last breath of fresh air!

The militiamen grew silent as they witnessed the spectacle, the faces of some of the younger ones displayed a horror beyond belief. Executing Tories was one thing, but this!

One of the onlookers suddenly stepped forward and grabbed John by both legs. He lifted his own feet off the ground and swung below him like a pendulum, adding his own weight to John's in order to hurry death along.

The grim-faced reaper, patiently waiting in the wings, now rushed forward eagerly to claim another victim. The inhuman sounds grew quickly fainter, the spasms less pronounced.

At the end, as darkness descended and the pain retreated, John began to grow still; the short spasmodic jerks of his body grew fewer and weaker. He drifted into his final sleep; he dreamed of Grainy.[87]

What happened to the real people in this novel?

Lt. Colonel Thomas Brown: After Savannah was evacuated, in July 1782, Colonel Thomas Brown joined the thousands of refugees who went to British Florida, only to be forced to leave when that province was returned to Spain in the peace treaty of 1783. Some Loyalists migrated to Nova Scotia, but Brown and many of his Rangers settled on Abaco Island in the Bahamas. Loyalists regarded Brown as a hero and elected him to the Bahamian legislature. He died in 1825 at the age of seventy-five.

Colonel Elijah Clarke claimed Thomas Waters's property by right of conquest. In the 1790's he was recruited by France to lead an invasion of Spanish Florida that never materialized. He then led his followers into the territory of the Creek Indians and established the Trans-Oconee Republic, an independent country, complete with its own constitution. When Georgia's Governor sent in the militia, Clarke accepted a pardon and abandoned the scheme. He died in Richmond County, Georgia in 1799.

Lt. Colonel John Harris Cruger died June 2, 1807 in London, England.

Brigadier General William "Bloody Bill" Cunningham died quietly at his home in the West Indies on February 9, 1813.

Lieutenant Daniel Ellis settled at Country Harbor, Nova Scotia on June 12, 1784.

Colonel Daniel McGirth continued fighting against the Americans in Florida even after the area was returned to Spain. He was captured and imprisoned by the Spanish in the Castillo de San Marcos in St. Augustine. Upon his release, with his health broken, he returned to South Carolina where, with his identity carefully concealed, he lived with his wife at the home of her brother, Col. John James.

Brigadier General Andrew Pickens: After the war, Andrew Pickens served in both the state legislature and the United States Congress. He died in South Carolina in 1817. It is said that he seldom smiled and never laughed.[88]

Colonel Thomas Waters escaped down the Chattahoochee River with remainder of his men and about 1000 homeless Cherokees. He died in England in the early 1800's

Captain Alexander Wylly lived the remainder of his life with his wife and children, among the plantation gentry on St. Simons Island, Georgia.[89]

The King's Carolina Rangers were disbanded in New York City and given land grants in Country Harbor, Nova Scotia in 1784. In a report to General Clinton in 1783, Colonel Brown stated that a total of one thousand two hundred men had served in the Rangers during the Revolution. Just over five hundred were killed in the course of their service.

Source Material

Bartram, William. *Travels.* Salt Lake City: Peregrine Smith, Inc. 1980

Cashin, Edward J. *The King's Ranger.* New York: Fordham University Press. 1999

Chiltoskey, Mary Ulmer. *Cherokee Words With Pictures.* Cherokee. 1972

Knight, Lucian Lamar: *Georgia's Landmarks, Memorials and Legends. Vol. 2.* Atlanta: The Byrd Publishing Co. 1914

Lumpkin, Henry. *From Savannah to Yorktown. The American Revolution in the South.* Columbia: University of South Carolina Press. 1981

McCall, Hugh. *The History of Georgia.* Atlanta: Cherokee Publishing Co. 1981

Mooney, James. *Myths of the Cherokee and Sacred Formulas of the Cherokees.* Cherokee: Cherokee Heritage Books. 1982

Scruggs, Carroll Proctor. *Georgia During the Revolution.* Norcross: Bay Tree Publishers. 1975

Swanton, John R. *The Indians of the Southeastern United States.* Washington D.C.: Smithsonian Press. 1981

(Endnotes)

1 Scruggs: Pg. 39.

2 A large, double-edged Scottish broadsword, still in wide use at the time.

3 The Georgia Rangers were later lured into an ambush and destroyed by Indians on the frontier.

4 In the absence of uniforms, supporters of the King wore a red cockade, or ribbon, on their hats to distinguish them from their enemies.

5 King George II, who died in 1760 and was followed by George III, the present monarch.

6 Near present day Clarkesville, Georgia.

7 Just south of present day Helen, Georgia in the Nacoochee Valley.

8 Those belonging to this clan were keepers of children's medicines and the caretakers of medicinal herb gardens. They were named for a medicine made from the blue holly.

9 Smallpox was common during this time period. The majority of people most likely had varying amounts of scaring caused by bouts with the disease at some point in their lives.

10 A block chair was simply a round log, smoothly cut to approximately 18" in length and turned on its end to be used as a seat.

11 A puncheon bench was made by simply splitting a two-foot length of log, usually 10" to 12" in diameter, down the center, and smoothing the split side as a seat. After drilling four holes on the rounded side with an auger, round pegs were inserted to serve as legs.

12 In the South at this time, it was customary to give the first born son the maiden name of the mother as a first name. Hence, the profusion of men with two last names during that era, such as Blackstone Mullis, Poole Hall, or Parker Pierce.

13 According to *Georgia's Black Revolutionary Patriots* By Carole E. Scott, about one-third of the defenders of Fort Cornwallis, in Augusta, Georgia, were black soldiers. They were routinely promised freedom when they enlisted to fight with either the British regulars or with Loyalist and militia units.

14 This is the same dance as a War Dance, but it was also used as a welcome dance on ceremonial occasions.

15 *Brighten Camp* is a fife tune that is commonly known today as *The Girl I Left Behind Me*. It is well known in US History as the tune favored by General George Armstrong Custer and his 7th Cavalry.

16 This melody is more familiar today as a Christmas song, *What Child is This?*

17 In 1779, the wage of a Provincial private was 6 Pence per day, minus 2 ½ Pence per day for food. At that time there were 240 Pence to a Pound Sterling, 20 Pence to a Shilling, and 12 Shillings to a Pound. Today, there are 100 Pence to a Pound.

18 During the Revolutionary War period beards were not in style. Men in the military were required to shave, just as they are today.

19   A toothbrush during this time period would have been made of a carved bone with bored holed for the bristles. The bristles were made primarily from pig bristles held in place by a thin wire. In the absence of one of these, a stick, mashed at one end to flair it, was used.

20   This was a plow made entirely of wood, except for an iron colter (cutter) that fit into a notch drilled into the pull bar in front of the wooden blade. The colters job was to cut roots and allow the wooden blade to push through the soil.

21   Mooney, Pg. 257.

22   Cracker was a term applied to lower class whites, especially those on the frontier who were constantly moving from place to place as they exhausted the soil on their small homesteads.

23   A Guinea was equal to 1 pound, 1 Shilling (5 pence)

24   This would be roughly in the neighborhood of Athens, Ga. today.

25   These were one style of women's caps that virtually always covered the hair of 18th century women. They were seldom taken off. If another hat, such as a sun hat were worn, it was usually tied on directly over this cap.

26   In the absence of ministers in the isolated frontier areas, couples would often hold hands and jump a broom to signify that they were married. Sometimes, but not always, the marriage would be formalized whenever a "Preacher" became available.

27   The Divine Right Theory of government stated that God chose kings to rule. Therefore, rebellion was not only treason, it was also a sin.

28   The description of Ebenezer, Georgia is from The 1780 Diary of Loyalist Lieutenant Anthony Allaire of King's Mountain: TNGenWeb Project

29   Surviving requisitions of the King's Rangers show them receiving shortened British or French muskets as opposed to the Long Land musket with a 46 inch barrel, or the Short Land musket with a 42-inch barrel. The longer muskets were the common muskets among British and Loyalist regiments.

30   Although the barrel of the British issued *Brown Bess* was .75 caliber, .69 caliber balls were used to ensure quicker and easier loading. Along with the ability of the musket to accept a bayonet, the ability to be reloaded quickly was an important advantage that the military musket had over the longer ranged and more accurate rifle. In a pitched battle the military preferred muskets primarily because of these two advantages. A third consideration was cost.

31   Today this position would be slightly to the east of Savannah's Talmadge Memorial Bridge, where it enters Savannah after coming over Hutchinson Island. Near the *Great Savannah Exposition*.

32   Although they are often depicted as wearing kilts, the 71st highlanders wore pants of blue or white.

33   A regiment was charged when one of its men had a stay in the General Hospital. It was not unusual in the British Army at this time for soldiers to be required to reimburse the regiment when they were released.

34   Rory is reciting a British ditty: "A friend before a messmate, a messmate before a shipmate, a shipmate before a dog, and a dog before a soldier."

35   Buttons on women's clothing were not in style at this time. Blouses were either pinned or tied.

36　Although they did not know why it worked, just that it often did, this was an accepted remedy. Actually, the moss contained trace amounts of penicillin mold.

37　At this time, digging entrenchments was considered as outside the realm of a soldier's job. They would receive extra pay for this work.

38　Coins were often designated as red, white, or yellow. Red coins were made of copper, white of silver, and yellow of gold.

39　British slang for the French.

40　This signal is used to indicate that prisoners are not to be taken.

41　An early form of the card game, Bridge.

42　d'Estaing survived this wound. He was guillotined during the French Revolution by the Paris mob on April 28, 1794.

43　Although not definitely proven, tradition claims that Henri Christophe, who became President of Haiti in 1807 and King of Haiti in 1811, served as a twelve year old drummer boy with the Chasseurs-Volontaires de Saint-Domingue during the siege of Savannah, Georgia. In October 2007 a massive bronze and granite monument to these Haitian soldiers was unveiled in Savannah's Franklin Square.

44　Like any battle of the Revolutionary War, casualty figures vary. However it is certain that the causalities sustained by the Allied armies in their assault on the Spring Hill Redoubt were well over 1000 and may have been as high as 1,200. British causalities were unusually low, somewhere between 7 and 55 depending on the source. No matter which figures you use, this loss greatly demoralized the Americans for the next six months to a year.

45　Swanton. Pg. 354.

46　Bartram, in his *Travels*, describes a pack train moving through Georgia. In his eyewitness account he recounts that the animals were not bound together with lead ropes, but simply driven along much like we think of a western cattle drive, albeit at a much more rapid pace.

47　A small metal strap containing a pin that fit across the fingers and helped remove the shuck from an ear of corn.

48　The tassels of broomcorn were combed of seeds and tied to wooden handles in layers, producing a surprisingly effective broom. Foxfire 3.

49　In these days with the lack of proper diet and vitamins, there was a common saying that a woman lost one tooth for each pregnancy.

50　Osnaburg is a natural off-white cotton fabric made by frontier women. It was used to make clothing and a variety of other articles such as sacks or kerchiefs.

51　Lipstick and rouge was made from the crushed bodies of female Cochineal Beetles. This is still used today in some cosmetics.

52　Hornpipes were popular dances of the day. Like today's dances, the steps were altered with every performance, usually in response to the cadence of the musicians providing the tune.

53   Traditionally, in the South at this time, weddings were generally celebrated at the bride's home at 11 A.M. followed by a party ending in a supper feast. Unless something unusual, such as has happened in this story, arose.

54   Beds of this day used a latticework of ropes as springs. When they stretched with use and began to sag, wedges were driven in under the loops on the sideboards to tighten the ropes and make the bed firmer. This is the origin of the old saying, *Sleep Tight.*

55   The officer was Captain William Martin. As Sergeant Hopkins had surmised, he was the rebels only experienced artilleryman.

56   This was the Muscogee name for the Cherokee. Literally, "people of a different speech."

57   "The King's Ranger" Page 118.

58   Today, the site of the White House is marked by a historical marker in Augusta, Ga. The story of the hanging of the 13 men is still told. Colonel Brown vehemently denied the allegations for the remainder of his life.

59   In 1780 the Georgia Royalist Legislature passed the Disqualifying Act that disqualified and rendered *traitors* incapable from holding or exercising any office of trust, honor, or profit in the Province of Georgia. It was an answer to the 1778 Act by the Patriot Legislature that did much the same for those who were suspected, or known, Loyalists.

60   Although his particular incident is fiction, Laodicea (Dicey) Langston is not. She survived the war, married Thomas Springfield, and died at the age of 75 in June, 1837. At the time of her death she was the mother of 22 children and 140 great grandchildren. For more information consult the Oct. 1975 edition of *National Geographic*, the Internet, or the DAR, which has had a medal struck in her honor. She is buried near her home in Traveler's Rest, South Carolina.

61   The shiny tin canteens of the British were often Japanned, or blackened, to keep them from being reflective.

62   The most commonly accepted number of Loyalist casualties at the Battle at Hammond's Store is 150 killed and 40 captured out of a force of about 250 men. According to the American General Daniel Morgan, the Patriots did not lose a single man. The Patriots touted this as a victory, but with such lopsided casualties it was almost certainly a massacre of unarmed, or surrendered men. It seems beyond belief that if the 250 Loyalist had put up even the slightest resistance, at least one man would have been able to fire a fatal shot. Even Colonel Tarlton's men suffered causalities at the infamous massacre in the Waxhaws, where they were accused of killing surrendering American troops.

63   Cherokee Words with Pictures by Mary Ulmer Chiltoskey Page 11.

64   Captain Alexander Wylly was the brother of Hester Wylly Habersham, the sister-in-law of Joseph Habersham, who had made Georgia's Royal Governor, James Wright, a prisoner in January of 1776.

65   Located just outside Augusta, Georgia.

66   Colonel Cruger, in command at the fort at Ninety-Six, South Carolina, had
      been sent an order to evacuate his post and merge his men into the defenses of
      Augusta, which was considered more valuable. Cruger was totally unaware of
      these orders since the message had been intercepted by the rebels in route to
      him.

67   A caponier is a covered trench usually used for communications purposes.

68   Porta crayons were nothing more than an early from of a mechanical pencil.
      They date back to the 1500's and during this time consisted of nothing more
      than a hollow metal cylinder, split down the side, with a round piece of lead
      inserted through it.

69   Although some of the Rangers, such as Colonel Grierson, were murdered by
      vengeful Patriots after the surrender, the majority were marched into captivity
      at Salisbury NC. They were exchanged in a general exchange of prisoners that
      summer and most were back on active duty by the end of the year.

70   John's victim was none other than Colonel Thaddeus Kosciusko, the Polish
      engineer serving under General Greene. He had been making an inspection of
      the works when the Loyalist attack almost captured him. He later described his
      wound as "inglorious."

71   The Pioneer Battalions of the Revolutionary War would be equivalent to
      the Engineer's of today's modern armies. Two of their major jobs were the
      construction of defensive works and keeping the roads and bridges in repair.
      A large number of these troops were ex-slaves who were given their freedom
      when they enlisted to fight for the British cause.

72   These Black soldiers were evacuated along with their white counterparts when
      the British withdrew from their old colonies. Their future was much brighter
      than most of the black soldiers serving in the Continental Army, such as some
      of those who served in the 1st Rhode Island Regiment who were returned to
      slavery after the war ended.

73   Cherokee Words With Pictures. Mary Ulmer Chiltoskey page 12.

74   Charleville was the common name used for the French supplied muskets during
      the Revolutionary War. They were called that after one of the arsenals in France
      that manufactured them, although the majority were actually manufactured in
      the St. Etienne Arsenal.

75   Chestnut trees were one of the main sources of nuts and one of the more
      common trees in the eastern forest during the Revolution. Early settlers relied
      on them for hog feed in the mountainous areas, and they allowed their animals
      to roam freely until they were rounded up for slaughter. A blight, introduced by
      imported Chinese Chestnut trees in the early 1900's decimated the American
      Chestnut. Within ten years they were virtually extinct. They remain so to this
      day.

76   A Stone is equal to 14 pounds, or 6.35 Kg.

77   A metal bar with hooks on each end and an eye in the middle that is used for
      hoisting animals and keeping their rear legs spread for cleaning. Primarily
      found today in abattoirs.

78 The Pine trees that cover the South today were not present in Grainy's day. She
    would have been familiar with the Virgin Pines which are all but extinct today.
    They still exist in a few places such as the Fernbank Forest in Atlanta, GA.

79 Early eyewitnesses tell of the Creek Indians using this hunting technique on the
    Omulgee River before the beginning of the American Revolution.

80 Writing paper.

81 When writing with ink, it was necessary to periodically stop and spread a light
    layer of sand across the ink to absorb excess liquid and cause the ink to dry
    more quickly. This prevented smears to some degree.

82 Myths and Sacred Formulas of the Cherokees, Moony page 415. This tree stood
    about six miles southeast of present day Clarkesville, Ga. It was a traditional
    meeting place for Cherokee war parties going to and from raids. It stood
    until the late 1800's when an unnamed white man girded and killed it so that
    it would not stand as a monument to the cruelties of the savages. The site is,
    today, under the asphalt parking lot of Chopped Oak Baptist Church.

83 The Border Wizard Owl was the Cherokee name for General Andrew Pickens,
    who always seemed to know where to intercept war parties crossing into South
    Carolina and Georgia.

84 Cherokee word for quiet. Pg. 20, Cherokee words with pictures, Mary Ulmer
    Chiltoskey.

85 Near present day Dahlonega, Georgia, later the site of the first gold rush in the
    United States.

86 This is what the Americans called the Rangers living among the tribes,
    accusing them of spreading false rumors designed keep the warriors angry
    enough to carry out raids against the border settlements. These lies included
    such things as telling the tribes that the Americans wanted all of their land and
    would not stop until they had pushed every Indian into the western ocean.

87 According to the history of Pickens County, Georgia, these hangings took place
    near the present-day town of Nelson, Georgia. The village of Long Swamp has
    been located just east of present day Ball Ground, Georgia.

About the Author

Gerald Stokes is a teacher in a rural Georgia high school. He received both a BA in History and an MA in Social Science from Piedmont College, located in Demorest, Georgia. Prior to entering the teaching field, he served as a Machinist Mate First Class onboard the nuclear submarine USS Simon Bolivar (SSBN 641), an Agricultural Inspector and a Correctional Officer for the State of Georgia, and as a captain in the US Army and the Georgia Army National Guard. *A Lesser Form of Patriotism*, his first published novel, was originally released in 2008.

Other Books by G.G. Stokes, Jr.

Historical Fiction

The Road to Bloody Marsh
Letters For Catherine
Loving Lynn Celia

Non-Fiction

Camp Toccoa: First Home of the Airborne
Massacre at Roanoke

Made in the USA
Columbia, SC
28 November 2020